Those
I Have
Lost

BOOKS BY SHARON MAAS

Of Marriageable Age
The Lost Daughter of India
The Orphan of India
The Soldier's Girl
The Violin Maker's Daughter
Her Darkest Hour
The Far Away Girl

THE QUINT CHRONICLES
The Small Fortune of Dorothea Q
The Secret Life of Winnie Cox
The Sugar Planter's Daughter
The Girl from the Sugar Plantation

SHARON MAAS

Those
I Have
Lost

bookouture

Published by Bookouture in 2021

An imprint of Storyfire Ltd.
Carmelite House
50 Victoria Embankment
London EC4Y 0DZ

www.bookouture.com

ISBN: 978-1-80019-621-6
eBook ISBN: 978-1-80019-620-9

Prologue

1946 – Vellore, India

The People Who Came in Cars

The people always came in cars, black Ambassador cars, great humpbacked beetles creeping along the potholed road outside the fence. You could see the silhouettes of their heads in the tinted windows, black shadows against grey. Sometimes they opened those windows and peered out, at the children gathering in the forecourt, shouting and waving. Sometimes, even, they waved back. They came in couples, a man and a lady, because that was what parents were: a man and a lady, a mother and a father. Real ones, not like Mother Maria and Father Bear; and they came to choose a child.

Most of the children prayed to be chosen. Anna-Marie and Luke prayed to be spared.

On that one Saturday Anna-Marie heard a familiar hum; she looked up and saw the black Ambassador creeping up to the gate. There was no time to pray.

'Run, Luke, run!' she cried. They jumped up and ran, zigzagging past the other children and around the girls' dormitory to the backyard. The other children ran in the opposite direction, towards the gate, shouting and laughing. They poured out of the buildings, ran in from the backyard and gathered at the entrance, controlling themselves just enough to stand back to allow the chauffeur to open the gate. Wheels crunching on the dry sand, the car crept into the courtyard and parked next to the rusty old school van.

The children swarmed around it, dancing, jostling each other out of the way, laughing, shouting and waving wildly.

The man, the potential father, opened the back-seat door and stepped into the scorching afternoon sun, into the swarm of children. Like all the men who came in cars, he wore a dark suit like the Englishmen in their schoolbooks; the jacket hung open and loose, but now he buttoned it up across the bulge of his paunch, straightened his tie and looked around. Simultaneously, the chauffeur opened the lady's door and she too stepped out, wearing a shiny silk sari in green with a wide, yellow-embroidered border. The man and the lady pursed their lips, frowning, and battled their way through the jostling children to join forces behind the car. The lady adjusted the pallu of her sari and pointed, over the heads of the children, to the girls' dormitory.

'I saw two children running away,' she said, in English, to her husband. 'One of them, a little boy, was very fair.'

The husband frowned. The chauffeur tried to shoo the children away but they ignored him and flocked around the couple, squealing in excitement, their skinny arms fluttering at their faces, calling 'Appa! Amma! Appa! Amma! Ammappammappa!' The man stretched out his arm to push them away, but they, thinking it to be a friendly gesture, perhaps the beginning of a hug, grabbed it, and swung from it like monkeys from a branch.

Mother Maria came hurrying up, hands joined in a welcoming namaskar.

'Welcome, welcome!' she cried, and 'children, children! Don't jostle!' She peeled the children away from the man's arm and swatted several backsides. To the strangers she said, 'They are little monkeys, aren't they! But so *sweet*! I am so happy you are willing to consider an older child. They are so hard to place, poor little creatures, and we have so *many* of them! Shoo, children, shoo!'

Sister Magdalena ran up to join the group, wringing her hands in apology for her tardiness. She herded the children away and organised them into two fidgeting lines for inspection, one for boys and one for girls. But the lady was not interested.

'I saw two children,' she said to Mother Maria. 'They ran away. Why did they run away?'

'Oh, that must have been Luke and Anna-Marie. Our Terrible Twins.'

'Twins?'

Mother Maria simpered and corrected the misunderstanding.

'Not *really*. Not real twins. Just good friends. They are very attached to each other but they are not related. They can easily be separated.'

'Could you find them for us? I'd like to have a closer look. One of them was a boy, you said? Luke?'

'Yes, Luke, four years old, a bit on the old side, but a lovely child, very sweet-natured, full of fun. Come, let's go and look for him.'

They set off in the direction of the dormitories, conversing as they walked.

'That little boy was very fair. Wheatish in complexion. Exactly what we are looking for. A bit old, though. We wanted a baby boy. Fair-skinned would be ideal.'

'A boy is a boy!' the man interrupted with a dismissive wave. 'Skin is only skin. Wheatish, blackish, it is all the same. Main thing, boy.'

'Well, we wouldn't want blackish, would we? But yes, it has to be a boy to take over my husband's business. We already have four girls and I cannot have any more children.' She launched into a detailed explanation of the devastating medical circumstances that prevented another pregnancy, finishing up with, 'It is unfortunate but after all, the Lord knows best.'

'Yes, indeed He does.' Mother Maria made the sign of the cross. 'You will love our Luke. He will make a very good Christian businessman. Highly intelligent, too, and very musical. He is our fairest boy.'

'Just what we are looking for!'

'An ideal son.'

'Your native place is Bangalore, you said? So your mother tongue is Telugu. No Tamil?'

The lady shook her head. 'Only Telugu, English and a bit of Hindi. The children do speak English?'

Mother Maria beamed. 'Of course! The Sacred Heart Catholic School is English-medium. It's the best school this side of Madras, and it is all thanks to our beloved Father Bear. He is a veritable saint.'

'We know. We heard,' said the man. 'That's why we came here. We'll send Luke back as a boarder when he's twelve.'

The lady repeated her still-unanswered question. 'Why did they run away when they saw us? I thought all orphans *wanted* to be adopted?'

'Ah, well, Luke and Anna-Marie are a little – well, a little *different*. They like to be together; it's a game. Once he… but no matter. Children will be children. *Anna-Marie! Luke!* Where are you? Playing your little games as usual! Come on out!'

The little group reached the backyard, a large compound shaded by coconut and papaya trees and dotted with the occasional scraggly hibiscus, bougainvillea or oleander bush, all baking in the sun. Chickens scratched here and there in the sand and picked among the weeds, and a calf, tethered to a coconut tree, gazed mournfully at the approaching visitors. At the back of it all stood the Baby House, a long low bungalow with a wraparound veranda thatched with coconut-palm leaves. In one corner, a vegetable patch where Pillai the assistant gardener squatted, planting onion seedlings; in the other corner a dilapidated playground with a tyre swing, a home-made slide of grey-parched wood sanded smooth, and a rickety climbing frame.

Another swing dangled from the branches of the mango tree, in pride of place at the centre of the yard. That swing was the clue; it shuddered, as if one of its ropes had just been released. As

if someone had just used it to hoist her- or himself up into the
mango tree's branches.

Mother Maria marched over to the tree, her generous bosom
wobbling to her stride.

'Luke! Anna-Marie! I *know* you two are up there. Come down
at *once*!'

The three adults gathered beneath the spreading crown of the
mango tree and peered upwards into a tangle of sprigs and twigs and
leaves: at body parts of children and parts of body parts glimpsed
through the foliage, at skinny brown limbs entangled with thin
brown branches; dark skin camouflaged as bark, arms and hands
and fingers clinging to boughs as if part of the tree itself, scraps of
colour from a faded dress and an old torn shirt like bursts of flowers
between the dark green of the leaves; and on closer inspection, two
pairs of bright eyes peering back with concentrated attention, alert,
immobile and petrified.

'Luke and Anna-Marie, come down *right now*!' cried Mother
Maria again, and, 'If you don't come down *immediately* I will send
Pillai up for you and he will beat you! You are naughty, naughty
children and don't deserve the kindness of these good people!
Luke, you are always following Anna-Marie! You're a bad little
boy! Come on down!'

She said this last in Tamil. The man and the lady looked at each
other and shook their heads. The lady leaned close to the man and
whispered. He whispered back.

Anna-Marie and Luke looked into each other's eyes and read
each other's thoughts. 'Go down,' Luke said to Anna-Marie. 'Go
up,' Anna-Marie said to Luke. And so they moved in opposite
directions. Luke carefully untangled his limbs from the tree and
slowly, smoothly, began to climb up higher. Anna-Marie, who
would never be adopted (Father Bear said so), slid herself down on
to the lowest branch, which was wide and thick enough for both

of them to sit upon on happier occasions. From there she leapt to the ground, landing lightly on the sand next to Mother Maria.

Mother Maria grabbed her wrist, her fingers tightening around it; she squirmed at the pain and tried to peel the fingers away, but they only gripped all the tighter. Finally, Anna-Marie gave up the fight, stopped squirming and stood demurely at Mother Maria's side. The grasp on her wrist relaxed.

The man and the lady ignored this scuffle and continued to gaze upwards, eyes fixed only on Luke.

'He's not coming!' cried the lady. 'He's climbing up higher!'

'Luke!' hollered Mother Maria. 'Where on earth do you think you're going? Come down here at once!' It was strange to hear Mother Maria shouting like that; usually she only ever spoke in muted tones, her voice as calm and placid as trickling water. Mother Maria could get cross, but you had to be really naughty to invoke her ire. Mostly, she was kind, so that some of the children even called her Mummy: Mummy Maria.

'Don't shout at him,' the lady said. 'If you're cross you'll only scare him away. You have to be gentle with him, coax him down.' Her voice changed. 'Come, little boy, come!' she wheedled, and held up her arms to the tree in invocation. The man followed her example.

'Luke!' said the man. 'Little boy Luke. Come on, jump into Daddy's arms! I'll catch you!'

But by now all that could be seen of Luke was his little bottom clad in ripped khaki shorts and skinny brown legs clambering upwards, fast disappearing into a forest of leaves. Lithe as a monkey, he grabbed the branch above him and swung his legs around it; hoisted himself up with knees and arms, scrambled up to the next branch and the next, up and up and up until he was so lost within the treetop not even a scrap of him remained to be seen.

Mother Maria screeched for Pillai. Pillai, a black lanky youth who could scale a giant coconut tree with his bare hands and feet in less than a minute, dashed over from the vegetable patch and, at Mother Maria's silent gesture, leapt up the mango tree. He too disappeared into its leafy heights.

Anna-Marie's heart pounded so hard she thought her chest would burst open. She could not bear to watch; she closed her eyes as tight as she could and prayed.

Don't let them take him don't let them take him please God don't let them take him for Christ's sake amen.

The lady cried out: 'There he is!'

Anna-Marie opened her eyes and looked up, craning her neck. There was no sign of Luke. The lady must have been mistaken. Anna-Marie tried to reach him with thought, but she was far too excited for that to work; Luke's thoughts could only be caught when her own thoughts were as quiet as a still pool of water, her mind smooth as a mirror. The lady cried out again:

'There he is, James, do you see him? There, look, look, on that branch!'

Anna-Marie looked upwards, craning to see. Sure enough, there was Luke. Her heart almost stopped, for Luke had crawled along one of the topmost branches that grew parallel to the ground and there he clung, near the very end and far above their heads. The branch was thin and bent down dangerously low, touching the branch beneath it.

'Luke!' yelled Mother Maria. 'Luke! Get back! Don't do that! The branch might break and you'll fall to the ground and kill yourself!'

Pillai, hidden in the treetop, called down: 'I can't reach him, Mother. If I go out there the branch will break. I'm too heavy!'

'Come down, come down! Don't chase him! He'll fall!' cried Mother Maria, and then screeched again: 'Luke, if you do not come down this minute I will tell Father Bear and he will flog you himself!'

But it was a lie, told to impress the visitors, because Father Bear never flogged the children. It was Mother Maria herself who would flog him.

'The poor little boy is terrified!' said the lady. 'If you threaten him it will only make it worse. Let us coax him down.' She raised her voice, calling out to Luke. 'Dear little boy,' she began.

'Luke,' corrected the man. 'His name is Luke, Anita. We have to entice him. He doesn't know yet what we have to offer.' The man cupped his mouth with his hands and, craning his neck, shouted up into the treetop.

'Luke, how would you like to have a *real* home and a *real* mummy and daddy? How would you like to come to live with us in Bangalore?'

Mother Maria switched tactics, adopting this new strategy. She shouted: 'Be a good boy, Luke. You are so lucky. So fortunate that these good people want you. You will live in a lovely big house with a big garden and have lots of toys and good food and sweets, and a real mummy and daddy and…'

'And drive in big cars! Did you see our lovely big car? You will drive in it!'

In reply it started to rain mangoes. Baby green mangoes, one after the other, pelted down from the top of the tree. Fortunately, none of them hit anyone, and soon Luke obviously ran out of available mangoes, for the downpour stopped.

'Bad boy, bad boy!' cried Mother Maria, forgetting the strategy. To the man and the lady she said: 'We do have other boys, you know. We have a very nice little boy called Thomas.'

The man and the lady put their heads together and whispered among themselves. It seemed they were willing to give Luke one more chance, for the lady once more turned her face upwards. 'Dear little boy,' she began.

'Luke. Luke,' the man said, and he too looked up. 'Dear Luke, we… *aargh*!'

Something splattered on the man's upturned face, and it wasn't rain, for it fell only on him and nowhere else.

'Oh my goodness, he's *wee-weeing* on you!' cried the woman. The man, howling in disgust, did a strange little dance involving feet, head, hands and a handkerchief, Mother Maria screamed at Luke and Anna-Marie covered her mouth to hide her giggles.

She felt sorry for Luke; he was always so embarrassed when he wet himself in moments of anxiety, sometimes even in class when he didn't know an answer and Father Bear looked grim and wagged a finger at him. The other children laughed when Luke wet himself, but never Anna-Marie; and she wasn't laughing at him now. She was laughing at the man, who right now was running, away from the tree, away from Luke, presumably in the direction of water, and his wife and Mother Maria were running behind him.

She looked up at Luke and waved. 'It's all right, now, Luke!' she called. 'It's safe.'

Part One

Before the War

Chapter One

The Day She Died

1933, Madras, India

The night before my mother died the brain-fever bird shrieked again, startling me out of sleep. That uncanny cry! A double screech, repeated again and again and again, ever louder, ever higher, ever more desperate, always in the silence of night, spiralling into frenzy, even madness. It made my heart race with a hollow fear; a groundless fear, for it was only a bird.

As always, I ran to Amma's room through the half-light and crept into bed with her. I could feel her smile as she said, 'Hello, Rosie, come closer!' And she pulled me into herself and I snuggled into her arms and my heart stopped its wild racing, and it was her last night on Earth. I was ten years old.

We rose, as ever, at dawn, and that last morning remains as clear to me as if it were only yesterday, the memory a precious jewel carved into my mind and locked there in a compartment of its own. Now and then I turn the key and enter, and bask in the keen sting of heartbreak.

It had started like any other day – Amma chattering away as she made breakfast for us both: idlis, like the Tamils, because Amma liked doing things the Indian way. She spoke Tamil like a mother tongue, and laughed it off when people said she should only speak English with me: 'But why?' she'd say, 'we are in India; this is our home. I am her mother, so she can call me Amma. I don't like this

Mummy business.' And she liked to cook herself, even though she had Thilagavathi, her right-hand woman in the house, to help her; 'Thila can't put mother-love into a dish,' she'd say.

I sat in the kitchen, watching her, listening to her, chatting with her while she made the idlis. Thila swept the veranda that wrapped our home, the swish-swish of her grass broom on the tiles providing a familiar backdrop. As ever, Amma had prepared the idli batter the day before, out of ground coarse rice and urad dhal mixed together; now, all she had to do was oil the idli steamer plates, pour the batter into the forms, and place them over the pan of boiling water. Soon we had a pot full of steaming hot rice-cakes.

Then laughter and birdsong on the veranda. Early-morning sunshine casting a filigree pattern through the bougainvillea trellis, like lace upon the tabletop. I can still taste those idlis. I never ate idlis again, after that day; they are exclusive to Amma.

And then I slung my leather bookbag – a present from Pa on my eighth birthday – over my shoulder, and she patted a strand of hair into place behind my ear, and walked me to the gate where Babu with his bicycle rickshaw waited on Atkinson Avenue, just like every other day. And I kissed her goodbye and she hugged me and we waved to each other as the rickshaw pulled away, and blew kisses; and she stood there waving and I laughed and turned in the rickshaw seat and waved back until we turned the corner into town. I remember her smile. Her eyes, drinking me in as if she couldn't get enough of me. That last view of her, waving, smiling, blowing kisses, remains etched in my mind as if it were a photograph.

And then I came home, and she was dead.

It was so sudden, they said. Just like that, a bolt of lightning. One moment she was alive, the next she was dead. They had taken her away to the hospital to do the tests.

A brain haemorrhage, the tests said. They didn't know why. Why her? Why me? Why us?

That day, I stopped believing in God.

It was Pa who told me, so distraught it all came out in broken lumps of words, gasping and bawling and snivelling. I'd never seen Pa cry before. He wasn't the type to show feelings. But that day he gathered me into his arms and howled out the truth. Pa, usually so collected, so distant, so unperturbed, now a blubbering wreck who clung to me as if I, a child, could bring her back. I didn't understand. *It can't be!* I yelled at him. *No, she's not. Not dead. Where is she?* I tore myself from his arms and raced to her room, but she wasn't there, she wasn't anywhere. She was gone, just like that.

And then I ran to my own room and flung myself on to the bed and buried my head in my pillow and I, too, howled; and he came and stood above me, and I felt his hand on my back as he tried to comfort me, and I heard adult voices, English voices, telling him to *let her be, let her cry it out, there's nothing you can do, Rupert,* and I vaguely recognised them as the voices of Uncle Robert, Pa's friend from the Connemara Hotel, and Uncle Rory, his colleague from the university.

Pa, in spite of his otherworldly air of being distracted – he's the typical absent-minded professor, Amma used to say – was also much loved in his own way. There was a kindness in his eyes, in the way he talked to people, that seemed to endear him to them, to be protective about him, and now they all rushed in to be helpful, colleagues and neighbours sending tiffin carriers filled to the brim with delicious meals, as if we didn't have our own cook. And cakes and sweets and a bottle of brandy, and themselves. Burrowed away in my room I caught this only on the periphery, of course; Thila told me everything.

Thila was almost as distraught as Pa and me. Amma had treated her more as a friend, or even a sister, than a servant, and like everyone else, she'd adored her; but being Indian she was also practical and kept the house running and me informed. It was her way of keeping me tethered to the Earth, to stop me drowning in the morass of my grief: she chattered away about all the comings and goings, brought food and tea and fresh lime juice and sliced mango and insisted on untucking the mosquito net, my tent of security, and hanging it up in a knot above the bed.

'You must go out, Miss Rose,' she said over and over again. 'I will take you to beach, no? I will make picnic, no?'

And always I shook my head and refused.

'Look! Lovely, lovely custard pudding! Mrs Lindsay send for you, Miss Rosie. You must try! Come, just one spoon!'

But no. Sometimes hunger and thirst did overcome me, and I ate a few spoons, drank a few sips of water; but it was all for sustenance, not for pleasure. Nothing would ever be for pleasure again.

It was all a jumble and a mess. They popped in and out over the following days; they and their wives. Four days later, Pa's older sister, Aunt Jane, and her husband Uncle Thomas stalked in, down from Delhi. They had taken the first train, they said; a three-day journey. Aunt Jane hustled to my side, made a lot of unnecessary fuss, and tried to talk sense into me, showering me with firm, sensible and down-to-earth advice. Her pleas to *come along, darling, you really have to eat!* rang with her inner frustration and came out as a reprimand. Finally, she turned to scolding. *Now pull yourself together, Rosalind. It's really time to be sensible.*

Aunt Jane had never had children of her own; she didn't like them, Amma had once told me. She didn't have a maternal bone in her body, and all she could think of now were *sensible* and *realistic* things to do. Her pleas and admonishments and rebukes fell on deaf ears. I wasn't listening, I didn't care. The only thing that mattered was that Amma was no more.

But one night on a visit to the lavatory I passed the living room and the door was ajar. Hearing voices, and hearing my name, I couldn't help but stop to listen.

'…but they had an unusual attachment, Jane, and I can't possibly…'

Aunt Jane's strident voice cut short whatever Pa was about to say.

'Rosalind really needs to snap out of it, Rupert, and so do you. These things do happen and when they do one has to be practical and think about the future. You really only have one option: boarding school. In England. She can stay with Beryl during the holidays; Beryl's children are only slightly older than her. Two birds killed with one stone: she'd be off your hands and get an excellent education. Moira House really is wonderful for young girls. Beryl's daughters are—'

I had to hold myself back from rushing in, shouting *No! No!* But Pa did it for me.

'I am *not* sending her to England! It's absolutely out of the question! Stop suggesting it!'

'But it's the only sensible thing, Rupert. Apart from everything else, she'd finally know what it means to be a proper English girl. And both sets of grandparents are there and would help keep an eye on her, mould her the right way. She could spend some of her holidays at Greystone Park, with your parents! Think of *that* advantage! You and Lucy have done her no favours; much too much Indian influence down here in Madras. Why, she's almost a *native*, the way she runs wild! You allow her to call her mother Amma, like some Indian ayah! Really, Rupert, you must…'

I wanted to rush in and pummel her to pulp, but once again Pa cut her off.

'Lucy kept her happy, and that's what counts. She was happy. And all I want is for her to be happy again. I'm not sending her to England.'

I had to stop myself from shouting *bravo, Pa!* at those words. But behind the rejoicing was deep frustration. Aunt Jane's voice was grating, her bullying of Pa despicable. I was glad he'd stood up for himself, for me, but really I was outraged on his behalf. But outrage with Aunt Jane was useless, a waste of a perfectly good emotion. I took a deep breath and held it and the emerging cry of vexation melted away. Amma had taught me how to do things like that. But now I wanted to burst into the room and fling myself at Pa and shout: *I will never ever again be happy! Not without Amma!*

'Children have to confront the world as it is, Rupert, not live in some fairy tale. Lucy was much too whimsical and otherworldly to be a good mother; not to speak ill of the dead, but—'

'Not a word more! I won't have you criticising my wife, and she's not even in the earth yet!'

'Calm down, Rupert. Don't raise your voice at me. So, if you flatly refuse to send her back to England, against my best advice, then you'll have to go with second best, boarding school in India. St Hilda's in Ooty is said to be quite adequate for English girls. Mind you, in the holidays you'd have to…'

'She is not going to a boarding school!' Pa roared. 'Aren't you listening? Rosie needs love and warmth, a *home*! I am not sending her to strangers! Are you mad? Have you no compassion, no understanding of a child's needs?'

I clenched my fists in excitement. *Hurrah!* This was a Pa I'd never known! If I had to choose three words to define my father, they'd be *soft-spoken, absent-minded, otherworldly.* I'd add *introverted; reclusive*, even, to that list. He never argued. Whatever Amma suggested, he went along with that. On the other hand, Amma had never suggested, would never suggest, anything as outrageous as packing me off to boarding school: not Ooty, certainly not England. Not anywhere. The Banyan Tree School was good enough for her, and for me. Of course, being only ten, I wasn't thinking, then, of words to describe Pa. I was only thinking, *well said, Pa!* I was simply delighted to hear him sticking up for me, confronting that dragon of an aunt. If he wasn't scared, then neither was I.

Satisfied that Pa was speaking up for me, I continued on my way, went to the lavatory and returned to my room, where I carefully lifted a corner of the mosquito net and crawled into the bed, tucking the net back in after myself. The room was bathed in moonlight, for the window was open to catch the balmy sea breeze that billowed gently against the ghostly white tent made by the net. The bed with the white net above it was an island, a safe refuge for me, a place away from the horrible world. But that night a cleft opened in the black cloud of mourning that surrounded me and instead of Amma, I thought about Pa. What would he do now? He'd be lost without Amma. That much I knew.

Chapter Two

Pa and I loved each other in our own way, but sometimes I wished I could enter his world, or he mine. He was a gentle, kind soul, who seemed to live in a different sphere altogether, a world of books and lofty ideas and languages. Words. Letters. Abstract concepts behind words and letters. Pa taught English at the University of Madras, but that was only how he earned his money.

His real work – Ma told me – was in foreign languages, mainly Asian languages. Pa had a special gift, she said, a natural affinity and a unique ability to learn the very languages that most Englishmen shied away from as being too alien. He had grown up in Delhi perfectly bilingual in English and Hindi, and when still a schoolboy had taught himself Sanskrit and Urdu. He'd studied all these languages at Cambridge, as well as a couple of European ones, French, and German, I believe, and his first job abroad had been as an English professor in Japan, where he'd learned Japanese in a matter of months. Then on to Kuala Lumpur, where he'd added Malay and Mandarin to his repertoire.

There he'd met Amma, my mother Lucy, whose senior civil-servant father had been transferred from Madras to the British administration there. With her as his wife he came, finally, back to Madras, to take up a similar appointment at the university. Here he'd learned Tamil in no time. They made a home right here, in the house in which Amma had grown up, and they'd had me twelve years later. He was thirty-five when they married, she just twenty-one. Which made him fifty-three when she died.

'So, how many languages does he know?' I'd asked Amma once, and she'd frowned and counted on her fingers. 'Ten, definitely,' she said, and laughed. 'But I'm sure I missed a few. Who knows? Probably Latin and Greek as well, and maybe a few more South Indian languages. Kannada, Telugu. I don't think he knows himself.'

Pa's great obsession was discovering obscure but grand and ancient works of literature in Sanskrit and Tamil, and translating them into English.

'It's all a bit useless,' Amma told me. 'Nobody will ever read them.'

'So he does it for himself, then?'

'Yes. He was given a small research grant – that means money, Rosie, money the university pays him to do this – to plunge himself deep into this world of lofty philosophical musings. I did try reading them once but – I think I'm just too dim to understand. Too stupid!' She laughed self-deprecatingly again. 'Pa lives in his own world, but he means well. He's the dearest sweetest man alive, but he lives behind a kind of a veil and he doesn't know much about the real world. That's why he needs me.'

And he did. Amma was the very opposite of Pa; outgoing, gay, gregarious, the kind of person who put a smile on everyone's face, who everyone wanted to invite to their parties, who people gathered around at those parties while she laughed and joked and kept them entertained. The kind of person you wanted to just – just hug. I needed her like I needed air, and in those dreadful days after she died I gasped and felt I was suffocated for lack of that air. I was lost without her love, without the warm cocoon of her personality around me. I suppose it's like this for every child who loses a mother.

Pa and I – we were both lost.

Pa's victory over Aunt Jane was short-lived. She was like a dog with a bone beneath its teeth. She wouldn't let it go. The next day, at lunch, she was at it again, this time in my presence. It seemed she had accepted Pa's refusal to send me away, but she had simply changed course, not given up on her interference. She'd had another brilliant idea.

'You simply have to make some changes, Rupert. You can't possibly manage all that Lucy did. And since you refuse to listen to good sense regarding Rosie's education, you must do the next best thing: you must employ a governess. I never knew why Lucy sent her to that common church school with the natives; this is as good a time as any to make a change. I can ask around for a suitable woman in Delhi; or rather, Robert can, through his colleagues at the secretariat. It might even be possible to have one sent over from England; perhaps an older and experienced no-nonsense spinster… No, that would take months. I'll have a think. Not one of those young flibbertigibbets, of course; they're all looking for husbands. They'd probably set their cap at you. I'm sure we can find someone suitable very soon. You'll have to employ more servants here, of course; a housekeeper, for one – an English one, of course, to manage everything. I mean, the house isn't very big, thankfully, but obviously with Lucy no longer here to oversee everything…'

Pa and I exchanged a surreptitious look. A smile played on his lips, and his eyes said, *don't worry, dear, I won't let this happen.* And I knew it wouldn't. I was safe. But not for long.

Pa tried to reach me. Once Aunt Jane had returned to Delhi, he made an effort to 'be sensible', as she had advised, to get over his own grief enough to try to comfort me and, horror of horrors, talk about the future. But how could there be a future without her? She was the rock on which our lives had been built. I saw my agony reflected in his eyes, and I knew he saw mine. There he sat, on the edge of my bed, looking down at me with eyes swimming with tears, and stroked my hair, and I looked back at him and that's how we stayed for a while, eyes locked and saying all that had to be said.

Finally, he spoke. 'Rosie, darling,' he said. An unusual thing for him to say; Pa was not given to endearments. In fact, I'd never heard him say the word *darling* before, either to me or to Amma, and as he gulped, sniffed, and started again, hesitant and faltering, searching for words, I wondered, beyond my grief, what new surprise was in store for me. But what he had to say, I already knew, because of my eavesdropping.

'Rosie, dear. Aunt Jane has gone back to Delhi and we now have to – to try and return to normal. Although – although there will never be a normal again, without her.' At those words his face quivered and stiffened and his eyes shut tight and his lips trembled as if he was trying with all his might to control a new and mighty wave of anguish. Pa, that calm, sanguine man who before now had seemed to float through life untouched by worldly emotions. I knew in that moment that appearances are deceptive. Pa's everyday demeanour of serene detachment was a mask for something more powerful than even I, for all my own grief, could imagine. I was only ten, but I knew, and I knew I had to help.

I sat up then, and put a hand on his cheek, and that's when he collapsed into me, flung his arms around me, pulled me to himself, and we both sobbed like babies, clinging to each other as if we were each other's lifebuoy.

But it helped. Once we were all cried out Pa began to speak, and his words came out with only a slight quiver and a mild stutter now and again. And I listened.

'They all, Aunt Jane and all my friends, think you should go to boarding school in England or Ooty. But you wouldn't want that, would you? I can't imagine how you would thrive away from – from – from *this*.' He made a spreading gesture with his arm, and I knew exactly what he meant. He said it, then. *Home.*

This was home. *This* was Shanti Nilayam – the Place of Peace, the name Amma and Pa had chosen for our home. Home – a sacred word. The only home I'd ever known. A sprawling garden of red-sand paths weaving between beds of canna lilies and hibiscus bushes and oleander. Wooden trellises up the side of the house bursting with bunches of bougainvillea in purple, shocking pink, bright red. Explosions of colour wherever your eyes roamed, colours vivid and clashing; or else the restful green above, of trees through which sunlight filtered, providing shade if you happened to be out when the sun was most blistering; or else the green palms of coconut trees towering against the vibrant blue of the sky, tall and thin, like matchsticks you could snap between your fingers yet resilient as the pond reeds that could bend double and never break.

Home was this house, a cool bungalow nestled within all this abundant foliage, shaded by two mango trees on one side and a tamarind on the other and a flamboyant tree to the front that dropped its brilliant blooms at the entrance to form a red carpet to the low staircase leading up to the wide veranda that wrapped the house in a cool ribbon of serenity, cooled by the sea breezes that wafted in from the east, vaguely fragrant with the scent of rose, jasmine and frangipani.

The grounds were spacious, extending back into a woodland area left untended; I loved to play there. There was also a patch of garden tended by our gardener, Babu, and his son. Once, in the heyday of the Raj, ours had been an elegant home to some very senior member of the Imperial Civil Service. The house had swarmed with houseboys and footmen and lady's maids and ayahs; you could even see the remains of a punkah, those huge fans operated by a uniformed lackey pulling a rope that swayed the fan back and forth.

Amma dispensed with all of that. She only had Thila and one boy who cleaned the house from top to bottom every day; or rather from right to left, as it was only one storey high, with its veranda where we could shelter in the shade on sunny days, or relax and play cards, or simply sit and chat with friends in the evenings.

Similarly, Amma dispensed with any furniture or decorations that weren't absolutely necessary. Some carefully selected paintings hung on the walls, and fittings were kept to an extreme minimum: beds and wardrobes and chests of drawers, of course; a dining table with chairs, a few comfortable sofas, and that was it. The veranda had by far the most sitting accommodation, because that was where we spent most of our time. Apart from Pa, of course; he had a study of his own with a proper desk and a chair and bookshelves, countless bookshelves, filled with books.

We also had a piano. Amma had taught me to play, a little. But it was singing she was most gifted at, and she sang with or without accompaniment, in the house and the garden and at the beach.

Not only was the house sparsely furnished; most of the rooms remained unoccupied. That Divisional Commissioner or whoever he was had obviously had a large family. With Amma, there'd just been the three of us. We occupied the living room, three bedrooms and Pa's office; two bathrooms completed the set-up. The kitchen was at the back, and next to the kitchen, as a separate annexe, Thila's room and bathroom. A little way behind the house stood the now empty building that had once been the servants' quarters, basically a row of rooms with a separate bath area and, behind it all, an outside latrine. Now, the building was almost derelict; the stonework was still intact and solid, but overgrown with creepers and the kind of weeds that can penetrate stone. If I had had brothers and sisters we'd have had such fun playing there: soldiers, perhaps, or some such thing. But there was just me, and this was home.

All this was encapsulated with Pa's gesture, in his succinct choice of a single word to convey so many meanings. Home was everything I'd ever known. It was love, family, mother, beauty, peace, safety, joy, mother, colour, serenity, comfort, mother, cosiness, protection, delight, laughter, hugs, heart, birdsong, flowers, mother… mother,

mother, mother. All this, and more, more than words could ever reveal, and it all came home to me in the instant that Pa spoke the word, and tears began to flow, but Pa – and I could see he was fighting back his own tears – took me by both my upper arms, held me away from him and shook me gently, and then he clasped me back into his arms, and then pulled away and continued to speak; a question.

'You wouldn't want that, would you, Rosie?'

And I sniffed and shook my head and looked up at him, hoping that my eyes could say all that was in my heart without my having to speak the actual words – for speaking, I knew, would bring on yet another rush of tears.

What I wanted to say was this: *what is home without its heart?* Amma was the heart of all this. She was what gave *home* its meaning. All those things that made home what it was: she had put them there. Without her, Shanti Nilayam was just a house. A house in a beautiful garden, it's true, but really just that. Its soul was missing.

Pa took a deep breath; I could see he was doing that thing Amma had often spoken of, pulling himself together. I knew she'd want me to, as well, so I tried hard, and somehow it worked and I was able to follow what he said next.

'But you see, it's difficult now. We have to somehow find a way to live on. We have to try, even though it feels impossible – a life without her. But it's what she'd have wanted. I can hear her now – can't you? *You sillies – of course you can manage without me! Just think of all the ways!* That's what she would have said, isn't it, Rosie?'

This time I nodded, my eyes still locked into his. His were so earnest, so tragic, moist with unshed tears, and looking into them made me only want to cry again but I did as he said and *pulled myself together,* and continued to listen.

'I want us to go on as before, yet somehow, without Amma. Thila of course will help, as she always has done. But there are things that neither I nor Thila have done yet because Amma did them and now she's not here. Well, really, Amma did everything, didn't she? That's the trouble, isn't it? She ran the whole thing, this place we call home, and now we have to run it ourselves. I mean, I have to run it. I have to learn to run it. And there are things – things she did – that I can't do, however much I try. She was your mother, Rosie darling. I can't be a mother, no matter how hard I try, because there was just something so special about her, about all mothers, I suppose, though not all of them have it…'

He stopped for a moment and I knew he was thinking of his own mother. Amma had told me about her, and about his father. She was a mother in name only, Amma had said; she'd never shown him love, and that's why he found it so difficult to show *us* that he loved us. 'But he does, Rosie, he does! I promise you that he does! He just can't show it, because nobody showed it to him! But it's right there inside of him, all locked up. Pa is a good man, Rosie, a man with the hugest heart ever, and you mustn't be hurt if he doesn't seem to care. He does. He cares desperately.'

So I knew what he meant when he said not all mothers had it. And I knew this was a special moment, a precious moment, when Pa was showing me that big heart Amma believed in, but that he could not show to anyone but her. So I nodded. I nodded vigorously to show him, *yes, Pa, I understand, and it's what she would want.*

'You'll continue to go to school, of course. You're doing well there and she would have wanted it. Your Aunt Jane wants me to take you out of school and employ a governess. But no – you'd hate that, Rosie. I had a tutor and I wish I'd gone to school. You like school, don't you? All your friends there? You're happy there?'

I nodded, but hesitantly. There was so much Pa didn't know about me. So much Amma had hidden from him! Amma had been adamant about my schooling; that I should stay in Madras and attend the Banyan Tree School and not be sent off to board like most other children of the Raj. The boarding-school threat was not a new thing in our home; it was a threat Amma had always resisted, a threat always hanging over her. I was one of a very few English children my age in all of Madras not to be sent to boarding school. Most, particularly boys, were sent back to schools in England, and didn't see their parents for years.

The girls were luckier than the boys. Most English girls in Madras were sent to St Hilda's boarding school in Ootacamund, the hill station, the one Aunt Jane had talked about, and that's where I should have been sent, along with all the other little girls with whom I'd gone to nursery school. From the age of six, one by one they had disappeared, returning only in the holidays, except the long hot summers when, instead, their mothers joined them in the coolness of the Ooty hills.

But even St Hilda's wasn't good enough for Amma. She had wanted me right here, here in Madras; and lucky for her, there was the Banyan Tree School. And Father Bear.

Chapter Three

Father Bear was one of Pa's closest friends – and as Pa had few really close friends, that was saying a lot. Father Bear was a Catholic priest; an Irishman, from Tipperary, and his full name was Father Bearach, 'Pronounced Bear-rock – but you can call me Barry or Bear, if you prefer!' he'd tell people.

We had always called him Father Bear, because that's what he was: a bear of a man, with most of the images that implies. *He's like a bear, isn't he, Rosie! A bear of a man, and so hairy!* Amma used to say. A thick shock of unkempt red hair on his head, a scruffy beard, bare hairy arms, muscular hairy calves poking out beneath the white lungi or 'lower cloth' he usually wore; like Pa, he dressed mostly Indian-style, the cotton lungi wrapped around the hips and tucked at the waist. Both, however, wore ordinary short-sleeved, front-buttoned cotton shirts instead of 'upper cloths', and even trousers and suits when occasion demanded it, or, in Father Bear's case, a cassock.

But the bear comparison failed when it came to personality. Father Bear was gentle and kind; forceful, but in a mellow, persuasive way, and determined, but in an understated, cooperative way. He got what he wanted by stealth, all the time convincing his persuadee that it was all their idea from the beginning. Father Bear could sell snow to Eskimos. Besides, he was funny and talkative and full of idealistic passion for helping the poor and needy; but also full of idealistic passion for God, whom he adored and worshipped and conversed with just as if He were real – which, to Father Bear, he was: the nearest of the near, not up in heaven but right here in his heart. 'God is made in the image of man,' he said, turning the Bible quote on its head. 'We create a human image of God, make him just like us, because that is the only way our puny minds can possibly conceive of that power and intelligence, of which we are only the smallest part.' Pa believed something similar; it's what he sought in those dusty books of his, so that's what made them friends.

As I grew up, I learned that Father Bear was no ordinary Catholic priest. He called himself a Christian freethinker: he declared openly – even in his sermons – that Christianity was just one path to God among many; a view he had developed through his long years living in India and observing the religiosity of Hindus, and reading their scriptures, and talking to them, and it was that view that formed the connecting link between him and Pa. He often came over to Shanti Nilayam in the evening; they'd spend hours sitting on the rattan chairs on our terrace, discussing God and religion and love and theology and charity and The Meaning of Life; debating the ins and outs of Christian theology versus the notions laid out in the ancient Vedantic texts, sipping their *stengahs* – whisky and soda – and smoking their pipes.

I would often join them, curled up in Pa's lap, the lull of their conversation, the twittering of birds, the whirr of the overhead fan providing a pleasant sense of comfort and safety. I loved the sound of Father Bear's voice; he spoke with a slow, melodic Irish lilt. If there was light enough, I would read one of my many books; sometimes I just listened to their voices until I fell asleep.

But sometimes Father Bear would address me. He loved children, and the twinkle in his blue eyes when he caught my attention always warned me when a joke was on its way, though his voice would be serious, so as to lure you into his trap. He had a strange magnetism; he told jokes and funny stories, analogies revealing religious wisdom, wherever he could, but it was the force of his personality that drew people to him. I loved his stories; I loved the way he spoke, in his soft, lilting Irish accent.

'Did you ever hear the one about the rarie bird, Rosie?' he once said, when I was about eight or nine. I shook my head. 'Oh! Well, let me tell you about the rarie bird. It's a called a rarie bird because it's so rare – it's only found in Ireland, in the magical Wicklow Hills, and it's a wee bird that often seeks human company – the Irish say it brings good luck, and if you find one hoppin' about in your garden, you have to make sure you put a feeder out, hang one from a tree, and the more you take care of your rarie bird, the more it'll trust you.

'Well, there was this big burly Irish fella from Wicklow called Sean, and he had a cottage and a garden and a rarie bird used to visit him every day, so of course he did what he was supposed to and put out a feeder for the bird and a bath for the bird. He and his bird became close friends, they did; the bird would hop so close to him he could almost touch her, but not quite. He knew it was a she because she had a nest, high up in the oak tree outside his cottage. And in that nest was a single egg. Just one. He climbed up the tree, he did, and he saw it, that egg.

'And one day the egg cracked open and a wee baby bird popped out. Sean, he climbed up that ladder and he was delighted! See, Sean didn't have a wife and he didn't have a child so he was very attached to that mama bird and her baby. So he would feed his wee rarie bird with bits of fruit and watch while the bird fed her baby, and that made Sean so happy. And the rarie bird would feed her baby and Sean would feed the rarie bird and watch her feeding her baby. Well, the baby bird grew and grew and it grew so big it was almost the same size as its mama. And the mama seemed to be getting worried because her baby bird refused to fly, and as well all know, one day a baby bird has to flee the nest, just as you will, one day, wee Rosie, though your da won't like that, will you now, Rupes? So this baby rarie bird kept growin' and growin' and was almost too big for the nest. Sean knew it and the mama bird knew it. Maybe the baby bird was scared, because it was on a branch quite high up and it was a long way down – maybe it was afraid of fallin' and hurtin' itself, maybe it didn't think it could spread its wings and fly.

'Well, the situation became quite serious. The baby bird was big, as big almost as its mama, and it still hadn't left the nest. By this time the mama bird had become very good friends with Sean; the two of them were so close, they knew what the other was thinkin', and one day when the mama bird came hoppin' up, Sean knew that she was coming to him for help. That baby bird had to fly, and even if he was thrown out of the nest, it had to be done.

'So Sean got a ladder out of his shed and carried it to the big oak tree and climbed up it to the next highest branch and then he climbed up some more to the next branch and that was the branch the nest was on. So he climbed on to that branch and said to himself, my, that's a long way down! I understand why that baby bird is scared! Still, there's only one thing to be done.

'And he reached over and tipped the nest so that the baby bird fell out; and the baby bird spread its wings and flew away. And Sean was so happy he began to sing a song – see, Sean was a singer, and he had a good strong voice, and his song went something like this…'

And Father Bear burst into song himself, and his song went: 'It's a long way, to tip a rarie, it's a long way to go!'

And Pa and I both laughed, and Pa's laughter was so rare I loved it when Father Bear came round because that's when Pa laughed the most.

Father Bear was a man with a mission, and his main mission at this time was the Banyan Tree School. It had all started many years earlier, when Eurasian members of his small congregation at St Kevin's complained that their children weren't getting a proper education.

All over India, children of mixed race – the offspring of liaisons, illicit and otherwise, between English men and native women – faced prejudice and rejection. These Eurasian children had no place in society, for they fell into the crack between English and Indian; respectable people of both races shunned them. Not quite British, not quite Indian, they did not fit into the tightly layered society of the Raj. Labelled half-castes, they were in fact the *out*castes of a cruelly elitist and prejudicial system.

Father Bear stepped in and managed to get the Eurasian boys accepted into St Michael's, the charity school run by the Roman Catholic Christian Brothers, the Irish missionary organisation that ran boarding schools all over India. This one in central Madras was for boys only: poor Indians, and Eurasian boys. That left Eurasian girls uneducated.

Poor Indian girls were anyway not sent to school, as they were required to help their parents at home, to run errands or look after younger children while their mothers did menial work. Eurasian parents, however, had higher ambitions for their daughters, and when Father Bear heard of this problem, he set himself the task of solving it. His thoughts went to a certain Miss Annie Besant.

Fortunately for Father Bear, Madras happened to be the home of the Theosophical Society, that bastion of progressive philosophical thought in India, and, arguably, the world. The Theosophical Society had among its aims the forming of 'a nucleus of the universal brotherhood of humanity without distinction of race, creed, sex, caste, or colour', and of encouraging 'the study of comparative religion, philosophy, and science.'

And so Father Bear had a 'wee chat' with his good friend Annie Besant. Annie, as he called her, had been president of the Theosophical Society since 1907, and schooling was right up her street. She had already established the Central Hindu College at Benares, based on theosophical principles.

The result of this 'wee chat' was a small school of initially five Eurasian girls aged six to ten years, who sat with their English teacher, a pretty young lady by the name of Miss Lydia Hull, under the enormous banyan tree in the luxurious grounds of the

Theosophical Society at Adyar, on the southern coast of Madras, and learned English and arithmetic. The banyan tree, already famous as the largest tree of its kind in the world, provided shade on hot days, for its branches spread out and sent shoots to the ground covering an area of 40,000 square feet, a perfect shady place to teach young girls. 'Just like the Buddha, they will gain enlightenment!' was how Father Bear spoke of these humble beginnings. On rainy days, the little group was granted permission to sit within a godown, or shed, elsewhere in the grounds.

It opened its doors wider, to girls from a wide range of Madras social strata. The English members of the Theosophical Society took note, and those who were parents realised that a private school for girls, run with the lofty principles of the Theosophical Society, was rather a good idea for *their* daughters too. For one thing, *they* were above the crass racism typical of upper-class British society in India. So why couldn't *their* daughters join the Eurasian girls of the Banyan Tree School? Soon, they did.

It was just a short stop from there. For the BT School – as it came to be called – also accepted the daughters of selected poor Indians who were eager for their daughters, too, to receive an excellent primary education. Gradually, the school grew. Other subjects were added to the curriculum, including Tamil, history and geography. More teachers were hired, both Indian and English, including a delightful lady called Miss Aditi Subramaniam, who taught Tamil and music. Members of the Society contributed generously, and a building was bought outside the premises where the fledgling school could grow and thrive – no longer a Catholic charity school but a semi-private one funded by a trust installed by the never-ceasing energies of Father Bear.

And this was my school.

As a child I knew nothing of Miss Besant, of course, but I knew that Amma was a follower and supporter and that it was she who had fought Aunt Jane and Pa's other sister in Delhi, Aunt Louise, who had both tried to insist that I should be sent to St Hilda's. Amma won that fight. It was a good school, and Miss Hull was a wonderful headmistress and Miss Brewer a wonderful teacher who had nurtured my mind since I was a tot of four. We all learned together and played together and from the outside we were a free-spirited, joyful group. Miss Subramaniam was my favourite teacher; I loved music, I loved her classes, I loved school. On the whole. But you couldn't see everything from the outside; you couldn't see Annabelle Relton. You couldn't see her reign of terror.

Annabelle lived at the other end of Atkinson Avenue. Her father was something Very Important in the East India Company and in the Theosophical Society and that made her Very Important, and she made sure we all knew it, and as luck would have it, her birthday was in April and mine in September, and normally she'd have progressed to the Senior Group the year she turned ten and I'd have waited a year, the cut-off date being 1 September; but Miss Hull, the headmistress, said I should go a year early due to my excellent test results; this made me the youngest child among the seniors.

To make things worse, my test results were even better than Annabelle's, which made me the butt of a thousand little jibes. On my own I was indifferent to another child's beauty or lack of it, or another child's clothes, and were it not for Annabelle I'd have grown up blissfully unaware of my freckles, the wildness of my dark curly hair, the fact that my mouth was too wide and my ears stuck out and my teeth were uneven, and that I was inelegant and clumsy and had knock knees. It was she who informed me, and the other children, of all these dreadful shortcomings. And she who sometimes hid my books or broke the tip of my pencil or spilled ink on my exercise book. Little things done behind my back that earned me a scolding from Miss Brewer, as well as earned me the reputation of being clumsy and forgetful and scatterbrained. Which I wasn't.

Not even Amma knew of Annabelle's subtle harassment. Miss Brewer's complaints were never too serious; she could laugh it off and put it all down to a scattiness I'd inherited from Pa, and it would never have occurred to me to tell tales. I bore it all in silence.

Which was why, when Pa now asked me if I were happy at the Banyan Tree School, I didn't nod right away. But I did nod, in the end, too polite to complain, too reverent of Amma's choice, and that settled it for Pa, for his next words were: 'I'll find a housekeeper. You'll stay here. I won't send you away to school.'

I threw my arms around him and sniffled into his chest and he squeezed me tight and I knew that somehow, we'd manage. We'd get through this. We'd stumble forward into this strange and lonely Amma-less life, together.

But it all sounded so desolate. It *was* desolate. We were desperate to make it work. Both of us. It had to work. We'd make it work.

And we tried: we did. Pa put out word among his colleagues and among the neighbours – those so-supportive people who came to our doors bearing cooked meals and condolences and offers to help however they could – and word spread. The word was that we were looking for a good English housekeeper, and within a few days the applications came pouring into the postbox attached to our gate, mixed in with the many condolence letters; some hand-delivered, some sent by post and even from as far away as Bombay and Calcutta.

Word spreads swiftly in the word-of-mouth network of the British Raj, and who would have known there were so many single women looking for housekeeper jobs! Mostly the sisters of established households, sent over on the Fishing Fleet from England to find husbands, Aunty Silvia told me later, much later, with a giggle and a wink: 'a youngish widower with a lovely house and only one child – an excellent prospect for a desperate spinster, Rosie!'

Chapter Four

But then Aunt Silvia herself arrived, unannounced, and that changed everything. Aunt Silvia had been Amma's best friend since her time in Kuala Lumpur. The daughter of a very senior functionary of the Foreign Office, who had been posted first to Singapore, then to Malaya, she had grown up in the Straits, and had met young Lucy, my amma, in Kuala Lumpur, taken her under her wing. They had been young girls together, pretty and gay daughters of senior English civil servants, much in demand with up-and-coming officers of the Raj, and both had been courted and won in that city, Amma by Pa, Aunt Silvia by a tea planter named Henry Huxley.

Both were eventually whisked away to, respectively, Madras and Ceylon. In Ceylon Aunt Silvia had produced three sons, the eldest born soon after her marriage, the middle one ten years later, the third a year before me. Amma, on the other hand, had thought herself barren as no child came along; and then, out of the blue, I had made my surprise appearance. Thus I was an only child. 'All the more precious, my little Rosie!' she'd whisper to me when she told me that story.

Now, Aunt Silvia immediately threw out all the letters. We didn't call a single applicant for an interview. She came, she saw, she conquered.

'Oh, Rupert, I'm sorry, I'm so very sorry – I only just heard! How absolutely devastating for you both! And Rosie – come, let me hug you, darling!' And she did, before she and Pa ushered me out to the veranda so – they thought – they could talk in private.

Her next words conveyed my fate. 'Rosie is to come and live with me. Of course she must. It's what Lucy wanted. I have it in black and white. Here.' And she whipped a letter out of her purse, a letter in Amma's neat handwriting, and there it was, literally in black and white:

> I know we spoke of this before, Sylvie darling, but I want to put it in writing: if anything should happen to me before she is grown up, I want my darling Rosie to be with you, a part of your family. Rupes adores her, and he'll object, the dear, but the truth is: he won't be able to offer her what she desperately needs: a family, the back-and-forth a growing child needs. He's an academic, lost in his work, and to pull him out of that world would destroy him. It will be best for both of them for her to come to you. She already adores you…

And I did.

Amma and Aunt Silvia, though settled in different countries, had kept in close touch. They exchanged letters regularly, and besides, Madras was not far from the island of Ceylon. It was hardly a day's trip for us to hop over and visit the Huxleys on their glorious tea plantation in the hills near Kandy, or, very occasionally, for Aunt Silvia to hop over with her sons Andrew and Victor, Graham, the eldest, being in England at boarding school. She was so like Amma! Just as warm and gregarious and embracing as her. The nearest thing to a real aunt I had, since Amma was an only child herself and Pa's sisters – well, the less said of Aunt Jane and Aunt Louise, or Aunt Beryl in London, the better. Amma dismissed them as old-school dragons, and that was that.

Secretly – I could hardly even admit it to myself, as it seemed a terrible betrayal of Pa – I could imagine nothing more enticing than being a part of her family, living in those paradisiacal hills of Ceylon. And now she was right here, and proposing exactly that.

Pa was distraught. 'How could she have said that! Even put it in writing!' For him, it was indeed a betrayal, Amma's betrayal of him. 'How could she doubt me! Of course I can care for Rosie!'

'Of course you can, dear Rupert!' said Aunty Silvia. 'But only at the expense of your work. You know how much your work means to you, how much you relish burying yourself in those old manuscripts! You can't do that and look after Rosie the way she needs to be looked after. You cannot replace her mother, Rupert. Neither can I, of course – but I can come close to doing so. A growing girl needs motherly care, not a housekeeper!'

'I can do it! I can! The housekeeper would attend to the house and I would attend to Rosie – I would!'

'I know you would. Lucy knew you would. But, you see, she saw beyond that. Being a mother is more than attending to a child, Rupert. It's—it's something far more subtle. Especially when it comes to a girl, a girl about to change into a woman. It's just – it's just different.'

I sat on the veranda, just outside the open window, listening. My heart ached for Pa, but I knew that Aunty Silvia was right. Pa's entire life was submersed in his books and papers. To picture him letting go in order to take over all of Amma's duties as mother – well, it seemed outlandish. Amma at the piano, singing children's songs with me, teaching me to sing. Amma and me playing hide and seek in the garden, Amma's laughter, Amma's sense of fun. Amma inviting the neighbourhood children for my birthday parties, Amma baking the cakes of her own childhood, organising the games she knew so we'd all be squealing all over the place: Simple Simon and Pussy in the Corner and Musical Chairs and The Farmer Wants a Wife. Amma and me walking down to the beach, hands swinging, bathing in the sea, frolicking in the surf. Pa didn't know all these things.

And I was ten. Amma had told me that I would soon start to become a woman and what that would mean, and that she would be there to help me. How could Pa help me to become a woman? It would be so embarrassing!

Pa was never happier than when buried in his books and his papers; the work he did at the university continued when he came home. Though he never complained when pulled out of his absorption in a particular text, you could tell by his initially confused and distracted expression, in the time it took him to 'come back to earth' – or 'come down from the angels', as Amma put it – that he'd been far away, in a different reality. He'd hem and haw, clean his glasses on his lungi – those ancient spectacles with their thick glass and metal frames held together with bits of wire and sticking plaster – blink several times and shake his head to dispel the cobwebs. 'What did you say, dear?' he'd say to Amma, and she'd laugh indulgently and repeat whatever it was; and if it was to come for a walk to the beach, he'd come; but one never got past the impression that he preferred that crumbling old book to the frothing back-and-forth of the sea.

And yet: 'Pa adores you! He adores us both!' Amma would say, and I knew it was true. I knew that though he could not give us much of his attention, there, deep inside, love for us both held him upright. And it was mutual. Pa, for all his distracted ways, was just Pa, and he was the third point in a triangle of love, the edifice that held us aloft. But now one pillar of that building had crumbled to the dust, the strongest of the three, because Amma was not just a supporting pillar, she was the very foundation. We were lost, and Pa had not the ability to rebuild the structure that had held us together. We both floundered. But while Pa could always retreat into and find solace once more in the dusty pages of those old texts, in words that held the power to sustain and nourish him, he lacked the ability to pass that on to me, to lift me up and nourish my growth.

That's how Aunty Silvia explained it to me later, much later; as a ten-year-old child, I could not grasp these subtleties. But even at the time, though I had not the understanding of how Pa functioned, I instinctively knew this truth: that Pa would flounder with me, but would find his feet on his own. And I felt his pain at the prospect of losing me, yet I knew that, left to himself, he'd be all right. And I knew that I loved him, and would miss him dreadfully, but that my days would quickly be filled with Aunty Silvia, my sadness comforted, the sudden void in my life replenished. I knew Amma was right.

As I listened outside that window, Pa's anguished cry was a knife into my heart: 'But why did she write *you* that? Why didn't she tell me? How could she make such a decision? Why? What brought it on? I don't understand! I mean, she left a will – why didn't she just put it in her will? Make it official? Tell me? Talk to me? Why? Why?'

His anguish leaked through every word; I longed to rush in and hold him in my arms and comfort him. I felt him floundering at the prospect of this new reality, whereas I... I felt almost guilt because for the first time since Amma's passing I could feel firm ground beneath my feet. A way forward. But it would come at the cost of Pa's pain.

Compassion oozed from Aunty Silvia's reply. 'Rupert, she did it out of love – love for you, and for Rosie. She knew it would pain you to even mention such a thing. How could she put such directions into a will – such a dry, uncaring document! No, she wanted it to come through me. She even discussed it with me beforehand, about a year ago. She had a dream, you see; one of those terrible dreams that seem as real as real life, a dream in which she was swept away by an ocean wave and drowned, and Rosie was left lying on the beach, and as she was swept away she screamed and screamed because another wave was sweeping down towards the beach and it would have taken Rosie with it, but just at that moment she woke up, in a terrible sweat and a terrible fear that she would die before her time, and Rosie would be left helpless.

'She told me that dream. I remember that day so well. It was a daytime dream. She had woken up from her afternoon nap, and as usual we were sitting on the veranda sipping tea, and Rosie was outside playing with Andrew and the ayah was looking after them both. Lucy was still trembling from the terror of that dream. It was all I could do to comfort and reassure her.

'If I die, Sylvie, you'll take Rosie, won't you? Look after her, like a real mother? Rupert won't be able to. I just know it. She needs a mother. Tell me you'll take her!'

'I tried to talk her down. I told her she wasn't going to die. We never really know, though, do we? We never know when our time is near. We just don't. We think we'll live forever. But Lucy knew. It seemed that dream really ate into her, made her certain she'd be taken, and soon. But I did argue, Rupert, I argued on your behalf.

'I told her, Even if it happens, Lucy dear – but it won't, I promise! – and how quick we are to make promises we can't possibly keep! – even if it happens, how could I take Rosie from her father? He'd be devastated! He'd never allow it! He'd need her more than ever!

'I know he'd be devastated,' she said, 'but only at first. He'd find his feet. Those old books, Sylvie – I don't understand it myself, but they give him strength. He'd need them more than ever. He'd need his work to keep going. But he couldn't do both. He couldn't immerse himself in them the way he needs, and give Rosie the kind of care she would need. It's true, Sylvie dear. I know it. I know him. Do it – do it for me. She can always go to visit him, in the school holidays, or he could come and visit you. It's not that far away, is it? It's not as if you'd be taking her away forever, away from him. He'd still be her pa, and she'd still love him.'

'I argued on Rosie's behalf, too. I told her that Rosie loved you, Rupert, and how could I tear her away from you? But she laughed that off. "Rosie's a child!" she said. "Children are resilient, and they adapt. It would hurt the first time but once she became a part of your lovely family, once she lived here, and had all this" – she waved her arm over the garden and the house – "once she got past the first shock, she'd be happy as a lark. She'd miss me, and feel pain, but she would find her feet eventually."'

Pa said: 'I can't believe the two of you spoke so casually about her death, and the aftermath!'

'It wasn't casual at all, Rupert. It was a dreadful conversation. I tried to dismiss it at first, but Lucy was deadly earnest. The way she spoke of it, why, it sent shivers down my spine! And afterwards I tried to put it behind me, pretend it had never taken place; after all, she recovered from the dream and was her usual gay and playful self for the rest of that visit. I thought it was all forgotten. But then came this letter. She had put it all in writing. She was that serious.'

'But the letter is not legally binding. You cannot take Rosie from me. She should have drawn up a document with a solicitor if that was what she wanted, and even then, as the remaining parent I could have the last word. That letter – it's worthless.'

'Lucy knew what she was doing, Rupert. She's smarter than you think. She didn't want some ghastly court battle for custody, which is what might have happened with a legal document; she didn't want you to fight for Rosie and win her through a judgment. She wanted your complicity. Your consent. Your understanding. She wanted you to agree that this is, in fact, the best arrangement.'

At that point I stood up and walked away from the window, into the garden.

It came to me in a flush of rightness, flooding through every inch of my being. Aunty Silvia was right. Amma was right. This was right. It was right that I should go with Aunty, away from Pa; that I would be happy, eventually, and so would Pa. I knew it was just a matter of time before Pa, too, understood and gave his consent. That Amma was speaking to him from beyond the grave, and to me too; I felt her now, felt her love and caring and vast wisdom. I remember her once telling me, long ago, when I was determined to go swimming in the sea even though there was a storm coming and the water was rough, and she said no. Sometimes you have to be cruel to be kind. Sometimes you have to say no and force people to do things they don't want. I cried and screamed that day but still she said, calmly, no. And Pa might kick and scream now – though he wouldn't, he wasn't the kind of person who kicked and screamed – but Amma's decision was right. And though nobody could force him to send me to Aunty Silvia in Ceylon, eventually he too would know it was right and he would give in and do what Amma wanted. And it was right for Pa. Right for me.

I said goodbye to all my friends. I returned to the Banyan Tree School one last time and said goodbye to my class and my teachers. Miss Subramaniam gave me a huge hug and then she said, 'Wait a moment, Rosie, dear.' She hurried to the staffroom and returned holding a long cotton tube and placed it in my hands. It was hard, and open at one end. Glancing up at her, smiling, I opened it. I knew what this was. It was her bansuri, her bamboo flute, the one she played for us sometimes.

'This is for you, my dear. You have such a good ear for music! Perhaps it can be your friend.'

I hugged her back and said thank you. She dried my tears with a corner of her pallu and wished me well. 'It's always a tragedy when a mother dies,' she said, 'but remember her in your heart and she will live on. And in time the pain you feel right now will be filled only with love, and love is joy.' I nodded, and I knew she was right.

Chapter Five

We left Madras two days later, in the pouring rain; the south-west monsoon had arrived with Aunt Silvia. Such a sad goodbye: Pa wept as he boarded the train with us, to make sure I was settled; and then he stood on the platform, outside the window, weeping as he waved, and I waved back, and leaned out of the window and waved for as long as I could see him, and then I wept too. Was I really doing the right thing? Would Pa be all right? Did he perhaps need me?

But Aunt Silvia managed to distract me; she was good at this, and it worked. This time, she told me the story of the *Ramayana*, the story of how Princess Sita was abducted by the demon king Ravana and taken to his palace in the hills of Lanka; of how Sita's husband, the Divine King Rama, rescued her with the help of an army of monkeys led by the monkey king Hanuman.

I had heard this story before, of course; both Amma and Pa had told it to me, along with the stories of Krishna and Arjuna and Karna from the other Hindu epic, the *Mahabharata*. But Aunt Silvia focused now on Hanuman, and his great leap from India to the island of Lanka, our Ceylon. 'When Hanuman was a child,' Aunty said, 'he thought the sun was a ripe orange in the sky, and he tried to jump up and catch it. He jumped really high and he nearly got burned, but the sun was impressed.' The sun gave Hanuman the gift of immortality, a reward for his courage and cleverness, and that's how he made the leap from India to Lanka to help rescue Sita.

'And,' said Aunty, 'that's how the monkey army came to Lanka, and how Rama rescued Sita.'

Though of course a faithful Christian, Aunty never had any compunction as to telling us children – me, and her sons – these Hindu stories. Like Pa, Amma and Father Bear, she thought that all the myths and anecdotes in both religions were to help us learn the deeper truths of life: to help us to be strong and caring people, who did not flinch before hardship and challenges.

But for me as a ten-year-old, they were just engrossing stories I could listen to again and again. And so we passed the hours, through the pouring rain, when little was visible outside the windows, down to Rameswaram at the very tip of the Indian peninsula, with me living through Aunty's highly embellished versions of the ancient myths. Oh, she was good at that, dispelling my sadness with stories of royal Indian palaces and kings and queens, and magic rings, and monkey armies swarming through the jungles to fight Ravana's demon army.

From Rameswaram we took the ferry across to Talaimannar, at the upper tip of Ceylon, and then another train down the coast to Colombo. There we went straight to the Galle Face Hotel, on the seashore, where we were spending the night; Aunty had a town house in the Cinnamon Gardens district, but, she said, it wasn't worth it to go there for just one night.

I longed to sink into bed, but still there was no rest. Exhausted as we were, Aunty insisted that we freshened up with a cold shower, after which she told me to put on my best clothes because we were going downstairs for dinner. Obediently I put on the Sunday best dress I wore to church in Madras.

So down we went to the restaurant. It was full of English guests and Aunty Silvia seemed to know half of them. She walked from table to table greeting people and introducing me as her new foster-daughter. I didn't like that. Not so much the foster bit but the daughter bit. Because I was still Amma's and Pa's daughter and Aunty Silvia couldn't just claim me as her own, but I was just a child so I said nothing except good evening.

Amma always said that good manners are important, especially
when you meet new people, and it seemed to work because everyone – well, the ladies, of course! – all said, *what a delightful child!*
Or, *what a pretty little girl!* I didn't know what to make of it. How
did they know I was delightful? And if they thought I was pretty,
why did they tell Aunty Silvia? And what did it matter? Anyway,
we sat down and waiters came and served us and then we ate. The
food was delicious; I had fish curry, a different kind of curry than
we had in Madras, just as good, but different. Aunty Silvia said
they use different spices here.

I almost fell asleep at the table, so Aunty Silvia took pity on me
and we went up to our room early. I fell into bed and was asleep
the moment my head touched the pillow. The next morning I woke
up to the thunder of rain on the balcony and the smell of rain and
the feel of the rain all over my body. And I shivered with cold and
excitement, because I was going off to my new home. The home
Amma had chosen for me.

We had an early breakfast, and then we went back up to the
room to get our luggage because Murugan had already come for
us. Murugan, Aunty Silvia told me, was the driver from Newmeads
estate and Uncle Henry had sent him down with the jeep to pick
us up.

But we didn't go straight home. Aunty Silvia couldn't resist
the opportunity to take me shopping in Colombo, to fit me out
with pretty clothes suitable for the new life I was about to begin.
Amma had let me dress like an Indian girl, in colourful cotton skirts
gathered at the waist, together with a tiny bodice, my midriff free. I
had several of these. I'd never known, before now, that Aunty Silvia
had always disapproved of Amma's chosen style for me.

But now she said this outfit would not be fitting in Ceylon. I had
to dress like the English girl I was. And so we spent the morning
being driven from this shop to the next, Murugan parking outside
while she and I hurried through the rain, Murugan holding an

umbrella over our heads, into the shop, where I tried on a variety of what she considered appropriate clothes: cotton shirtwaisted dresses, with tiny flowered patterns, pleated or slightly gathered, and belted at the waist. I didn't like them at all, but I said nothing. After all, I was the guest, and only a child, and it was not my role to complain. So I bore it all bravely and wondered how I would ever be able to climb a tree in this get-up; with my flowing Indian skirts all I had to do was tie them up, tuck them into my knickers, and I was free as a boy. Perhaps that was the part Aunty Silvia objected to.

After the shopping Aunty Silvia was hungry, so we returned to the Galle Face for lunch, and there she ran into another old friend of hers just back from England, and we spent another hour or two in the lounge while they exchanged news and gossip, me sitting quietly at her side. And then: 'My goodness, look at the time! How it flies when one is in town! We have to set off for home, dear Cynthia, we don't want it to be dark when we arrive – the hills can be quite treacherous, especially in this rain! Come on, Rosalind!'

Murugan picked us up in the lobby, held an umbrella over our heads, and bundled us into the jeep waiting outside. And at last we were off.

I'd made this trip a few times before, with Amma, but today it seemed ten times longer, up and down, circling and curving through the lush green hills that lay between Colombo and Kandy. The rain made the journey twice as long, because it lashed down on the jeep and the windscreen wipers could hardly keep up, slashing back and forth in a hopeless battle against the onslaught of water cascading onto the glass. Murugan leaned forward to peer through the window, the view distorted by pummelling rain, and the jeep creaked and groaned on its way upwards, round this hill and that. I tried to peer out of the windows but there was nothing to see except grey wetness.

I knew, though, that the hills were covered in tea plants because I'd been here before and I remembered. I remembered the Tamil women, bent over in the fields, plucking tea, or walking down the streets with great baskets on their head, filled with tea leaves. I remembered the colours of their saris, bright reds and blues, and though the clothes they wore might be threadbare the colours seemed something bold and brave, a defiant fist raised to the sky. And I wondered what it was that placed me in a white body privileged by wealth and status, and them in dark, almost black, bodies bent double in the sun. And I knew that even my boredom was a privilege, and I understood then why Pa buried himself in books in which he hoped to find answers to the puzzling enigma presented by human life on Earth. Why, why, why? What made me *me*, and them *them*? Why was I here, and they there? And I wondered if Pa would ever find answers.

All this came back to me on that endless journey into the Kandy heights, cooped up in the safe dry bubble of the jeep. The rain beat an incessant tattoo on the vehicle's roof, which helped lull me into sleep. I slept and woke up and slept again, never quite rested, filled with a strange mixture of boredom and nervous energy and vain philosophising, mulling over questions that had no answers. Even Aunty seemed exhausted; she had run out of stories, it seemed, and she too slept and woke and slept again and snored. Now and then we stopped at a roadside stall, where we drank tea, and once we stopped for a full meal at a hotel restaurant down a little side road. But apart from those breaks the journey seemed interminable.

And then at last: my new home. The jeep turned off through open wrought-iron gates and onto a sandy driveway, and at that very moment the rain stopped and the clouds parted to reveal the golden ball of the late afternoon sun, and Aunty Silvia cried out in joy: 'See! Even the sun is welcoming you to Newmeads! Welcome home, Rosie!'

The two-storeyed building they called home stood before us basking in glorious sunset radiance, golden light sparkling on the water that still graced the leaves and the flowers surrounding the building; droplets on hibiscus and lilies and bougainvillea, on puddles in the sandy forecourt, on the surface of the birdbath, filled to the brim, beside the short flight of steps leading up to the veranda. I couldn't help but gasp at the sight.

'Isn't it beautiful?' said Aunty Silvia. 'You see? Even the house is smiling for you! Welcome home, Rosie!'

Chapter Six

I slept like a log, but woke up once in the middle of the night, my cheeks wet with tears and a terrible sense of loss in my heart. I missed her so much. I missed him so much. What was I doing here, so far from home? Had it all been a terrible mistake? It was raining again, and the steady drumming of water on the roof above me seemed to intensify my sadness. But eventually it put me to sleep.

The next morning I woke up to a ray of sun on my cheek, warm and welcoming, the despair of last night washed away with the rain. I sat up in bed, yawned, stretched, and then ran to the window, which overlooked the orchard at the back of the house. In all my storybooks an orchard consisted of apple or pear or peach trees – *this* orchard was of oranges and limes, and the leaves, still wet from the rain that had fallen all night, glistened in the sunlight. To one side was the magnificent mango tree, branching out from close to the earth to spread out in the most delightful climbing frame any child could wish for; and it was then that I remembered Andrew and Victor and rushed out to the bathroom so as to wash and dress for the day and meet my friends.

Really, I'd known Aunty Silvia's sons, the Huxley boys, all my life. One of my earliest memories was of Amma taking me back to England on a ship, together with Aunty, Andrew and Victor. We were going to visit my maternal grandparents near Tunbridge Wells, while Aunty was going to spend time with Graham, who was at boarding school in Eastbourne, as well as with her parents-in-law, Uncle's parents, who had retired to England, the country they called 'home'. They stayed with the boys' grandparents, in their sprawling mansion not far from Graham's school.

I was only four, but I remember well how impressed I'd been with the ship; how I and the two boys had run around the decks and passageways, up and down the steep narrow staircases, in peals of laughter, escaping from our hassled mothers (who feared we'd fall overboard); hiding from them behind curtains and pianos and lifeboats, being as naughty as we possibly could, all under Victor's leadership.

I don't remember much of my grandparents, once we arrived; I believe they were rather cold and, though pleased to meet me, had little idea what to do with me. The same with my Aunt Beryl, who lived in Lewes and came to visit. I was very shy with them.

Of course, our mothers met regularly; we would often travel down to Eastbourne, which was hardly an hour away, to stay with them and the boys' grandparents in their mansion in the Meads area of Eastbourne, just a five-minute walk from the sea.

How I loved those visits! Uncle's parents were so very different from Amma's; they loved children and knew how to entertain us all. They had three Labradors, which we took for walks on the South Downs, and friends with ponies we were allowed to ride, and it was all such fun. I loved the sea, in spite of its shingle beach and water too cold to bathe in (at least for Amma and me) – so different from our own ocean at Shanti Nilayam. But you could spend a whole summer's day there, picnic on the pebbles, enjoying the mild English sun. You couldn't do that at the beach in Madras. It was just too hot. And the seagulls, oh, those naughty seagulls! Trying to steal our picnics, pooing all over our car; but I adored their raucous cry. Even now I can conjure it up in my mind; a cry that, to me, symbolises those halcyon days in Eastbourne.

But really it was just being together, all of us, that was so very lovely. And being with Graham, the big brother they'd all come to visit, all the way from Ceylon. It was the first time I'd met Graham, and I'd been in awe of him: he was so tall, so grown up, it had seemed to four-year-old me! He must have been about sixteen at the time, and mature enough, our mothers thought, to be put in charge of the rest of us, even little me. I suppose they were happy to spend time alone doing whatever it is young mothers on holiday at the seaside do when given a few hours' respite from their rambunctious children. And Graham was, indeed, mature, and had a certain quiet authority, even over Victor, which Aunt Silvia lacked. Perhaps it was just the fact that he was *male* that Victor respected; he wasn't in the least bossy or overbearing, yet he never had to yell, the way Aunty did, to keep Victor in check. In the absence of the two fathers, Graham was the adult male in our little combined family group.

To me, he was just kind and gentle, always considering my short little legs when the other two boys ran ahead, and staying close to me. To me it seemed that he must know everything. He certainly seemed to. One day we were out on the South Downs to the south-west of Eastbourne and, running behind the boys and the dogs, I put my foot into a rabbit hole and stumbled and fell, and cried with pain. Graham simply lifted me up and carried me home, and when they took me to hospital he came along and asked the doctor questions Amma had not thought to ask, and inspected the X-ray as if he could read it, which I don't think he could. But he certainly wanted to.

I hadn't seen Graham at all since then. The five of us had stayed in Sussex and Kent for the whole of that glorious summer, and well into the autumn, before taking the return passage to Colombo. Graham stayed on at boarding school, in the Huxley family tradition, like his father before him. Aunt Silvia visited him every two years, and I remember her vowing never to send another of her children 'home' for their education; this, Newmeads, *was* home. And Amma swore the same, concerning me. No: Victor, Andrew and I were to be educated close to home, and at least once a year Amma and I visited the Huxleys at Newmeads. Victor and Andrew were my big brothers. I couldn't wait to see them again. Graham, meanwhile, had finished school and gone to university on a scholarship without ever returning to his parents' home. This had been, apparently, a bone of contention between him and his father, as he had been ticketed to follow in Uncle's footsteps as a tea planter, heir to Newmeads, but he'd chosen medicine instead. So it was left to the two younger brothers to eventually take over the plantation.

Now waking up on that first day back at Newmeads, my first excited thought was of them. I'd not seen them yesterday after our arrival. I'd been vaguely disappointed but so exhausted after the journey I'd almost collapsed as I tumbled out of the jeep, sinking to my knees. I dimly remembered, now, Murugan lifting me into his arms and carrying me into the house and laying me on the bed where, in the past, Amma and I had slept. I must have fallen asleep immediately, and slept deeply all through the night.

But now I was eager to meet the boys. They were perhaps the main reason I was here, the main lure. I'd always wanted brothers and sisters and the prospect of joining a ready-made family had cheered me just a little. Wallowing in grief, and then missing Pa dreadfully, was utterly exhausting, but the prospect of reliving the glorious days of yore gave me just the spark I needed to run out into the new day with the boys.

In the bathroom I looked in the mirror and saw a face smeared with dried tears as if snails had slid over my cheeks. I must have cried in my sleep – again. And my hair was in a mess of tangles. I stepped into the shower and turned the tap and the cold water not only sloshed away the last remnants of sticky sweatiness from my body but cleared the mental fatigue. At last I felt fresh and eager to start the day in my new home and meet my old friends again.

Newmeads was delightfully situated in a wide, long valley between the velvet green hills below Kandy, hills covered in the parallel lines of tea plants, dotted with moving specks of colour: the Tamil women who plucked the tea buds and carried them to the factory in huge baskets strapped on their backs.

The house itself was tucked into several acres of forest, at the end of which was a lake where as a girl I'd gone boating and fishing with the boys and almost, but not quite, learned to swim. It was an idyllic setting; up there in the hills the climate was perfect, never swelteringly hot as in the city, cool in the winter months, cold, even, at night, so that we'd need blankets and shawls and cardigans; but never subject to extremes of weather – except, of course, for the downpours that came with the monsoon.

The house itself was surrounded by a glorious garden. Casuarina trees, gently ruffled by breezes scented with spices and flowers, provided shade at the sun's zenith, while tall flame-of-the-forest trees lined the entrance drive, sprinkling, in season, brilliant scarlet blossoms on the pale-yellow sand so that the entrance to the property was a wide red carpet. Songbirds chirped and warbled and sang all day long, and now and again a bright green parakeet flitted from tree to tree.

Although Aunty and Uncle modestly referred to it as a bungalow, Newmeads, as a home, was the exact opposite of Shanti Nilayam and actually a mansion. It had an enormous front hall and a wide staircase leading to the upper floor, where at least six bedrooms were to be found, one of them, now, my very own. Downstairs were several reception rooms, a music room, a library, Uncle's study. There was also, of course, a billiards-cum-games-room, where Uncle would play billiards with his male friends and Aunty would play bridge with her female friends; plus a downstairs nursery where, when we were young, I and the boys had been looked after by Sunita, the Tamil ayah Uncle had brought over from India along with her whole family.

Now Sunita was head housekeeper, in charge of a veritable army of barefooted houseboys in stiff white uniforms, a footman for Uncle, and varying numbers of kitchen staff depending on which family members were at home. Unlike at Shanti Nilayam, each room was crowded with heavy dark furniture, and various ornaments stood on sideboards and tallboys and tables, creating more than enough dust to be cleaned to a sparkle each day.

'Staff! I can't keep count of them! Sunita, you take charge!' Aunty would cry, fanning herself in exhaustion, and Sunita did take charge, not only of the house-staff but of the grounds-staff: the yard-boys, the gardeners, the chauffeur, the dhobi, and myriad other servants who came and went, silent on their bare feet so that you never heard them. I never learned most of their names, except for the houseboys and the yard-boys, who were all referred to by the adults as 'boy'. I did learn their names. It would have embarrassed me to call out 'Boy!' to a person only slightly older than I was myself.

But now I had other boys in my sight. My friends, Andrew and Victor.

Andrew was my age exactly, a month or so older, and Victor was two years older. That made them ten and twelve. Victor, being the elder, had been our undisputed leader, and he was fun and funny and full of ideas for interesting things we could do and discover; and he was a little bit naughty, often getting us into trouble, fearless and daring. Whereas Andrew was softer, more amenable and somehow just nicer, less brash.

Now, I ran around the veranda until I came to the kitchen, where I found Aunty Silvia, Rajkumar and Sunita preparing what they called a 'full Ceylonese breakfast' consisting of egg curry, potato curry, dhal, coconut sambol, and puffed-up puris.

Sunita gave me a smile that spread from ear to ear, revealing a set of perfect pearly-white teeth.

'Rosalind!' she cried. 'What a big girl you are now! You're almost as tall as me!'

As ever, she spoke Tamil. I ran to her and hugged her. I'd known her all my life; she had once had a double role as ayah when I was smaller. I snuggled into her, delighting in the signature coconut and jasmine scent, as familiar to me as the sense of being embraced by an enormous embodiment of love itself, sweeping me up into a place beyond grief. In my eagerness to meet the boys I had forgotten Sunita – now it all came back to me and, pulling back from her embrace, I looked into her big brown eyes, now moist with compassion.

'I'm so sorry,' she whispered. 'So sorry about your dear mother.' And we hugged again.

Aunty Silvia stepped up. 'She has grown, hasn't she? Now, back to work, Sunita, that coconut needs grating. How did you sleep, Rosie?'

'Like a log!' I said, as I gave her, too, a hug. Then, 'Where are Andrew and Victor? I can't wait to see them!'

'Oh!' she said, startled. And then, 'Didn't I tell you, dear? Didn't your father? I thought you knew – I thought – well, they're in Kodaikanal, in India, at the Kadai school – they're boarders there!'

My face must have shown the utter shock I felt, for immediately she said, 'But they'll be back in the hols. Don't worry, dear, it'll be soon. It's not as if they've gone off to England for years, like Graham. Only a few more weeks and then you'll all be together again. In the meantime, you'll make other friends. The Camerons live not even a mile away and they have a daughter about your age – maybe a bit younger. And…'

Priscilla. I remembered her. She was two years younger than me and quite a spoilt little thing, who didn't like running barefoot or getting her dresses wet or her hair untidy, or even losing a ribbon from her tidy plaits. My disappointment knew no bounds, and somehow I knew, I just *knew*, that Aunty Silvia had known all along that if I'd known that the boys weren't here, I would never have come.

'But didn't you tell Pa there was a tutor?' I'd been too devastated, at the time, to follow their conversation fully, but I knew for certain I'd heard her say something about a tutor for all the planters' children.

'Yes, dear, I did. There *is* a tutor – for the girls. There's you and the Cameron girl for a start –what's her name again? Priscilla? Penelope? Something with P. And the Penningtons have twin girls, a little older than you, and Dorothy Cook, our factory manager's daughter, she's about your age. And a few others. All from the English planter community in the area. I mean, there's a school in the village but it's for the locals; that wouldn't do, and so we all banded together to create our own little tutorial ring. It's hardly a school, but the man is excellent, I've heard. And later, you can go to secondary school in Kandy. Don't make such a face, dear, it's unbecoming. You look as if you're about to burst into tears. It can't be that bad, surely…'

I was and it could, and because I didn't want her to see me cry I turned and ran out of the kitchen, which I'm sure was terribly rude and probably worse than staying.

What was I to do now? I felt as if Aunty Silvia had pulled the carpet out from under my feet. I'd imagined coming here and being in a family and having brothers to play with. I knew about how Amma had always longed for more children, and couldn't have them. And how Silvia herself had always longed for a daughter, and would treat me as her own.

And now, I just wanted to die; or at least return to Pa. I rushed out into the garden and down the sandy drive that led to the main road. I had no aim – I just wanted to get away from the house, from her. I heard her calling me from the veranda but I did not turn around. Terribly rude, I know. I just kept running.

The drive was a long and sweeping one, curving around a cluster of coconut trees, their palms, silhouetted against a vivid blue sky, perched atop impossibly tall and thin and unwieldy trunks. The last time I'd been here, when I was nine, Andrew, Victor and I had been learning to climb the coconut trees, taught by Satish and Karthik,

Sunita's two younger sons, who could scale even the tallest trees like monkeys. Andrew and I still used belts tying us to the trunks, but Victor had managed to get to the top of one of the shorter trees without any aid, and he'd cut down water coconuts for all of us with the knife he'd tucked into the waistband of his trousers.

Victor was like that – just like a native, wild and free; he never wore shirts outside the house and ran barefoot like Satish and Karthik, just as he followed their example in everything, all unbeknown to Aunty Silvia. She'd have been horrified to see him wield a long sharp knife to cut the coconut stems, and to see the way he expertly slashed the tops off the water coconuts with a machete and cut holes in the inner core so that we could drink the delicious water, tilting back our heads, the green nuts pressed to our lips, the water leaking out and splashing off our cheeks. She was always berating him for his dirty bare feet and reminding him to keep his shoes and his shirt on. His feet were already calloused like Satish and Karthik's, and his body tanned bronze, and she didn't like that either, nor the fact that both boys spoke Tamil as fluently as if they were natives. As did I, of course.

All of this was the whole *point* of being here. As much as I loved Amma, as much as I loved the flowers and the singing and the gentle, peaceful, wholesome life we led at Shanti Nilayam, I really only came into my own in the rough-and-tumble of Newmeads, where every day an adventure seemed to lurk around the corner, where Victor was never short of some new derring-do, some new tree to climb or waterfall to discover.

And so I ran on down the drive, feeling sorry for myself; and that's why I almost ran into her. Her. A tiny slip of a girl, walking down the middle of the drive, a milk canister in each hand, both obviously full, because dribbles of white seeped out from beneath their lids. The girl was of very dark brown complexion and didn't look any more than six. She wore the native dress of a long gathered skirt similar to the ones I used to wear back home, only hers was faded, with a flowery pattern that had obviously once been brightly coloured in reds and greens, and a short bodice buttoned up the front, equally patterned but equally faded. Her hair was thick and black and straight, pulled away from her face and falling down her back in a heavy plait that reached almost to her waist, and decorated with a twist of jasmine and marigold, a piece of a garland. And she was beautiful – oh, so beautiful. She was a vision, an apparition. I skidded to a stop before her, and she too stopped and gazed at me with the most enormous, blackest eyes I'd ever seen.

I was just about to say '*wannakum*', the Tamil greeting, but she beat me to it by saying, 'Good morning, Miss!' in a pleasant lilting voice. I returned the greeting and then we introduced ourselves – her name was Usha – and I turned and walked back with her to the bungalow, and as we walked, we talked.

We both spoke English and Tamil fluently; her school had given English lessons as part of the curriculum, as most of the children would go on to work for English employers. Her English was almost as good as mine, but enhanced with a lilting Ceylonese accent.

Usha was the daughter of Rajkumar and Sunita, and she wasn't six at all, she was nine, just a year younger than me; and the reason I had never met her before was that until recently she had been living with Sunita's sister in the village so that Sunita could live with Aunty Silvia and the family at Newmeads. Up to now she had attended the village school, but now her parents thought she had had enough schooling and she was required to help in the kitchen instead, in preparation for her marriage.

'Marriage!' I said in shock. 'You're not getting married, are you? You're just a child!'

She giggled at that. 'No, of course not! Not now! But one day, of course.'

'Oh,' I said, relieved, but then something else occurred to me. 'Let me carry one of those,' I said, pointing to the canister nearest to me. 'They look heavy.'

She reacted with shock. 'No, Miss! Of course not! I am just a servant, I cannot let you do my work!'

'Don't be silly, you're not my servant! Come, give it to me!'

And I reached out and put my hand on the handle and at first she tried to gently pull it away, but the danger of it spilling was too great so she let me have it.

It was heavier than I'd expected. Much heavier. 'Oh, it's so heavy!' I said.

She giggled again. 'Not as heavy as a pail of water!'

'And you bring milk every day?'

'Yes. There's a dairy farmer, Govinda, who sets up a milk stall down the road every morning, and all the women come to buy milk from him. It's good milk, really creamy, because he treats his cows well.'

Already my arm was beginning to hurt, badly. I stopped and put the canister on the ground to give my muscles a rest, and wrung my hands together because the wire handles had made them sore. Putting down the canister was a silly thing to do, because immediately Usha grabbed it again and walked on with one in each hand, as before. She gave me a cheeky grin. 'Come on, Amma's waiting for the milk.'

'Give it back to me!'

'No!' she said. 'It's too heavy for you and it will take too long. Amma is waiting.'

She spoke with an air of confidence and firmness that was unusual in a girl so small. And in a native; they were usually so deferential. But she was right, I couldn't manage. I couldn't believe that such a little girl, so skinny, her arms like sticks, could carry the canisters with such ease, and I told her so.

'You're so strong!' I said.

'Yes,' she said simply. 'Work makes you strong.'

Chapter Seven

Over the next few days, the next few weeks, Usha and I became friends. It wasn't the usual kind of childhood friendship in which you just play, for most of the time Usha had to work. So I had to adapt myself around her duties, and sometimes I even helped.

The monsoon brought yet more rain, every day, but rain or shine Usha brought the milk and fetched water. She'd go off to the well whenever there was a pause in the rain. And I would go with her and stand watching while she lowered the bucket into the depths below, letting it dangle down, down, down. When it was full she had to wind the pulley to bring it back up, now slopping water over the edges, and that was when I could help a little, holding the clay containers steady while she filled them from the bucket. They were pot-bellied vessels with narrow necks, so she had to pour carefully not to miss the opening, which was hardly more than three inches wide. But she was good at it, and really, I felt quite useless – I had the feeling she was doing me a favour, rather than I her. When all the water vessels were full – there were several of them – she'd hoist first one and then a second on to her hips and walk back to the house like that, her arms slung around the necks of the vessels and the rounded part supported by her hips.

Which was odd, because, being still just a child, she really didn't have hips; yet she'd mastered the art of balancing the jugs against her body so naturally it seemed easy. It was at this point that I felt the most useless, because try as I might, I could not help. I would have gladly carried two more pots, but she flatly refused to let me, and besides, when I did try, once, to lift one of the jugs I could not support it, as she did; it simply slipped down to the ground, tilting dangerously so that water slopped out. She only laughed at that and filled it up again, and we walked back to the house, me empty-handed beside her and feeling terrible for that fact. I felt so sorry for her, but she seemed not to mind, walking with a graceful swinging gait, arms slung around the pots, or sometimes, even, on her head, which probably accounted for her perfect posture and grace of movement. She could carry loads on her head with no hands; I tried that myself, and always failed. I felt so stiff and awkward beside her!

But I did help her with other tasks. We'd sit on the veranda preparing vegetables, peeling potatoes or sifting through rice to remove tiny stones and weevils, or shelling peas, or cutting carrots and lady-fingers, or trimming string beans. Neither Sunita nor Aunty Silvia approved of me helping Usha at first, but Aunty Silvia quickly realised that I needed some kind of an occupation until I started school in a few weeks, as well as someone my age to talk to after the disappointment with the boys, and quickly changed her mind. Especially now, with the house enclosed in a curtain of rain day after day, Aunty knew that Usha was my best distraction from boredom. Sunita's disapproval never ceased, though; whenever she looked at us, sitting together and chatter-ing, she frowned, but there was nothing she could do as long as Aunty Silvia acquiesced.

And how we chattered! After she had overcome her initial shyness, Usha showered me with question after question: about my life in Madras, about Pa, about Amma, about the Banyan Tree School, about what I knew and didn't know, about English habits and customs. She had a probing, engaging curiosity: she wanted to know everything, and even the questions about Amma, which might have brought me pain if asked by anyone else, were neither awkward nor embarrassing, and I was able to tell her about Amma with an ease and a sense of acceptance I had not known before, and in this she helped me more than a little to move to a place beyond grief.

Of course, I too asked her questions, but her life was simpler and more obvious and I was wary of questions that might highlight the difference in our status and wealth; I did not by any means want her to feel any sense of inferiority. That was something both Amma and Pa had drummed into me, as well as the teachers at the Banyan Tree School: in spite of our different roles in life, our different status, we, the English, were not superior to the Indian or Ceylonese people. Both my parents had a sharp and disapproving eye for racial arrogance, so normal in our English circles; they'd point it out to me whenever it reared its ugly head and made sure I did not adopt such attitudes. And yet, the difference in our situations was so obvious it hurt, and I hated the fact that I was, socially, above her.

It was she who didn't seem to mind, who took it all as a given. She was relaxed and open and so very natural! Her questions were candid and without embarrassment, and in time I began to be equally candid. I did not hide from her the fact that I was shocked that her parents were already keeping their eyes open for a suitable husband for her: that they would choose, and she would have little say in the matter, and marry early.

'But I do have a say!' she said, laughing. 'They will show me a photo, and if I don't like him I'll say so and they'll choose another. They won't make me marry someone I don't like! My parents love me and will choose well. I trust them.'

'But it's not just the photo!' I cried, snapping open a pea shell with frustration. 'What about love? I wouldn't want to be married to anyone I didn't love!'

'But I *will* love him!' she answered. 'Once we live together we will learn to know and to love each other.' She made it sound so simple, so obvious. In fact, she was shocked at the fact that in England, we choose our partners ourselves.

'But how do you meet someone? Do you just go up to someone and tell them you want to marry them? How does it happen?'

I actually had no idea. I was only ten, and knew nothing about marriage beyond what I'd seen with Amma and Pa. I knew their story; Amma had told me a hundred times.

'Well, you might be at a party and you see someone and you fall in love with them so you ask to be introduced. And then the man courts the woman and then they marry.'

'What does that mean – he courts her?'

'Well, he might take her out for a walk. Or on a boat trip. Or to a restaurant. And he lets her know he likes her, and then he asks her to marry him, and if she agrees, she says yes.'

'But how do you even *meet* someone?' she insisted. 'How can you just leave it all to chance? What if you never run into someone suitable? It's all so… so…'

She searched for a word, and I helped: 'Random?' I suggested. It was a word she didn't know, so I explained, and she nodded.

Usha thought about that for a while in silence, shaking her head slowly as she shelled the peas. And then she said, 'I think our way is better.'

And nothing I could say would change her mind.

Usha lived with her parents and youngest brother Satish in a row of cottages at the back of the grounds at Newmeads, the so-called servants' quarters, a label I abhorred but she didn't seem to mind. Murugan, the driver, and his wife Binu also had a cottage there, as did Ram, Uncle Henry's personal servant-cum-butler, and his wife Anjali, Aunty Silvia's personal maid; unlike the other servants, Ram and Anjali were from North India; all the others were Tamils, just like all the tea pluckers who worked on the plantation. I never understood why so many servants were needed; Amma had only ever had Thila, who lived in her own room at the back of the house, and not only cleaned but cooked; plus a dhobi, who came and went to deal with the laundry as needed. I'd never even had an ayah, a minion all the other English mothers seemed to regard as indispensable. But then, there were only three of us, whereas the Huxleys when all at home were five-plus-me.

Usha's two oldest brothers were by now married and worked in Colombo and Kandy respectively. Her other brother Karthik, meanwhile, had found work as a trainee cook at the Galle Face Hotel in Colombo, a job facilitated for him by Uncle Henry. Satish, the youngest of the four brothers, worked as our gardener; he had always had a knack for growing things, for caring for plants and tending them till they flowered, and it was his magic touch that had made Newmeads such an oasis of colour. Both Usha and Satish worked hard and much as I'd have loved to spend more time with Usha, she simply didn't have the time; unless I joined her in her work – and that without distracting her – she had not a minute spare for me.

The thing was, I was bored, and Usha helped relieve that boredom. Aunty had decided that I should not yet join the neighbourhood tutorial group – I was still in mourning, after all, and she thought it better that I get to know the other girls involved first, play with them, become friends. Yet she never made any attempt to introduce me to them, but simply left me to my own devices. I should join the group after the summer holidays, she said, and just concentrate on enjoying myself and feeling at home. But with nothing to do all day, Usha became my raft to tide me over the long and empty days. Which meant that I had to blend myself into her life, rather than vice versa. What was for her work became play for me.

However, sometimes she was able to extract herself from household duties, especially in the early afternoon and the evening. Uncle Henry had his lunch at the plantation's factory several miles away, which had its own little canteen, so Usha often got this time off, and then we'd sit together in the rose pergola and I would read to her from my beloved storybooks, and sometimes she read to me from the same books. She could not read as well or as quickly as I could, however, for her schooling had been limited by her household duties in her aunt's household in the village, mostly tending her younger cousins. Yet she was eager to learn more, and she learned quickly, and I made it my job to ensure she always had a book to read. And so, in the three weeks between my arriving at Newmeads and the boys' return from Kodaikanal, Usha and I became firm friends.

But then the boys came back.

I ran excitedly into the kitchen. 'Usha! Usha! Come quickly! They're back, they're back!'

She knew exactly who 'they' were. I hadn't stopped talking about the boys for days. I'd told her all about the fun we'd all had and how much fun she'd now have, with all of us together. I was looking forward to introducing her to them and to having another girl join the gang.

But Usha only looked down at the pot she was stirring. 'That's nice,' she said, without looking round at me. 'But I have to work now.'

'It's all right, you can come! She can, can't she, Sunita?'

Sunita and Usha exchanged a glance, but Usha's back was to me so I couldn't read her expression. Sunita frowned, though, and said, 'I have some more work for her; with the boys back, there is more to do.'

'Oh, please, Sunita, please! Just for a few minutes! I just want her to meet them! She can come back right away! I promise.'

Another exchange of glances. I grabbed Usha's hand. 'Come on, Usha! You can come back in a minute! I'll help if you like!'

I tugged at her. She met my eyes for a second, shook her head very slightly, then turned again to her mother. Sunita sighed, and said, 'Very well, then, Usha, you may go, but only for a few minutes.

Please come right back here – and, and – be a good polite girl! Remember your place!'

'Hooray!' I cried, and once again tugged at Usha. She let go of the wooden stirring spoon and let me draw her away from the stove. I felt her reluctance, and I knew the cause. I decided to reassure her.

'You don't have to be shy with the boys! I promise they'll love you as much as I do! I know that you think you're a servant and shouldn't be mixing with us, but we're all children and it doesn't count! It really doesn't. My amma and pa always said all humans are equal, and we whites are not above the natives. It's just different roles we play in life, but we're all of equal value, really! I know Aunty Silvia doesn't really agree but she won't mind, I promise! The boys will persuade her to let you play with them, just like I persuaded her. She does everything the boys tell her – look, there they are! Andrew! Victor! Wait!'

They were walking away, down the drive, obviously eager to reclaim their home and find again all the hidden corners of the grounds, all their secret places. All *our* secret places.

I started to run to catch up, letting go of Usha's hand, then noticed she wasn't running, so I stopped to let her catch up again. I called again: 'Andrew! Victor! Wait for us!'

The boys did stop then, and turned around to let Usha and me catch up, Usha still a few paces behind me. I had of course already greeted them when Murugan had driven them up in the car and helped them unload their luggage. It had been so exciting, with Aunty Silvia fussing around and them talking nineteen to the dozen! But I was excited for another reason too. I'd told them there was someone I wanted them to meet and ran off to fetch Usha. It was a little disappointing that they hadn't waited, but I could understand – they were just too eager to be off, and it had taken me a while to fetch her. They'd just been impatient, that was all.

'This is Usha!' I said as I ran up, and turned to gesture towards my friend, who was slowly walking up. 'Sunita's daughter.'

'We know,' said Victor, frowning. 'Mummy told us.'

'She's great fun!' I said. 'And I bet she can climb a coconut tree faster than you, Victor!'

I'd said it with a laugh, teasing him, but he didn't seem to appreciate it. He stood there, sullen, while Andrew fidgeted on his feet. Usha stopped in her tracks and didn't come nearer.

'Well? Aren't you going to say hello?'

At last I picked up on everyone's awkwardness. I looked from the boys to Usha and back again. I knew it was the boys' duty to welcome her – it was only polite. But they weren't doing it. Victor still looked surly, and Andrew– well, Andrew looked embarrassed. I was sure that had it been him alone, it would have been different, but Andrew always took his cues from Victor.

Finally, Victor remembered his manners. He raised a hand and said gruffly: '*Wannakum.*' And then he immediately turned and marched away. Andrew stood for a few minutes, looking from Victor walking away, to Usha, and back again. She had placed her hands together in a namaste and bowed her head and whispered '*wannakum*' back.

Andrew said, 'Nice to meet you!' but he too then turned and ran after his brother. And then Usha turned and walked back towards the house. I looked from the boys to her, back and forth, for a few seconds, and then I cried, 'Bye, Usha, see you later!' and ran after the boys.

For a while after that awkward meeting I felt guilty at deserting Usha, but I was delirious with joy that the boys were back and soon it was as if we had never been friends. I convinced myself she didn't mind at all, and silenced that guilty conscience by telling myself that it was always me who had sought her out, never the other way around. That Usha anyway chose work over play, duty over friendship. But deep inside I knew I'd abandoned her. And that I must have hurt her. Yet she never showed that hurt. When the boys returned to their school at Ooty at the end of the holidays, Usha and I picked up our friendship as if it had never been interrupted. She made me no reproach, and I never apologised. And so we settled into a strange on-and-off relationship: off when the boys came home, on when they returned to boarding school. Somehow it worked.

The boys' return was all that I could have wished for. Once again, I was at home; once again, it was us against the world, Victor our leader, Andrew and I his eager acolytes. They didn't mind having me, a girl, tagging along, and I was eager to prove that anything they could do, I could do, if not better, then just as well. Never as well as Victor, of course, who was far and away the fastest, strongest, most intrepid, most adventurous, most daring of us all. But Andrew and I – we were equals in every way, and I was pleased to see that this time around I could climb higher than he could up a coconut tree. That's because I had taken lessons from Usha, who by now was almost as good as Satish. Victor would have been mortified had he known how she could shoot up a tree, as quick and lithe as a monkey, not needing a belt because she was so small and light. But I never told him, and he never knew.

Chapter Eight

That embarrassing episode with Usha exemplified the difference between the two boys. Victor and Andrew were, in fact, the exact opposite of each other. Andrew was soft and gentle; Victor was hard, tight-balled muscle, and rough in manner.

Take music, for example. Aunty, who had as a girl dreamed of being a concert pianist, had given all her children piano lessons. She had taken on a few other children as music pupils, too, the children of other tea planters who lived nearby, and she had helped me with my own playing, giving me more advanced goals. I'd been a willing pupil, competent but not extraordinarily so.

Andrew was an easy, good pupil and had loved the lessons. He had a natural gift for all things musical, poetic and lyrical.

Victor was different. He had rebelled against lessons, against the piano, against his mother. She had struggled with him from the beginning, tried to force him, and the more she forced, the more he rebelled. Even I, a child myself, could see that forcing him only made it worse, but she was adamant; she wanted to break him, but she couldn't. Even worse was comparing him with Graham.

'Graham wasn't particularly gifted either, but he worked hard!' she lectured Victor. 'Diligence is what it takes! He didn't have a musical gift, like Andrew, but he took his lessons seriously! You should emulate Graham!' And she made him sit at the piano and practise endless scales.

'Oh, Graham! Your model eldest son, your perfect Graham!' Victor would retort. 'But I'm not Graham!' He'd slam down the cover of the keyboard and simply run off.

'Never again! I'm never going to teach another child the piano!' said Aunty one day, and that was that.

Completely different characters. Yet Andrew adored Victor and emulated him, perhaps because of Uncle Henry, who praised Victor to the skies for his manliness, and disapproved of Andrew's 'sissiness'.

That was a pity, because in fact Andrew had by far the better character, and I am not at all convinced that raw brawn actually equals strength. Andrew had a strength of his own, a moral strength, an ethical strength, which I was convinced would one day distinguish him as a man of substance. Once Andrew's heart was won, it was won forever, through thick and thin, and he would fight any battle for the sake of whatever had won his heart.

To begin with there was Flopsy, the ginger kitten. Shortly after I moved into Newmeads – those first school holidays, in fact – we went to visit another planter family, the Carruthers. They had a cat, which had just had kittens, a large litter hardly two weeks old. All except one were robust little things scrambling to drink at their mother's teats. But one was tiny, and weak, a runt. Mr Carruthers said he was going to kill it, and the only reason he had not done so yet was because his daughter, a girl about five years older than me, had begged him not to. But he was determined. 'Nature takes care of the weakest, and so must we humans,' said Mr Carruthers. And that was that.

But Andrew fell in love with that runt. He held it and stroked it and, on the way home, begged his mother to rescue it and give it to him. At first she refused but Andrew begged and begged so much, promised so much good behaviour, practised his piano so diligently, studied voluntarily at home in subjects he was weak in, that she eventually relented, and Flopsy was brought home four weeks later. Flopsy was a poor little thing, but Andrew adored her. He cuddled and kissed her, played with her for hours on end. He was besotted. And even though Victor teased him, Andrew loved that cat as a mother loves her child.

And the love was mutual. Flopsy became the best-behaved cat I'd ever known. The moment Andrew came through the door, Flopsy would be there, twirling around his legs until he picked her up, purring and closing her eyes in utter bliss. Flopsy loved no one but Andrew. She followed him all over the grounds; wherever Andrew went, there Flopsy would be. She came when called. She brought him dead mice and laid them at his feet. If he read a book, she'd sit on it, purring away until she had his attention once again. And though she'd started life as a runt, she grew into a big strong cat. Flopsy lived to a good old age, and to her very last days she slept on Andrew's bed, whether he was at home or not.

Victor, though, despised that cat, and curled his lip when he saw her clamber on to Andrew's lap and stretch out to be belly-stroked. Victor was a dog person. There were two mongrel dogs belonging to the estate, and Victor trained them as attack dogs, obedient only to him. Just as Flopsy adored Andrew, so too did the dogs – Spike and Devil – adore Victor. And they liked no one else. I loved dogs myself, more than cats, actually, and would have loved to make friends with the Newmeads dogs, but it was impossible; they just snarled at everyone, and so eventually I left them alone. They were really guard dogs, not pets, and good guard dogs too. Uncle approved: 'You never can tell with the natives,' he used to say. 'They've been known to turn against the planters, bite the hand that feeds them. It's good to have dogs to keep intruders away.'

Yet Victor did not *love* his dogs. He'd pat them on the head to reward good behaviour, but that was it. Once I saw him kick Spike, who ran away whimpering. No dog-lover kicks dogs. I knew that, and I knew then that to Victor the dogs were merely things of utility, appendages to enhance his own sense of power.

Then there was the bird. Unfortunately, Flopsy did not only catch mice. Once she brought a bird home and laid it at Andrew's feet as an offering. The bird was still alive; its wings fluttered and its tiny beak opened and closed.

'Oh, Flopsy, you naughty girl!' said Andrew, bending down to pick it up. He loved birds as much as he loved cats. This bird was so pretty. It was blue all over, and round and plump, and utterly adorable. 'The poor thing!' said Andrew, stroking its head. 'I'm so sorry! But Flopsy was only doing what's in her nature – please don't be cross with her!'

He walked over to the group of wicker chairs and continued to stroke the bird, cooing to it. For once he did not allow Flopsy to crawl on to his lap; sensing her master's disapproval, Flopsy jumped instead onto the swing sofa and fell asleep. I sat down next to Andrew, and managed to get a stroke of the bird's head in. 'It's a dull-blue flycatcher,' Andrew told me. He had a bird book and could identify most of the feathered creatures that frequented the garden. The conflict between cats and birds was a living agony for him. That much I knew.

That was when Victor came bounding up and plonked himself down on one of the free chairs. 'What you got there, Andrew?' he asked. Andrew held up the bird, enclosed by his hand with just the head showing. 'A dull-blue flycatcher,' he repeated. 'Flopsy caught him and he's injured. Poor thing.'

'Oh well, That's what cats do. Hand him over, I'll do him the honours.' He stretched out his hand to take the bird. Andrew pulled it swiftly away.

'What do you mean?' he asked warily.

'Wring its neck, of course! I don't suppose you're up to it.'

'Don't you dare!' cried Andrew, and got up and ran away. I followed him; he went to the rose arbour, hidden behind a high wall of latticework covered in purple bougainvillea.

Andrew was almost in tears. 'He wanted to kill my bird!'

That's how sentimental Andrew was. He nuzzled the bird, kissed it. 'I can feel it fluttering!' he said excitedly, then cautiously opened his hand so that it stood on his open palm. It fluttered again, tried to fly, and fell to the ground. Andrew picked it up, stroked it some more. Again and again he repeated the process, and each time the bird flew a little bit further. On the fourth attempt, it seemed to gather all its strength, and flew away.

'See, Rosie?' said Andrew. 'Never give up! That's the power of love.'

Chapter Nine

Aunty Silvia's promise that I could 'go home to Pa in the holidays' was of course made worthless by the fact that the boys only came home in those very holidays. So it was another choice I had to make: go home to Pa, or stay with the boys? And I made another guilty decision: I chose the boys over Pa, just as I had chosen the boys over Usha. It was unpardonable, how rapidly I stopped missing him, and home.

Whereas my grief for Amma never left me, a permanent wound carved into my being, missing Pa soon faded into the background. There was so much going on in the foreground! I could, and had to, learn to live with the wound of grief for Amma; I had lost her physical form, and all that remained was a manageable pain. But I hadn't lost Pa; I knew he was right where he belonged, at Shanti Nilayam, alive, in the world, living in the place he had known her and loved her, doing the things that made him happy. The more I settled into life at Newmeads, the more I knew I was more at home here than in the place where Amma was embedded in every stone, every shadow, every silence, hauling me backwards into a sadness that could never recede as long as it was reinforced by memories.

Somehow, too, I didn't *want* to go back, back to the place where she would always live, where I imagined she'd pop out around every corner, where I'd see her so vividly, bending over to deadhead the roses, picking a low-hanging mango for me, laughing, always laughing, or singing: we especially loved the English Country Garden song. We learned the words by heart and sang it together, and we'd laugh together because we never knew any of the flowers in that song, or the birds, or the insects. 'We should rewrite it for India, with hibiscus and oleander!' she'd once said. I missed her more than words can say. I ached for her.

But I'd miss her more at Shanti Nilayam, because she was there and yet she wasn't. The sadness there would be everywhere. Newmeads was free of her ever-presence, and so I could find happiness in this new home, and did. Amma stayed in the background. I'd never forget her, but in my new home she did not haunt me.

Pa and I wrote to each other weekly. My letters were full of energy, of my everyday adventures. In the beginning, I'd told him about Usha, our conversations, what we did, about the water-bucket and filling the jugs at the well and about cutting vegetables: I wrote veritable missives about my new life. Now, I told him about the boys, and the choice I had to make between Usha and them, and how I managed my conscience, and what we got up to now.

His letters, on the other hand, were succinct and, I have to admit, boring. He had nothing new to say, ever, as *his* adventures took place within literary annals of which I knew nothing, and in which I had no interest. And so his letters, that first year, were never more than a few paragraphs long, reiterating the daily schedule of a life where almost nothing changed from day to day, a programme I already knew by heart.

Now and then in the early years of our separation there was a snippet of actual news: when Father Bear, for instance, left Madras to set up an orphanage in rural Tamil Nadu, the Banyan Tree School being now established and running well under the headship of Miss Hull. It was only later that all this changed, and Pa finally stirred out of his languid complacency.

That first year, 1937, I did manage one visit to Pa during the long August holidays, Aunty Silvia delivering me at the start and retrieving me at the end, like a packet. I stayed for two weeks, during which time we reinforced our loving relationship; I told him long stories about my life in Ceylon, he listened attentively and nodded along; and at the end of each holiday I was always eager to return home, and he was always eager to sink back into his books. It worked, and it became our annual tradition; and over the years a warm and intimate relationship developed between us.

We both knew by now that Amma's provision for me, so painful at the time, had been almost prophetic in its wisdom, for I was happy at Newmeads, and Pa was happy buried even deeper in his ancient Sanskrit and Tamil scriptures. He was by nature a hermit, but even a hermit needs human interaction, and the way ours worked – at a distance, through letters and words, with only occasional physical contact, and that limited to just two or three weeks at a stretch – was perfect for our needs.

Amma herself, meanwhile, lived on in my heart. That may sound soppy, but it's true. I could almost hear her voice, giving me advice, or comforting me when I missed her and felt sad. 'Don't cry, Rosie, dear, I am always here, watching over you.' Or I could hear her singing to me: as I lay down to rest, those lullabies she had sung when I was small came back to me; or the sweet little songs she'd taught me, about English country gardens and songbirds and maidens with bonny brown hair, and darling Clementine, who was lost and gone forever. I hummed them to myself, sometimes, to remember, or played them on the piano. Amma had been such a good singer, while Aunty was the brilliant pianist.

Time moves slowly when you're young, but move it did as one year slipped into the next. On the home front, there were many gradual changes. We were all growing up. I and the other girls in my tutorial group moved to a small, private secondary school for English girls in Kandy when we reached the age of twelve, Somerset Academy.

At first, Aunt Silvia said I could be a boarder, but then Mrs Cameron, Penelope's mother, said that she would move into her Kandy town house and all five of us could live there with her during the week, and come home at the weekends. This was an ideal solution. I loved going to school and was a good pupil; my real strengths proved to be not in languages, like Pa – though I was pretty good at those – but in science, with biology being my favourite and best subject. I was a keen member of the Science Society, the school's leading academic society, which enabled us science students to bloom.

In Kandy, too, I made friends beyond the close circle of family and planters' children I'd known up to now, girls my own age, and I blossomed through friendship, too, becoming less shy with strangers, more outgoing. But my best friend was still Usha, and though we now saw each other far more rarely, we never ran out of subjects to talk about, and Usha never stopped learning, receiving in great gratitude all the schoolbooks I had no more use for. And she never held against me the fact that I'd once deserted her, choosing instead to play with Victor and Andrew that first day, and for the rest of that holiday, and every holiday since. It's as if she understood that I had to juggle my friendships, and never held that against me.

Now, though, Victor and Andrew were growing up and going their separate ways. We were no longer an inseparable gang when they came home for the holidays; their very different personalities were establishing themselves. Home life in the hills proved too boring for Victor, who often went off to stay with a friend in Kandy. The Lord only knew what he did there; sometimes he spoke of karate lessons, karate being, to my understanding, some sort of Japanese fighting skill. And he couldn't help showing off what he'd learned. One evening he demonstrated his skill to us.

'See!' he said, placing a thick block of wood between two brick towers. And with the side of his hand he chopped the wood in two as if the bare hand had been an axe.

Uncle was perturbed.

'And that's a *Japanese* skill? You learned it from the Japs?'

Victor only laughed. 'We could learn a thing or two about fighting from the Japs!' he said. 'That chop could kill a man, if you know how.'

'We shouldn't be taking examples from the Japs!' said Uncle sternly. 'They've invaded China. They're our enemies.'

Victor only laughed. 'All the more reason to learn their martial skills,' he retorted. 'The English are such – such chickenhearts, with all their moral inhibitions!'

I said nothing, but I was disturbed. Did Victor really think this way? That moral compunction was a thing to be ashamed of? A sign of weakness?

Victor was by far the more handsome of the boys, with his tall, blond, blue-eyed good looks, and had a certain undeniable classical charm, which attracted a lot of female attention. As I grew older, some of the girls in higher classes started to enquire after him and ask for introductions. I never complied. Female adulation would not improve Victor's already questionable character, I felt.

He had developed a certain insensitivity – arrogance, even – towards others that distanced us even further. I now generally avoided contact with him, particularly since he liked to tease Andrew for his less rough-and-tumble ways. Andrew and I, on the other hand, became close friends. He had a sensitivity that reminded me of both Amma and Pa; and he was cultured. He was musical, liked reading, and painting, and writing poetry. He was a lot like me, in fact. No wonder we became such fast friends.

As for Graham, the eldest, after boarding school he had not returned to Ceylon but had gone straight to university in London and was now studying medicine. And so I did not see him in my early years at Newmeads. But in 1938 he returned to Ceylon, having completed his medical studies, and enrolled in the medical college in Colombo for further training as an orthopaedic surgeon, and now he came to Newmeads to visit his parents. Only occasionally, because he and his father did not see eye to eye, whereas his mother adored him, her firstborn and only child for many years, and went to visit him in Colombo regularly. She could combine this with catching up with her friends, shopping, and certain amusements not available in the Kandy hills: tea-parties, and extended dinners at the Galle Face Hotel, and picnics on the beaches close by.

To me, Graham seemed particularly distant, and I'd never felt the urge to crack that shell of his. I remembered vaguely that one holiday in Eastbourne, when I'd seen him almost as a father figure, him shepherding us younger ones all over the place. Now, he seemed to have taken on a stature way beyond even that and that holiday was all so long ago. I wondered if he even remembered me; the little girl he'd had to babysit, the little girl who'd stupidly fallen into a rabbit hole and whom he'd had to carry home, a day I remembered so well. I was sure that even back then, the X-ray of my sprained ankle had been more interesting to him than me and my tears.

I wondered what kind of a doctor such a man would make; surely it was a vocation that required not just medical skill but a certain ability to connect with others on a personal level? Which Graham patently lacked. He seemed cool, and even a little stand-offish. No, I corrected myself: that was unfair. I remembered now that he *had*, back then, dried my tears with his handkerchief and comforted me so that I stopped crying. In spite of my awe, I'd felt cared for.

But I didn't spend much time speculating about him because, well, for me he was basically a stranger, an enigma. I'd found more rapport even with Uncle Henry.

Secretly, though, I admired Graham's choice of career. To heal others! What a wonderful vocation! And secretly I was wondering if I, too, could go that route, since – as I had found out from my favourite mistress at Somerset College – Ceylon Medical College had been accepting girls as students since the last century. Me, a doctor! It seemed a goal far out of my league – but then again, why not?

The last person I would have mentioned this ambition to was Aunt Silvia, who thought little of girls being educated beyond a certain age. Somerset Academy only taught girls up to the age of sixteen, after which it was thought they should prepare for marriage at an appropriate finishing school, and that's what Aunty thought I should do.

'Just look at this!' she said one day, waving a brochure in my face. It was for a finishing school for English girls down in Colombo, at which the principal subject was domestic science.

'I'll come with you!' she went on. 'We can live in the Cinnamon Gardens flat during the week and come home at the weekend.'

Aunty had grown particularly attached to me over the years. I felt now that she really did regard me as a sort of daughter; she sought out my company, and most evenings roped me into playing gin rummy with her in the games room, or whist, and, when a couple of her planter-wife friends came to visit and they needed a fourth player, even bridge.

Only later did I realise that behind it all was an ulterior motive; that Aunty had secret, far-reaching plans for me. Right now, to me it seemed that my role was similar to that of 'lady's companion', one of very few jobs accessible to a young woman of my standing, and far removed from my own plans for myself. Very gently, I dissuaded her from this domestic science idea. No. I was mostly happy to please her, but I wouldn't go that far.

Instead I chose to continue my academic schooling, particularly in the sciences, by moving to Girls' High School in Kandy for my finals. I was set on course for, one day, starting my medical studies. It was to be my secret, and Pa's, for the time being; for now, I simply told Aunty that I'd be staying on at school. I knew she was lonely at home; without me she was bored, reduced to playing patience all by herself, or reading her romance novels. The latter, I think, gave her a strange notion.

'Rosie,' she asked me, hesitantly, one day, 'is there – you know – someone *special* in Kandy? Is that why you want to go back to school?'

I was able to reassure her. Other girls in my class seemed concerned with boyfriends: not me. I was determined to do well so as to win a place at university. I had no doubt that it would not be easy for a girl to get in. I was certain that boys would be given preference. My teachers at Girls' High told me as much. 'The competition is strong,' they all reminded me, and I could almost hear the silent '…and male!' at the end of the sentence.

And so I had no time for boys, no ambition to marry in the near future. One day, perhaps, but not now. As well as this indifference, I did not keep up with fashions and paid little attention to my looks, beyond cleanliness and basic neatness. Yet I had friends; they teased me, a little, but we enjoyed good times together. It wasn't all work and no play; I relaxed now and then by going with friends to the cinema, and for walks in the Botanical Gardens. The years passed swiftly enough.

There were other things I could not mention to Aunty, as I discovered during a conversation with Andrew, a conversation that had started out casually enough but soon set my heart racing.

'…but what do you want to do, Andrew?' I'd asked one evening as we sat on the veranda. 'With your life, I mean? Are you going to go to university, like Graham?' It was 1937; Andrew was almost fifteen, like me, but had never spoken about the future.

He sighed. 'I suppose it all depends on what Victor does. One of us has to take over the plantation. That's Father's plan for us, but Victor doesn't seem about to comply. I can't really see him as a planter myself.'

'What do you think Victor will do if he doesn't take over?'

I also couldn't see Victor as a planter. Having seen Uncle at it over the years, I knew it was as much a vocation as medicine.

Uncle came from a long line of tea planters; he'd grown up on his father's tea plantation in India and moved here, along with an entire troop of Tamil staff, a year before he'd married Aunty, to establish Newmeads and grow it from scratch. He had succeeded eminently; tea, you'd think, flowed in his blood. Not so with Victor.

'Can I let you into a secret?' Andrew said now.

'Of course!'

'Mother must never know. She'd be scared out of her wits. But you know there's war brewing in Europe, don't you?'

Pa had mentioned it; there was, apparently, a new chap in Germany who was making trouble. Pa's letters to me had changed gradually over the years. World developments seemed to be pulling him out of his inwardly-turned contentment, and he'd started to share with me his observations – and his concerns.

'We have to watch Germany,' he wrote, more and more. 'I know it's far away, on another continent, but whatever happens in Europe has repercussions all over the world. I don't like this new man, this Adolf Hitler, who's scrambling to the top – not a bit.'

In the past, he had read the newspapers only once a week – the *Hindu* was his paper of choice – but now, he told me, he was having it delivered every day, and following developments carefully. Anyone who knew Pa would know that him not only paying attention to the world stage but focusing his interest there – which was exactly what was happening, as he related to me in ever-longer letters – was extraordinary.

'Yes, Pa has mentioned it in a few of his letters,' I said now to Andrew. 'This fellow with the moustache: Mr Hitler. Pa thinks he's dangerous. But that's Europe; so far away.'

'The world is small, Rosie. If one domino falls in Europe, we'll all be affected. Even here in Ceylon. It's what Victor wants, in fact. Victor told me he wants to be a pilot. He's hoping for war, so he can be just that. A fighter pilot.'

'No!'

Andrew nodded. 'I'm afraid so.'

'Who would want war? They just had a war, in Europe! Who would want another one?'

'Victor does. Not for political reasons but just because he wants to fly. He sees himself as some kind of fighter-pilot hero.'

'But he'll get himself killed!'

'That's why you mustn't tell Mother.'

'I won't, of course I won't. But oh, Andrew! Let's pray there won't be a war. It just sounds so – so absolutely ridiculous. It sounds insane!'

'This Hitler fellow sounds insane, from what I can gather.'

'What does your father think of it all?'

'Father? Oh, he dismisses it all. He thinks it's all hysteria being whipped up. And anyway, like you, he thinks we're much too far away to be worried.'

I hoped against hope that Uncle was right, and not Pa. War! It couldn't happen. Not even in Europe. And even if it did, surely we were safe here in Ceylon. But, according to Andrew, we wouldn't be safe. Japan had been haranguing China for years, and was making nasty noises. I knew in my guts that, should war break out, even on a faraway continent, Victor would do exactly as he'd threatened. And then we would all be involved. A long, disturbing shadow crept through my being. Cold, and sinister, it invaded all my thoughts, all my feelings, and I could not shake it off. It clung to me like a long black, nebulous, shapeless leech. Always at the back of my mind.

To my relief, apart from Andrew nobody at Newmeads was concerned at all. Germany and Europe could be on a faraway planet as far as Uncle Henry and Aunt Silvia were concerned, and if I ever mentioned it, they scoffed and brushed Pa's concerns aside.

'Rupert has always been a bit of a fantasist,' Uncle Henry proclaimed. 'Always his head in the clouds. If he wants to get involved in politics then he should be more concerned with this Gandhi chap than with Hitler. If you ask me, it's Gandhi who'll destroy the world, not Hitler. The British world, of course.'

But Pa did also speak of Gandhi. I would never tell Uncle Henry this, of course, but Pa actually admired Mr Gandhi and his goals, and had attended one of his talks when he came to Madras. Uncle would have been shocked to know that Pa supported the goal of Indian independence: a traitor! He had, of course, to keep this all under cover, but he told me: 'The Indians are right. Who are we, a little island, to step in here and pretend we know better and we *are* better? India needs to fight for its dignity and its rights. Gandhi is the man.'

In retrospect, and with the wisdom of hindsight, I believe that Pa was prophetic in his apprehension. I think he knew. I think he had a sort of second sight, and had not only an inkling of how much the world was going to change, but a very clear insight. I might even go so far as to call it clairvoyance. Though I strictly do not believe in clairvoyance and all that humbug. But Pa *knew.* 'The world is going to go to hell in a handcart,' he wrote, as early as 1938. A year when everyone still hoped and prayed for appeasement.

A year later, on 1 September 1939, Hitler invaded Poland. I'll never forget the moment when, two days later, we gathered around the wireless to listen in shocked silence to Neville Chamberlain's speech:

> *This morning the British ambassador in Berlin handed the German government a final note stating that unless we heard from them by 11 o'clock that they were prepared at once to withdraw their troops from Poland, a state of war would exist between us. I have to tell you now that no such undertaking has been received, and that consequently this country is at war with Germany.*

Pa had been right. The world *was* going to hell in a handcart, and we in Ceylon, though far away from the present action, were not to be spared. Europe's shadow fell on us, too.

1939: The year I turned fifteen. The year Andrew and Usha fell in love.

The year this whole mess started.

Chapter Ten

1939

Sunita knew what she was doing by keeping Usha kitchen-bound, never allowing her to enter the main living quarters of the house. This was easy, since the kitchen was in a separate annexe, connected to the house by a covered passageway, along which meals were carried or wheeled to the dining area. Beyond the kitchen was the utility area, where coconuts were chopped open and grated and logs for the fire were split and all the arduous activities for the preparation of food were carried out. The well was at the back of this area; there was a storage shed for rice and other staples, and a small herb garden and, at the back, a vegetable patch. When the boys and I were children, it was the best and most exciting area to play in the whole place, with the tallest coconut trees and the branchiest mango tree, and the well. Victor would pull up buckets of water and we'd pour it, screaming with joy, over each other. But as they grew older and more dignified, the boys were expected to keep away, and they did.

This area was well shielded from the prettier parts of the grounds, and apart from sporadic visits from Aunt Silvia, I was now the only household member who ever went there. My friendship with Usha crossed the traditional boundary between staff and family, and I was only slightly aware of the unease this created. And I didn't care.

The boys, however, no longer crossed that boundary. And neither did Usha.

Except, one day she did.

Usha's beauty had only blossomed over the years. As she ripened into womanhood, her pure loveliness, so striking when she was nine, had matured the way a rosebud opens up into full splendour, one petal at a time. Though still only fourteen, she had shot up over the last few years, and those skinny limbs had turned long and lissom. Her thick silky hair, tied primly back in a single heavy plait, touched her waist, and soft black curls framed her face. It was a face that would have not been out of place on a hoarding for one of those monumental Indian epic films, a face whose unadorned beauty drew your gaze so that you could soak it in, become a part of it. If I could say this as a young girl myself, how much more would it be felt by a boy?

I doubt that Andrew would have seen her at all in the years between that first awkward meeting when she was a child of nine, and now. Sunita kept her daughter jealously guarded from all males – I knew this from our conversations, for she and I were still the best of friends. A propitious wedding was being arranged for Usha, through the intervention of her brother Karthik, who still worked at the Galle Face Hotel: she was to marry the son of the head cook there, a boy named Arun, as soon as he had completed his own training as a chef and had found work. No dowry was required; a photograph of Usha was all that was needed.

Men, I realised when Usha – somewhat astounded herself – told me this, are like that. They see female beauty, and they want it. They have to have it. They have to own it. They give no thought to the character behind the face. Perhaps they believe that beauty of face reflects beauty of character; this, I have since discovered, is a fundamentally wrong assumption, for beauty of face can easily be a catalyst for vanity, and vanity can lead to a multitude of very unpleasant characteristics.

But not with Usha. She seemed – no, she was – completely devoid of vanity, ignorant of the power her beauty had over others, particularly men. Usha had had many suitors, many contenders, seen many photographs, received many proposals, and had chosen this Arun.

'A *photograph?* That's *it?* You won't even meet him beforehand?' I asked, very astonished.

She only laughed. 'Of course not! That would spoil everything: the magical moment when he lifts my veil at the wedding, and our eyes meet for the very first time. From that moment, love will grow. It's like the planting of a seed.'

'So you judged him entirely on his good looks? How shallow!'

She laughed again. 'No, of course not! Good looks don't matter at all!'

'But you just said…'

'I said I'd look at his photograph. Don't you know what *look* means?'

'Of course! But…'

'*Looking* is more than seeing, Rosie! The whole person is captured in a photograph, and it's important to look beyond the form, beyond the image. When I looked at his photo I took him inside me, into my heart, and held him there. Then I asked my heart. I did it with all the five suitors. To *this* boy, this Arun, my heart said yes.'

I shook my head sceptically, but said nothing. Usha could be stubborn. There was no point arguing with her; we had had this conversation many times, and she had always won. There was no changing her. So that was that: Usha was betrothed, and as a betrothed woman she had to be kept out of the sight of other men, men being what they are.

But then a series of coincidences changed everything. First of all, Sunita's mother fell ill and she was required to go back to the village to take care of her. The village served Uncle's tea factory; it was where most of his staff lived, the workers who separated the tea buds, graded them, packaged them for sale. It was therefore close to the factory, which was about five miles from Newmeads, down the narrow road that led off the main road towards Kandy. Even beyond the village were the rows of primitive domiciles inhabited by the tea pluckers and their families, known as the lines. I'd seen these hovels: once, and never again. I knew full well that they were disgraceful, that no human should live in such conditions, especially not humans who lived in such luxury as we did. But I was just a child, just a guest; it was not my place to question Uncle and his way of life. I held my tongue.

Sunita had arranged a replacement for herself, a cousin from another village, who was assisted by Usha just as Sunita had been. In this very same week, Andrew broke his leg at his boarding school in Kodaikanal. Aunt Silvia rushed to his side and brought him back in a wheelchair to recuperate.

Sunita had not warned her cousin that Usha was not allowed in the main living area of the house. Why should she? As far as she knew, all the boys were safely far away from Newmeads, in Colombo or Kodaikanal.

The cousin did not know the family. Did not know that Andrew was young and handsome, and that Usha should be kept away from him. Or else she simply did not think. Or else she was too busy, too distracted, to consider that it would be wrong to send a young, beautiful, betrothed girl to serve a young man. Whatever the reason, the cousin did just that. Usha, too, must have been oblivious or forgetful of the required propriety, for she simply obeyed the order. She found us on the veranda outside Andrew's room, Andrew, sixteen years old and handsome, with his one leg, fat and white in its coat of plaster-of-Paris, up on a footstool.

It being a school-free Saturday, I was keeping Andrew company, defeating boredom by reading *The Three Musketeers* to him; of course, he was perfectly capable of reading it himself, but, he said, he preferred to be read to, and I was enjoying the story as well as the breezy, sun-filtered ambience of the veranda. Aunt Silvia was not at home; she had gone to Kandy to visit some friends and enjoy a round of bridge at the Planters' Club. So apart from the servants, Andrew and I were alone in the house.

I looked up and smiled as Usha approached. Andrew also looked up. But he did not smile.

Aware of a subtle change in the atmosphere, I stopped reading, and looked up again. Their eyes were locked. I started reading again, but I knew at once he wasn't listening. I paused, and looked from one to the other. They seemed locked into a silent gaze which began to feel awkward; it was going on far too long. Usha standing there, holding the tray. Andrew sitting there, staring at her. This was inappropriate, even I could knew it. It was far too – I searched for the word – too intimate. Too *intensely* intimate.

I had only read of love and romance in novels, but even I could feel it in that moment. The lightning bolts that shot from him to her. And back again.

Usha suddenly jolted back to reality from wherever she'd been floating.

'Your lunch, Master Andrew,' she mumbled. She set the tray down on the wicker table before Andrew's chair, turned, and fled.

Andrew made as if to get up and rush behind her, forgetting the plaster cast weighing one leg down and the fact that he was not yet allowed to put weight on it; he stumbled, and I had to leap from my own chair to catch him.

'Watch it!' I cried. I held his arm and he lowered himself back into his chair. But he wasn't listening; he reached out for his crutch, which was leaning against the latticed veranda railing, and even before I had sat down again he was struggling back to his feet, with the help of the crutch this time.

'Who is she?' he shot at me.

'It's only Usha. You know, Sunita's daughter. You met her a few years ago.'

Recollection flashed across his face and he nodded. 'Oh. Yes – Victor was so rude that day.'

'So were you, Andrew!'

He had the grace to blush. 'Well, I was just a little boy and I took my lead from Victor. It's different now – oh, Rosie!'

'What?'

'That's the girl I'm going to marry, Rosie!'

'Don't be ridiculous, Andrew. What a silly thing to say!'

'But I know it! Something just happened—when I saw her—I just—it was like an electric shock. An intuition, a knowledge. Rosie, I have to see her again! I'm going after her!'

He hopped forward. I leapt up and grabbed his arm.

'No. Andrew, you can't!' I cried.

'Who says I can't? Does she work in the kitchen?'

'Yes, but…'

'I need to see her, Rosie. I'm going after her.' And he started hobbling away, propping himself on his crutch.

I sprang forward and intercepted him.

'No, Andrew, no! You can't! She's staff!'

'What d'you mean, I can't? This is my home – I can do what I like, go where I want! I'm sick and tired of this master–servant nonsense. Let me go!'

For I had grabbed his other arm to hold him back. He tried to shake me off but I held on even tighter. We stood there, facing each other, he with his weight on one foot, the other leg bent at the knee to keep the weight off, the crutch supporting him.

'It's not, not about that, Andrew! I know her – she's my friend. She's not allowed to speak to boys, to any males. She's betrothed – engaged to be married!'

'Don't be ridiculous, Rosie! She's not even your age – she can't be *engaged*!'

'But she is, she is! You know the local customs, Andrew. Parents arrange marriages, quite early.'

'So she doesn't know him yet? So she can change her mind.'

I almost wept. 'Don't interfere, Andrew! Please don't!'

He stared at me, for the moment no longer struggling against my lock on his arm.

'You don't understand, Rosie. Something just happened. I just know I'm going to marry her! I can't explain it. But you've heard of it, surely? When you just know something?'

And I *did* know. Pa had told me, once: something just like that had happened to him in Kuala Lumpur when he saw Amma for the first time, standing next to the piano and singing, accompanied by Aunt Silvia. He had just known he would marry her. It was a clear flash of knowledge, he'd said, just like Andrew. But he had been a mature man with excellent prospects. Andrew was a schoolboy of sixteen. I couldn't possibly take him seriously.

'What happened? I know she's beautiful, but that can't be... Andrew, sit down. We have to talk. You can't just run after her. Trust me, you can't. I know her; you'd terrify her if you just came after her. You have to respect her.'

I held on to his arm, pushed against him, trying to get him to back away. Thankfully, he didn't try to pull away. We stood there, facing each other.

'But I do respect her! It's not just her looks, Rosie, her beauty! It was...' He hesitated, obviously searching for words. Then he sighed, hobbled back to his chair, and sat down.

'Have you ever met someone, seen someone, Rosie, and you recognise them, somehow, and you just know, you simply know, that...' he shrugged here, lost for words. '...it was something in her eyes, when they met mine. I recognised her. I knew that she belonged in my life. I can't explain it, but it happened.'

'That's not love, Andrew! You don't even know her! How can you love someone you've only seen for a moment?'

'I didn't say it was love! Don't put words in my mouth. I said I know, I just know, I'm destined to marry her. I know you don't believe in things like destiny, Rosie – you're far too clever. But I do. Sometimes it's real and you can feel it working in you, through you. It's… well, just a *knowing*. A feeling, so strong… as if she is part of my life, part of me! It happened in a glance – just like that!'

He snapped his fingers to demonstrate, and looked at me, pleading for understanding. There was something in his eyes I'd never seen before and all at once I knew that he was right, that something strong and mighty had happened here, at least to him, if not to Usha; and I was terrified – terrified for all it meant. For Andrew, for Usha, for our comfortable life at Newmeads. Terrified of the consequences.

'And the thing is,' he continued, 'she felt it too.'

And then he sort of slumped, his shoulder sagging on to the crutch tucked under his arm, the tension in his body, and in the atmosphere, slacking, the fire in his eyes losing its spark. He met my eyes, and this time his look was not defiant, but pleading.

'You have to help me, Rosie. Please. You have to help us.'

'I can't, Andrew. Really, I can't. You don't understand. We can't get involved in their traditions. It's all been planned, and—'

'And we have to stop it.'

'No! We can't! And anyway, what would Aunt Silvia say! She'd never allow you to marry a servant!'

'Don't you call her a servant! She isn't! She has as much value as you or me and I know Mother's a snob but she can't dictate to me, and—'

'Andrew, you're only sixteen. You can't get married at all. You'd have to wait a few years.'

'Waiting doesn't bother me. I can wait forever. Because I know it's going to happen. But I need to see her again – soon, and that's how I want you to help. You have to arrange it. You will, won't you? Please say you'll help!'

'You don't even know if she wants to meet you. You can't decide for her!'

'She does. I know she does. I saw it in her eyes, Rosie. You can't imagine – if you haven't experienced it, you can't imagine.

It's nothing like those soppy love stories Mother reads. It's real, so real! Like a… like a bomb! A bomb going off in the heart. And you know, with every fibre of your body, you just know!'

I shook my head slowly. I knew Usha. Better than he did. Usha would never give in to such nonsense. She was such a level-headed person, well in control of her emotions, not given to moods or changes of heart. Her path was straight ahead, no detours. It did not allow for bombs going off in the heart.

He read my scepticism. 'At least talk to her. Promise you'll talk to her.'

I sighed. 'All right. But don't get your hopes up, Andrew. She's tough, and stubborn, and has some fixed ideas. You won't like it.'

I was right, as I'd known I would be. I found Usha sitting cross-legged on the kitchen veranda, shelling peas with unwarranted vigour, shooting them out of their shells into the brass bowl. I set myself down beside her and laid a gentle hand on her knee. She looked up at me. Her face was tear-stained but her eyes were fierce. Determined.

'Usha,' I said. 'Talk to me.'

'Did he send you?' she said with gritted teeth. 'No. I know he did. To interfere. Rosie, I want you to stop interfering.'

'I'm not interfering,' I said mildly. 'Don't shoot the messenger.'

'I don't want the message!'

'You don't even know what the message is.'

'I do. And I know you'll take his side. You white people are all the same.'

That hurt me. We were in conflict already and I hadn't even delivered the message.

'Usha, I will always be on your side. I *told* him that you are engaged.'

'And it's final!'

'I know, Usha. I know. I told him.'

'And what did he say to that?'

'He said he wants to meet you, to talk to you. Just once.'

'To get me to betray my fiancé!'

'Just to talk, Usha. Talking can't hurt.'

'Of *course* it can! Just *seeing* has hurt! Just… just…'

Tears leaked from her eyes. She briskly brushed them away with her bare arms; but more came, and she lifted the end of her dupatta to wipe them off.

'The thing is, Rosie, and you probably don't understand this because you are English, but it is possible to be unfaithful with a single look. Eyes can speak, you know. Sometimes louder than words.'

It all seemed so overwrought to me; after all, it was just a look, wasn't it? But I knew how Usha felt about eyes, and what they can reveal, and what even a glance can convey. How she felt about eyes meeting for the first time, and how that first meeting was, in fact, like a marriage; how important it was for a girl not to look into a man's eyes, because of the intimacy of such an occurrence. It's what her culture taught her.

And perhaps it was exactly this that had captured Andrew. An intimacy revealed through the eyes. Andrew had always been so very sensitive. Had he really felt something genuine?

'You Westerners don't understand, can't understand,' Usha had once told me. 'But there are layers to ourselves, hidden by veil upon veil. We keep our true selves hidden behind veils. When we look into each other's eyes at the moment of marriage, it is like an unveiling, not just the bride's actual veil being lifted. It is pure light, pure joy, and that is the moment of marriage. That's why it is a sacred moment for us. The veils are stripped away and our true being is revealed. That is the moment love is born. It must be nourished and cared for, but once it has shown itself it is everything.'

Yes: love at first sight. Hadn't I read of it, in many a Greek tragedy, in Shakespeare? Something beyond logic and human understanding. But was this really love? I doubted it. Even Andrew had said it wasn't love but simply a knowledge that they belonged together.

I nodded. 'I do understand, because that's exactly what happened. I saw, Usha. I was there. I saw that... that exchange.'

'Two souls meeting,' she whispered. 'Souls who already know each other, have known each other.'

'You mean, in a past life?'

She nodded, but I did not want to go into that. It was too uncanny for me. But Usha certainly seemed convinced that she and Andrew were two souls who had once been together, and had met again: and she was determined to fight it.

She sniffed. I stayed silent for a while, waiting, then I said, very quietly, 'So what shall I tell him?'

'I cannot meet him. It can't happen. Don't you see? It cannot happen! Never!'

'I explained that to him, Usha. That you are engaged; that it's all arranged and final. And even if you weren't, I know for a fact that Aunt Silvia would never allow it. I've heard the way she talks about mixed marriages. She's a bit of a snob in that respect.'

Usha gave a sarcastic chuckle. 'In *every* respect, Rosie. Your aunty is a terrible snob.' She took a deep breath. 'Anyway, Rosie, I cannot meet him again. It is against the rules. I can't believe I looked him in the eye – it was an accident! I can't see him again and if he insists on chasing me, I'll have to leave. '

'Leave? Oh no, Usha! You can't run away! Please don't go! Where will you go?'

'I have no idea.' She was still shelling peas, not looking at me. 'Amma will help. I will tell her everything. Thank goodness she returns tonight. I will tell her, and she will make sure I am removed from this place. And, Rosie, you must tell him to forget me. Forget this ever happened. Wipe it from his mind, just as I will from mine.'

She looked up from the peas, then, and stared into my eyes, and held my gaze without blinking, as if to prove the power of her decision. And I saw it. She had done exactly that: wiped the – whatever it was – from her mind. Turned away from it, and moved on, right there and then. She said it: 'I am not going to be a victim of my wayward mind! He caught me in a moment of inattention. But now I know. That is my message to him. Go, Rosie. Go now, and tell him.'

I did tell him, but he would have none of it. The following morning saw him stalking into the kitchen, leaning on his crutch, which, thank goodness, meant he could not move quickly. I was at his side, pulling at his sleeve, begging him not to do it.

He ignored me, and simply walked in.

Usha had her back to us, thank goodness. She was at the stove, stirring a large pot of milk.

Sunita, returned, was kneading dough at the central table. The moment she saw Andrew she rushed towards us, arms spread.

'Out! Out with you! Do not come near to my daughter!'

Sweet, mild Sunita, speaking to the mistress's son like that! But of course, Sunita had once been Andrew's ayah. She'd known him since he was a baby, corrected him and told him off a million times; and Andrew had submitted to her authority a million times – as he did now.

Behind Sunita's spread arms I saw Usha's quick glance behind her to see what the commotion was, and then her hasty flight out of the kitchen door.

By midday, Usha was gone. A day later, she was replaced by Parvati, a young married woman from the village, a cousin of Sunita's, thankful for the job. I later heard that Usha had found work on the Penningtons' plantation.

It would be years before I saw her again.

*

Andrew spent the next few weeks moping and sulking and blaming me. But then the term ended and Victor came home from Kodaikanal, and offered his brother a remedy for lovesickness: he swooped Andrew off to Colombo, where, he said, there were 'girls galore' for him to love. I could tell by the twinkle in his eye that Victor's interpretation of the word *love* was a universe away from Andrew's. All the same, Andrew went with him.

They were all gone: I was alone. I took the opportunity, now that the long holidays had started, to visit Pa. But even at Shanti Nilayam, there were changes.

Pa was different. He welcomed me home with his usual quiet warmth, but the very first night, he sat me down for a serious talk.

'Rosie,' he said, 'I've been thinking. We know that your mother was right to make arrangements for the event of her death, and I've decided to do the same.'

'Pa!' I cried. 'You don't…'

He chuckled. 'No, I haven't had a dream or anything, not like her. And of course, you're much older now; not a ten-year-old child. But you should know a little about our circumstances, just in case. After all, there's a war brewing in Europe. I don't expect India or Asia to be drawn into it, but there is a chance; the Japanese are up to no good, I fear. They invaded China and instigated a full-blown war there. They're a very clear danger.'

'But not to us, surely, Pa?'

'Not at the moment. But the Japanese are just as expansionist as Germany. If they get ideas into their heads… They're ruthless. We need to be prepared.'

'Prepared for war? Surely not, Pa?'

'Well, we'll leave war preparations to our political leaders and the military. I meant prepared in a more personal sense. Here's what you need to know: this house is yours. Your mother was given it as a wedding present by her parents, your grandparents, and she left it to you in her will, giving me a right to live here for the rest of my life. As for me, if anything does happen, there is a bit of property in England that as an only son— well, you don't really need to know all the details at this time. It's all in that file over there,' he pointed, 'the one labelled Legal. The name and address of my lawyer is on the first page. It's all taken care of, and in case of anything, of course your aunts would be there to help. My sisters. All busybodies, I'm afraid, but well-meaning, as you know!' His eyes twinkled, and we both remembered Aunt Jane's intervention when Amma had died. How long ago that seemed now! Like a different era.

'But why now, Pa? What's brought this on?'

There was something in Pa's demeanour I couldn't put my finger on; a new spark, a new life, a new energy. Which he was quick to confirm.

'It's just, Rosie, I've been doing a bit of self-inventory recently. Looking at myself with a bit more awareness, a bit more criticism. I've not been a good father, have I?'

'Oh, Pa! Of course you have! You're just – well, you're just *you*! I wouldn't have you any other way.'

'No, no, Rosie. I haven't been really me, have I? Buried in books. I think I was actually searching for me all the time, but I'm not there, am I? *Who am I?* Isn't that the key question? Who am I, *really*? Where do I find myself? Not in those books.'

'Pa?' Now, this was new. Pa's books were everything to him.

'Yes, well. I've now decided to stop the reading and actually do what the books say. Books don't have the answer I'm looking for, Rosie. They can point to it. But I have to do the actual work.'

'I still don't understand.'

'No, no, you wouldn't. I don't understand it all, myself, but I'm beginning to. I'm on the cusp of understanding. What the books say, Rosie, what all of them eventually say, what they point to again and again over thousands of words, is this: the answer is inside. Inside me. Here.'

He pointed to his chest. 'I'm really looking for myself. But they all tell me, all those old Tamil scriptures, all the Vedas and Upanishads and other ancient texts, they all say: look inside and you will find the answers. It's all inside, Rosie. Every happiness, every joy, every fulfilment. But it's hard work getting there. I've made a beginning, though. I've started to meditate.'

'Really? You?'

I don't know why I was so surprised. Wasn't Pa exactly the type: introverted, otherworldly, reclusive? Surely this was just the next step.

'Yes, me. And, surprisingly, it's changed everything! It's actually quite exciting!'

'Hmmm. Looks rather boring to me.'

'That's because you're seeing it from the outside. You're not actually *experiencing* it. Anyway, it's as if I'm starting off on a whole new journey. An adventure, but an internal one.'

I must have looked sceptical, because his next words were defensive. 'It's true, Rosie. Don't be so judgemental!'

'If you say so, Pa!'

'Would you like to learn?'

I didn't hesitate. 'No, Pa. Really, no.'

He smiled then, and it was his old Pa smile. I breathed a sigh of relief. His next words, too, were the old Pa again.

'Shall we get up early tomorrow, walk down to the beach and watch the sunrise together?'

'Oh, Pa! Yes, let's!'

We hadn't done this for years. It was what Amma and I used to do, and Pa and I had taken up the habit in the first few years after her death, on my annual visits. We had both slacked off in the last years, preferring a lie-in, but now, it sounded like a wonderful new beginning for us.

*

Over the next two weeks I had to admit it: if this new Pa was a result of this new hocus-pocus he was engaging in, then maybe there was some value to it after all. He was far less distracted, far less... dusty might be the right word. He listened when I told him of the drama with Andrew and Usha, and gave his opinion: Usha was wise beyond her years; it could never work and good that she had the strength to resist. At only fourteen!

We spoke of my future.

For the last year or so I had held my secret, not telling anyone outside of school, and now, Pa was the first person beside my teachers to hear of my hesitant speculation: could I be a doctor? He was immediately enthusiastic.

'*Of course* you can! You must, Rosie! What a wonderful idea!' And my heart swelled and I knew I'd made him proud, and is there anything more satisfying than knowing you've made your parent proud? Even though I wasn't even there yet, even though it was just a nebulous idea in my head?

But then his face darkened.

'But, Rosie... The war.'

'But that's in Europe...'

But Pa only shook his head. 'Japan!' he said. 'Japan is still at war with China, and who knows what they will do? Military strategists say that the Japanese Emperor is likely to sign treaties with Hitler. Maybe even attack America. Who knows, Rosie, who knows? All I do know is that you'd be better off not making any future plans right now.'

'But surely, Pa, Ceylon is safe?'

'Who knows? I hope so. And I hope Uncle Henry will know what to do, if and when danger threatens. Of course, you can all come here if there is an emergency. You'd be safe here.'

I sighed. I thought Pa was making a big fuss about nothing. I wanted to believe Uncle Henry, who despite the war in Europe was bent on denying any danger to us at all. I wanted nothing to change. I changed the subject.

It was around this time that I at last started to teach myself to play the bansuri, the bamboo flute Miss Subramaniam had given me when I left the Banyan Tree School. It was a lateral flute and it was quite difficult for some people to even create a sound, to get just the right amount of air at the right angle into the blowhole, much less to sustain that breath in order to play a tune. When Miss Subramaniam had brought the flute to class and passed it around, I was the only one who managed it. I suppose that was why she gave me the flute. Now it was up to me to learn to play it, so that her generous gift would not be in vain.

But I found that learning to play, with the help of an old dog-eared booklet called *Teach Yourself Bansuri* that I found at a marketplace bookseller, was more than a duty owed to my old teacher: it was a joy. I learned to love the sweet, hollow, yearning sound the bansuri made; it conjured up feelings I'd never known I had from the depths of my being, and playing it, even in my stumbling, cautious way, actually brought me closer to myself, to a *me* I never knew existed, a beautiful, whole, happy me. A me without worry about the war or an uncertain future. From that day I took the flute with me wherever I went.

At the end of my stay, Pa dumped yet another surprise on me.

'Rosie,' he said, 'I'm going away for a few weeks. Just so you know; I won't be writing you in this time and I won't get your letters. So please don't think I'm ignoring you.'

'Really? Where are you off to?'

Pa very rarely travelled; he had done little of it even when we were a family of three, and since then, as far as I knew, he'd not gone anywhere at all.

'Well,' he said slowly, 'I don't expect you to understand. It's to do with what I told you, about an internal adventure. I need to see a few people... people who've, well, gone the whole route, you could say. There are a couple of them in India, and, well, two especially stand out and I'm going to stay with them for a while.'

'Who are these people? Where are they? You mean, gurus?'

He shrugged. 'If you want to call them that. One's a woman saint, up in the Himalayas. I'll go there first, for a while. Then I'll come back. The other one's nearer to home; in Tamil Nadu, actually. A couple hours by bus from Madras.'

'Oh, Pa! You know they're all just charlatans!'

Pa and I had been to listen to Jiddu Krishnamurti last year when he gave a talk in Madras.

Krishnamurti was a charismatic speaker and writer who had been groomed during the 1920s by Annie Besant and other Theosophists to become the new spiritual World Teacher. They had founded an organisation called the Order of the Star in the East to support him in this role, and promoted him vigorously in both East and West. There was no doubting his extraordinary personal magnetism and spiritual vision, and he spoke out vehemently against the proliferation of gurus in India. They weren't necessary, he taught. I'd thought Pa and I were in agreement on this.

Both Pa and I had been impressed by Krishnamurti's talk, Pa much more so than me. I assumed that this proposed trip was something along the same lines. Pa was far more deeply invested in all this than I'd assumed. I was deeply disappointed. But his mind was made up and off he went. I was quite downhearted as I returned to Ceylon. This was a Pa I didn't recognise at all. Not only his talk of war, his fears for me, his awakened political interest; now this, rushing off to see some Indian fakir or the other. It just didn't make sense.

I returned to find Andrew and Victor in a bit of a spat; in fact, I walked right into the middle of it. Victor was laughing at Andrew.

'You always were a pansy!' he said. 'Oh, hello, Rosie. Tell me, don't you agree? Isn't Andrew a washout?'

I frowned. 'What do you mean?'

He laughed again. 'Well, I won't go into detail, but I took him to Colombo to have a good time. You won't know anything about the pleasures of the flesh, Rosie, but it's important for a man, to become a real man. Andrew's sixteen; high time to be broken in... but would you believe it, he backed out!'

I blushed; I knew a little of what he was talking about, women who sold their bodies, temporarily, of course, to anyone who paid the right price.

'I don't think Andrew would like that,' I said lamely.

Victor roared with laughter. 'Right, right! He's a good boy, isn't he? All airy-fairy with his art and music and poetry. But girls don't like that, do they, Rosie? They like bad boys, like me. Tell him that! Go on, tell him!'

'But Andrew isn't looking for a girl,' was all I could manage. Victor was so very intimidating, so very aggressive in his teasing. I didn't like it at all. I wanted to whisk Andrew away.

'Ah yes, I forgot. He's fallen for this Indian girl, this servant, right? Well, I'll tell you a secret. Girls like that, servants, are a dime a dozen. You don't even have to pay them.'

And he guffawed, pinched my cheek and walked out. 'Little sissy!' he called as he left the room.

Over the next few days the spat continued, as Victor continued to mock and disparage Andrew. Uncle Henry took Victor's side – Andrew had to become a man, he said, and what better way than in the pleasure houses of Colombo. Aunt Silvia, meanwhile, sympathised with Andrew, her baby son, but thought it absolutely imperative that he purge 'that girl' from his mind.

The spat snowballed into a major conflict between them that continued throughout the holidays. We had anyway all grown apart since childhood; long gone were the days when Victor would lead us on adventures into the wild. Victor, now almost eighteen and practically a man, had other interests and spent much of his time in Kandy where, I'm certain, he indulged in certain manly pursuits. Victor and I were civil to each other, but I'd never regarded him as a brother I could feel close to and confide in and certainly didn't now. That role was Andrew's.

I felt for Andrew. He was still completely convinced that Usha was the girl he would one day marry. I couldn't understand it; but then, I'd never known a thing like this, a sudden flash of intuition when you just know.

My role, now, was to distract Andrew. And since tensions were running high at Newmeads, I thought the best way to distract him was for us both to go on a little holiday, together. A trip to the seaside.

The one thing I missed about Shanti Nilayam – apart from Pa, of course – was the ocean, practically on the doorstep. I believe that anyone who grows up near the sea develops a lifelong love and longing for the pounding surf, the sweet sound of water sucking sand, foaming and frothing as it laps on the shore. The vast expanse of water reaching to the horizon; the sun rising or setting against a vision of infinity.

'You need a break,' I said to him. 'A pause. Let's go away, just you and me. I've never been down to the south-coast beaches, Galle and Madiha and Talalla. Have you?'

'No, we only ever go to Colombo. The only beach I've ever been to is Negombo.'

'Well, then! Let's go! Just you and me. A little holiday. Let's get away from all this talk of war and pleasure houses and Victor harassing you.'

Andrew was all for it. 'Yes!' he said. 'I can get back to my painting! I always wanted to try a seascape!'

'And I can practise the flute. Perhaps the sea will give me more inspiration!'

'And maybe I can compose some more poems. I'd like to try love poems.'

'Oh, Andrew!' I sighed. But I didn't try to argue. Let him compose his love poems. Nothing would come of it.

Of course, we had to ask permission of Aunt Silvia. And we'd need money so we could stay in hotels along the way; it would not be a cheap trip. I had some money of my own – apart from the money he paid my guardians for my maintenance, Pa paid regularly into a bank account for me; I'd never touched that money before and it had accumulated over the years. I was ready to splurge a bit.

But Andrew had to ask his mother not only for permission, but for money too. We both assumed there'd be no problem, but to my surprise she was horrified. I didn't understand it until she took me aside for a quiet talk in my bedroom.

'Are you out of your mind, Rosie?' she said.

I frowned.

'What do you mean, Aunty?'

'Isn't it obvious? Do you really think the two of you can just swan off on a romantic holiday and I'd give permission, just like that?' she clicked her fingers.

'Romantic? Aunty! No! Of course it's not a romantic holiday! Andrew and I, we're like brother and sister!'

'Oh, Rosie! I wasn't born yesterday and neither were you. You're of an age now that you should understand. And you do, don't you? Deep inside?'

'Understand what? Oh, Aunty! I can't believe you…'

'Look, I do have your best interests at heart. I agree that you and Andrew would make a perfect couple, and I always thought – hoped – that you'd end up marrying. Well, either Andrew or Victor, but Andrew seems more likely, and—'

'Me, marrying Andrew? Why, Aunty, it's never once occurred to me. It would be, well, it would be like *incest*!'

'Nonsense, my dear! You don't have a drop of common blood. But, you know, it's what your mother would have wanted. What we, as young mothers, always dreamed about. When you were born, we both thought it was perfect. Me with three boys, and you, a little girl who could one day take your pick. If all went to plan. Dear Lucy thought it was brilliant!'

'But, Aunty, I told you: I grew up with them! They're like brothers!'

'They are NOT your brothers! Really, Rosie, don't you have any imagination? I mean, at your age I was swooning at film stars, imagining marrying one of them one day, being in his arms. Both Andrew and Victor are very good-looking – both are a catch. Don't tell me you never once thought of snagging one of them?'

'Never! It never crossed my mind, Aunty!'

'I actually thought Victor would be perfect for you, and you for him. You would have such a steadying influence on him. He is a bit on the wild side, and you are so mature.'

That notion was so preposterous I couldn't respond to it. I changed the subject, away from Victor.

'And Graham?'

She flapped her hand. 'Don't be silly, Rosie, Graham's much too old – twelve years older than you.'

Of course, I knew this. I was quite in awe of Graham, and knew he was far out of my league in age and calibre. Still, I needed to probe Aunty's rationale.

'Uncle's more than twelve years older than you. Same with Amma and Pa.'

'Yes, and that's exactly why I advise against it. And besides, I have someone else lined up for Graham. Either Andrew or Victor for you, I thought.'

'Trust me, Aunty: it never occurred to me.'

'Well, it should have. It's only natural. This brother–sister thing, you both need to grow out of it. Now more than ever. This little drama with Usha – Andrew has to put it to the back of his mind, and what better way…? Now let me think.'

She was silent for a while, and I sat on the edge of my bed biting my bottom lip. What a perfectly preposterous idea! Me and Andrew! She was mad. Who would have thought it? But it now appeared that Aunt Silvia had been dreaming of my wedding to Andrew or Victor right from the start. I now understood some of the hints she'd been dropping. It seemed she'd been carefully watching for any signs of romance between us; between any of us. It was what she and Amma had dreamed up when we were tiny. I'm certain that Amma had long forgotten any such romantic girlish dream, but Aunty had not. Thus she had completely misinterpreted our plan to visit the beach.

Finally, Aunty spoke.

'Dear, I do see I've misunderstood. This whole time I thought you and I were on the same track; that you were secretly in love with Andrew. I know I would have been, in your shoes! So when you suggested the two of you go off together, naturally I was shocked, because that's certainly not the way to do it. Obviously you're too young for intimacy with a young man at fifteen, and obviously once he'd enjoyed intimacy, he'd lose interest. That's why I was so perturbed. But it was, I see now, only a misunderstanding. However…'

Here she paused, and I said nothing, waiting.

'…however, in principle it's a good idea. But you need a chaperone, for the sake of propriety. We don't want tongues wagging; you know what people are like. I'll go with you. You and I can share a room. A little holiday would be wonderful for all of us and, well, the sea air, the romantic atmosphere, that should take his mind off that little minx. You'll be right there, in a bathing suit, distracting him…'

And nothing would persuade her otherwise.

*

'If there is heaven on earth, this is it!' said Andrew.

'I agree wholeheartedly!' I said.

We were sitting on the beach at Hiriketiya, having driven down the coast from Colombo the week before. The main advantage of having Aunty as unnecessary chaperone was that we were able to travel in the car, with her as chauffeur. We had driven from town to town, stopping for a night or two in each place, and this was our last day before turning round to return the way we'd come.

It was a glorious time. Andrew had brought his paints, brushes, and an easel, and everywhere we'd been, he had painted a different seascape.

'So, what d'you think, Rosie?' he'd say when he finished each one. 'Think I'll make it as a professional artist?'

'Hmmm,' I'd say each time, examining the painting and rubbing my chin. 'What about a few big splashes of red here and there?'

I loved to tease him about his painting, but secretly I thought he had talent, and here on the glorious beaches on the island's south coast that talent was beginning to show.

'It was a good idea to come here,' he said now. 'The sea really inspires me,'

'Me too!' I said. Just as he had brought his paints, I had brought my bansuri, and had created a whole new set of tunes, bouncing, happy melodies. The sea had always made me happy, but here it was even prettier than the ocean on our doorstep at Shanti Nilayam.

Hiriketiya beach was in a horseshoe-shaped bay and was perhaps the most beautiful beach we'd visited, well protected from wind and swell throughout the year; the waves being not so high, and under Andrew's patient tutelage, I finally learned to swim.

'I wish I didn't have to be a tea planter!' Andrew sighed. 'I'd love to go to art school and learn to paint properly, professionally.'

'Can't you discuss it with Uncle?'

'Never! If Victor doesn't take over the plantation it's my duty. No escape from that.'

Andrew seemed perfectly resigned to this fate so I didn't argue, but secretly I thought it such a pity. I could well imagine Andrew as a bohemian artist, perhaps living in Paris, or an artists' community in Cornwall…

'When Usha and I are married, we'll come here for our honeymoon!' he said suddenly and I was jolted back to the here and now.

'Andrew!' I cried. 'Stop that right now!'

But he only chuckled. 'You'll see!' he said, pinching my cheek. 'You can't fight destiny.'

Aunty, meanwhile, preferred to sit in cafés in the seaside villages, the ones frequented by English wives, or memsahibs – 'mems' – like herself, and chat about life. She encountered several women she already knew, and met several others newly arrived, and she loved nothing better than helping these new mems to settle into their new lives. She had mountains of advice on tap, and could spend the day gossiping. She refused to bathe, beyond a quick 'freshening-up' dip now and then, after which she would quickly run back to shore to get dressed. She'd never sit in the sun; it made her brown, she said. But Andrew and I revelled in the sun on our skin, and the sand under our feet and the cool water washing over our bodies.

It was, as Andrew said, heaven on earth.

We returned at the end of August. A letter from Pa was waiting for me.

'My dearest Rosie,' he wrote.

> It was wonderful having you with me, and I hope you, too, found this time together agreeable. Following your departure, as you know, I went on a sort of 'pilgrimage' and that was extremely enriching, and only confirmed, for me, the matters we spoke about. I know you disagree with the direction I have taken, and probably even

think me slightly mad, but I'm convinced that if you'd approach the matter with less prejudice you might see my perspective…

Be that as it may, I have some more news for you that might upset you quite a bit, and I'm sorry to say I can't go into any detail. I am going away for a while, on a journey that will take me far away from Shanti Nilayam. I might be gone for a good while, a year, years, even. I cannot say at this time, nor give you any details as to my whereabouts or further movements. This will be my last letter to you for the time being; please do not reply to it as I will be gone by the time your letter arrives.

I am closing down Shanti Nilayam, but only partially. Thila will remain here, and be staying in her own room and have use of the kitchen and bathroom. She will keep the place running in a reduced way; it is, after all, her home as well. The gardener, too, will ensure that the grounds are kept in order. You are, of course, welcome to come and stay whenever you want, as it is above all your home. But Thila does not have a forwarding address for me, nor will she know my whereabouts. Nobody does.

I've also told Father Bear he can stay here whenever he's in Madras, as he does visit from time to time. I'll give you his address near Vellore – as I have told you, he has opened a rural orphanage and has now moved there permanently. It seems he's having a bit of bother with his Catholic Order. He is such a maverick. But in my opinion, they should take their lead from him; the Church could do with some reform, and he could teach them a thing or two about truly following Christ, walking in His footsteps. I met him (Father Bear – not Christ!) recently – he stayed with me here – and I have given him a spare key; I hope you, as the official owner, don't mind! But I know you won't.

But I digress. I really just wanted to say that this is goodbye, but only for the time being. In case of emergency, please contact my lawyer in Delhi, whose address you will find at the bottom of this letter. I'll also add Aunt Jane's address as I'm not sure if you have it.

I'm sorry to be so secretive, my dear, but it is for the best. I do wish you much strength and courage for the coming years. Hopefully the war will stay confined to Europe and both Ceylon and India will be spared any involvement. You will be safe…

There followed the list of addresses and telephone numbers he had promised, and some encouragement to pursue my ambition to study medicine as soon as circumstances permitted, and some details about money to pay for such an education and how to access it. There was a short note for Aunt Silvia in the envelope.

And that was it.

Needless to say, I was shocked. By the secrecy of the whole thing, meaning he did not trust me enough to confide in me. Because it was obvious what was going on, and where he was headed. The very structure of the letter told me everything. He had joined up with one of the gurus he had told me about, decided to link his fortunes to them. My bet was on the female 'saint' in the Himalayas, judging by his wording *on a journey that will take me far away from Shanti Nilayam*. The other one was in Tamil Nadu, he'd said, not far from Madras itself, so that was ruled out.

I feared for Pa. Had he got himself involved in some kind of a sect? One did hear of such matters, of normal people suddenly being seduced by a self-appointed 'enlightened being'. I would have thought Pa far too sensible to be attracted to any kind of outlandish, half-baked religious humbug, but it seemed these people were able to draw in people even of high intelligence. Their power was uncanny. And usually all they wanted was money. At least Pa seemed to have ensured that my financial security was not compromised, though.

Aunt Silvia was equally upset.

'I can't think what has got into Rupert,' she said when I told her the gist of my letter, and she had read her own, less detailed, note. 'But then, he was always a dark horse, wasn't he? Head up in the clouds, little connection to reality. Without Lucy he'd have been lost, the dear man, floating ten feet above the ground. That's what Lucy knew when she made her arrangements for her possible death. He was always likely to fly off into the unknown. A bit of a bohemian. No roots in himself.'

Now, it was all very well for me to have my doubts about Pa's mental condition, but I was not going to have Aunt Silvia criticise him.

'Pa is one of the finest linguists in the world!' I said firmly. 'He's highly respected in the literary world! He's fluent in *at least* ten languages, some of which he taught himself! He's brilliant!'

'Oh, I don't doubt his brilliance!' said Aunt Silvia with a rather patronising smile. 'It's just that his brilliance isn't actually very useful, is it? Give me a man with some practical brilliance any day, a man who can run a profitable tea business, like your Uncle Henry. I did warn Lucy, at the time – but, ho-hum. She made her choice. Made her bed and had to lie in it.'

'She loved him! And was happy with him! And he is practical; he earns money at the university.'

'Ha!' she replied. 'You obviously have little inkling as to the renumeration earned by English professors. If it weren't for his estates back in England your father would have been a poor man indeed. Even the house was not his. Thank goodness for your mother! On his own, he'd have housed his family in some mud hut in the sticks of South India, lived like a peasant. You can be thankful that you had sensible grandparents on both sides, ensuring that you, at least, will not suffer financially.'

It was a long speech, and it infuriated me because, somehow, I knew she was wrong. She might have been right about Pa's teaching and research work but she was wrong, so wrong, about... well, I couldn't quite figure out what exactly she was wrong about. I suppose it was just the derogatory way in which she spoke of Pa. That was wrong. I knew, I just knew, that Pa was a very fine man, the finest of the fine; and even though I myself had been indulging in derogatory thoughts myself concerning my father, her little pricks ensured that I reversed my opinion entirely and now fought tooth and nail on his behalf. I cried: 'Pa is the finest, most upstanding, caring, most thoroughly *good* man I've ever met!' (And that includes Uncle Henry, I thought, but didn't say.) 'I don't know anybody who can hold a torch to him! And in the end that's what matters, isn't it? Character!'

'Ha!' said Aunt Silvia. 'Character! There you've hit the nail on the head. Character, strength of it. I'm sorry to say that your father is of weak character, as this running off to join some nebulous sect proves. You said so yourself, just a minute ago.'

She got me there. I had shared with her my suspicions as to what Pa was up to and where he had gone, and I now had no reply. I had given her the ammunition to defeat me. I walked away.

But from that day onward I could no longer regard Aunt Silvia as an ally. Her disdain for Pa rankled within me, and I had to distance myself from her in order to maintain some sort of personal integrity.

This was when I started going to the waterfall, before dawn, to play the flute. The waterfall was a fifteen-minute walk from the house, hidden in the forest that surrounded Newmeads. There, on the hillside that led down to a beautiful lake in the valley below, a stream splashed over a rock into a shallow pool where the water was as clear as glass, and fresh and cool, where I'd often bathed with the boys in our younger days.

It was a small pool, a narrow waterfall, but the sound made by water entering water was simply delicious: so soothing, so fresh and clear and pure, the constant splash pleasing to the ear and to the heart, seeming to wash away all cares.

That sound formed a backdrop to my playing. Like an unbroken flow of oil, it provided a steady baseline upon which I could improvise a thousand tunes, each one as new and original as the dawning day. Coming here to play in tandem with the water's fall became a daily ritual that refreshed and rejuvenated me and made me fit for the day: a kind of meditation that tuned me for the coming day just as a violin is tuned before playing; an essential part of my life.

Chapter Eleven

1939–1942

Meanwhile, I continued to thrive at Girls' High School. Since my last conversation with Pa, and knowing I had his support, I was more determined than ever to pursue my decision to become a doctor, and was strongly encouraged by several of my mistresses. I hadn't yet mentioned this seemingly outlandish ambition to Aunt Silvia, who had continued to try to persuade me to go to finishing school until I asked Pa to intervene and he wrote her a very stern letter, after which she desisted.

She did not desist, though, from her efforts to persuade me that I should marry one of her sons. Her approach was one of watchful waiting, covert and sly rather than overt. After the debacle before our holiday she was far too smart to actively attempt any more direct approach in her matchmaking, for as a devout reader of Jane Austen's novels she was well aware that such vigorous attempts to push matters along often ended in disaster. But it was obvious that she believed that our close proximity would do the trick.

Unfortunately, it was exactly this close proximity that actually annulled any romantic developments – we three were like siblings, and nothing was going to change that; neither of them were marriage material in my eyes. Of course, like any young girl I hoped to fall in love with someone wonderful one day, but it wouldn't be one of *them*. Anyway, my eyes for the time being were fixed on a different star, that of becoming a doctor.

Besides, Andrew still had his hopes pinned on Usha, even in her continued absence. He could not be talked out of it; I no longer even tried. Despite his youth, he 'just knew' he was to marry her one day. As for Victor, he'd made a name for himself in Kandy as a Romeo; half of my friends from Girls' had had their eyes on him, and vice versa, and rumours of this out-of-bounds escapade or that often scalded my ears and seriously put me off him.

And as for Graham, the eldest, he was never in the running as far as Aunty was concerned. For him, she had other plans: our neighbours the Carruthers had a daughter, Gwen, just two years younger than him – a perfect match, in more ways than one. Two plantations, two families becoming one, who couldn't see the advantage? Aunty told me of this plan quite unabashed, while swearing me to secrecy. Graham must not know. 'You know what men are like! I'll guide him gently in that direction, once he is in a position to marry.' (I didn't know what men were like, but that didn't seem to bother Aunty.) And so Graham breezed through life unaware of negotiations made on his behalf between the mothers and, I believe, Gwen herself.

But we saw little of Graham anyway, as Uncle Henry violently disapproved of him training in medicine when he had been supposed to take over the plantation. So strange, I thought; medicine sounded to me like the perfect career.

I was still in awe of Graham, not only because of his chosen profession and his defiance of his father but, perhaps most of all, because of his character. When we did see him he was always so silent, so incapable of small talk; so unresponsive in conversation. Graham, to me, was unfathomable.

Part Two

The War Years

1942 onwards

Chapter Twelve

When war in Europe was first declared in 1939, Aunt Silvia had breathed a sigh of relief that Andrew and Victor, both still at boarding school in Kodaikanal, were not only not in England, but too young – apparently – to enlist; young Englishmen, no matter where in the Empire they lived, all seemed desperate to run off straight into the arms of Hitler and fall down dead on some French cornfield.

But not her boys. Or so she believed. She immediately brought them back home, where they were to finish their schooling at Trinity College in Kandy as boarders. At home in Ceylon they'd be protected. With Graham also back on the island that year as a fully-fledged doctor, her family was complete and out of harm's way, and, she smugly believed, untouchable.

But she hadn't reckoned with Victor.

Victor was eighteen when war in Europe broke out and due to sit his final exams the following year, before joining Uncle Henry in managing the plantation. But unknown to his parents he had already been investigating his options, making enquiries in all the right places and with all the right people, demonstrating a hitherto undetected determination and decisiveness.

There was no conscription in Ceylon, but young men, both British and Ceylonese, were encouraged to volunteer for service, and before any of us knew a thing Victor had joined the Commonwealth Air Training Plan and was off to Australia to train as a fighter pilot at a training school in Victoria. Aunt Silvia, frantic at his sudden disappearance seemingly off the face of the earth, received the news in a telegram the following week. We all had to deal with the fallout: days of wild hysterics. It took her a week to calm down.

Andrew, meanwhile, rejected in love, excited by a romantic notion of war, by the chance to flex his muscles and prove his manhood, joined the National Cadet Corps, a voluntary youth organisation for secondary school students.

Aunt Silvia was apoplectic at this. 'No! Andrew, you're much too young for this war business! I refuse to give my permission: you're only sixteen!'

'Not a child any more, Mother. What do you say, Father?' He turned pleading eyes to his father.

'I think it's an excellent idea and of course I'll give permission! Splendid! I'm glad to see you're at last thinking of becoming a real man. It's a chance for you to do your bit for Britain without risking your life.'

The Cadet Corps, Uncle said, would keep Andrew happy with basic military training in small arms and parades, make him feel like a real man, a proper soldier, but in a non-combative and thus harmless way.

But in particular – as he read aloud from the brochure Andrew handed over: 'it will enable you to – now listen carefully, it's what I've been saying all along – develop "character, courage, sportsmanship, self-reliance, discipline, and civil-mindedness, spirit of adventure, responsibility and comradeship to be a human resource of well-trained youth, capable of providing leadership in all aspects of life."' He wagged a finger at Andrew.

'None of this namby-pamby, softy-wofty, bleeding-heart business!' he declared pompously, and I knew this was in reference to Graham's choice of a medical career. With Andrew and Victor back from Kodaikanal, his hopes had been reinvested in his younger sons. *They*, he had thought, would be his successors to Plantation Newmeads.

But Victor was now gone, and Andrew, too, had been showing signs of 'namby-pamby softy-wofty' weakness, with his predilection for painting and reading novels and poetry. And worst of all:

'It'll help you take your mind off things. All this falling in love with unsuitable girls, like some romantic hero in one of your mother's novels.'

So this, for Uncle Henry, was a step in the right direction. He turned to Aunt Silvia:

'This ridiculous war will be over soon anyway. No need to worry. Britain will send that little Hitler fellow packing with his tail between his legs. Both the boys'll be home soon, stronger and better than ever before.'

Uncle himself was a member of the Ceylon Planters Rifle Corps, a regiment attached to the Ceylon Defence Force. It was a volunteer regiment based in Kandy, made up of only Europeans, all tea and rubber planters from the hill country.

Like many of them, Uncle Henry was too old for active duty, but it gave him a patina of patriotism and a camaraderie with his planter friends; they could discuss the war and share their acquired knowledge with their families. He assured Aunt Silvia that the war would not last long. 'It'll be over by Christmas,' he proclaimed. 'And here in Ceylon we're perfectly safe.'

But it did not seem that way. The war was not over by that Christmas, nor the next. Travel down to Colombo (the highlight of Aunt Silvia's life) became more and more hazardous, as Britain seemed to think our island was the perfect base to face the threat posed by Japan. Petrol began to be rationed, which meant the curtailment of such trips anyway. More and more military bases were established, both in and around Colombo, and on the other side of the island, in and near Trincomalee. It became normal to see British military tanks and trucks passing by, soldiers marching. Who would not feel trepidation? Who would not worry? I certainly did.

Andrew and I often discussed the threat. Andrew, of course, was well informed, and explained: Malaya and Singapore, and, indeed, Ceylon, were rich in rubber. With the likelihood of war, Japan would be eyeing these countries; rubber would be needed for aircraft and land vehicles; rubber was vital to the war effort for both sides.

'Word is,' he told me, 'the Straits are crawling with Japanese spies. We're not safe, Rosie. The Nips are a formidable force. Ruthless; even more so than the Germans. We need to take the threat seriously.'

The shadow that had lain across my back since the outbreak of the war in Europe seemed to wrap cold dark arms around me, pull me even deeper into its darkness.

'Uncle Henry says that we're perfectly safe. That Singapore's a fortress that can't be broken,' I said.

'Ha!' said Andrew, shaking his head. 'He's forgetting about Siam. An attack from the north is more than possible. Don't underestimate the Nips, Rosie. They're clever, and good at outwitting their enemies. Pa's foolish to dismiss them.'

Aunt Silvia's younger sister and her mother were both still in Kuala Lumpur, and their letters to her confirmed Andrew's fears.

Then there came the point when even Uncle Henry could no longer hide his head in the sand; all the wishful thinking in the world could not obscure the truth.

On 7 December 1941 Japan bombed Pearl Harbor, and immediately became our official enemy. The war in Asia had begun.

Two days later, the Imperial Japanese Armed Forces invaded Malaya; British and Commonwealth forces tried to resist but were swiftly decimated. Like a house of cards, the Malayan island of Penang, designated by the British as a fortress, fell, the Royal Air Force base in Butterworth blown to bits. It was an unmitigated disaster for the British. We listened in shocked silence to the BBC reports; Aunty, fearful for her relatives and many friends in Kuala Lumpur, sent cable after cable: 'You must flee!' she insisted to them all. 'Get down to Singapore! You'll be safe there!'

But she received no reply.

Dreadful accounts reached us of atrocities in Malaya; a British family massacred in their home. Streets bombed. Hordes of people fleeing south, to Singapore. Singapore was our last chance to hold the peninsula.

Uncle clung to his faith in British invincibility, and we clung to that faith. Surely he, if anyone, would know? He now spent hours bent over the newspapers: *The Straits Times*, *The Times of India*, the *Ceylon Observer*, even, when he could get his hands on a copy, *The Times of London*. Every news titbit about the war, he devoured, and when not reading the newspapers he listened to the BBC. But both his reading and his listening were selective; he only absorbed the news that fed his own hopes.

'The Japs can't possibly take Singapore,' he proclaimed, and went into great detail, giving us lectures at the dinner table, information he had picked up from the Planters' Club in Kandy and the members of the Ceylon Planters Rifle Corps: 'fifteen-inch guns line the coast – a seaborne invasion is absolutely impossible. As for this rumoured attack from the north, through Malaya, preposterous: Malaya's covered in rainforest, utterly impenetrable. And a backbone of impassable granite mountains, protecting the city. Those puny Japs wouldn't dare to attack Singapore. We've got a hundred thousand crack troops upcountry waiting in defence, and they bloody know it! No, that balloon's not going to go up.'

But it did.

Uncle was correct in that Singapore, off the southern coast of Malaya, was heavily fortified on the seaward side; every report confirmed that these fortifications were inviolable. Singapore was after all the 'Gibraltar of the East'. It was Britain's most vital military base in South-East Asia, the key to British imperial interwar defence planning for this area and the South-West Pacific. It simply could not be taken by direct attack.

Yes, Uncle said, the landward side was in theory vulnerable: 'But realistically, they can't!' he scoffed.

We pored over maps of the area, diagrams supplied by the newspapers, and saw that Uncle was correct: the Japanese would have to traipse through five hundred miles of thick jungle, the length of the Malay Peninsula, to get to Singapore from the north. They'd have to cross rivers and fortified positions. And then they'd have to attack Singapore itself, the keystone of British defences in the Far East. Impossible, surely?

Nobody in their wildest dreams had imagined the simple solution with which the Japanese Imperial Army solved the jungle problem: Bicycles. Later, it was nicknamed the Bicycle Blitzkrieg.

Chapter Thirteen

1942

The year 1942 arrived with a literal bang, and the end to all our hopes. I was eighteen, and had recently graduated from Girls' High School, when the Japanese invaded the so-called inviolable fortress. Singapore fell on 15 February.

Aunty finally received a telegram from the island, followed, weeks later, by a letter from Australia. Her sister and mother were safe. They had, at the last minute, taken a train down from Kuala Lumpur and were able immediately to board an evacuation ship, bound for Australia. Her brother-in-law was not so lucky, her sister wrote:

> It broke my heart to leave poor Theo behind, but we had to. Only women with children were allowed on the ships; men had to stay behind. I'm in an agony of worry. I can only say, thank goodness Father passed away last year when he did. I don't think Mother would have left without him. So many of my friends had to stay behind, because they had no children! What will become of them, Silvia? What will become of us all?

All through this terrible period Aunty and Uncle received news from friends and relatives posted in the Straits. Terrible accounts of Japanese marauders bursting into the homes of people they had known, massacres of whole families. But her sister also sent devastating news: that a good friend of theirs had been slaughtered in her home, a rubber plantation in Malaya. This, combined with the fear for Aunty's own sons, was almost too much to bear. But what could we do? We had to bear it. We were the lucky ones.

But who really knew – would Ceylon be next? Would there be a Japanese invasion of our beautiful island? It certainly seemed that this was exactly what the Allied forces were preparing for. More and more warships sailed into Colombo's harbour. Other ships, too: ships bearing refugees from Singapore, who poured into the city, and had to be housed. On the other side of the island, an airbase had been established, the China Bay Airport, where, Uncle informed us, the RAF were building up a base of Spitfires and Hurricanes.

'They're a lot better than those useless Brewster Buffalos the RAF tried to defend Malaya with!' said Uncle, who couldn't help commenting on every single event. They should perhaps have made him Commander in Chief of the war, because he always knew better. But it was all out of helplessness. We were all helpless, here in the Ceylonese hills. It was all so terrifying: would we be next? Ceylon had valuable commodities: above all, rubber, needed for any war effort, but also tea, jewels, spices. And our position, just at the tip of India, was surely strategic. Would they be after us, India, the whole of Asia? The world? Whole continents falling to a German–Japanese Empire? My imagination ran away with me, down avenues of sheer terror. Germany and Japan, Lords of the Earth! The very thought made me tremble. For the time being, we were safe. But for how long? The citizens of Malaya and Singapore had also thought themselves safe. Look at them now!

Other, more personal, more terrifying bits of news trickled in. A good friend, a doctor who had been working in the Queen Alexandra Hospital in Singapore, had been slaughtered in cold blood, along with almost the entire staff of the hospital and the patients, the hospital turned into a veritable bloodbath. The beautiful city of Singapore was now a warzone, with rampaging Japanese soldiers swarming through the streets, through the houses; Chinese and Europeans, massacred even after surrendering.

'So much for the Geneva Convention!' said Uncle. 'The Japanese just don't care. And why should they, if they win this war?'

Finally, he conceded that we had lost. Singapore had fallen. The stronghold boasted of as being inviolable. The Empire of Japan had overpowered the British Empire, and Britannia no longer ruled the waves.

Yet in the midst of all these terrible events, all this devastating news, Aunt Silvia had one overriding concern.

'Do you think Victor will come home now?' she asked me. But I knew as little as she did. We knew he'd been dropping bombs on German battleships – that much we'd divined from his rare letters. Would he now be brought nearer to home? Aunt Silvia longed for this with all her heart. And for her sake, I, too, hoped for news of him. Meanwhile we kept our ears glued to the wireless, as one terrible snippet of news followed the next.

But then, to make it all much worse for her, in early February Andrew followed Victor's example and he, too, ran off to war. His cadet background put him in good stead; he volunteered to join the British Army at a recruitment office in Kandy. I was the only one he told in advance. He had been given a date a few days later to register down in Colombo. I tried, in vain, to talk him out of it. He was determined.

'I accept now that I can't have Usha,' he told me. 'Perhaps I was fooling myself, that she's the girl I'll marry. But it seemed so clear at the time! But I just can't get her out of my mind. I've tried and tried and nothing works. I've met other girls and they all leave me cold. It's her I want. So what's the alternative? Hanging around at home and moping? I might as well be a hero and die bravely. Isn't it what Father wants? For me to be a hero?'

'Oh, Andrew, don't talk like that! You'll find someone else. Please don't do anything rash!'

But he only shook his head. 'I don't want anyone else. I know what Mother wants – me to marry some respectable British girl, preferably you, and carry on the noble tradition of us being the exalted ones and *them* – wonderful girls like Usha – being beneath us. But I won't play that game. It's the principle of it, Rosie. The *principle!*'

And at last the penny dropped. Clinging to Usha the way he did was Andrew's private rebellion. His parents had always slotted him into a role in life, told him what he should do and become: run the plantation, join the Planters' Club, marry a decent English rose of a wife, carry on in the carefully honed role of a planter's son. A role Andrew was simply not made for.

I recalled a conversation I'd once had with him, when we were fifteen, before Usha had entered his life: 'When I take over the plantation I'm going to change everything!' he'd said.

'What do you mean? How?'

'Well, have you seen how they treat the workers over there? Those poor women, working all day in the hot sun. They're paid by weight, Rosie; did you know that? And they're paid a pittance. I'm going to pay them a living wage. And I'm going to tear down those awful hovels they live in – have you ever seen them? It's a disgrace.'

I had, and I agreed with him. I'd been shocked when I'd seen the awful living conditions: the lines of dilapidated shacks for the Tamil workers, not fit to keep animals in.

'I'm going to demolish those hovels, and build nice cottages for them, clean and decent. And give them free healthcare and education for their children, and pay them pensions when they're too old to work, and…'

On and on he'd gone, outlining all the projects he'd initiate once he'd taken over Newmeads.

'That sounds like a charity, not a tea plantation!' I'd laughed.

'It is a business, you know!'

Though I approved of all of Andrew's plans, I had to make him see reality. But Andrew was a visionary; he dreamed of a better world, and he was going to be instrumental in making it.

'I hate the way they – I mean the British – look down on the Tamils, treat them as lesser humans,' he'd said. 'I wish there was something I could do! But what can I do, one man alone?'

I realised now that Andrew was not just an idle dreamer or a visionary. He was an anarchist, but a clandestine one. He'd never openly challenge the inhuman institutions he loathed, he'd undermine them from within. He was a rebel by stealth, not by open attack. He'd realise his plans by taking over a plantation, only to dismantle it completely.

And: by marrying a native girl, a Tamil, of the servant class. What better way of shocking them all, without directly telling them to their face that he rejected every one of these pre-packaged roles? Usha was his escape card. Not that this was something he'd overtly planned; he hadn't chosen her for this reason. But it was the perfect slap in the face to the Planters' Club and all it stood for.

And if he couldn't have her, then he'd rebel in another way: by becoming a soldier, fighting a war, something completely alien to his nature. I saw right through him. And there was nothing I could do to stop him. Andrew was not the kind of rebel who'd openly show his hand. He had to do it his way. Even if it meant risking death.

Usha had written to me soon after she'd moved away, and since then we'd carried on a vibrant correspondence. We really were genuine friends, and I missed her company desperately. True, I had made friends among the other girls at Girls' High, but I only felt really close to Usha, and not having her at Newmeads meant that I was alone much of the time. She was now working as an ayah for a planter family near a village halfway between Kandy and Colombo, taking care of two children, one a girl of three and a baby boy.

I still couldn't believe that she'd soon be married to a stranger, but she was adamant. Her wedding had been planned for May this year – 1942 – just after her seventeenth birthday, and so was imminent. She had obviously still not met the lucky groom; she sounded more convinced than ever that the moment of truth, the moment of love, would arrive at the wedding when her new husband lifted her veil and they looked into each other's eyes.

'In that moment, everything will be erased. All previous infatuations. They will all be gone,' she'd written a few months earlier. I immediately latched on to the 'previous infatuations' mentioned.

'It was a strong meeting,' she had admitted in an earlier letter. 'And I admit that it awoke in me loving feelings that I found hard to dissipate.'

I was keen to get her to admit that those strong feelings were still not in the past. I wrote back: 'So you still think of him?'

She replied in her next letter:

Of course I still think of him! It's hard, so hard, to erase him from my mind. If only I had not looked up that day, met his eyes! It's the eyes that did it, Rosie! Eyes are so dangerous! Far more dangerous than a physical touch, because through the eyes souls meet and merge, and that's what happened. It's a thing that should only happen with my husband. It's like marriage yet it's not, and that's the painful thing. It is what I was saving for my wedding day, when my husband, the man I am to marry, lifts my veil. I am only hoping against hope, praying and praying, that it happens once more at my wedding, when Arun looks into my eyes for the first time. And that second glance will erase the first.

It was the most candid confession she had made in regard to Andrew in all these years, and it broke my heart. It seemed so unfair, so cruel, that these two should be kept apart when they so plainly belonged together! But now, talking to Andrew and hearing his determination to run off and get himself shot, I reached a decision that I knew was wrong. That I knew, even at the time, would have serious consequences.

I don't know what got into me. I just had to. It was as if I was overcome with a righteous wrath against the stupid, insidious, cruel rules of culture and religion that were keeping these two apart. It was as if I thought I could break apart that rigid wall between them. Perhaps I wanted to give them a chance, a tiny chance, and by doing that, perhaps, save Andrew's life. Perhaps I had a hopelessly romantic vein myself that I had not known of, and was compelled to promote vicariously a thing I had never known myself; for I had never been in love. Perhaps I yearned for such a wonderful thing, yearned to see its fulfilment in people I cared about, and who loved each other with a love so strong it had not faded a bit in all these years.

Whatever it was, I did it. I said it.

'Wait here,' I said to Andrew that evening. I went inside, opened my address book, and scribbled Usha's address on to a page of my writing pad. I tore it off, returned to Andrew.

'Go,' I said, handing him the note. 'Go to her. Maybe you can work it out together. She loves you too.'

I have no idea what I was thinking. An elopement? Them running away together, a secret marriage? Usha being 'spoiled' for a traditional marriage, so that it could not take place? Give Andrew a hand-up on the galloping horse of his rebellion?

I must have been overcome with some sort of lunacy to involve myself in a matter of such magnitude.

He thanked me with moist eyes. 'Look after Flopsy, Rosie!' he said, and I promised I would. The next day he was off before breakfast, leaving a letter for his parents.

Aunty opened it at the breakfast table. Her eyes opened wide as she scanned the few short sentences. And then, predictably, the wailing began.

'My boy! My baby! My youngest! He's going to get himself killed!' She swayed in her chair so that I thought she'd faint and fall: Uncle and I both ran to support her. She didn't faint, though. It was just another bout of hysterics.

I knew very well why Andrew had not had the guts to tell her himself: it was to avoid exactly a scene like this, her screaming and crying and even throwing things. I thought it was cruel of him not to say goodbye properly, but I understood his motives.

Uncle Henry accepted the news with more composure. He picked up the discarded letter, read it, and said, 'Well, well, well, I'd never have thought it of Andrew. Good show, my boy, good show. This war will make a man of you yet.'

'But what if he never comes back?' Aunty screamed.

'Now, now, dear, calm down, calm down,' he said to that, predictably to no effect. But even he had paled a little.

Chapter Fourteen

Burma was the next to fall. Cutting off the Burma Road, the one remaining land supply route to China, was the Japanese goal, the key to which was the occupation of Siam. Japan and Siam had signed a treaty of friendship in mid-December 1941; the very next day the first Japanese troops entered Burma by the narrow land bridge connecting the Malaya Peninsula to the rest of South-East Asia, thrusting in to invade Burma. Uncle, his ear always to the ground or stuck to the wireless or the phone, listening to his network of pals in the Rifle Corps, kept up almost a running commentary.

'They're moving up from the southern tip of Burma,' he'd explain, opening yet another map on the dining table to show us the route the Japanese would take. 'They want to occupy this string of British airfields that connected Burma with Malaya.' He'd jab at the map to show us exactly where these airfields were. 'Now they've taken Malaya, they'll advance towards Rangoon. All according to plan. If that happens, we're done. Goodnight, British Empire.'

Uncle was correct. The Japanese Imperial Army arrived in Rangoon in early March, and the city fell on 8 March. Singapore, Malaya, Burma… Would Ceylon be next? Would we one day soon witness Japanese soldiers with bayonets running down the drive towards the house, yelling their battle cries? I shivered with fear, night after night. I couldn't imagine what Aunty was going through, in agony not only for herself but for Victor, for Andrew. Two of her sons, sucked into the vortex of this terrible war. Already a bag of nerves since Victor had left to fight in Europe, she must be out of her mind.

But then something happened to swing her in the exact opposite direction: Victor came home on leave.

He simply walked in while we were having dinner, looking extremely dapper in his RAF uniform. In one moment Aunt Silvia was a changed woman. She leapt from her chair and flung her arms around him and wept with joy. 'My boy! My boy!' she cried over and over again. Victor grinned over his shoulder at his father and at me and rolled his eyes, but it was obvious he was enjoying the exuberant welcome.

Aunt Silvia managed to pull herself away and sit her boy down at the table, then rushed into the kitchen to summon up food for him, allowing Uncle Henry to express his own delight at his son's safe return. Now he wanted to know details, which Victor was not allowed to give. He had written home sporadically over the years, never saying exactly where he was or what he was doing; all we knew was that he was flying, most probably in Europe, and loved flying, and was a very good fighter pilot.

Now, again, there were few details Victor could give about his past missions and future assignments. We could only assume that, Asia finally being engulfed in the war, he would be flying missions closer to home; at least, he hinted at that.

'Oh, and by the way, I ran into Andrew in Colombo,' he said as an aside. 'He sends his love and apologies for running off so suddenly like that.'

'What? You saw Andrew! How was he? What was he doing?'

'Oh, we practically ran into each other in the street! We went to a little café to catch up, and then we met again the next day as he had something to give me. So my little brother's going to be a soldier! I didn't think he had it in him. Surely you wanted to keep him safe at home, Father, introduce him into the business? Now that I'm gone, and Graham's going to be a doctor.'

Uncle Henry shook his head sadly. 'That was the plan. As you can see, it failed.'

Aunt Silvia started to weep out her anger and fears about Andrew, but Victor just swept them away.

'We're at war, Aunty. I'm glad my little brother's showing some mettle. I really thought he was a lost cause, a bit of a limp rag.' He looked up at me then. 'Oh, by the way, Rosie, he gave me a message for you. I'll give it to you later.'

I nodded, and excitement flooded through me. It would doubtless be news of his meeting with Usha. I don't know what I'd been expecting – maybe that the two of them had run off together; but I suppose he couldn't very well do that, having just enlisted. That would be desertion, wouldn't it? And desertion was a serious matter. But surely they had reached some decision.

'How was he?' I asked, as casually as I could.

'Very well indeed!' said Victor. 'I've never seen him so jolly. Oh, and I saw Graham too – went to visit him. He says he's coming to visit in a few days. I'll be gone by then, but it's something you can look forward to, Mother.'

'How long is your leave?' Uncle Henry asked.

'I've got three more days and then I'm returning to base,' Victor replied.

'In Ceylon?' Uncle asked.

Victor glared at him. 'You know I can't tell you that.'

'And then you'll be flying again!' Aunty wept. 'Oh, Victor, darling! Promise me you won't do anything dangerous!'

He chuckled. 'I won't make any promises I can't keep, Mother! It's all dangerous. It's dangerous every day.'

Uncle frowned at him, but he took no notice. He seemed to almost enjoy torturing his mother this way.

'It's what makes it all so exciting – the knowledge that each mission could be your last. Waking up each morning and not knowing if you'll see another. The thrill of it all! It's what I've always wanted. Out here in the sticks is no place for me. But that... it's exhilarating! Gets my blood flowing.'

I looked up at Aunt Silvia. She was as white as a sheet. I felt very cross with Victor. Really, he was so very insensitive! How could he say such things to his own mother?

But he wasn't finished. 'But don't worry, Mother. With a name like mine, how can it possibly go wrong? Mind you, another fellow I knew with the same name crashed into the sea just the other day. Oops!'

He burst into laughter. That was too much for Aunt Silvia. She stood up so suddenly her chair tilted dangerously, and ran from the room.

Uncle Henry shook his head in exasperation. 'Did you *have* to upset her like that? She's already out of her mind with worry because of Andrew.'

'Well, Father, she might as well get used to the idea. We're at war, and we've got a few very ruthless enemies. Young men falling like flies. I could very well be one of them. Andrew as well. Your sweet sensitive baby Andrew. Heart broken by a little Indian tart.'

'What are you talking about?' said Uncle Henry.

'Wait a minute – you and Mother don't know? That he went to see her again, just a few days ago?' He looked at me. 'I know *you* know, Rosie. You and she are the best of friends, isn't it so? I thought he'd be over it by now, that little infatuation, but no, still as besotted as ever. I wonder what's happened. He wouldn't go into any detail, but... hmmm.' He frowned, as if trying to figure something out. Something to do with Andrew and Usha.

'I have no idea what you're referring to,' said Uncle Henry. 'And I insist that you go after your mother right now and comfort her. Really, Victor, I don't know what's got into you. Go and talk to her.'

'Very well, Father.' He got up, and glanced at me. 'Will you be in your room later, Rosie? I'll come to give you his message.' He left the dining room, and I breathed a sigh of relief. My growing aversion deepened. What was it about him that I did not like, did not trust? That inner hardness, veiled by the slightest veneer of good manners: a veneer that sometimes slipped. I remembered the first time we'd met Usha – how rude he'd been, when she was only a small child.

And the way he disparaged Andrew for loving Usha. I was sure, then, that Victor had never loved anyone, could not love anyone. He loved only himself.

But he had a message for me, from Andrew, and I looked forward to that. I certainly wasn't going to cross him.

Chapter Fifteen

Victor came to my room later; I had started a letter to Usha and had just prepared the envelope when he knocked and, without waiting for a reply, walked in. I stood up to face him. He handed me a small envelope. I recognised Andrew's handwriting: *Rosie*, was all it said.

I took it and placed it on the desk. Hopefully he'd leave now so that I could read it in peace. I had no desire at all to socialise with him, not even after his long absence; not after the way he'd behaved at dinner. I had to calm down before I could talk evenly to him. Writing to Usha had been helping, but I wanted to read Andrew's message before finishing my letter. I just wanted Victor to go.

'Why's he sending you a message when he only left here three days ago, I wonder? What's going on?'

'Nothing's going on at all.'

'You can't fool me, Rosie. The fellow went all dotty when I asked about that girl, admitted he'd been to see her but didn't want to say more, stuttered around for a bit. I thought time would be enough to quash that little affair. Seeing as the brothels of Colombo didn't help in the short term.'

He chuckled. 'Poor Andrew. He was quite horrified at the idea. Seems to have some crazy exalted view of women.'

And then his eyes narrowed, and he glared at me. 'So he's still lusting after her. And she's encouraging it, the little slut!'

'Victor! Don't talk about Usha like that! You don't know anything!'

He gave a dry chuckle. 'I can put two and two together. Look, I know she's your friend, Rosie, but you should never have got yourself involved. It's not your business. You're a guest here, you should at least respect our family!'

He paced the room, walking from one end to the other. Nervous energy poured from him, infecting me as well. His words woke ire in me. I shot back: 'I'm *not* a guest! Your mother's my foster-mother. I'm part of the family. She's always said so.'

'Just being kind. And manipulative. Mother's very manipulative. You know, of course, Rosie, that she wants you to marry one of us. Andrew or me. So which one would you choose? Though I suppose you don't have a choice any more, since Andrew's so besotted. But I'm still free, you know!'

He chuckled, lewdly, and looked me up and down in such a way that made me feel decidedly uncomfortable. I'd never felt completely at ease with Victor, even when we were young. As much as I'd looked up to him as a child, as much as I laughed at his outlandish jokes and gasped at some of his daredevil antics, there was just something thorny and prickly about him, something aloof – I could never really get close to him. Even before the boat incident; much more so after that.

I was eleven at the time, my second year at Newmeads. I had never learned to swim, because Amma couldn't and the Indian Ocean near our house was anyway too shallow for swimming; we only paddled and splashed around. But the lake in the valley below Newmeads, that was a different matter. Both Victor and Andrew had learned to swim there, taught, I believe, by Satish and Karthik, Usha's brothers. It was perfect for swimming, the water, even quite close to the shore, only reaching my shoulders, so that I could always touch the lake floor.

There was a short pier jutting into the lake, and a rowing boat Uncle had procured for the boys a few years ago, and which they used to row across the lake – always wearing life-jackets, as Aunty warned us again and again, each time we went out; she came with us usually. But sometimes she didn't. And if she didn't, we didn't bother with life-jackets. Victor said they were for sissies, and of course Andrew and I agreed. It was easy to comply with Victor. It made us feel wised up, above average, different.

So on that day Victor rowed us out to the middle of the lake, all of us without life-jackets, on a fishing expedition. Each of us had a fishing rod; Andrew sat in the prow, I in the middle, Victor at the back of the boat, next to the rudder. But Victor never had the patience for fishing for very long. If he had not caught anything in fifteen minutes, he'd get bored. He declared he was going swimming.

'Coming, Rosie?' he asked.

I shook my head. 'I can't swim properly yet.' I was coming along quite well with my swimming by now; Andrew was teaching me, very patiently. I could swim on my back and float quite well, but I still found it difficult to coordinate arms and legs.

'The best way to learn to swim,' Victor said now, 'is to just plunge right in. That's how I learned. The survival instinct is alerted, and you just do it, like that.' He clicked his fingers. 'Why not try it, Rosie?'

I shook my head. 'No,' I said. 'I'm not confident enough.'

'But that's how you'll get confidence, when you see you can do it! Just tell yourself you can, and you can!'

But I was adamant. 'No, I won't.'

'Righty-ho. But I'm going in. Coming, Andrew?'

'Of course!' Wherever Victor went, Andrew was never far behind.

'Can you come back here, then, Rosie, and take care of my rod for me, in case I get a bite? You can surely manage two rods? I'll fix mine to the boat so you only have to reel it in if there's a bite.'

'Yes, of course,' I said, getting up. I stood up and stepped over the bench I'd been sitting on, into the gap between the two benches.

But before I knew it, Victor was standing next to me and with a quick motion had grasped me by the waist and chucked me into the water.

Oh, the panic! I could not even think of trying to float or do a backstroke. I floundered, plunged underwater, flapped my arms; my head bobbed up above the surface, I gasped, wanted to cry out but couldn't. I tried to wave for help, but couldn't. I tried to think, but couldn't. Just water and choking and floundering and sinking and drowning. But suddenly strong arms grasped me under my own arms, lifted me over the water's surface, and I could breathe again. Andrew's head appeared next to me. His arms, hooked under mine, pulled me along. And then the boat was right there in front of me, and a hand was reaching down for me from it: Victor's hand. I grasped it and he pulled me up, laughing all the time.

'Well, that didn't work too well, did it?' he said, still laughing, once I was in the boat.

Andrew climbed in beside me. 'You shouldn't have done that!' he yelled at Victor. 'She could have drowned!'

'Oh, no fear of that,' said Victor. 'If you hadn't dived in, I would have. Of course I wouldn't let our little Rosie drown!'

He boxed me in the ribs with mock fondness, but I flinched away. I didn't find it funny at all.

'Don't tell Mother, though!' said Victor, as an afterthought, as he reeled in his rod and we prepared to return to the shore.

After that day I never trusted Victor again.

It was different with Andrew. If I had been in the least inclined to take Aunty's advice of trying to 'catch' one of them, it's Andrew I would have gone for. Andrew, with his winning smile and his chivalry and kindness. It was always Andrew who helped me navigate the trickier branches of the sprawling mango tree that grew in the backyard, Andrew who held my hand to steady me when a foot slipped off a slippery branch, Andrew who'd help me down, Andrew who seemed to actually care.

But it was a friendship without the least hint of romance; he was like a big brother to me, always had been. While the thought of Victor as a partner – well, it gave me the creeps.

Now, he said: 'Actually, you've grown into rather a nice little piece yourself, Rosie. Three years ago you were still one of those silly knock-kneed hockey girls. You're quite a woman now!'

He walked over to where I was standing, near my desk, and stood right in front of me. I stepped back, but he only stepped forward. He raised a hand and I thought he was going to touch my breast, and flinched away, but thankfully he didn't; he only lifted a swathe of my hair and let the strands fall slowly from his fingers. Which was unpleasant enough.

'Nice shiny hair!' he said, and chuckled again. 'So what about it, then? You and me? We'd make a handsome couple, don't you think? Mother would be so happy. We could take the initiative now and make a baby. What say you? So that if I do die on my next mission, Mother would at least have my child.'

'You're disgusting!' I snapped. 'Go away and leave me alone.' I turned away, sat down at my desk.

'Ah! Writing letters, I see. Got a sweetheart somewhere, little Rosie? Let me see…' He leaned over and picked up the envelope I'd just finished addressing.

'Aha! So you write to that little slut, do you? And she writes back, I assume. I wonder – did the two of you plan this together? Is it because of *you* that Andrew went back to her and is now so full of hope? I thought he'd given up, but now… well, well, well.'

'Give that back!' I cried, and snatched at the envelope. Thankfully, he willingly let me recover it, but then he picked up my writing pad and began to read my letter to Usha, holding out an arm as a shield to keep me at bay even as I pummelled it.

Laughingly, he replaced the letter on my desk. He had no shame, and no manners left at all now – what had the RAF done to him?

'Well, dear Rosie, since you don't seem keen to accept my courtship, I'll leave you to your own devices.' He gave a slight bow. 'Goodbye, little Rosie! See you tomorrow!'

The moment he left the room I grabbed Andrew's envelope and tore it open. Inside was a slip of paper, with only a few words written across it:

> Thank you, a million times, Rosie. The meeting went beyond my wildest dreams, and it's all thanks to you. Andrew.

But instead of feeling relieved and thankful that their meeting had gone well, all I felt now was fear. The meeting having gone beyond his 'wildest dreams' – what did that even mean? Had Usha agreed to break off her engagement? Could she even do that at this late stage? But what then, with Andrew off to war? What if something happened to him? What if my playing Cupid for them would actually spell disaster?

Perhaps it would have been better to simply let sleeping dogs lie. Let Usha marry her Arun next month. Let Andrew go off to war, not caring if he lived or died – not because he was a natural daredevil, like his brother, but because he had lost the will to live. Had I really meddled in a matter that was not my business? Did the consequences fall back on me? If it all went wrong, was it my fault?

I finished the letter with a few concluding words:

> I've just this minute read a letter from Andrew! Such a happy letter, Usha, and I'm delighted things went so well for you both. To tell the truth I was worried – I still don't know if it was my place to mediate between you two – I just felt so strongly that the two of you should at least

be given the chance to meet, just to see what happened; if there would be closure of some kind, one way or the other. A final NO from you, or, just maybe, a YES. I conclude, from his letter, that it was the latter, and I'm relieved but very worried. What will you do now? He's off to war, and if you break off your engagement – what then?

Please write as soon as you can: I'm hungry for details. This is such a precarious time. I just want you to know that whatever decision you make, I'm here for you.

I folded the letter, put it in its envelope, and went to bed.

Chapter Sixteen

The following day I decided not to be at home, so as to avoid Victor. I took my bike and rode off to one of the plantation houses an hour's ride away, to visit one of my school friends from Girls' High. I returned before dusk, only to find that Victor had already left, after a row with both his parents.

Aunty was frantic. 'He didn't even say goodbye!' she cried to me. 'Not even here for a day and off again!'

'And he took the Vauxhall, without asking. He knows we need the car! Drove off in a roar of exhaust.' Uncle seemed more upset about Victor taking the car than that he himself was gone, but I put it down to him never being able to find fault with Victor himself, and needing to find a tangible reason to be cross. Victor's rudeness to his mother – to all women, in fact – seemed to bypass him completely.

I comforted Aunty as well as I could. This was her long-lost son – I could hardly speak ill of him.

'At least you know that he's alive!' I said, putting an arm around her. 'At least he came to visit – at last!'

'For one day! ONE DAY!' she kept repeating. 'And when he goes back on duty it's the same thing, the same old worry. How will I survive?'

I was amused by those last words – Aunty worried about her own survival, when two of her sons had gone off to war. But it was just her way, and I was sorry for her – what if he were truly killed on one of his next missions? In wartime people should really attempt to stay on good terms with their close relatives. One never knew. But I myself couldn't live up to that high-minded concept, for I breathed a sigh of relief that he was gone. I'd dreaded running into him again.

There was also a letter waiting for me: from Usha! I tore it open.

Dear Rosie,

This is just a short note to say thank you for bringing me together with Andrew. I now know that I've been resisting something tremendous that just has to be, because it is. That is really as clear as day now. I love him, and I cannot marry another. I'm writing to my parents today to let them know that the engagement must be dissolved. I cannot be a true and worthy wife to Arun if I belong to another in my heart. I don't know when I'll see Andrew again and it breaks my heart to know he's in danger, but I believe our love and my prayers will bring him back to me. For the time being, I have my job and though my parents will be furious, I feel strong enough to face their wrath. They cannot force me to marry. I hate to do this to them but it simply cannot be.

However, I beg you to keep this matter private. Memsahib must not know of it. I doubt Amma and Appa will tell her, so it's up to you. I know I can trust you.

Yours sincerely, Usha

My heart swelled, and all doubts left me. Yes, it had been a good thing, bringing them together. And Usha was being so very brave! She, always the obedient daughter, respecting her culture's traditions, breaking away with such determination! She was now alone in the world, and would be until the war ended and Andrew returned safely to her.

And if he doesn't? a little voice nagged inside of me. But I knew the answer. If he doesn't, if it all goes wrong, I told myself, I will be responsible for her. I will do all I can to help her.

That night I went to bed feeling much relieved, and slept like a baby.

The next morning I was surprised to see not Sunita serving us breakfast, but her cousin, the girl who stepped in now and again whenever Sunita was indisposed. I wondered if it had something to do with Usha – had she received the news of her defection already? And again, a sense of guilt rose within me. It really wasn't my place to interfere in this family's future. But I pushed those feelings aside and went for my usual morning walk, through the forested hills to the waterfall – *my* waterfall, as I'd come to think of it. Over the past few weeks I had taken to coming out here at dawn to play my flute. Doing so calmed me; the medley of rushing water and the flute's sweet voice was enormously soothing, and prepared me for the coming day and whatever terrible news it might bring.

Now more than ever I turned to the flute for solace. I had nobody any more: Pa, Usha, Andrew – all the people I'd been close to in the past had all moved on. I alone was stuck here, at Newmeads, I alone had no specific task. While out there a war raged, and people were being killed, here was I, in the safety of an opulent mansion, living a life of comparative excess. The flute brought peace to me, and its pure, sweet music merged well with the steady rushing of the waterfall. I had once dreamed of becoming a doctor, but the war had torn those dreams into tatters. Was there another task, another mission, for me, somewhere? The peace the music and the water brought, I felt, would give me the answers I sought, point my way forward.

But I had not even been playing for five minutes before I was interrupted by a loud yell.

'Hey!'

I looked up, astonished. Before me stood Satish, the youngest of Usha's brothers, arms akimbo, his face a picture of unmitigated rage. I liked Satish, always had. He was a good fellow of balanced personality, always helpful and always polite. But not today.

'How dare you!' he shouted. 'How dare you meddle in my family! We know it's you!'

'Satish! What? What do you mean?' I feigned innocence, which was of course devious of me. I knew exactly what he was referring to. I was now well and truly involved in his family affairs, his family honour.

'Don't pretend you don't know! You know exactly. Who else could he have got her address from? You white people, why do you always think you know better?'

'I don't—'

'You got a letter from her yesterday too, didn't you? Don't deny it – I'm the one who brought it into the house. I know she tells you everything.'

'Satish, please, calm down. Can we please just—'

'Don't tell me to calm down!' he roared. 'Do you know what this means to my family? Do you know what a disgrace it is to dissolve an engagement? How can we ever hold our heads up high again? How will Karthik and I be able to find brides, when everyone knows about my sister?'

'I only want her to be happy!'

'It's none of your bloody business!' Satish never swore. That he did so now was a measure of his fury. 'Her happiness lies in doing her duty by her family! And you have ruined that! How will we ever live this down?'

'She and Andrew belong to each other. It would be wrong for her to marry Arun. It would break...'

He would not let me finish. 'Who cares about her broken heart? It is just a bloody English fantasy! She has broken her mother's heart, her father's heart! It was all perfect, and she has ruined everything. She is on her own now; my parents have disowned her. She is no longer their daughter. She is no longer my sister. If Andrew is killed in this bloody English war, she is on her own, thanks to you!'

And with that, he stormed off again, leaving me in a state of trembling shock. I picked up my flute again and tried to play, but my fingers trembled and my breath was short and shaky and I could not play two notes together. Guilt overwhelmed me. If I could take it all back, now, I would. I had meddled in something that didn't concern me at all. I packed away my flute, stood up and returned to the house.

I now had no doubt whatsoever that I had indeed rushed in where angels fear to tread. Usha's marriage was not my business, and I'd been a fool to try to prevent it. I should have left well enough alone. Especially in the middle of a terrible war, whose outcome lay in the shadows of the future. For I had no doubt that worse was to come. We were only at the beginning. Perhaps my little dream of bringing these two lovers together was my way of consoling myself, of finding a smidgen of something positive among the detritus of this terrible time. A way to lift my own heart. How terribly selfish of me.

Chapter Seventeen

In March 1942 an Evacuation Advice appeared in the newspapers:

> All persons not normally resident in Ceylon and who are not employed in essential war work must arrange to leave as soon as passages are arranged for them. This includes the wives and children of Naval, Military and Air Force personnel.
>
> With regards to residents of Ceylon, non-Ceylonese women with young children who are not employed with war work are advised to leave as soon as they can conveniently do so.

That was it, then. Ordered to leave. Unless... unless we were employed with war work. Now that was an idea, although not new to me at all as I'd been wondering for some time if there was something, anything, I could do. With both Victor and Andrew off to defend our country, and all plans for further education disrupted due to the war, I was feeling rather useless.

'I'm not going!' declared Aunt Silvia immediately, after Uncle read the notice aloud at the breakfast table. 'Let me have a look.' She snatched the paper from Uncle, perused the notice and looked up, jabbing at the page. 'And I don't have to. See: *non-Ceylonese women with young children.* I don't have young children, so I'm staying.

You too, Rosie,' she said, turning to me. 'Don't you go rushing off. You don't have young children.'

'Yes, but I could be engaged with war work. I'd like to do something – anything – to support our troops. I've been thinking about it for some time. It would probably mean moving to Colombo.'

'And leave me here, all by myself?'

'That's too dangerous, my dear,' said Uncle. 'I can't let you do that. And, Silvia, I can't risk you staying here. Did you hear about that English family in the hills of Burma – rubber planters? Slaughtered in their home. No, no! You both have to leave as soon as possible. I will go down to Colombo tomorrow and see when I can book a passage.'

However, this proved an almost impossible mission, because every English husband on the island had the same idea, and by the time he arrived at the booking office in Colombo there was no berth available for the wives and children. Many of the upcountry families were in the same position; they would have to book passages on later voyages, when the ships had returned from their safe haven, ready for a new shipment of mems to be evacuated. He finally managed to get a passage for late April, two months after the initial evacuation order.

Chapter Eighteen

Easter Sunday, 5 April 1942

The telephone call came just as we were sitting down for Easter Sunday dinner. We had returned from church in Kandy, and Rajkumar and Sunita had prepared the meal, the nearest thing to the kind of Easter dinner Uncle Henry had grown up with, back in Eastbourne.

I'd always loved watching them cook, the way they silently synchronised each step of the process to achieve culinary perfection.

There were no sheep in Kandy (or probably in the whole of Ceylon) and thus no roast lamb, so chicken had been chosen as a substitute; you might think it inadequate, but only until you viewed, smelled and tasted the result. This one had been marinated whole in a paste of coriander, cumin, fennel, fenugreek, mustard seeds, cardamom, cloves and cinnamon, all rubbed into the skin and the flesh, diffusing their diverse savours. The spices had all been freshly ground by Sunita sitting in the tiled area outside the kitchen shed, rolling the pestle back and forth on the grinding stone to produce the orange paste that made the difference between a meal and a feast. The oven itself was in a room of its own, walls blackened by smoke; a huge stone igloo heated up for hours by burning wood within its bowels, the still-glowing embers eventually scraped out, the prepared chicken inserted and left to roast. The result, sitting now before Uncle Henry, was glorious: a golden-brown chicken, crisp and succulent, giving off an aroma so utterly scrumptious it felt as if I'd fallen into a sensual heaven where taste and smell combined to float one off into a Shangri-La. Who needed church, when paradise could be created at home? The juices in my mouth were flowing.

We – that is, Uncle Henry, Aunty, me, and the Rutherfords (a planter couple who were our nearest neighbours) had all settled down at the heavy oak table (yes indeed, oak; it had been imported from England, from Uncle's childhood home) and Rajkumar had just placed the steaming chicken before Uncle Henry, who lifted the carving knife and fork ready to do the honours, when the telephone call came: shrill and unnecessarily loud, and, somehow, threatening, in hindsight at least.

'Oh dear, how inconvenient!' sighed Aunt Silvia. She was still trying to pretend there was no war on, and had banned all talk of 'the situation' from the meal. 'Rajkumar, please go and answer it; tell whoever it is we're not at home.' To us, she said: 'I do hope it isn't Marjory Craig – she does prattle on for hours and it's impossible to shut her up. She wasn't at church today and I suspect she has news of her daughter – I do hope nothing has happened, no new bombs on London. She's expecting a baby any day now and Marjory must be frantic with worry – she always said she was glad she didn't have sons, but having a daughter in a London Hitler's trying to bomb into oblivion must be just as frightening. I wonder if she'll agree to being evacuated?'

It was ironic, she complaining about Marjory Craig when she herself was such a chatterbox!

Rajkumar returned, bent low and whispered in Uncle's ear: 'Excuse me, Sahib. It's Master Graham.'

Poor Rajkumar. He spoke quietly and with great dignity, but we all heard, and all looked up. Uncle had already removed a thigh from the chicken and placed it on a plate, and that plate had been passed around the table and ended up before Mrs Rutherford.

'Excuse me,' said Uncle, and scraped back his chair. We all sat looking at each other, exchanging puzzled glances. Whatever could Graham want?

Aunt Silvia took over, scraping back her chair and standing up. 'Well, I don't know about anyone else, but I'm hungry!' she said as she walked to the head of the table, picked up the carving knife and fork, and proceeded to finish the job Uncle had started, keeping up the hearty small talk all the while.

Plates loaded with chicken thighs, wings and breasts, we all helped ourselves to the various vegetables and chutneys: lady-fingers, roast potatoes, pumpkin, spinach. As always, Rajkumar and Sunita had created a banquet fit for royalty.

Aunt Silvia was just telling us about the scandalous marriage of a Lady Something to a Ceylonese architect – 'as black a Tamil as you can imagine!' – when Uncle reappeared. He stood in the doorway, saying nothing, possibly waiting for a pause in Aunty's description of the man in question, but his silence seemed louder than her speech and somehow, gradually, all heads turned towards him and her stream of words slowed to a trickle and stopped. When he had all of our attention, Uncle finally spoke:

'Colombo has been bombed,' he said. 'The war has arrived in Ceylon.'

Chapter Nineteen

Nobody had much of an appetite after Graham's telephone call. In fact, I felt sick. The day we had all so dreaded had arrived. Ceylon, our home, was now a nation at war.

Of course, we had all long known that sooner or later Ceylon would be sucked into the conflagration that was already devouring Europe and creeping like a plague of locusts through North Africa and Asia. With Japan's entry into the war, and especially after the fall of Singapore, Ceylon had already become a frontline British base. The Royal Navy had moved their East Indies Station to Colombo and Trincomalee, on the north-eastern coast of the island, with fixed land defences at both locations, and the RAF occupied a civil airfield near Colombo.

As with the Pearl Harbor bombing, the Colombo attack came out of the blue. It was vicious and sudden and came in waves over the day; it being Easter Sunday meant that many parishioners were in church during the second wave.

Graham gave his father no more than a basic account that day: *that* it had happened rather than *how* – and that he was safe, which was the main thing. But the following day we learned more of the details, as the *Ceylon Daily News* reported the raid in full:

> Colombo and the suburbs were attacked yesterday at 8 o'clock in the morning by 75 enemy aircraft which came in waves from the sea. Twenty-five of the raiders were shot down, while 25 more were damaged. Dive-bombing and low-flying machine-gun attacks were made in the

Harbour and Ratmalana areas. A medical establishment
in the suburbs was also bombed…

Luckily for us, that 'medical establishment' was not the hospital
Graham worked at, but we could no longer hide from the fact that
it was all so much closer to home. We were no longer safe. Not that
we'd been safe before the attack, but there's a difference between fear
of an attack and an actual attack, and now that we'd been attacked
that fear escalated into fear of an invasion, such as had happened in
Malaya, Singapore and Burma. Japanese soldiers, bayonets in their
hands and murder in their eyes, swarming through our beautiful
island and bathing it in blood. My imagination ran away with me: I
visualised the worst and trembled at the possibilities. Uncle Henry,
too was afraid, though he refused to show it. He kept repeating:
'Thank God I'm sending Silvia away!'

All this, on top of my worry for Andrew and Usha, and my
meddling in their lives. I regretted it all wholeheartedly, now. I
had no right to bring them together, especially at such a precarious
time. The Japanese would win the war, I felt sure of it. We were
doomed. Andrew would die, and what would become of Usha?
Would her family take her back?

In the light of all these fears, my own destroyed future as a
doctor – utterly impossible in the light of the crisis – seemed
nothing more than a pinprick. Of no consequence whatsoever.
Chilled to the bone by the stories of horrendous massacres, I knew
we'd be lucky to escape with our lives.

No wonder I sought a different escape: my flute. I ran to the
sanctuary of music. I found refuge in its sweet, exquisite voice
and healing in the soft tendrils of sound it wrapped around my
anxious heart. I did not play any known music; I made it up as I
went along, listening to the waterfall and the stream as I played,
letting the water's music inspire me, letting my notes dance and
leap in harmony.

Three days after Graham's telephone call I was doing just that. I had skipped breakfast; instead, I'd poured myself a glass of coconut water from the jug in the Frigidaire, helped myself to the plate of newly peeled and sliced mango sitting there, and gone out to my favourite place. Sitting on my rock by the waterfall, my eyes closed, my upper body swaying as my fingers danced upon the body of the flute, I let the music fill me, move my fingers and my breath. Yet another tune welled up from inside of me, a pure expression of all that I felt: all the heartbreak, the loneliness, the grief, the guilt, the fear, Pa's abandonment, all merged with a deep yearning for peace and joy and love, a longing to be freed from mental strife. And beneath it all, the *shruti* note, the constant unchanging flowing stream that upheld it all. Carried away by the music, I did not hear that someone was approaching. But when at last I stopped, removed the flute from my lips to gather new breath, he spoke:

'Wonderful! That's truly exquisite, Rosie!'

I jumped, and looked up. It was Graham Huxley. He stood there, hardly a metre away from me, in such a relaxed way that I was sure he'd been standing there, unnoticed, for quite some time. Not the Graham I'd always thought of as cold and distant, either, but a smiling Graham with warm eyes, who now squatted down next to me.

'Thank you!' I said, blushing, overcome with shyness. 'When did you arrive?'

'Late last night; I crept in so as not to wake anyone, but I didn't sleep much and slipped out at dawn. What was that you were playing? It's neither Western nor Indian music. Who's the composer?'

I smiled. 'It doesn't have a composer,' I replied. 'I was simply improvising, making it up as I went along.'

'Really? Well, then, *you're* the composer, and you're very good! How long have you been playing?'

'For years, really. I learned a bit of music when I was at primary school, and was good at it – piano and flute – but I stopped for a while after Amma died and I moved to Ceylon. I brought the flute with me, though, and started playing again a few years ago. And coming here to play, it's so lovely, so calming!'

'It is,' he agreed. 'The waterfall in the background – it's like a *shruti* note, isn't?'

I broke into a huge grin. 'Yes! Exactly! That's just how I feel – I listen to that *shruti* note and then the music just kind of takes on a life of its own. I don't even feel that I'm the composer – it's as if it composes itself. It just bursts out from me as I listen to the *shruti*.'

'That's the way it should be,' he said. 'That's the sign of a true musician. A true artist. But, you know, the way you play – it's so eloquent. It's like a cry from the heart. There's so much joy in it – and yet deep sadness. All at once. Bittersweet.'

I took a deep breath. 'Yes, I know.'

'Can I have a look at it? It's beautiful.'

I handed him the flute. 'My music teacher gave it to me when I left Madras.'

'Is there a name for it?'

'It's called a bansuri,' I told him. 'It's been used in Indian classical music to accompany the sitar and the tabla for ages. For thousands of years.'

He inspected it, let his finger dance over the holes, put it to his lips but did not blow into it.

'It's bamboo, not wood, yes?'

'That's right,' I said. 'It's made from a single reed of bamboo.' I paused, then went on: 'They say it's the kind of flute Krishna used to enchant Radha – you know that story?'

He chuckled. 'I certainly do. It's beautiful. Krishna, the incarnation of God, played his magic flute and all the young girls who heard him adored him. But Radha was his one true love, his beloved. The story is supposed to symbolise the longing of mankind for the divine; that we all, men and women, should fall in love with Krishna. With God. All the pictures of Krishna have him holding his flute, one just like this.'

He handed it back and I placed it in its cloth bag, which lay on the rock beside me. A silence hung between us. I drew my knees up and hugged them and listened to the sweet splashing and gurgle of the water flowing beside us, and the twittering of birds up above. It was a comfortable silence, and I felt no need to break it. But he did.

'You're obviously going through a lot. I heard your father disappeared.'

I nodded, and kept my head down, afraid my eyes would give away too much. That they'd glisten with tears.

'That must be hard. Especially now that we're at war here in Asia.'

'It's very hard,' I whispered.

'You don't know where to find him?'

'He doesn't *want* to be found, Graham. That's the hard part. He knows where he could find *me,* though, so obviously he doesn't care.'

'Oh, Rosie!' he said, and that was all, and I was glad. Glad that he was sensitive enough to know that I didn't want to talk about it. That next to my mother's death, my father's desertion was the single deepest wound in my being. Deeper even than the fear of invasion. It's not a thing I'd shared with a single soul in the years since he'd gone, and it was something I hardly dared to admit to myself. I'd kept that wound plastered over with all kinds of distractions: school, and exams, and ambitions, and more lately the war, and news of it, and Andrew, and Usha, and then the drama with Victor, and then Satish. All matters and problems that kept my wound hidden. But now, with this man, virtually a stranger, it threatened to all come out, and I couldn't fight it, couldn't deal with it, couldn't hold it back. I tried, but a tear or two escaped.

He handed me a handkerchief, and I dried my tears.

'If you would like to talk,' he said quietly, 'I'm known as a good listener.'

I shook my head fiercely.

'It's not good to keep things bottled up inside,' he said, and at those words the dam burst and I broke into a torrent of wild, loud, ugly sobbing, knees drawn up, face hidden against my thighs, back quivering and heaving as I emptied it all out.

He said nothing all this time. At one stage he laid a hand on my back and left it there. It felt good, so good, as if strength poured from it, entering my body and stabilising my mind. After a while the sobs subsided and I became quieter and quieter, and finally stretched out my legs again. He withdrew his hand.

'I'm sorry about that,' I said as I leaned over to dip his hand-kerchief in the clear cool water. I wiped my face with the wet cloth and took a deep breath and looked at him and attempted a smile. 'I don't know what came over me.'

'I think it did you good!' he said. 'A good cry is sometimes the best medicine for a troubled heart.'

'You should know,' I said. 'You're a doctor.'

'Yes. And I've often found that healing the heart is the first step towards healing the body.'

'Can you heal hearts?'

'No. I think we can all only heal our own hearts, because that kind of healing comes from inside. But I can point the way. Sometimes it only needs a word or two – like a key, to open the door where all the hurt is buried.'

'Is that what you did just now? With me?'

'Not intentionally,' he said with a chuckle. 'I mean, when I first heard you playing I didn't even think there was anything that needed healing. Your music is wholesome, pure, good. I suspect it's *that* that mostly heals you. That's why you come here to play. The water and the music…'

'But I've never cried like that before.'

'Maybe you just needed a last nudge. Someone to help you break through the dam.'

'More like, push me over the edge! Like falling down a waterfall.'

'Whatever it was, I bet you feel much better now.'

'I do. But, well, a little embarrassed. It's not as if I know you well enough to… well, to dissolve like that in tears.'

'Ah, well, we need to rectify that.' He held out his hand. 'Graham Huxley, pleased to meet you!'

I laughed as we shook hands. 'The pleasure is mine! Rosalind Todd, Rosie for short.'

'So now you can cry as much as you like.'

'God forbid!' I said. 'That was enough crying for one day.' I paused, then asked, 'What's the time?'

He looked at his watch. 'It's almost eight.'

'Already! We should start walking back to the house,' I said. 'Aunt Silvia will want to see you – I can't believe you haven't seen her yet! She'll be over the moon.'

He sighed. 'Don't I know it!' He stood, stretched out a hand. I took it, and he helped me to my feet. I slung my bag over my shoulder and we started down the path through the woods.

'Poor Aunty! She's had quite a few shocks to the system recently, with Victor and Andrew both off to war.'

'And she's going to get another shock once we have time to talk. You're the first to know it but I've signed up for the Ceylon Volunteer Medical Corps, part of the Ceylon Defence Force, and it's very likely I'll be posted abroad very soon.'

I stopped walking and gasped. 'You too! Oh, Graham, you're the last of her sons! You can't just run off to war like that – it would kill her!'

He stopped too, faced me, and said: 'She'll have to come to terms with it, because it's done. How was I to know that Andrew would be signing up? He's the one who should stay here to hold the fort. Nobody was expecting him to join up. He's the last person I can imagine as a soldier. Victor, now – that's a given. And as a doctor, well, I'm only doing my bit. But Andrew's role was to be to be trained in the tea business. I thought he'd accepted that. I had no idea, when I signed up, that he'd run off. I only found out a week ago, when he came to say goodbye at the Colombo house.'

We walked on again.

'Did he tell you why he was running off like that?' I asked.

'No, but when I met Victor a few days later, I heard it was to do with some girl? A Tamil girl, no less. Star-crossed lovers, a broken heart, and a death wish?'

'Something like that.' I gave him a brief account of what had taken place over the last week. 'I shouldn't have tried to play Cupid,' I sighed. 'I guess I was trying to kill two birds with one stone – get Andrew not to run away…'

'Too late for that. He'd already signed up. Leaving now would be desertion.'

'And I also ruined Usha's family. I feel so terrible about that. Sunita's furious with me, and we always got on so well.'

'It was Usha's decision, though, to break off the engagement.'

'She wouldn't have if I hadn't practically pushed Andrew her way, knowing that if they met properly— well, I think I just *knew* and wanted them to be together. I didn't think of the consequences.'

'You meant well.'

'But it might well mean disaster for her. What if – I hate to say it, but – what if Andrew does get killed? What then?'

'Awful thought, for all of us. But it's done now. I think you'll just have to hope and pray for the best. No point worrying about the worst, which may never happen.'

'But – sorry. We were talking about you, you going off to war as well, and how Aunt Silvia will take it. '

'I'm dreading telling her. She'll be in hysterics.'

'For the third time in the last few weeks.'

'What to do? The decision's made and it was the right thing. Every man is needed.'

I said nothing. We walked on a few paces, and he must have noticed my quandary, for he said, 'Rosie?'

'Yes?'

'What's troubling you now?'

'Oh... well.' I hesitated. How perceptive he was! 'It was when you said every man is needed. What popped into my head was, "and every woman". I've been reading articles about women in England, how they're all doing their bit, as they say, working in factories, making ammunition, driving ambulances, even flying Spitfires. And me? I'm living in luxury and safety on Plantation Newmeads.'

'We don't have jobs like that for women in Ceylon. Don't blame yourself.'

'Yes, but—' I stopped.

'But what?'

'The other day I saw an ad in the newspaper. It was placed by the Department of Civil Defence. They're looking for ladies to make first aid dressings for the ARP casualty service. They asked volunteers to check in at the Girl Guides Headquarters in Colombo.'

'So that's what you're planning to do?'

I nodded.

'Well, good for you! You've left school, I heard, so you're free. Mother mentioned it in her last letter, complaining that you didn't want to go to some domestic science college, but that's out of the question now.'

I gave a wry chuckle. 'It never was a question. The truth is, Graham, up to now I'd planned to train as a doctor, just like you. I heard that Ceylon Medical College accepts female students to study medicine. But the war's put an end to that, for now at least. I might as well make first aid dressings. A good preparation!'

'You'll make a wonderful doctor, Rosie! We do need more women as doctors, it's just that the time is wrong. So if you feel like volunteering in the meantime, go ahead.'

I nodded. 'I think I will. I also read about something called Voluntary Aid Detachment – VAD – and they train women to support the war effort in any way they can, such as nursing assistants, ambulance drivers, chefs and administration. The nursing assistant part would be good practical training for later, when the war's over, and I can start my studies in peacetime.'

Somehow, I could now speak almost with confidence of when the war is over, rather than wallow in fears that we'd lose to the Japanese. That's how healed I felt. How strong.

'That also sounds like an excellent idea. I've heard of the VAD. They do essential work.'

'Exactly. I really want to pitch in. I'd do anything. Maybe administrative work. Just to know I'm not cowering in the safety of Newmeads.'

'That's just how I felt; it's why I've decided to volunteer.'

'Then you understand… for me it's so difficult, making these decisions alone. If my father was around— but he isn't.'

'You can talk to me all you want.'

'Thank you… but you're never here! And it seems you're about to be posted overseas. Is that right?'

He shrugged. 'I have no idea where I'll be posted. There's talk of a hospital ship.'

I shuddered. 'Don't ships get torpedoed all the time? I keep hearing of this ship and that ship being attacked. From below and from above. It's terrifying to think of you out there, on one of them.'

'Some do, some don't. It's just luck, I suppose.'

'You're not afraid?'

'Of course. It never really goes away, the fear. Like a beast at the back of the mind, ready to pounce. The trick is to keep it there, leashed, and not let it overtake you completely.'

I sighed. 'I'm trying.'

*

That evening, in the sitting room after dinner, Graham told his parents. I stood up to leave the room, thinking this should be a private family moment, but he gestured for me to stay, and so I sat down again.

He didn't beat around the bush. He simply broke the news that he had signed up and would be involved in the war effort, as a doctor.

'No!' screamed Aunt Silvia. 'No, no, no! I won't let you go! You're the last of my boys.'

She made to stand up, but stumbled and fell back into her armchair. Graham stood up and sat himself on the armrest, next to her.

He leaned close to her, took her hand and squeezed it, rubbed her back, and for the first time I noticed their strong resemblance: he had exactly her own warm hazel eyes and glossy, slightly wavy, mahogany hair, whereas Victor and Andrew both had the blond hair and grey eyes of their father. His voice was kindly, without being condescending:

'I'm sorry, Mother. I'm truly sorry, but I have to do it. I have to go.'

'Not you too! Please, not you too! How could you do this to me?'

'I didn't know Andrew had signed up,' said Graham, 'but anyway, it would have made no difference. I have to go. I have to do it, Mother. I'm sorry. So sorry.'

'All my sons, all my sons, off to war! What if you all get killed? What will I do? What will I do?'

My heart broke for her. I sat there, next to Uncle Henry, and felt so helpless, so useless. Uncle and I exchanged a glance and on his face I saw the very same anguish, a pain he was struggling to contain. Even though he and Graham had been so at odds over the last few years, faced with this new departure he must have been as devastated as Aunty.

Uncle Henry did what he could to console her. In vain. 'You should be proud of our sons, Silvia!' he said. 'All three of them, doing their duty like real men. And I have to say, Graham, I'm very proud of you. Finally doing the manly thing.'

And he actually stood up, walked over to Graham and held out his hand. Graham shook it, but he was obviously embarrassed, letting go quickly to continue gently rubbing his mother's back. Uncle returned to his seat. Aunty continued to sob, but quietly now, her face buried in her hands while Graham's hand rested on the nape of her neck. I thought, then, what a caring son he was; the only one of Aunty's sons to deliver the terrible news in person, directly, and in a compassionate way. The other two had both simply run away without a goodbye, unable to brave her hysterics.

Graham leaned forward now and rested his forehead against the side of her head, put an arm across her shoulders and closed his eyes, pulling her close. It seemed to me a most moving and tender gesture. A son, comforting his mother in her sorrow. Now, their heads together, she weeping silently into her hands, he gently massaged her shoulder with one hand. She removed her hands from her face and grasped his other hand. She held it so tightly the knuckles of one hand turned white, while the other slowly moved up and down along his wrist. I felt as if he was actually giving strength to her, silently, through his hands and his heart and, I guessed, through prayer. Her face, now uncovered, reflected quite plainly her struggle for calm.

Uncle coughed and I glanced at him. He gave me a rather desperate signal: *shall we leave?* I guessed he was highly embarrassed by the intimate nature of their interaction, the acute silence apart from an occasional snivel from Aunty, for this was a family in which physical touching was rare between parents and children. I supposed he wanted me to say something, break the spell when he could not.

But no, I would not interrupt. Yes, it was intimate, yet not awkwardly so. Though Aunty's emotion was raw, it was open and unashamed and to see it somehow absorbed by Graham was a moving experience. It was something so precious; a moment, I felt, of healing, not only for her but extended to all of us. It worked, too. Gradually the sobs receded. Her erratic breathing relaxed. She drew away from him then, and, now holding both his hands in hers, said: 'Please, please, Graham. Come back to me. Please come back to me. I can't bear to lose you. This terrible war. This terrible, terrible war, stealing our sons away!'

It was the moment Uncle had been waiting for. 'I think we all deserve a drink!' he announced, and pushed himself up from his armchair.

We retired to the veranda. Uncle poured himself a stiff *stengah*, and looked at me. 'Ready for a sundowner, Rosie?' he said, whisky bottle poised. It was the first time he had allowed me to drink hard alcohol. 'It's supposed to be half and half whisky and soda,' he went on, handing me the glass, 'but it's more like water with a few drops of whisky for you. You're going to need to drink to survive this war.'

I took a sip, and choked, but then the whisky began to work its magic and a sense of acceptance settled into me. He poured Aunty her favourite drink, gin and bitters. As she sipped at it, she began to sob again, but it was a resigned, accepting kind of weeping now, as if she had surrendered to the inevitable; she would face her trials with tears but they would be tears laced with patience, with stoicism.

And there was nothing anyone could do to comfort her, relieve her pain, because, after all, she was right. She could lose any one of her sons at any time, even all of them, and there was nothing anyone could do to change that reality; the reality faced by millions of mothers of sons caught up in this dreadful conflict. No matter what side of the conflict a mother was on, the terror and the dread must be the same, I thought. I could not think of a worse situation for a mother than to send her beloved child – for a soldier is still a child to his mother – off into an unknown that could very well end his life.

I too wanted to cry. But this was *their* time, an intimate family time, not the time and the place to display my own deep despair. I stood up and slipped away, unnoticed by them all. I went to bed and cried into my pillow. I cried for them all, for us all.

Chapter Twenty

Over the next few days Graham and I spoke many times, and I understood how much I'd misjudged him in the past: how could I ever have thought he was stand-offish?

Once I knew him enough to tell him that, he laughed his head off. 'Oh, Rosie! Me, aloof towards you? Not at all! What you were seeing was shyness! I hardly knew you, and yet I was supposed to be your big brother, and I had no idea how to fulfil that role! What do big brothers actually do, what do they say? You were such a lovely girl, so intelligent, so mature – not at all like other girls I'd known. With you I was for once lost for words!'

I laughed too, and I understood. What I'd taken for coldness was really just awkwardness. Graham was not a gregarious person, not an outgoing kind of man to whom people were instantly drawn and who went out of his way to chat with them. He didn't talk much, but when he did speak it was with depth and understanding.

In fact, he was a little like my father, easily misjudged for not being the life and the soul of the party, lurking, rather, on the side-lines; but once you got to know him, you tapped into a wellspring of kindness and caring. Once you scratched Pa's surface, too, you understood that; that was why he had so few friends but those he did have, the ones who really knew him – like Father Bear – were as close as could be.

Graham was of that ilk. I'd once thought he must be a bad doctor because I'd thought him cold. I now realised he must be an excellent doctor because of his ability to get beneath the surface of another person, see the inner hurt. To listen, and care.

My decision to one day become a doctor myself drew us together and he told me of his belief in the symmetry of body and mind, and how very often the healing of the mind was a precursor for the healing of the body. 'Sometimes,' he said, 'all it is, is a longing for love. An inner hole, yearning to be filled.'

'And can you fill it?'

He chuckled. 'Usually it's not their doctor's love the patient longs for, but the love of a specific person. A husband, a mother, a child. But the doctor's understanding can go a long way.'

'But now you are causing Aunty so much pain!' I said. 'By going off to war.'

Immediately the smile dropped from his face and his forehead creased in wrinkles. 'I know, and there's nothing I can do about it. This war is causing pain to everyone and I'm afraid Mother is another victim. My heart breaks for her, but it won't change my mind. It's not as if I can un-volunteer myself anyway.'

I reached out and squeezed his hand. 'Please, Graham, stay safe!'

He squeezed mine back. 'I'll do my best.'

The next day, Uncle drove Graham to the train station at Kandy and we all went along to say goodbye. It was the most emotional send-off I'd ever experienced, Aunty once again breaking down, Uncle doing his best to be stoic, and me standing there with tears streaming down my cheeks.

Graham hugged me. 'Goodbye, dear Rosie,' he said. 'It's been wonderful getting to know you. Look after Mother for me.'

'Come back soon,' was all I could manage through the tears; and then he was on the train and waving to us from the window, and the train was chugging out of the station, and he was gone. I cried, silently but helplessly, all the way home, filled with a melange of sadness and fear; I realised only now how very fond I was of him.

Aunty was an emotional wreck. 'I've lost all my boys!' she kept moaning, and I felt deeply for her, and did my best to suppress my annoyance at her constant weeping and wailing. Two of her boys now actively involved in a deadly war, and her third son volunteering as a frontline medic right in the midst of the conflagration; who could blame her for falling to pieces? All of a sudden, she'd been left with just me. My role was to provide comfort and internal sustenance. But it wasn't so easy. All her great dreams crumbling apart. She was devastated – yet somehow found it within herself to blame me. I could have 'done better'.

'But you're such a pretty girl!' she'd told me, so many times, in the past. 'You could easily have, you know, taken the initiative a bit. Why did you have to be so, well, so *boyish* all the time with them? That was the problem from the start.'

I knew exactly what she meant. Almost from the day I moved to Newmeads, I had learned to be one of the boys. With Amma, it had all been flowers and dancing on the beach and butterflies and singing twee songs about all things bright and beautiful, which is all very well, and all very uplifting, but moving to Newmeads had brought a seismic shift to my life that had seen me yearning to leave all that behind, to abandon the sensitive, rather otherworldly realm that had been my life in Madras and move forward into a harsher reality; to grow from a delicate flower into a tree that could withstand any storm, a tree of tough bark and deep roots.

It had been easy with Andrew and Victor; they just dragged me along, without any sentimental stroking of my wounded feelings, any of this 'oh, you poor darling!' nonsense. And I appreciated it. They'd been such fun, such adventure-loving, rough-and-tumble rascals.

But in Aunt Silvia's eyes it had been my duty to behave like what she saw as a 'proper' girl, to make either Andrew or Victor fall in love with me.

'You could have married one of them!' she wailed now. 'Either Victor or Andrew. I'd have approved, of course I would have. Maybe you'd have had a child by now and they would have felt the responsibility and not run off like madmen. And there would be a little one to distract me and keep me sane! I can't take it!'

She wept out her own story, then, and at last I understood. Two of her elder brothers had been volunteers in the last war, and both of them had been killed. This was where her terror of losing her boys to war came from. It was a fear that haunted her day and night, a fear she could not shake off, and no wonder. She had doted on her brothers, just as she doted on her sons, and her wish to see at least one of them settled with a suitable woman – me! – was nothing more than a misguided attempt to keep them safe and, possibly, have another being to love and to raise, a grandchild. It was my fault this had not happened.

I comforted her as best I could. This was not the time to tell her that one of her sons was a complete scoundrel: that I loathed Victor, and would not have married him for all the tea in China. I told her – uselessly – not to worry but to pray, and promised my support. This was also not the time to tell her that I was about to move to Colombo, to join the war effort. With all her plans falling apart, that would be the last straw.

But she had to know sooner or later. When I finally revealed my intentions to Aunt Silvia she had another breakdown and beseeched me to stay on, just for a while longer. 'You're all I have now!' she wept, and I conceded. She needed me; her life was turning rapidly upside down.

On top of all her boys being off fighting this terrible war, Uncle Henry had now laid down the law and booked her a first-class passage to South Africa on an evacuation ship due to leave Colombo in ten days' time. All her weeping and wailing would not change his mind.

'It's just not safe here!' he said. 'I won't have you here. One never knows what those Japs will be up to next. Not even the jungles of Burma and Malaya held them back.'

'And what about Rosie? Why can't she come with me?'

I shook my head and was about to speak, but Uncle spoke for me. 'You know Rosie wants to be a volunteer in Colombo. She's a young girl with no children; she'd doing her duty, as she should. So, my dear, she stays, you go. You won't be at all lonely. Almost all the planters are sending their wives away, so you'll have company on the journey and in South Africa. Evelyn Carruthers will be on the ship; I'm sure the two of you will be happy to have time together without husbands! Her daughter as well. I wouldn't be able to relax if you were here, stuck by yourself at Newmeads.'

And so Aunty was to be dragged, kicking and screaming, to South Africa. Over the next few days I helped her prepare the house for the diminished residency: Uncle alone would be remaining, so fewer members of staff would be needed. The furniture in the entire upstairs floor had to be dust-covered, the downstairs guest room prepared for Uncle, arrangements made for staff to be temporarily packed off home, with a lump sum in severance pay as a bribe to keep them available as soon as Aunty returned, hopefully in a few months' time. Only kitchen staff and two cleaning boys remained for the house, as well as the gardener and driver.

Satish and Karthik, I learned, had both volunteered for the Ceylon Armed Forces, as had their older brothers and a number of Uncle's male staff at the factory, a fact that caused him much distress. But he stoically accepted it, as it was, after all, only temporary: 'We'll soon send those little Japs packing.'

Yes: notwithstanding the Fall of Singapore, Uncle's faith in Britannia's rule of the seas and the colonies was inviolable. I could only hope he was right. I feared for everyone involved: Graham, Andrew, even Victor; Satish and Karthik; Aunt Silvia, travelling by ship across an ocean known to be riddled with enemy submarines, under a sky crossed daily by enemy warplanes looking for moving targets to torpedo. They all were in my prayers. Yes, even Victor.

My only solace was the flute. Without the hours of calm granted me by music I would have floundered, unable to help myself, much less another person in need who was waiting for me just around the corner.

Chapter Twenty-One

A week after Graham's departure I received a letter from Usha. It was the first letter in many weeks, and I'd been concerned. She had not replied to my last letter, written the night I'd had my confrontation with Victor, the letter expressing my pleasure that she and Andrew had finally met again and declared their love for each other; that she had broken off her engagement. Since then, of course, I'd seen how much disruption and anguish this had caused her family, how much anger there was towards me as the mediator. So when I saw the envelope lying there on the silver plate on the sitting-room side table, the meticulously rounded writing I knew to be hers, I immediately grabbed it and retired to my room.

> …sorry I have not written for so long. Oh, Rosie, my family is so angry. I have ruined everything. They have now disowned me for bringing this shame on them. But even knowing this I do not regret my decision. There is no going back anyway. I could not marry Arun knowing I love another.
>
> Luckily the English family I live with are on my side and up to now have supported me. I have a nice room and I enjoy looking after the children and all is well from that point of view. The mother and children are about to be evacuated, but the husband says he will keep me as a housekeeper as their present one has serious health problems – the poor thing.

But, dear Rosie, I now have another, more serious problem. I cannot write it down. I need to talk to you. Is it possible that you could come and see me? Very soon? I really need to talk.

I wrote her back immediately: 'I'll come as soon as I can.' But then I thought, *scrap that*. I crushed the letter in my fist and threw it into the wastepaper basket. *I'll take the car and visit her tomorrow.*

It was an old green Vauxhall, the same car Victor had driven off in in a huff and left in Colombo for Graham to return in. Aunt Silvia sometimes drove it to Kandy herself for her bridge club meetings, or to visit friends. Sometimes we were chauffeured here and there. I had only learned to drive it a year ago, and was still somewhat shaky, especially on those narrow, winding mountain roads. But I had driven to Kandy with Aunty a few times for practice, and so my decision to visit Usha meant taking my fear in hand and summoning all my confidence. I found a map of Ceylon in the hall sideboard, and took it to my room to find out where, exactly, Usha lived. It took some time to find the village's name, but eventually I did. It was on a side road that meandered off the main road to Nuwara Eliya. There I could surely ask for directions to the planter's home where Usha lived.

I would have to lie to Aunt Silvia – I could not tell her I was going to visit Usha. So I said, instead, that I was going to visit a school friend who lived near Nuwara Eliya; and because I disliked lying, I decided to drive on after my meeting with Usha and *really* visit her. She had written to say she and her family were going to be evacuated – on the very same ship as Aunty, it so happened – so I said I was going to say goodbye.

So, taking my heart in my hand, I set off early the next day. The sun was just rising over the red-blossomed flame-of-the-forest trees that lined the Newmeads driveway, and the world seemed bathed in glorious light. It was so hard to believe that, out there, nations were bombing each other to smithereens, people were dying, soldiers as well as innocent civilians. It was all so unreal. But it was true. Once I had discussed Usha's problem with her I looked forward to a long talk with my friend about what she was going to do. We were, basically, ladies of privilege, relatively untouched by the calamity that engulfed the world. My friend had a very political streak, and I was sure she'd have some pertinent ideas. Her plan, while at Girls' School, had been to study law in Colombo, but I was sure that she, too, would have been forced to put her ambition on hold. What would she be doing now? I looked forward to finding out.

I drove slowly, and very carefully, my knuckles sometimes turning white as I navigated some of the sharpest curves and edged past the few cars I met. But a few hours later, I had arrived at Usha's village in one piece.

I stopped in the centre of the village, parked the car and got out. I asked in a small grocery shop for directions to Plantation Somerset. The shop owner, a thin, balding Sinhalese man, gave me directions in broken English and I thanked him and continued on my way.

I found the plantation easily enough. It was tucked away in the hills and, like Newmeads, it had a long driveway lined with tropical shrubs in full flower, at the end of which stood a deep-verandaed bungalow, shaded by thickly profuse bougainvillea that seemed determined to spread all across the roof in the most glorious of colours. Usha had obviously landed on her feet here; what a beautiful home she had! Since her employers were also, according to her, good, caring people, I wondered what her problem could be, but I felt sure that together, we could solve it. I thought that it must have something to do with her family. I could only imagine her pain at being cut off from her parents and brothers. She had always been that dutiful, respectful daughter, happy to oblige them in every way, so for her to rise up in rebellion in this way must have been a shock to all of them, causing much grief on every side.

I parked the car and got out. A dog ran out, barking madly, but as he approached me crouched down, started wagging his tail and edged forward with lowered head and slinking body, a welcoming grin on his face. I liked dogs; I patted his head and walked up to the house, up the low, wide steps, and crossed the veranda to rap at the front door.

It was opened a second later by a petite maid wearing a blue dress under a crisp white apron, who, upon seeing me, said with deference, 'Good morning, Miss. I'm afraid Madame is not at home. Would you like to leave a message?'

I realised then how unusual my visit was, and perhaps inappropriate: a white person visiting a member of staff, a Tamil, a subordinate. Having been raised not to take such differences seriously, I often overstepped my role, and this was just such an occasion. I blushed – another thoroughly inappropriate reaction – and said, apologetically, 'Oh, no, no! I've not come to see your mistress. I'd like to see Miss Usha – the ayah.'

'Oh!' said the maid, taken aback. She needed a second or two to think, and then she said, 'Usha is with the children on the back veranda. Kindly come with me, Miss.'

She did not take me into the house but led me along the veranda, which apparently wrapped the entire house, for we turned a corner and then another corner. The bungalow was much larger than it appeared from the front, and at the back branched into a wing, this time without a veranda; the place seemed to be L-shaped, with the L-wing situated at the back of the main building. The veranda stopped at this junction, with an area sectioned off by a latticed wall of bamboo with a door in it. Vines grew up the lattice, so it was only when the maid opened a door set into it and gestured me to come through that I saw her: Usha, sitting on the floor and playing with two young children, one a toddler and the other a girl about three years old. The older child was bent over drawing something with crayons and Usha was absorbed in building a tower with wooden blocks with the toddler; she only looked up when the maid called her name. Seeing me, she leapt to her feet and flung herself at me, all smiles and hugs. 'You came! So quickly!' she cried. The maid, visibly taken aback, murmured something and quickly retreated. She was perhaps not accustomed to seeing white people so familiar with the help. But I couldn't care less. I was delighted to see Usha again.

There was a bench against the wall and Usha asked if I'd like to sit there with her, but I shook my head and told her the floor was fine, and we both sank down to the ground just the way we'd sat together on the Newmeads veranda.

We were obviously in a play area set aside for the children, the latticework forming one of three walls, the other two walls formed by the main building and the wing jutting out from it. The veranda opened up to the garden, which also was sectioned off from the main garden by low bushes, forming a play area containing a shallow pool, a sandpit, and a swing hanging from the overhanging branch of a mango tree, as well as a wooden climbing frame. Long low steps led from the veranda to the playground. This was obviously a family that cared deeply for the happiness of its young children; I'd never seen such an arrangement before. Through the open door in the wall behind I could see a rocking horse and a playpen: obviously an indoor nursery. These little ones were well provided for, and I commented to this effect.

'Yes,' Usha agreed. 'Mrs Harrison is a very kind lady and she adores her children. She is often out here with me, playing with them. She's very young, and we get on well – though we will never be friends, the way I am with you. But she also has to manage the household, which is quite a large one. A spinster aunt has come to stay, and also an older daughter – a bit older than you, I think.'

'An older daughter? I don't understand.'

'Well, Mr Harrison is a great deal older than Mrs Harrison, and she is his second wife. He has three older children, two girls and a boy, with his first wife, who died. The boy – he volunteered for active service – is twins with the girl who's here now. The other girl is a bit older and married to a rubber planter in the north. Mrs Harrison and her stepdaughter went out today to do some shopping in Nuwara Eliya.'

She hesitated. 'Maybe you know the girl. She used to go to your school in Kandy. Girls' High School.'

'Unlikely,' I said, 'if she wasn't in my form. And how are you, Usha? You look well!'

She did. She was obviously well fed; she had gained weight since she had left Newmeads and was no longer an ethereal teenager but a fully-grown woman, softly rounded, more beautiful than ever. Her eyes seemed to have grown larger yet, and contained still more depth: those eyes which, she was convinced, contained the portal to true marriage. Those eyes with which she had 'married' Andrew. I longed to talk about Andrew's visit, but she was obviously stalling, not eager to discuss her problem yet, whatever it was. There was so much we had to catch up on! Three years had passed since I'd last seen her, and this was her third job since then. She had not seen her parents in all this time and was eager to hear of their well-being.

'I'm afraid I can't tell you much,' I said. 'I'm still very much in Sunita's bad books. I don't think she'll ever forgive me. Satish certainly hasn't.' I told her of how Satish had berated me, which made her visibly uncomfortable so that she veered the conversation, once again, away from that contentious matter.

She offered me tea and got up to make it. 'Can you stay here with the children while I go to the kitchen? It's just through that door.'

I turned my attention to the younger child – the older one had hardly given me a glance, so absorbed she was in her drawing. I built a tower with the little boy, which he immediately knocked down, laughing his head off, and so I built another one, and a third, by which time Usha was back with the tea.

I asked her about her job, and she told me it was the best job she'd ever had. She enjoyed looking after the children, and Mrs Harrison was so nice. It was a pity they had to leave, but it was for their safety.

'Do you have set hours, or are you on the job twenty-four hours a day?'

'I look after the children every day until supper time,' she said. 'I have supper with them in the nursery, after which Mrs Harrison takes over. She enjoys getting them ready for bed, reading them stories. Then they go to bed. One of the maids sleeps in their room in case they wake up, and if they do, she summons me. I have my own room, next door to the nursery. It's very pleasant. It's that window, there.' She pointed to a window just visible beyond the lattice wall, its green shutters opened back against the wall.

'Do you ever have days off?' I asked, and she nodded.

'I get Sundays off. I like to go for walks on those days. Or bicycle rides. They've got an old bicycle they let me use, and there's a lovely lake not too far away that I can ride to. It's very relaxing. I'm so lucky!'

But her face told a different story. Her face looked anything but happy; it was the face of someone *trying hard* to look happy. She was definitely stalling. Her letter had seemed so desperate, yet now she seemed to be putting on a face, keeping to small talk, not coming to the point. Her smile seemed false, and she was avoiding not only my eyes but the obvious subject. It was up to me to raise it.

'And… Andrew?' I said. 'I'm so glad to hear it went well.'

She looked up at me directly, then, and the anguish in her eyes was written there clearly.

'Yes,' she said. 'I love him.' And then she lurched forward and flung her arms around me and broke into wild, convulsive sobs.

'Oh, Rosie!' she blubbered. 'I've done everything wrong! And I don't know what to do now!'

'Why, Usha? What's wrong? Is it because of your parents?'

The word 'parents' unleashed a new flood of tears. She was incapable of words, and simply clung to me, weeping. The little girl left her drawing and came over to us, patted Usha on the back. 'What's the matter, Usha?' she said kindly, and then 'Don't cry, Usha!' She stood watching for a few seconds, and then shrugged and returned to her art.

The toddler, meanwhile, was also intrigued. He stood up from his bricks, took a few steps closer, and pointed. 'Usha, crying!' he said. 'Usha sad.' I smiled at him; he toddled off into the garden, picked a marigold and brought it back and handed it to Usha. 'Flower!' he said. Usha was in no state to take it, so I took it from him and stuck it in Usha's plait, and thanked him. He returned to his bricks, having done his best. Such sweet, caring children!

I still believed that she was upset because of the rift between her and her family. I had already decided that since it was me who had caused the rift, I had to do something to help heal this family. Her parents had to see that it was wrong to force her into a marriage with the wrong man. Surely they had to see that! Sunita was so sensible, normally. Surely she didn't really want to cast her only daughter out forever. And Andrew was a good man. It wasn't the first interracial marriage anyone had ever heard of. Yes, there'd be a scandal at first, but surely they could work something out? It was so unfair!

Or maybe Usha was afraid for Andrew. What a time to decide that *he* was the one, just before he plunged off to fight for his country! Andrew could be killed; and what then? She must be terrified for him. I knew I was, and I'd seen Aunty's terror. And if he *was* killed – what then? Well, Usha would just have to do what thousands of other wives, fiancées, sweethearts did: learn to live with the pain. Perhaps she only wanted to talk it over with me, the one who brought them together. It must be awful, I thought, keeping that anguish locked up inside.

'It's all right, Usha. We'll work something out. It's all right,' I murmured again and again. 'I'm here for you. I'm your friend. You can count on me.'

But then Usha pulled away from me. The fire in her eyes shocked me.

'Stop saying that!' she cried, her voice fierce and commanding. 'You know nothing! Nothing at all!'

'Usha, I only—'

'I know, you only want to help but you're just making it worse and you know *nothing!*'

She almost spat out the last words. I'd never seen Usha this angry; in fact, I'd never seen her angry at all. But it wasn't anger, I was to realise with her next words. It was sheer desperation.

'I'm pregnant!'

I left the Harrison home only an hour later. I most certainly did not want to encounter the lady of the house, as my presence would be hard to explain. I decided not to visit my friend in Nuwara Eliya after all; I would not be able to concentrate on small talk, or even not-so-small talk. I needed to think. I needed to digest what Usha had told me. I drove straight home.

Of course Usha's admission had shocked me, but only at first. I had never once thought that Andrew, sweet, shy Andrew, would have taken advantage of Usha in the short time they'd had together. That was the shocking thing; but on second thoughts, it was understandable. He was off to war and who knew if he'd even survive. After so many years of pining his heart away for Usha, she had finally confessed her love for him. That must have been momentous! Of *course* he'd been carried away, overwhelmed not only by her finally opening up to him, but also by the fact that they had so little time left. And the fact – bury the thought but there it was – that this might truly be his very last, his only, chance to be

with her. He might die, and never see her again. And she would
have been overwhelmed by those very same ideas. Flooded with
emotion, in fact. I knew so little about love and romance, but this
is how I imagined it. I could almost visualise their meeting. Usha
told me they'd gone to the lake together, that Sunday, and had a
picnic. That must be when it had happened.

And now, this. Usha, expecting a baby. Andrew's baby! On the
one hand, such a marvellous thing. On the other, a disaster. An
unmitigated disaster. And, yes, shocking. A Ceylonese girl, cast out
by her family, unmarried, the father a young man who had rushed
off to war and might very well be killed. No marriage, no security.
It would be bad enough if Andrew was here and they had to have a
shotgun wedding. But as a young single mother? What would she do?

Of course, there were other options. I might be just an innocent
young girl myself, but everyone knew that in the cities there
were women who 'took care' of inconvenient pregnancies. But
everyone also knew that that was a risky option, unsafe, carried
out in backstreets in unhygienic conditions. That those women
quite often died. But most of all that it was illegal, and carried dire
consequences, not only for the abortionist but for the pregnant
woman too. It was out of the question. We both knew that.

We had talked and talked but had come to no conclusion, and
I had driven home with a heavy heart. But later that evening, it
came to me. The perfect solution. A solution almost too good to
be true. First thing the next morning I wrote to Usha:

My dear Usha,

I know exactly what we'll do. We'll go to India, you and
I. I have a house in Madras, standing empty, but with a
housekeeper with little work to do. She is trustworthy.
I'll take you there and there you'll live, and your baby
will be born there.

The thing is, I know just the person to help you. His name is Father Bear, and he is an old friend of my father, a family friend, a Catholic priest whom I would trust with my life. I shall write to him about your problem and ask him to meet us in Madras. He will certainly be able to help; the Catholics deal with this problem all the time. Father Bear himself runs an orphanage. Perhaps Father Bear will keep your baby there until Andrew returns from the war and you are married, and then you can reclaim him or her! Isn't that a marvellous idea? I don't know why it didn't occur to me right away, when I was with you!

Usha, I am so excited by this solution! Just let me know when I can come and pick you up…

Her answer came by return post:

My family are going to Colombo on Thursday, so that Mrs Harrison and the children can catch the evacuation ship. I'm going down to Colombo with them to help with the boarding. Can you meet me there?

How convenient! Aunty and Uncle were also driving down to Colombo so that Aunty could board that very same ship. It was the easiest thing in the world for me to go with them, to say goodbye.

I had no doubt that I'd find Usha, even in the hustle and bustle of a massive evacuation of white ladies about to embark on a new adventure. I knew I'd find her. And I did.

Chapter Twenty-Two

'Oh, this is so beautiful!' Usha cried as the rickshaw deposited us at the gate of Shanti Nilayam. As for me, my heart swelled with nostalgia, and tears pricked my eyes. Yes, it was beautiful, yes, it was home – but it was empty. In previous years I'd had to deal with Amma not being there; this time, Pa was also not here and for me, it seemed just an empty shell. I could not rejoice.

'Not any more beautiful than Newmeads, or the Harrisons' place!' I said. 'They are all beautiful.' The English, the wealthy English, certainly knew how to create paradise, even in the midst of poverty and ugliness, I thought. Not too far away from our paradisical home was one of Madras's ugliest and dirtiest slums. This was India: the juxtaposition of opposites. There was nothing you could say about India to which the very opposite did not also apply. All extremes, thrown together in a hotchpotch that somehow, in some unexplainable, almost supernatural way, functioned.

'Come on,' I said, as I picked up my canvas bag and opened the gate. Usha followed me into the grounds and up the sandy drive to the bungalow hidden among the bougainvillea, as always in full flower, bunches of vividly coloured blooms covering the lattice walls that shaded the wide veranda.

'Thila!' I called as I walked up the wide low stairs leading to the veranda. 'I'm back!'

A moment later, Thila came running up, beaming. 'Oh, Miss Rosie!' she exclaimed. 'I didn't know you were coming! I would have prepared a welcome meal for you! And I haven't made the bed, and...' Her gaze lifted to take in the slight figure just behind me.

'Oh!' she said, and fell silent.

'Thila, this is Usha. She used to work for Aunt Silvia, and I've brought her here to stay for a while. Please welcome her, and help her to feel at home.'

Time enough to explain Usha's predicament, and the role I had foreseen for Thila herself, later, when we had settled in. Not now.

Thila and Usha eyed each other, somewhat suspiciously, I thought at first. I had surely broken some delicate rule of Tamil etiquette, bringing in a woman who had basically been a servant herself in my house and expecting Thila to treat her with the deference due to a guest.

But Thila knew that we, my whole family, had no time for such up-and-down divisions of people. We had always treated her as a family member and a friend of equal value; her role of caring for our home and the people in it was not an indication of her value as a human. As Pa had always said, 'It's only a role. People fulfil roles, but they remain of equal worth, regardless of their role. It's character that counts.' And now, Thila demonstrated that she had taken this to heart by giving Usha her widest smile and holding out her hand to take the small bag she held.

'Welcome, Usha!' she said, and it was a greeting from the heart. 'Come on in and have a seat. I will make tea for you both – or would you prefer lime juice?'

'Lime juice for me, please!' I said. 'It's scorching out there in the sun, and I need something cold.'

Usha, who seemed to have lost her voice, nodded in agreement when Thila looked at her for confirmation. I deposited my bag on the veranda for the time being, took her by the elbow and led her into the main sitting room. It was exactly the same but, again, strangely empty because Pa was not here to fold me into his arms. I could have wept. *Where are you, Pa?* my heart cried. *Why have you deserted me?*

We sat down on the wicker sofa. Thila had switched on the overhead fan as she disappeared into the kitchen, and it slowly began to whirl, gathering speed as it turned its weary circles, doing little more, at first, than unsettling the dust that had gathered on its wings and strewing it into the stagnant ceiling air. Gradually, though, it generated a gentle cool breeze that wafted around us. I must remind Thila, I thought, to hang up wet sheets at all the windows to mitigate the heat burning in from outside. Later. Now, it was just good to be home.

Thila returned with a tray on which stood a jug of lime juice, two tall glasses and a bowl of ice. On one of my last visits Pa had proudly shown me one of his very few modern acquisitions, a Frigidaire, which made a world of difference, especially in the hot dry seasons. Thila served us both, placing ice in the glasses and filling them to the brim with lime juice. Usha still seemed embarrassed. 'Thank you,' she whispered, and Thila looked kindly at her.

'You're very welcome,' she said. 'I hope you feel at home here.'

'Could you please make up the guest room for Usha?' I said. 'She'll be here for quite a while. I'll be returning to Ceylon in a few days.'

'Oh?' said Thila, her eyebrows raised in curiosity, but I said no more. Not yet. Let Usha settle in first.

'Oh!' Thila repeated, and as she turned round she looked back and said, 'There's a letter for you! It came yesterday.'

She retrieved the letter from the telephone table against the wall, along with a letter-opener, and placed it in my hand. I looked at the address on the back, and smiled up at Usha.

'Father Bear!' I said. 'That was quick!' I slid the blade of the letter-opener under the seal, sliced it open and removed the letter. It was short and sweet. I looked up at Usha and smiled.

'He can help,' I told her, 'and he'll be here tomorrow. He said to tell you not to worry. Everything will be all right.'

*

After we'd had a rest and a snack of freshly peeled and sliced mango, Usha and I went down to the beach. It was Usha's first time on a beach; before our trip yesterday, to Colombo and up the coast to take the ferry over to Rameswaram, she had never seen the sea. The beach was almost empty; dusk was approaching and most people had gone home for the day. Ours was an east-facing beach, so we could enjoy the sunrise but never the sunset, and the sky was now a bluish grey, the water dark blue with white foam where it lapped the sand.

'Come on,' I said. 'Let's wade!' I took her hand and led her running towards the water's edge. I didn't even bother to tie up my long skirt; I simply plunged right in, screaming with joy. I had been living in a sort of panic-box for weeks, I realised, ever since the bombing of Colombo. Worry after worry, one after the other: the attack, Aunty's anguish, worry about evacuation, Andrew running head-first into danger, Victor's aggression, Graham, too, rushing off into the fray, Usha's plight, had all swamped me, and I had lost track of who I really was behind it all. I was a ball of tension, tightly packed. And now, as I leapt over a frothing wave, a bit of that tension relaxed, and I laughed, turned round and called to Usha to join me in the sea. She stood at the water's edge, hesitant; but then she ran forward, into the tiny waves lapping at the shore, and very soon we were leaping and dancing, and, yes, laughing! Laughing in abandonment, laughing with glee as, for just this window in time, we let the vastness of the ocean wash away our cares. Soon we were soaking wet, but it didn't matter.

Eventually it grew darker but then the moon made its welcome appearance and there it shone above us, round and silver and somehow magical. Wisps of clouds passed over it; it came and went, and the vastness of moonlit sky and the gently rolling ocean seemed to absorb all care and whisper to me: all will be well. We sat on the sand, huddled together, and I placed an arm around Usha. 'All will be well, one day,' I said, and I was sure of it.

At last we went home, where a delicious meal of rice and sambar awaited us, served by Thila. And then we went to bed.

I slept more soundly that night than I had for weeks.

The next day, I waited nervously for Father Bear to arrive. I had still not told Thila why Usha was here, and the role I expected her to play over the next few months. I was worried about how she'd react. Thila, of course, had had a traditional upbringing, and a baby out of wedlock would surely be a shocking thing for her; something unheard of. In her world, such a thing just didn't happen. It was morally wrong. What if she refused to be a handmaid to a thing sinful beyond imagination? What if Thila, in fact, walked out on me? I realised now that in my immature enthusiasm I hadn't thought the matter through; I had simply made a decision without regard for the wider implications for others. I was, as usual, being a busybody and making decisions for others, in matters that did not really concern me.

Because of the stigma attached to illegitimacy, Usha's pregnancy would have to be kept strictly secret, and she would have to spend the next seven months hidden away at Shanti Nilayam. Thila would have to do her shopping for her. No doubt she'd be able to cook for herself, but all communication to the outside would have to be done through Thila. Nobody must know. In effect, Usha would be a prisoner in the house. It wasn't even advisable, after yesterday's joyous dance in the ocean, for her to go to the beach, for there'd be people coming and going all day long and she'd soon stand out as a newcomer. Once her pregnancy showed it would anyway be out of the question.

I realised that I didn't even have the right to request such a thing of Thila. Thila was Pa's employee, not mine. I was barely a woman; still in my teens, in fact. How could I ask someone to do a job that would surely conflict seriously with her conscience? More than ever, then, I was desperate to talk to Father Bear. Perhaps he would have an alternative solution. I remembered hearing once of a Catholic home for unmarried mothers. Perhaps that would be a better place for Usha. But the very thought made me cringe. No, no, I thought, she must stay here. This is perfect. But I needed Father Bear's advice on how to manage the whole business.

Father Bear appeared just before lunch. I had never before been so happy to see him.

There he was, striding up the garden path, his beard bushier than ever, his ubiquitous straw hat more tattered than ever, his grin visible yards away! Usha and I were sitting on the veranda in wicker chairs as he approached, and I leapt to my feet and ran to greet him just as I had done as a ten-year-old.

'Father Bear!' I cried. 'It's so good to see you! How are you?'

'Grand, grand – and yourself?'

He didn't really look grand. He looked… tired. I hadn't seen him now for eight years, and as I grew closer, I could see that he had aged; his face creased into wrinkles around the eyes as he smiled, and his hair had turned almost completely grey, which I noticed as he removed his hat in his ever-polite way, before replacing it and flinging his arms around me and attempting to swing me around in a circle as he had done years ago. But he couldn't.

'Oof!' he groaned. 'You've grown! Where's my wee girl gone? Look at you! A real proper lady now!'

I laughed. 'That does happen, you know, after a few years!'

I took his hand and led him on to the veranda, where I introduced him to Usha. He looked at her with keen interest and soft eyes.

'Rosie been tellin' me about your wee plight,' he said. 'but don't worry. There's ways forward you can walk, and nobody here's lookin' to judge you.'

I frowned. That was the crux of my present matter. I might as well plunge right in. 'That's just it, Father,' I said. 'I'm worried about Thila. I don't want her thinking the worst of Usha. What if she refuses to take care of her? What then?'

'Now just don't you be worrying your wee head,' said Father Bear. 'That's all taken care of. Now let's not talk about problems for now, after I haven't seen you so long. Tell me how you've been doing, over there on the island? I been worried when I heard about the bombing – them bloody Japs! Hoped you hadn't been affected, but here you are, safe and sound. I read they were evacuating all the women and children?'

So the talk turned to my life in Ceylon since I'd last seen him, and then gradually moved on to Pa. I asked, bluntly: 'Do you know where he is, Father?'

Father Bear shook his head. 'I do not, unfortunately. He simply disappeared into the night. Very unlike him, I have to say. He never liked going anywhere, and to vanish for years without a word to anyone all this time... well. Strange.'

'I always thought he might have joined one of those strange sects. Somewhere in the Himalayas.'

But Father Bear shook his head. 'Not your father. He has his head screwed on very tightly. And he loves you so much – why would he abandon you for a sect?'

I shrugged. 'Sect people do strange things, so I've heard. They abandon their families overnight. A bit like your Catholic monks and nuns. Don't they, too, have to renounce family ties?'

But he was adamant. 'I know him as well as anyone, and I promise you, he'd never do that. In fact...'

He glanced at Usha, then, who all this time had sat silently listening. I'd had the feeling for some time now that she wanted to leave us to chat, since our conversation had nothing to do with her, but was too polite to ask to be excused. But now, she took the hint and stood up.

'I'll go and see if I can help Thila with dinner,' she said, and made namaste to both of us. 'It was very nice meeting you, Father Bear.'

'We'll have a more useful talk later,' he said. 'Rosie and I were just catching up.' She smiled, nodded and walked away.

'In fact, what?' I asked.

'Well, the last time I saw him, just before he went off, he asked me specifically to keep an eye on you. He gave me your address and said you'd have mine, just in case.'

'Just in case of what?'

'Well, I suppose in case of emergency. War had just broken out, after all.'

'That's just it. What a strange time to disappear. Almost as if he went into hiding.'

'I think we should stop speculating. All will become clear one day, Rosie. These are strange times and people are doing strange things. I do have my suspicions, but I'm not going to give them sunlight. Actually, I been wanting to talk to you about something else that your pa and I agreed on the last time I was here.'

'Oh. Oh, yes, indeed. I'd love to know.'

'It's about Thila. And what you said earlier, about worrying about if she'd accept Usha's predicament and help. And I wanted to reassure you that yes, she absolutely will. And to share a little secret with you. I know you're discreet, and you should know this.'

'A secret?'

'A secret, indeed. You see, Usha isn't the first young woman Thila has supported in this way. There was someone else. A young lady with the same problem. I wanted to help and discussed it with your father, at our last meeting. And it was his suggestion that she stay here after he left, and that Thila look after her. Which she did. You see, Thila is a child born of just such circumstances. Why do you think she isn't married?'

I frowned. 'I hadn't thought about that at all!'

'I thought not. And this of course is entirely confidential: Thila was born illegitimate, in one of our Catholic homes for unmarried mothers. I was a young priest at the time, newly arrived in India, full of zeal, and I gave pastoral care to all those who needed it, whether or not they were Christians. After all, we all worship the same God, just in different ways. So I used to come and talk to the young mothers-to-be, all of whom, of course, were distraught about their situations, knowing they'd have to lose their babies. And I'd try to find good homes for the babies given up for adoption, and comfort the mothers, give them hope. I was especially concerned about them because there were some rather scandalous rumours circulating in Ireland at the time about unmarried mothers and babies.'

He shook his head sadly. 'Really horrible things been going on; it's one of the reasons I left Ireland. I couldn't take it. And I felt a certain responsibility to do better here in India. Anyway, Thila's mother grew especially attached to me; we had long conversations. She was a well-educated daughter of a prominent Hindu family and I enjoyed discussing many things with her. She could not keep her child after the birth; it would have disgraced her family. But she asked me, as a special favour, to keep an eye on her. I promised, and I did. I found a good adoptive family for her, an older, childless couple, who both, unfortunately, passed away when she was sixteen. Your parents had just married and were looking for a live-in maid, so…' He hesitated, and then concluded, 'Anyway, Thila knows her background and so she is not one to judge another woman in the same situation as her mother.'

'Does she have any contact with her mother?'

He nodded. 'She does. She visits her on her days off. But it has to be kept secret; the mother is married to a respectable man who does not know of her past, and would be horrified. But that's life. Messy.'

'Well, that's a relief!'

'There's more, though…' He hesitated again, and I noticed a nervousness to him I'd never seen before. Father Bear was the very epitome of confidence. Was he actually blushing?

'You see, I made a mistake. Well, it wasn't a mistake. I don't regret a moment of it. But, well, it happened—' He stopped then.

'Father Bear, please don't tease me like this! If you're going to say something, say it, or don't!'

'I fell in love. With an Indian young lady. A wonderful, delightful young lady. And she with me. We got a little bit too close. I suppose it was the clandestine nature of the relationship that did it. And…'

He stopped again. I waited.

'She got pregnant. It was an impossible situation. I didn't want her to go into that Catholic home for unmarried mothers-to-be. I mean, it's the only resort for most girls in Madras in that situation, but no, I could not allow Aditi to go into that place. I had enough of that, in Ireland… terrible places, some of them. I discussed the situation with your father – he was, of course, very understanding and open-minded. He said, "Well then, she must come here. To Shanti Nilayam. For as long as it is necessary." And that's what we did. He gave instructions to Thila, who was very willing to be complicit, and discreet. She stayed here right up to the birth, and even a few weeks after, with her baby.'

'And then?'

'And then, unfortunately, she had to move on. She asked her parents to find a husband for her – she had, years ago, refused to marry, as she wanted to be a teacher, and she did become a teacher, a very good one. But there was no future for her as an unmarried mother. And having lost one child, she wanted another, so she decided to marry and give that little girl up for adoption. I heard of a struggling Catholic orphanage up near Vellore and I decided to move there, to be as far from Aditi as possible, and to take our daughter there and see her raised in a good, caring environment with hand-picked nuns. And that's where I am now. All that orphanage needed was some good management.'

I was almost in tears. 'Oh, Father Bear! That's such a sad story! Couldn't you have just – well, just married her?'

'You mean, leave the priesthood? Might as well go the whole hog, be hanged for a sheep as a lamb and all that. I suppose so. But what then? I'd have had no means to maintain a family. And she could not find work as a teacher again, not in that situation, married to an ex-priest and all that baggage. We discussed all that, believe me. I would have given up everything for her. But we could not build a life together, neither here nor in Ireland. We'd be outcasts. Our child would grow up with the stigma of scandal – that can be terrible.'

'But… just a minute.' I held up a hand to stop him going on. I needed to think. 'You called her Aditi. I'm not sure, but wasn't that Miss Subramaniam's name? I remember the younger children called her Miss Aditi, because her name was too long for them…'

He smiled wryly. 'Well deduced!' But then his face crumpled again. 'Well, that's that.'

'And the child? Was she never adopted?'

He shook his head. 'I managed to avoid it. Perhaps it's a selfish decision. Maybe she'd have been better off in a stable home with two parents. But frankly, it wasn't hard to avoid. Most children go when they're babies, but boys are preferred. If her skin had been light, because of being biracial, it would have been different, but she was indistinguishable from other Indian girls. Maybe not as dark as most Tamils, but still, a nice healthy and completely normal brown. She's still with us. The light of my life.'

'Does she know you're her father? Do the nuns?'

He looked horrified. 'No, of course not! And I definitely don't play favourites. I treat Anna-Marie the same as I treat all the children. She has a good life – for a life in an orphanage, anyway, and compared to other orphanages. She's just two years old, obviously too young to know what she might be missing. I mean, a proper mummy and daddy. I suppose when she gets older she'll pick up on that, though. They all do. The older orphans. They all want to be chosen when prospective parents come to look for a child. Invariably, though, those couples want a baby. The older children, especially girls, get left behind.'

'That's so sad!'

'Anyway,' said Father Bear, thumping his glass down with some finality. 'That's that. I wanted you to know. Seeing as how you were wondering about Thila, and how she'd react.'

I nodded. 'Yes. Thanks for telling me all that.' I paused and shook my head slowly. 'And I'm so, so sorry. You and Miss Aditi! I would never have guessed. I'd have thought you were too old for her.'

'I look older than I am. It's the grey hair and paunch that do it. I'm forty-eight. She's thirty-five. She looks younger.'

'Did she ever have any more children? You said that's why she agreed to marry?'

'Yes. She had two, in fact. A girl and a boy. She married a childless widower, an Indian who had emigrated to Australia and was looking for a new wife of childbearing age. They found each other through the matrimonial pages of *The Times of India*. Exchanged letters, photos, agreed to marry. So off she went to Australia to start a new life as a wife and a mother. She said she couldn't bear to be in the same country as Anna-Marie, wanted to put an ocean between them. And she did. I've heard through the grapevine that she's happy. All in all, she didn't do too badly. I won't ever see her again.' He sighed. 'Well... Would you like to call Usha over, and we can talk it all over.'

And that's what we did. Usha said nothing the whole time, but simply sat there, listening and nodding. When the part came about her baby being taken into the Good Shepherd Orphanage, tears came into her eyes and she bit her lip but said nothing. But I could see she was holding back something, so I asked her directly.

'Will... will he be given away?' she asked. 'Will somebody adopt him? Or her?'

Father Bear nodded. 'Sadly, that could happen. Once you have given birth and handed the baby over to us, you also have to sign over your rights as a mother, allowing us to find good parents for him or her.'

I squeezed Usha's hand in sympathy. I had a question of my own. 'But what if the war comes to an end, and the baby's father marries Usha? They will want their child, surely?' I looked at Usha, reached for her hand. 'That's what you're worried about, aren't you?'

Her eyes were swimming in tears. She only nodded.

'Well, in that case, let's hope that the child is still with us, and not yet adopted. There would be nothing against them adopting their own child. That would be a happy ending, of sorts. Of course, it's never happy for mixed-race couples but if that's what they want…'

He was obviously thinking of his own unhappy story, but I thought it would be different for Andrew. Surely, once the war was over and he was ready to take over the tea plantation, his parents would have no other option but to accept his choice of wife, regardless of the scandal surrounding the whole thing, regardless of her race and background. But it would be problematic.

I could just imagine Andrew turning up at Newmeads a year or two from now – or whenever the war ended, and having survived – with a Ceylonese wife and child in tow. Aunt Silvia would need the smelling salts again. And the entire planter community would be in uproar. They would be ostracised, for certain. Did Andrew have the stamina and the guts to deal with the backlash? Would Uncle Henry even have him back? Surely that would put paid to the plan for Andrew to take over the plantation; the planter community would not stand for it. These were all questions I could not answer. There were so many *ifs* surrounding the future. The biggest *if* being when the war would end, and who would be the survivors. Which of us. What frightening times we lived in.

Thila brought us a tray with tea and sandwiches, then, and I asked her to stay and sit, as we had something to discuss with her.

Which is what we did. And just as Father Bear had said, she took it all in her stride. And so it was arranged. Usha and I would stay at Shanti Nilayam for a while; Usha would stay home up to the birth to avoid questions and gossip, and I would return to Ceylon after a few days and look for war work.

Or perhaps not. It now dawned on me that I was, at last, a free woman. True enough, only eighteen and so not yet fully of age, and a war raged out there, curtailing my opportunities, but this was my home, my beloved real home, even without Pa's presence, and I felt little inclination to return to Ceylon as yet. Yes, I wanted to do my bit, but surely I could do more than roll bandages, which was what waited for me in Colombo? My mind began to whirr with possibilities. India, or Madras in particular, seemed to have been spared the wholesale panic that had enveloped Ceylon. Perhaps there were opportunities here not open to me in Ceylon. It was time to think seriously about my future, and the role I could play in the war.

I wished Graham were here, and I could talk it all over with him. In Pa's absence, he was the person whose advice and guidance I most welcomed. Father Bear might know a lot about schooling and young unmarried mothers and raising orphans, but had little to say, I found, when it came to opportunities for a young woman such as me to engage in useful war duties. But Graham was far away, on some warship or other on the Indian Ocean, in danger of being blown to pieces any day. My own problems were minuscule compared to his, my own future almost cosy compared to the danger he was in. I would not bother him with my trivial decision-making, I would have to work it out for myself.

That's what I did, and eventually I decided on a course in shorthand and typing. There were a number of good schools for that sort of thing right here on my doorstep. I would acquire those skills, and then return to Ceylon to finally do my bit, but with a proper qualification.

Chapter Twenty-Three

I returned to Colombo three months later as a qualified bilingual stenotypist. I moved into the Huxleys' house in Cinnamon Gardens, an elegant two-storey colonial mansion that had been converted into two flats. Graham usually lived in the top flat, which was now empty. An English family usually occupied the bottom apartment but the wife had been evacuated along with her two small children, and now only the husband, who worked in a reserved capacity with the Apothecaries, lived there, along with his father, a widower, a retired admiral.

With the intervention of the aforementioned admiral, and after a series of interviews, I was given a job with the Far East Combined Bureau. This was an outstation of the British Government Code and Cypher School, which had been set up in 1935 to monitor Japanese, Chinese and Soviet intelligence and radio traffic. Initially set up in Hong Kong, it had later moved to Singapore, Colombo and Kenya and then returned to Colombo. Pembroke College, an Indian boys' school, was requisitioned as a combined code-breaking and wireless interception centre.

That was where I found work as a secretary to the code-breakers, in a long low hut among several similar huts, where all this top-secret essential work was carried out. I had to sign the Official Secrets Act and I wore a white uniform to work, which was all rather exciting: I was working with spies!

Back in March there had been an influx of refugees from Singapore and Burma, for whom accommodation had to be found, and soon both flats in the Cinnamon Garden house were occupied by refugees; below, a mother and three children had moved in with the two gentlemen, while above, in our flat, a mother and her teenage daughter, Mrs Grantley and Pamela, had found refuge. I found them very pleasant indeed, and I was happy not to be living alone. Mrs Grantley's husband had been a rubber planter in Singapore, and she was in agony not knowing what had, what would, become of him.

'They say that all British men have been sent to Changi Prison,' she said, 'but I've not heard a word and I doubt if they'll allow him to write.'

She told chilling stories about the Japanese; her account of the massacre at the Alexandra Hospital on 14 February made my blood run cold. She had not wanted to leave, but there had been no option, especially with a young girl in tow.

Pamela and I got on well, and when I had time I showed her a bit of Colombo and the surrounding areas – her mother was not inclined to come with us. Eventually, once they had settled, they both decided to make themselves useful and volunteered for war work. Mrs Grantley was a trained nurse and she immediately got a job in that field, working long shifts, while Pamela worked as a nurse's assistant, mainly fetching and bringing items to doctors and nurses as they worked, rolling bandages, emptying and cleaning bedpans. After that we all saw less of each other; they were hardly ever at home.

Meanwhile, Colombo was becoming more and more militarised. Soldiers everywhere. Naval ships came and went, discharging soldiers, loading new ones. Warplanes sped past above our heads, and I always automatically looked up to be sure they weren't Japanese. Everyone lived in a permanent state of heightened tension. The Galle Face Hotel was a hive of activity; ever the centre of expatriate social life, it somehow managed to keep going as a meeting place for everyone who was anyone, desperately trying to convince themselves that life must go on and there would always be an England. I, personally, avoided it.

And then, out of the blue, Andrew turned up with a friend, both in army uniform. The friend wore some insignia on his epaulette; I had no idea what it meant. He also wore a few medals on his chest. But the most arresting thing about him was his eyes; so dark, almost black. They immediately caught my attention and I had to stop myself from staring. His skin was very dark, but he wasn't Ceylonese, or Indian: his hair was of a stiff moss-like texture, and so I guessed he was African, from what I'd seen from photos of Africans. But it wasn't so.

'This is Freddy Quint,' Andrew said, 'Or rather, Lance Corporal Quint. Freddy, this is Rosie – I told you about her.' Freddy held out his hand to shake, and I took it. His grasp was warm and somehow familiar, and perhaps a second too long. He smiled, and I returned the smile, and we stood smiling at each other while Andrew continued with his explanation: 'His people are in South America, a place called British Guiana. He's got leave and nowhere to go, so I invited him to come with me. We're going up to Newmeads tomorrow. Care to come?'

'I'd love to!' I said without hesitation. 'I'll come up on Saturday, I've got this weekend off.' Meanwhile, my eyes kept being drawn to Freddy Quint's, and I was struggling harder than ever to avoid his gaze. It wasn't that he was staring at me, it was just that our gazes had met and locked and it all seemed, just like the handshake, so absolutely familiar. As if I'd known him all my life and this was simply a long-due reunion. I couldn't explain it, but I understood now a little of what Usha had always told me about a meeting of the eyes, and why looking into a young man's eyes should be avoided.

No, it wasn't the instant marriage that Usha believed in. I wasn't that irrational. But it was there, all the same. A sense of deep, comforting intimacy. I had to give myself a little nudge to bring me back to reality.

'I'm so sorry, where's my hospitality? Can I offer you both tea? Nimbu pani? Something to eat – though, sorry, I've really got nothing – oh! I think there's a mango in the Frigidaire – I could slice it, and…'

'Nothing to eat, thanks!' said Freddy. 'Nimbu pani would be just right, after the heat out there.' It was the first time he'd spoken, and his voice was as warm as his eyes, and had a quaint lilt to it, an accent I'd never heard before, an up-and-down intonation, almost musical. I'm sorry to say I blushed, after which I looked at Andrew – who said, 'Same for me, thanks' – and rushed off to do the necessary.

We no longer had a live-in maid in the flat; she had returned to her family upcountry after the bombing. The three of us, the Grantleys and I, did our own cooking, and there was a permanent jug of lime juice in the Frigidaire from which I could make nimbu pani. I poured three glasses, placed them on a tray and hastened back to the sitting room, where the two men had settled down next to each other on the wicker sofa. I placed the tray on the glass table and sat down opposite them, trying desperately not to look at the newcomer. It wasn't easy.

Andrew would no doubt have a horde of questions regarding developments over the last few months, and I could tell he was dying to hear about Usha, but that would have to wait; I ignored his leading questions because what I had to say was far too serious to be discussed at a first catching-up conversation. Andrew knew nothing at all of Usha's pregnancy and approaching birth, and I wanted to tell him when we were alone. So I deflected his question, seemingly casual, as to whether I'd seen her recently, and changed the subject to life in Ceylon since the bombing.

'And you know that Graham has joined up?'

'Yes, Mother wrote me about that. She must have had a fit. All of her sons gone off to war.'

He shook his head sadly.

'You didn't have to go, you know, Andrew,' I said. 'Tea planter is a reserved occupation. She'd have had at least one son at home – it would have been a comfort.'

'You know why I had to go.'

'You didn't have to, you wanted to. You were running away.'

He chuckled. 'I don't regret it. It's making a man of me. Father will be pleased. By the way, Freddy ran away too. He was too young to enlist properly.'

I'd managed to keep my eyes on Andrew all this time but now they involuntarily swerved to Freddy. And there, waiting to meet them, was his calm, warm gaze. Again. Only instead of making me calm, it made me nervous. I had to look away and say something. Talking would distract me.

'You did?' I asked.

'Yes. How couldn't I? All of my elder brothers had signed up. All seven of them. Well, six, actually. One of them was rejected, so that was a comfort for my mother.'

'I can imagine!' I said. 'Seven sons off to war! Does she at least have a daughter as well?'

'No,' he said. 'No daughters. At least—'

He stopped in mid-sentence, then, and said, 'It's a long story, but I think that's right. No daughters.'

'You think?' I wanted to probe, but I noticed the ghost of a frown and realised he didn't want to talk about it. Andrew must have noticed too, for he changed the subject.

'So Freddy's got three years on me,' he said. 'He was fighting Nazis in Europe, and Africa, and only recently got posted to Asia. They put us in the same battalion, and we hit it off right away.'

'Where did you—?' I began, but Andrew immediately and brusquely stopped me. 'We can't talk about it,' he said. 'Absolute radio silence.'

I understood. Everything military was bathed in secrecy. We chatted on in a superficial manner – me all the while desperately trying to avoid Freddy's eyes, and mostly failing – for a while and then Freddy declared he was desperately tired and needed a nap. The flat had three bedrooms, so there was one free; I let

Andrew show him to it. After which Andrew and I were at last together, alone.

He swooped right in with the question that had no doubt been burning away at his heart.

'Have you heard from Usha? Where is she? I haven't had a letter for six months and I'm so worried.'

I knew this. I'd argued with Usha, telling her she had to tell him about her pregnancy, he had a right to know, but she only ever shook her head.

'No,' was her invariable reply. 'It would only worry him.'

So it was left to me to break the news, a task I did not relish at all. Annoyance welled up in me: why did Usha have to be so coy?

Now, I said to Andrew: 'Usha is in Madras, at Shanti Nilayam.'

'What! At your place? Why, that's marvellous! I was imagining the worst! I can't think why she didn't write to me, though. Why didn't she tell me herself? Maybe she didn't get my letters?'

'Probably not those sent in the last two months,' I said. 'They would not have been forwarded. Mrs Harrison, her employer, was evacuated, you see, and I hardly think Usha left a forwarding address for Mr Harrison, or that he would bother forwarding even if she did.'

'Oh, I see. So you helped her out when she lost her job. That's so kind of you, Rosie. So what's she doing in Madras? Has she found work there?'

I shook my head. There was no longer any avoiding saying it.

'No, Andrew. She can't. She's going to have a baby. *You're* going to have a baby.'

I swear that Andrew turned as white as ash at those words. It was as if he didn't even grasp their meaning.

'A-a-a *baby*? A real baby? Not, you know, a baby to look after, as an ayah?'

I thought he was going to faint, and moved closer to him and took his hand. Ideas were pouring into my head.

'Yes, a real baby. It's due in about five months' time. You're going to be a father, Andrew! And I've been thinking, if you were to go over to Madras now, maybe you two could get married before the birth and then she wouldn't have to put it in an orphanage, and then—'

'It can't be true! It's not true! How could she? I don't understand!'

'You surely know how babies are made. You made one, Andrew.'

'No! No, I didn't! Stop saying that! I didn't… I would never… it's not possible! How?'

An expression of pure shock, horror even, eyes wide open in disbelief, spread across his face.

'What do you mean?'

'I never touched her, Rosie! Not like that! I wouldn't. I never would! Not before we married! We were going to… we planned…'

Now it was my turn to be filled with shock.

'You didn't… what are you saying, Andrew?'

His voice was loud and clear, and so very firm.

'I'm saying I did not touch Usha. Not in any way that could get her pregnant. Unless it's possible to get pregnant through the eyes. Or from holding hands. Because that's the farthest we've gone. Physically.'

'Then how…?'

'Since you seem to have spent so much time together, surely she told you how? Or more precisely, *who*?' A hard, scathing voice. A face as white as chalk. Cold eyes, demanding an answer.

I raked my memory. Had Usha even once spoken of Andrew as the father? Or had she simply accepted my own assumption that that was the case? And I soon realised: I had blithely chattered on about Andrew and fatherhood and she had never corrected me. Never once. And so I had taken for granted that they had crossed that line. But, obviously, she had hidden the truth from me. Because the truth was, it seemed, even more scandalous than what I had assumed. This was terrible.

'She let me believe that you're the father.'

'Well, that was obviously in her interest. I wonder who the lucky chap is.' His voice was now bitter.

'Oh, Andrew! Please don't believe the worst of her! There must be some explanation. I know she loves you. She does.'

I said this with absolute conviction, and yet... Once more I combed through my memory, trying to recall just how Usha had spoken of Andrew since her pregnancy. And now that all the veils were dropping, I realised that behind her understandable fear of the future and what it might bring there had been an ineffable sadness; before, she had spoken so convincingly of love and marriage and what it all meant to her and how inviolable the marriage vow was, and how looking into Andrew's eyes had sealed it all. But afterwards there'd been a caginess to everything she'd said; and, now I came to realise it, a sense of loss.

I thought then that I'd known it all along, but in an unconscious way, and had been determined to just believe the obvious, the simple explanation, the fact – as I saw it – that only Andrew could be responsible for Usha's condition.

But if he wasn't, then who?

Andrew bent forward, hiding his face in his hands, elbows resting on his thighs. He was crying.

'I can't believe it! I just can't! How could she?' The words came out in little gasps, pleas for me to deny it all, to say it was all a cruel joke. All I could do was place a hand on his back and murmur words of comfort. I knew no more than he. I could not answer his questions. I was as dumbfounded, and disappointed, as he was. Usha had fooled us both; rather, she had fooled me, allowing me to believe a lie, engaging my help under false pretences. I felt duped.

But as I sat in silence, allowing Andrew to cry himself out, I asked myself, did it really matter? Whatever she'd done or not done, her predicament remained the same. Would I still have helped her, had I known that Andrew wasn't the father? Wasn't she my friend, and wasn't it a friend's duty not to judge, but to help in all circumstances? And what if Usha had been afraid, terrified, that if she confessed whatever it was she had to confess, I would judge her and not help? Wasn't I the only person she had in the world to turn to? Where else could she go? What would she have done if, as she may have feared, I'd rejected her call for help because she'd betrayed Andrew? She knew how close I was to him and she must have thought I'd turn from her in scorn and recrimination. Might I have? I asked myself again and again, and the answer came with resounding clarity: I would have stood by her, no matter what. She could have confessed to me. My help would always have been there for her.

But now it was Andrew who needed my help, but there was none I could give besides sit there with my hand on his back.

Eventually he stopped sobbing and rose to his feet, stumbling slightly.

'I must go to bed,' he said. 'It's been a long day.' He looked exhausted, drained. Freddy, in the guest bedroom already, was asleep, lost to the world. 'He hasn't taken leave for over a year,' Andrew whispered to me as I helped prepare a bed for him. 'His people are too far away, he's nowhere to go. That's why I brought him. You'll see more of him tomorrow. He's such a decent chap, Rosie!'

But I didn't. The next morning, I rose to find a note on the kitchen table:

We left early. Come to Newmeads tomorrow, if you can.

And I knew I would. There were too many words left unsaid, too many misunderstandings. And then Freddy's eyes, luring me home to the hills.

Chapter Twenty-Four

I too had not taken leave since I started work, and it wasn't difficult to get a weekend break. I took the bus up to Kandy, rather than the train, because it stopped at the junction leading to Newmeads. From there it was a half-hour's walk. I'd be back tomorrow evening, Sunday. I noticed on the way up that all street signs had been removed, obviously an attempt to confuse the Japanese in the event of an invasion. I'd heard they'd done this in England when it had seemed the Germans were about to swarm inland. In spite of all that had gone before, nothing brought home to me the stark reality of the danger we were in as much as this. I imagined hordes of murderous Japanese soldiers swarming up and down the hills, not even caring where the roads led to, carnage in their minds. Once more my imagination ran wild, fuelled by stories I'd read of the massacres in Malaya and Burma.

Up and up and up, along narrow curving roads, the bus rollicked along at a pace I found crazy; the driver seemed to never slow down, only slightly so when approaching a steep hairpin curve in the mountain. It was the same in the city: the Ceylonese drivers seemed to have an innate spatial sense, and though I'd heard many English people complain of them being bad drivers, I thought the opposite was true: they were excellent drivers. Accidents were rare, though brutal when they did occur.

We climbed up the hills for many hours, winding in and out among the emerald tea fields. How beautiful they were, the tea plants undulating in parallel lines over the hills. The tea pluckers, in their saris of brilliant hues, dotted among the lines of tea, already at work at this early hour – I supposed the earlier they started, the cooler it was and the more they could pick.

And so, through breathtaking views of green hills stretching to the horizon, I gained some equanimity of spirit, and by the time the bus reached the Newmeads junction I'd calmed down and retrieved a sense of proportion. The Japanese weren't coming. Ceylon was well protected. But then I remembered Singapore, supposedly inviolable. But no, it wouldn't happen. I had to retain my faith.

I felt a strange excitement as I descended from the rickety vehicle and made my way along the narrow lane leading to my adopted home. On both sides stretched the Newmeads fields, belonging to the Huxleys. The sun was quite high in the sky now, and I broke into a sweat; the first thing I'd do when I arrived, I decided, was go to my secret place for a refreshing dip.

Andrew and Freddy were nowhere to be seen. I caught a glimpse of Sunita on the kitchen veranda, grinding spices, but she ignored me. I knew she was still furious with me; it was probably a permanent state.

A quick survey upstairs showed me that the bedrooms were still dust-covered, except for Uncle Henry's single room. There were two guest bedrooms downstairs; one had already been prepared for the two men. The other would be mine for the night.

I stripped off my sweaty clothes, wrapped a sarong around my body, and made my way through the woods to my waterfall. I wondered where the men had gone. There weren't, in fact, many places to visit around here. Perhaps Andrew had taken his friend to Kandy, to do some sightseeing – but no. With petrol rationing in place, he'd hardly make such a frivolous trip. Perhaps they'd gone to the tea factory. During our conversation yesterday it had emerged that Freddy's family was involved in sugar cultivation; they owned a sugar plantation and factory, and he had shown much interest in how the tea he'd been drinking all his life was produced.

But I was wrong. I heard their joyous shouts and their laughter and raucous splashing long before I arrived at the waterfall, and there they were, leaping and dunking each other in the pool, having the time of their lives. There was no way I'd be going in there amid such frolics; I smiled and sat down on a rock beside the pool, just waiting and watching. So intent were they on apparently drowning each other, laughing and pouncing on one another, that they did not notice me for quite a while. Two fine young men, in the prime of life, their strong toned bodies leaping and whirling and bouncing in and out of the water, their obvious delight in their game – it was refreshing for me, too. It was especially good to see Andrew laughing again, after the shock of Usha's betrayal.

It was Freddy who saw me first. 'Oh!' he said, 'Hello there!' and started to move towards me; Andrew, following his gaze, came too. They both climbed out and sat themselves down beside me on the rock, dripping wet. I'd brought along a second sarong to use as a towel and I offered it to them now, but they were in no mood to dry off.

'Go on in, Rosie!' said Andrew. 'The water's wonderful!'

I stood up, and laughed. 'Yes, now that you've made room for me!'

'You should have come in, joined in the fun!' Freddy said. His brown skin glowed as if oiled; he was as dark as mahogany. His face was wreathed in smiles; it was the smile of someone who had at long last deposited a cumbersome burden and was exulting in a delicious sense of freedom and utmost joy. I'd never seen such a smile. But then, I'd never seen a man returned from the horrors of war, from killing fields where blood and gore and death were the order of the day and you'd never know if you'd see the next dawn; returned and been deposited into a perfect paradise. He was a fine figure of a man; handsome and strapping yet trim, slightly taller than Andrew, who was also slighter of build. Both wore khaki shorts; I recognised Freddy's as an old pair of Andrew's, frayed at the hem.

I dipped my toe in, and recoiled slightly from that first shock of cold. The water came straight from the Earth, not yet warmed by the sun. But I hesitated only a second, then took a deep breath and dropped into the water, crouching down until I was completely submerged; it was just over one yard deep. I stayed under as long as I could and then shot upwards, gasping for air. The men sat watching, laughing.

There was no room to swim in the pond. If plunging about and ducking your friends wasn't your cup of tea it wasn't a place you'd stay in for very long. What I'd always liked best was standing under the waterfall and letting it beat down on my head and shoulders, and that's what I did now, leaning forward slightly to let it pummel my back. That felt good; a sorely needed massage after hours of sitting still on the bus, after months of sitting on a hardback office chair, typing away day after day. I raised my face upwards and let the water pound that, too, and that too felt good, as if a million tight muscles loosened up, as if millions of compressed cells were set free. Tingling all over, I finally emerged from the waterfall and joined the men on the rock.

They'd moved to a sunny spot and their skin was already dry, sprinkled only by a few glistening drops of water. Their shorts, too, were no longer dripping. The sun was at its zenith now, and I joined them in its radiance, still wrapped in my sarong. I decided not to change it; I'd return home just as I was, and let the sunshine do its drying work. I felt so much better. So did we all. Normally I'd have felt shy, allowing a strange man to see me in such an indecorous state, the wet sarong clinging to my body, my shoulders bare, as well as the upper part of my body, from my neck down to the knot of the sarong above my breast. But somehow, it did not feel improper in the least, just as Freddy did not seem a stranger. He felt like a part of the family, like someone I had known for a very long time. Known forever. The shyness that had overcome me yesterday in Colombo had completely disappeared, washed away, perhaps, by the water and the waterfall. Even Andrew seemed to have put his drama with Usha behind him.

That concerned me a little. Poor Usha, I thought. So quickly can a man's eternal love dissolve into nothing. I knew that her love was not so fickle. I knew with an instinct perhaps only a woman can understand that she still loved him, deeply, eternally. I had no explanation for her pregnancy but I knew there must be one. And I would find it out. She'd be more alone than ever now that Andrew had deserted her. She only had me. And, I reminded myself, Father Bear.

We all lay in silence for a while, the men with their eyes closed (yes, I peeped) and me musing and pondering and wondering about this and that. And more and more, my thoughts kept going back to Freddy. I was intensely aware of his presence, lying not two yards away from me, flat out, spreadeagled on the sunny rock. The sun was past its zenith, but the heat of its rays were filtered by the overhanging trees they passed through, so that we lay in a filigreed pool of light and shadow, not too hot and yet still warm enough to warm our skin and dry our clothes. I turned on to my stomach and let the warmth and light rest on my back. It was delicious. I began to dream. And what I dreamed of was – Freddy's eyes. Their warmth; as gentle as the sun, and lighting the darkness within me that more and more had become a part of me. Freddy was – well, I could find no other words for him but a breath of fresh air, clichéd as it might be; the sense of coming out into the open after being locked in a stuffy room for aeons. I couldn't wait to get to know him better. But I didn't have much time to do so; tomorrow I'd be returning to Colombo. I might never see him again. This was war.

Chapter Twenty-Five

Dinner was early; we were all famished. Sunita had prepared a delicious Ceylonese chicken curry with several side dishes and a pot full of steaming rice, and served us all. I thought her behaviour so strange – where was the smiling, friendly Sunita of old? – until I realised that her fury would of course extend to Andrew as well as me, him being the devil who had broken up Usha's marriage. And Freddy, of course, was a complete stranger, so it would have been wrong for her to be particularly friendly towards him, beyond the courtesy expected towards a guest. I missed her usual warmth, and it was somewhat awkward, but there was nothing any of us could do about it and so we just continued as we always had, complimenting her on the meal and ignoring the stony silence and sullenness. She really was being overdramatic, I thought.

It was just the three of us for dinner; Uncle Henry had seen the two men last night, but had to work again all day today; he wouldn't be home until late that evening, Andrew told me. But he'd be home all the next day, Sunday, and had suggested we all go to church. I agreed. We all needed comfort and solace in these desperate times. Flopsy jumped on to Freddy's lap and stayed there all through the meal, being stroked and fed little titbits. I could hear her purring from across the table: utter and absolute contentment.

After dinner the three of us retired to the evening veranda, the area on the western side of the house that was fully enclosed by wire mesh and thus mosquito-free. It was cosily furnished with wicker chairs, a double wicker swing and a wicker sofa, all generously fitted with plump matching cushions, grouped around a large carpet.

Small tables were sprinkled around this inviting area, and Freddy and I soon made ourselves comfortable, he on the sofa, I in the swing (a favourite place of mine since childhood), while Andrew went inside to the bar to fetch our drinks –*stengahs* for him and Freddy, nimbu pani for me.

Alone with Freddy for those few short minutes, a new wave of shyness fell over me, completely disabling my ability for small talk; I fell into silence. But he seemed not to notice, chattering away about this and that as if there was no particular magic between us. He asked me about Madras, and my life there, offered condolences about Amma's death, commiserated with me about Pa's disappearance, asked me about my work in Colombo; lots of questions, to all of which I gave staccato replies. Luckily, Andrew was soon back with the drinks on a tray, which he set on one of the larger tables. He handed us our drinks, sat himself down with Freddy on the sofa, and the atmosphere returned to normal. Probably it had been normal the whole time and all of the awkwardness had been mine.

The evening continued. More *stengahs* arrived. The two men talked amiably, and I listened to the buzz of conversation, contributing nothing.

I sat rocking the swing gently back and forth with one foot, the other curled beneath me, cradled my nimbu pani, and let them discuss the intricacies of tea-production, the different grades, how it is sorted and graded and packaged for sale and export. I knew this all already, of course, and so I added nothing to the conversation. I simply sat, swaying gently in the swing, enjoying the familiar atmosphere of chirping night creatures, the lull of the men's voices. Now and then, Freddy's eyes and mine met, but never for long, for I trained mine to look away, beyond him, into the darkness of the garden beyond, all silvery moonlight and shadows.

Far away, a brain-fever bird called. It was a sound that always took me back to my early life in Madras. When I was a child, this bird-call used to haunt me. It's not at all pretty. It starts with a fairly simple ta-*ta*-ta call, but then repeats, again and again, with a mounting sense of drama, of something terrible about to happen, a rising cry of frenzied desperation, ever louder, more shrill, spiralling out of control. It used to give me goosebumps as a child; I'd climb out of bed and run to Amma, and she would comfort me.

In the daytime, Pa would laugh it off and explain; it's a hawk-cuckoo, he said, and they're very common. He also told me that in Hindi, they translate its call to 'where's my love?', in Marathi to 'the rains are coming', and in Bengali to 'my eyes are gone'. To me, as a child, the Bengali interpretation seemed to most capture the sheer hysteria of that chilling call. That's exactly what the bird was lamenting: *my eyes are gone! I'm going blind! Help!*

I'd seldom heard this bird at Newmeads; in fact, I couldn't remember ever hearing it here. The call stopped, but then started again, much closer, and much louder; so loud, now, that Freddy looked up and into the darkness beyond. Andrew was just explaining how freshly plucked tea leaves are laid out to dry for several hours, to 'wither' and lose some of their moisture content.

'This makes them flexible and supple,' he was saying, 'so they won't crumble when being processed. And—'

'What's that?' Freddy interrupted. 'That noise. A bird of some sort?'

For the first time, I spoke. 'The brain-fever bird,' I said. 'I've never heard one around here before.'

'It's almost creepy,' said Freddy, and I nodded.

'It used to terrify me, when I was a child,' I said. 'When you wake up in the middle of the night and hear that sound... well... It used to give me the jitters.'

I then explained the various translations of the call. He laughed, and mimicked: 'I lost my eyes! Where are my eyes? My eyes! Oh hell, my eyes are gone!'

We all laughed. 'That's exactly it,' said Andrew. 'Brain-fever is the right word – it sounds like a delirium! I only ever heard it at your place in Madras, Rosie. I bet you were scared!'

Meanwhile, the brain-fever bird called out again and again, just beyond the wire screen. He could have been calling just for us, so near it sounded, over and over, that frantic dry ascending in shrillness and anguish. We listened in silence. Finally, Freddy said, 'I think we should be a bit more generous. Maybe the Hindi interpretation is the right one. *Where's my love?* Can you imagine, losing your love and being so broken-hearted you can only cry out with such utter torment: *where's my love? Where's my love? Where's my love?*'

A pregnant silence fell between us three. The brain-fever bird cried on. And then stopped. Silence.

And in that silence Andrew said: 'Yes, I can well imagine it. *Where's my love? I lost my love!*'

Chapter Twenty-Six

I yawned. The gentle swaying of the swing was lulling me into a pleasant doze. I hadn't realised just how exhausted I was, but it was too early to go to bed, so I made myself comfortable in the swing by drawing up my legs, leaning on an arm extended along the backrest, and curling up against its soft cushions.

My eyes closed, I half-listened to the buzz of conversation. The others talked on; seeing that I appeared to be dozing off, their talk turned to war. I suspected their minds must automatically return there whenever possible. I also suspected that Freddy and Andrew wanted to spare me the details of what they had gone through, deeming it all too harsh for a woman's ears. The more they talked, the more I listened – eyes closed to make them think I'd fallen asleep – the more I learned of the horrors they'd never tell me. Everything else, I imagined, all pleasantries and chatting and drinking and entertainment must be just a distraction from the terrifying reality they must face, day after day. I listened as they exchanged tales of this and that situation they had lived through. How had they even survived? It seemed a miracle that they had both lived to tell these tales, and it was more than frightening to think that in a few days they'd be plunging right back into the fray.

I gathered, now, that Freddy and Andrew had met during jungle warfare training here in Ceylon: that was interesting. So Andrew had been right here on the island for most of his time away. The talk moved on to Burma. Freddy said:

'The whole brigade marched through those foothills. We had to cut off the Japanese supply lines.'

'You were acting company commander still?'

'Yep. Dense jungle everywhere. We killed twenty Japs in close combat. I heard Gurkhas shouting "*Ayo Gurkha!*" – so chilling. Even the Japs were scared. Those Gurkhas, they used their kukris right up close, the first time I'd seen this. They went straight for the throat. The Japs ran away. Later, we had to bury the dead Japs. They couldn't fit in the foxholes because of rigor mortis, so those Gurkhas just chopped up the dead bodies to shove them in the holes. It was macabre.'

More anecdotes. More grisly details. More snippets of the ordeals they'd survived.

'…I had malaria; I was delirious, and not fit to march…'

'Leeches. Leeches. Those leeches, oh my! They'd get through any part of your body that was open. We kept the openings on our trousers and shirts closed but they still got in. You couldn't pull 'em off because the head was still stuck on your body. You had to get a lit cigarette and burn those buggers off.'

'The Nips came in the middle of the night, marching in a column down the road. We were ready and waiting, the perfect ambush. It was pitch-dark but we just fired into the darkness. Some escaped and crawled away, but we got most of them…'

And so on. It was macabre; hearing my childhood friend, the gentle, artistic Andrew, talking so casually about 'killing Japs' as if it were the same as killing flies – that gave me a jolt, and I realised just how much participation in a war can change a man's entire character, numb him, not only toughen him but roughen him. And all of this they hid from me. I couldn't stand it; I shut off internally and began to dream my own dreams.

I wanted to see Freddy again, alone. There was so little time. All these years I'd been growing into a woman, listening to my friends talking about falling in love and growing excited about this chap or that, but I had never felt the excitement of romance. I'd been so intent on performing well at school, so serious about my future, there just had been no time for boys. Had I wasted my youth? It would never come back, and now at last there was someone who interested me; but I'd be saying goodbye to him tomorrow and watching him walk off into an uncertain, and very perilous, future. Although, of course, it would be me who was walking away, boarding the bus back to Colombo. Tomorrow! Oh, how short was the time left to us!

The looks we'd exchanged – they'd been so knowing! Surely he felt it too? And yet we knew so little of each other. There was so much I wanted to know about him – not so much facts, but who he was, what he thought, what he felt. What he was going through. I found myself thinking of him constantly, watching him as he spoke – hopefully unobtrusively! – basking in the sound of his voice. I had the sense that I could not waste even a single minute. Would we get a chance to be alone tomorrow? Surely it would be possible. I determined to make sure we did find the time and the space. I drifted into sleep listening to his voice.

Uncle Henry came back at about nine, slamming doors and loudly announcing his presence. Immediately I was wide awake and greeting him. I had not seen him since the day we'd said goodbye to Aunt Silvia at the dock, and I was eager to hear how she was getting on. She had sent me a card for my birthday with just a few sentences to say she was fine and to apologise for not writing more often. I couldn't blame her; I imagined that all her concern these days was for her sons and she wouldn't be much interested in writing long missives about her daily life in Durban. I had written her a few letters from Colombo, letting her know how the city was coping with its new reality as a strategic military centre. So now, my first question for Uncle Henry was, 'How's Aunty? Is she well settled over there?'

'Yes,' he said. 'She's rented a cottage with Mrs Carruthers and her daughter, so that's worked out nicely. The English contingent over there seem to have found each other and formed quite a clique. Of course, they all can't wait to come home.'

'I can imagine,' I said. 'It all seems so far away.'

'Yes, the family is scattered. The boys all who-knows-where, she down in South Africa, me rattling around in this palace with nobody for company. It's good to have the three of you here.'

'Do you know how long they'll be down there?'

'Nobody knows. Until the war ends, I suspect, and who knows when that will be. You boys probably have a better notion of that than I do.' He looked from one to the other, and both shrugged. The implication was clear: no one knew the future. For either of them, the war could end in a heartbeat. In the thrust of a bayonet, in the blast of a bomb. In bloodshed and mayhem. My own heart quivered. This endless waiting, waiting, waiting. Waiting, it seemed, for something terrible to happen, for an end that seemed eons away. It seemed to have gone on forever, and would indeed last forever. How many of us would survive? When would we ever breathe freely again?

The talk inevitably drifted back to war. To those ghastly details, those gruesome anecdotes. I couldn't take it any longer. I excused myself and went to bed.

The next morning I rose early, slipping out of the house just as it began to grow light. I had brought my flute with me, and couldn't wait to sink into the healing balm of its music. I sat myself down on my usual rock and began to play. On and on I played as the day grew lighter and a few rays of dawn sunshine filtered through the trees and I felt it on my skin and I opened my eyes and saw the sunlight playing on the water and there, sitting silently to one side, was Freddy. Cross-legged on the very same rock, not close to me but also not far, watching and listening.

I lowered the flute from my lips and met his gaze.

'Beautiful,' he said. 'So beautiful.'

I had nothing to say. I merely looked at him and allowed my eyes to speak. Usha would have been proud of me. I was actually *experiencing*, here and now, the truth of what she'd always insisted: one doesn't need words to speak, to communicate. There is eloquence in silence. If two people can speak the language of eyes, then everything can be said. Everything. Not chit-chat; everything that really, truly, matters.

What happened next defies all logic, all morality, all psychology. Before this day, I had lived a perfectly ascetic life. I had never understood, as a pupil of Girls' High School, all the talk of falling in love and having crushes on boys; I'd never wondered what it felt like to kiss someone, or more; but there would never have *been* more, because I wasn't interested. I had assumed I'd one day marry and have children, because it was simply what one did, as a girl, as a woman. I'd listened with some amusement to Aunty's marriage-making plans for me and her sons, but never taken it seriously. If I had married one of them, it would have been because I liked him enough to believe I could live with him and raise his children.

But first and foremost in my mind through all the years had been my ambition to become a doctor, stalled only temporarily because of the war, and the pressing need to 'do my bit'. I had never, for a moment, let myself be distracted by the occasional single man I'd come across. And of course, intimate relationships before marriage were completely out of the question. I would never even have considered it.

Then why, now, as Freddy moved closer to me, edging effortlessly across the rock, did I not raise a hand to tell him to stop? As he took my hand, why did I not pull it away? As he gently stroked my cheek with his other hand, with a touch as soft as a feather, why did I not slap him away?

As he moved his face towards mine so that I felt his breath, warm on my cool dawn skin, why did I not recoil in umbrage;

leap to my feet, perhaps, and scold him in prudish indignation? Protect my honour? Defend my modesty? Most of all, why did I not make the slightest move to preserve my chastity?

I cannot explain it. I cannot endorse it. I cannot remotely understand what happened that dawn at the waterfall. It was so far out of character it was as if a different *me* had inhabited my body and responded, oh! How I responded! To that feathery touch, that mingling of breath, and most of all, to the eyes that seemed permanently locked into mine as if there were not two people gazing at each other but only one: a single gaze, a single person, a single soul; and that since our souls were one, somehow merged in a spirit that encompassed us both, and the two entities, Rosie and Freddy, somehow became absorbed into that one spirit, a spirit blissful beyond words, rapturous, even, how could our bodies not join?

I have no recollection of the minutiae of what happened thereafter. I do not recollect the discarding of clothes. The rock on which we lay must have been hard and cold – why did I not feel that hardness, coldness? Why was I oblivious to the discomfort of our surroundings? Why was there no fear that we could be suddenly, rudely, interrupted? No embarrassment, that a man, a virtual stranger, should see me unclothed?

Why do I recollect only the silkiness of his skin that gave the lie to the sheer strength and toughness of the tendons that lay beneath the surface, the resilience of his long brown limbs, the grace and beauty of his movement? Why did the nakedness of our bodies, long-stretched together as in a single entity, seem not sinful but perfectly natural, as if it had always been this way?

Why did the sheer exhaustion of the previous weeks and months and years, gathering force and lying like a thick murky coating upon all that was free and sweet and beautiful in me, all the fear, all the anxiety, all the darkness that came with the onset of war; above all, all the loneliness of the time before: why did it all, that morning, peel away, dissolve into nothing? Why did I suddenly become myself in Freddy's arms, free from constraint, and beautiful beyond measure?

Not a word was spoken. Our eyes spoke, and then our limbs, our bodies spoke, as if our bodies' language was a natural evolution from what our eyes had said. Every movement flowed as smoothly and naturally as if pre-rehearsed a thousand times, as if we had known each other, loved each other, a thousand years, a thousand lifetimes. He was me and I was him. It is as simple as that.

It is all, even now, beyond comprehension. It just happened.

And never, never once, never for an instant, have I regretted it.

At some point we separated and, exchanging slightly shy but knowing smiles, we dressed, and, still without speaking, made our way back to the house, Freddy leading down the forest path.

As we stepped on to the veranda everyday reality cut through the half-daze that still enfolded me; Uncle Henry and Andrew were there, obviously engaged in a post-breakfast cheery conversation – or as cheery as anyone can be, when the horror of war is hovering just beyond the horizon, and one of the two is about to plunge himself right back into that horror. They were laughing at some joke. It was obviously their way of escaping from that dreadful reality, just as Freddy and I had escaped in our own way just thirty minutes ago. I landed back into that reality with a thump.

Uncle Henry welcomed us back with gusto. 'You two missed a delicious breakfast!' he said, and pulled at the bell-rope that would summon the kitchen staff. 'But I'm sure Sunita can rustle up something equally scrumptious for you.'

Andrew looked at his watch. 'It's late – what have you two been up to?' He gave us each a mischievous grin. In reply I lifted my flute, and that was my answer. It was none of Andrew's business what had just transpired.

'I'm not really hungry,' I said, 'I'll just go to my room and have a bit of a lie-down. I slept badly last night.' It wasn't a lie. But it was an excuse. I could not bear to sit there, chit-chatting with them all as if nothing had happened. I needed to be alone, to digest the whole episode. The thing that had fallen like a bomb into my life.

Bomb might be a strong word, especially considering the precarious political situation, but it was the right word. A bomb *had* fallen into my life. But it was a benevolent bomb, a bomb full of goodness and light, transporting me back to the person I really was, the person I was meant to be, before all the horrible things had happened. And only alone could I revel in it, digest it, let it nourish me, before I could allow drab and ugly reality to seep back in.

'Church is in one hour!' Uncle called as I turned away, glancing and smiling at Freddy as I did so.

'I'll be ready,' I called back.

And I was. We all cycled to the chapel in the village where the English people who worked for Uncle gathered on Sundays for a little service, and I partook in the usual hymns and prayers without a morsel of regret, without a hint of a sense of having sinned. Because I hadn't.

Once, though, tears came to my eyes and I struggled to suppress an outrush of emotion. It came as we sang that one hymn that always grasped me by the jugular, 'For Those in Peril on the Sea'. The refrain never failed to awaken a rush of deep emotion within me:

> Oh, hear us when we cry to Thee,
> For those in peril on the sea!

And I prayed, sincerely and reverently, for all our soldiers in peril on the sea, like Graham. But not just those on the sea but those on land, too, and in the air – even Victor. And those who, in a matter of days, would be hurling themselves right back into that peril, that horror. Andrew, and Freddy.

*

The rest of the day passed as in a dream. I was amazed at how quickly Andrew seemed to have overcome his shock at Usha's betrayal. In fact, he seemed more animated than ever, laughing and joking with his father, inviting Freddy to another bath at the waterfall. I did not accompany them this time. Once, he looked at me and said, 'What's up, Rosie, you're very quiet today?' but I only smiled and mumbled something about being exhausted. I wondered if Freddy would confide in him what had transpired between us, and blushed at the very thought: it really wasn't for external ears; it was far too private, far too intimate. Far too sacred.

But rationally, I thought he would. Just as, if I'd had a close female friend, I'd have had the need to simply open myself to her, to share that part of the experience that could be described in words. If Usha had been nearby I'd have told her; Usha would certainly understand. The old Usha, that is, the Usha I'd trusted, the Usha I'd thought was devoted to Andrew. Not the new Usha, who'd betrayed him. I did not know this Usha.

The time for me to say goodbye came all too soon. Andrew and Freddy walked me to the bus stop, the two of them chatting away as usual. I did not speak at all. In fact, I never spoke another word to Freddy. When the bus arrived we shook hands, chastely, as I said farewell, and he managed to lean forward and whisper: 'I'll write, when the war is over, if...'

He left it at that. At that ambiguous *if*. I knew what he meant. I nodded and climbed into the bus. I did not look back.

I wept all the way back to Colombo. A searing, biting pain consumed me, as if a red-hot poker had been plunged into my being, tinged with snippets of sheer, uttermost joy and beauty yet smothering those exquisite wisps of memory. And yet I knew they, those tendrils of memory, had the power to live on, live on forever, never fully extinguished; that they would accompany me all my life, establish themselves as my own gold standard as to what was worth living for in this short life of mine.

At the back of it all I feared, I felt, I knew, that I would never see Freddy again.

Chapter Twenty-Seven

Back in Colombo, life returned to normal, except that it didn't. My own *normal* had changed, because I now carried a wound within me that would take time to heal; if it ever did. And as the days passed, another concern began to plague me. We had not even vaguely thought of taking precautions. What if I were pregnant with Freddy's baby?

Concern changed to anxiety as the days dragged past, only withdrawing temporarily during the time I was at work. If it were so, then what? Would I end up in Usha's position, hiding away in my own house in Madras, giving birth secretly, handing my baby over to an orphanage? The moment that notion popped into my mind I struck it away: NO! Never! Never would I give away any child who resulted from that glorious morning! I would keep and love that child and know that it was the fruit of something perfect. But… me unmarried with a child; and, to complicate things, a half-caste child! One of those dreaded Eurasian children everyone spoke of in shocked whispers, behind fans, turning up their noses! I didn't mind my own disgrace, but my child's expulsion from society – that would be devastating.

Something swelled within me at the thought and I knew I would fight to the death for my child's honour and dignity. I would. I would not hide or cower. I would speak up, loudly! I would force people to listen: how can you call yourselves Christians, when you reject these children born out of wedlock, born of two races? Are we not all children of the same God?

A stubborn hope remained: that the war would miraculously end, that Freddy would return to me, that we would marry. I knew it was hopeless, but I clung to it. A remote happily ever after for me, for us.

It got to the point where I was absolutely convinced, though there was no biological evidence whatsoever, that I was with child, that I would do exactly as Usha had done, that Father Bear would be there to guide and help me, that everything would work out. I grasped that imaginary future with both hands – it was a tangible way to cling to Freddy – and prepared myself to face the cruel world, no matter what. And then my period came and the dream-edifice of fears and hopes collapsed. I realised now that the hope had surpassed even the fear – what more wonderful thing than to have Freddy's child! But it had all been an illusion.

Someone once said that for those living through a war without being an actual participant, for those of us keeping the home fires burning, it's a long, seemingly never-ending stretch of nothing happening, just the same old everyday slog. And then: bang! Something terrible happens and your whole life is thrown out of kilter. Or it could be something not-so-terrible, something good, even, but at least something different, something to interrupt the tedious anxiety-infused monotony. And then the dust settles and the long slog starts again. Right now, I was in the wartime waiting room, doing my very best, but in a constant state of worry as to what would be the next event to shake up my life.

The monsoon started soon after the departure of Freddy and Andrew. Great sheets of water hurling down from above, the thunder of rain pelting the roof above. Normally I loved the monsoon; I loved the freshness and the sense of being enclosed in a cosy dry bubble, safe and sound and protected from the elements. But this year, the rains only darkened my mood. I could think of nothing good that might happen in the near future. It was all gloom and doom, and the relentless rain only augmented that sense that from now on, only disaster waited for us.

The next bit of news to break the monotony was a letter from India, and the news only helped to depress me further.

> Oh, Rosie! My heart is broken, completely broken. I had my baby, a beautiful little boy.
>
> His name is Luke and he is healthy and thriving and I love him so much, so very much, but I must give him away. It is the only way, Father Bear says. If I do that he will help me get on my feet again. If I refuse – then what is to become of me? I am allowed to breastfeed him for a few weeks to give him a good start and then they will come and take him away.

This was devastating indeed; I could not begin to imagine Usha's pain. But then again, I was cross with her. I had not written to her for ages, not told her that I knew Andrew was not Luke's father. I did reply, to congratulate her, and tell her to listen to Father Bear as he would surely help her, however hard life might become.

Usha's next letter, four weeks later, was short and to the point and laden with sadness.

> Luke is gone. A nun called Sister Agnes came with Father Bear and took him away. She said they would love him and look after him. So it is over and I must move forward. Father Bear has advised me to take up training of some sort, and I've decided to train as a nurse. I can do this at the nursing school affiliated with the Christian hospital in Vellore, the Christian Medical College hospital. Wish me well, Rosie.

I had heard about the CMC from Father Bear. It had been founded in 1900 as a one-room dispensary by an American missionary, Dr Ida S. Scudder, who had trained as a doctor specifically to provide female-led medical services to Indian women bound by caste and religious restrictions. From there it had grown into an institution renowned not only in the state of Tamil Nadu but in all of India. It seemed a wonderful step forward for Usha. But I was still cross, and did not reply. Why wasn't she honest with me about Luke's conception?

Usha wrote again, shortly after that:

> Oh, Rosie! I cannot forget him though I try so hard! He is a part of me! But I know I did the right thing. I have to give him a better life than any I could offer. If only the war was over and Andrew would come back; we could marry and adopt him together. Please write to me. I need a friend, someone to console me!

She mentioned nothing about training to be a nurse this time. I assumed that was secondary to her deep desire to mother her child.

And I realised as well that she did not know that Andrew already knew she had betrayed him. I wondered what she was thinking, with all this talk of marriage and adoption. Was she so certain that Andrew would forgive her, put it all behind them, and continue as if nothing had happened? Was she so very naïve? I wondered if I should write her and tell her that I knew, that Andrew knew, the truth. If I should force her into an admission.

It was all very puzzling. She was still trying to fool me: but how could she even dream of fooling Andrew? It made no sense. I longed to rush over and visit her, but that, of course, was out of the question for the time being. Once again I repeated the old refrain to myself: when the war is over. When the war was over everything would sort itself out. I had to believe it. And the war *would* be over. One day. In the meantime, I kept the silence. I did not reply to Usha's desperate plea for support. I had personal secrets and troubles of my own to deal with.

I had hoped that Freddy would write to me. While on the day itself we had both been lost for words – and, indeed, words had seemed superfluous, interfering, even – surely, once emotions had died down due to time and distance; surely once we had put the matter into perspective, we could reach out to one another? I certainly would have loved to write him a short note; nothing gushing, just a quiet confirmation of the intimacy I felt towards him. But I did not know where to write. He, however, knew my address: not the one in Colombo, but any letter addressed to me c/o Newmeads or Huxley Family would have reached me. But he didn't write. Or rather, I received no letter.

Andrew wrote, however, heavily censored short letters, letters without addresses, sent from some unknown military base. So much was crossed out – had he told me something important, but sensitive, about Freddy? I wondered, and hoped it was so.

But then, in early January of 1943, came the letter that dashed all hopes. Again, it was heavily censored, but the remaining words told me all I needed to know. As usual, he sent it to the Cinnamon Gardens flat.

'Our mutual South American friend,' it said, and then much blacked out, and then 'missing'. After 'missing', four more words were blacked out and I knew what they said: 'In Action. Believed killed.'

Never had a piece of paper caused me so much despair, so much anguish. On first reading it a kind of icy-cold winter ran through me – me, a young woman who had never known winter, never really known cold. I actually, physically, shivered, and seemed to fall into a sort of rigor, devoid of feeling, devoid of any emotion except this cold, blank nothingness. An internal void.

The letter fell from my hands. I'd been standing just next to the front door, and had torn it open – as I always did Andrew's letters, hoping for news of Freddy – as soon as I'd removed it, along with other envelopes, from the letter box hanging on the inside of the door. Read it, standing just where I was, on the ornately patterned red-and-gold Jaipur carpet Aunt Silvia had chosen decades ago. I think I may have let out a gasp. But everything else was… frigid. I had turned to stone. Cold stone.

For once, our refugee, Mrs Grantley – or Eileen, as I now called her – was at home, for her day off, and had just finished her breakfast. She noticed at once that something dramatic had occurred and came rushing up. 'Rosie! What's happened?' she cried, placed a comforting arm around me and led me over to the sofa. She gently helped me to sit. I was still speechless, tearless. She glanced at the letter on the floor, decided instantly that it was insignificant, and asked me if I'd like a cup of tea.

'Or, perhaps, a brandy?'

To the latter, I nodded. Tea would not be sufficient to wake me out of my stupor.

Brandy did, in fact, do the trick, more than required, because at last I could feel myself, and that was when I broke down. I collapsed internally and externally into a mess of wild, blubbering sobs. Not like me at all; Eileen must have been surprised to see me, always so rational and controlled, like this, but she rallied herself and calmed me down, handling me as if I were a baby who needed a bit of coddling.

'There, there, my dear, why not lie down in your bed, much more comfortable? And you can cry your heart out, don't mind me! Come on, do you need a hand?'

I did, and nothing seemed more inviting than bed at that moment, notwithstanding it was hardly nine o'clock in the morning.

'I-I have to go to work!' I stuttered, even while standing up, with her help, to stagger over to my room.

'Nonsense!' she replied. 'I'll give them a call and let them know that you're ill. And you are. Work can wait. Now, dear, it's up to you. I can leave you on your own to cry your heart out and preferably cry yourself to sleep. Or, if you prefer, I'll sit right here on the side of your bed and you can tell me all about it. A trouble shared and all that. Just as you wish, my dear.'

I chose to speak. It was the first time I'd told anyone about Freddy – after all, who was there to tell? – and for some reason just putting it all into words, and placing those words into another person's keeping: it helped. It helped relieve the tremendous pressure that had been building in me ever since that cherished weekend. I told her all about it. Poured out my heart, as they say. I'd never realised before just how apt a description that was, and how immeasurably healing it can be to let another, trusted, person know the most intimate secrets of one's soul.

She was everything I could ever have desired in a confidante. 'And it was your first time, was it, dear?' she asked, and when I nodded there was no judgement, no condemnation in her reply:

'The first time is a watershed, for most girls and women,' she said. 'It's as if you've opened the most intimate part of yourself to another, isn't it? And then there's the fear that he might not treasure it, might not respect what you've just done, might take it all for granted. But in your case, it seems even more than that. It seems…'

She struggled for the right word, and so I supplied it. It wasn't at all hard. 'Magical,' I said. 'It was magical. As if a spell had been laid on us, something completely out of this world. As if we were lifted up into some enchanted fairy tale. No, even that sounds childish, inadequate. I can't describe it, Eileen. I can't find words. It's not what I expected at all. I mean, I've read about it of course, but nobody ever said…'

I broke down again and she patted my back. 'And now he's dead!' I cried out. 'Dead! He can't be!'

'Well, *believed* dead,' she said. 'I suppose there must be *some* hope. We must never give up hope. We women who stay behind, we must always nourish hope, because without hope we have nothing. I, too, live in hope.'

I remembered then that her own husband was in Changi Prison, living under abominable conditions, and all of a sudden my own breakdown seemed selfish, petty. She had never broken down – why should I?

'I'm sorry,' I said. 'I must seem so childish to you. I don't even know him properly – I only knew him three days – and I'm behaving like some spoiled prima donna. And you – your husband, your George...'

'No, no, never compare,' she said, 'and never put yourself down for the intensity of your feelings. Being able to feel intensely – it's a good thing. It's not a weakness. It can only happen to those of us who have not been dulled by misfortune, or by rejection, or by being unloved, or by the horrors of this ghastly war. It's good to be sensitive. But we must not let it *become* a weakness by allowing it to dominate our lives – to cripple us. I think that you and I, we can work something out. Cry as much as you want, my dear, and I'm here for you. But the thing about pain is that we need to not let it destroy us. We need to grow from it. And then pain can be a catalyst for a new, and better, life. For regrowth. For maturity. Even death can be such a catalyst.'

But I was not yet in the mood to hear her sensible thoughts about moving on and spiritual growth. Not yet. For the moment I just wanted to wallow in my grief, in my hopelessness. Moving on – that would have to come another day.

Chapter Twenty-Eight

Yet somehow, over the next few weeks, I slowly found a way back to myself. First and foremost, I immersed myself in my work. I shut out the world and worked, worked, worked. But for Eileen that just wasn't good enough: 'All work and no play, and all that,' she proclaimed, and, 'It's time, my dear, for you to have some good old-fashioned fun.'

In her eyes, that meant, in the wake of losing Freddy, distracting myself with other men. I myself had always been shy with young men and their flirtatious advances, having grown up in such a secluded environment.

'Don't worry about that,' she said. 'Leave it to me. Nothing easier than to fix you up.' I soon understood what 'fixing me up' meant.

The expatriate community of Colombo, and Ceylon in general, had always suffered under a dearth of young females. We were a minority among the English, and what with the increased injection of young soldiers since the Pearl Harbor attack – well, there was no lack of men willing and eager to escort me here and there, and Eileen was the consummate matchmaker. Men were looking for sweethearts and wives, and, in her opinion, I was an excellent candidate. I just had to get out there more. She was determined to facilitate my emergence into society.

At her job in the first aid tent she was surrounded by them – young male doctors, young male patients – and when they flirted with her, as inevitably happened, she'd laughingly let them know that she was too old for them and anyway, she was 'taken', but that she had a lovely young friend who happened to be single – and that was me. Reluctantly, I followed her advice.

I went to parties and balls and dinners and days out to Galle for swimming. One young man after another. Yes, it was quite fun. But I realised in those few months that there's a difference between *fun* and *happiness*. Fun is a temporary pleasure, evoked by some external event or activity: dancing, swimming, a lovely meal at the Galle Face Hotel. It is dependent on that thing you're doing, external to yourself. Happiness is different. It wells up from deep within; it feels integral to oneself, whole and complete and autonomous, not down to any external stimulus. You do not need to do anything to know happiness. It stands independent: it simply is; evoked quite simply by the power of love. Of loving someone, and knowing that they exist, whether near or far.

I had no doubt that this was love. That love was happiness, in and of itself. That as long as I could treasure that love in my heart, I'd remain happy, even if longing for reunion with my lover. But now that that had been ripped away from me, I could not be happy again. Not for a long time.

But I could have fun. And that's what I did. At first to please Eileen and stop her nagging, but then for my own sake because, after all, fun was fun, a welcome distraction, and certainly preferable to brooding and mourning and covering myself with misery. The young men who escorted me here and there were also in search of a distraction; they needed to laugh, and joke, and frolic about, and dance, and smoke, and drink, and we did all those things together.

Yet I can hardly remember a single name; certainly not a single surname. There was a Geoff, and a Roland, and a Charles, and a Soames; but frankly, their faces and names rolled all into one over time and none of them stood out. They were all, every one of them, eager to take the relationship further, to let it grow. But I wasn't. My dance card is full, I'd have to laughingly say to decline a further invitation, as if I were a Jane Austen heroine at the local earl's ball.

It was a situation weighed heavily in favour of us girls and young women, and the men knew it, and accepted such refusals gallantly. I wished them all well. Occasionally one of them would tell me more, speak of his fears and his family, and I'd feel guilty, knowing how much having a sweetheart of his own could help him through his next mission. Give him hope, and something to live for. But I could not pretend, and it was, I thought, less cruel to let him move on to find a lovely girl who could be there for him, wait for him. The most I could do was pray for them. And I did. After every assignation, I would, before I got into bed, kneel at my bedside and pray most sincerely for that young man's protection. I never knew what became of them. They came, enjoyed their moments of leave, their time of distraction, and they'd be off again, into the fray. It was perfectly dreadful for them, and I could only hope to provide a few short memories of something good. It was, really, tragic. The fun we had was nothing more than cheap gilded gloss on a stinking turd.

But then: boom. Boom. Boom. Three utterly devastating events that threw 1943 into a category of its own. It was the year the war finally came home to us at Newmeads, in the most personal way ever. The year the war took the Huxley boys. All three of them.

The first to go was Andrew. I received the news through a telephone call from Uncle Henry. A telegram had been delivered to him. He read it out to me: 'Missing in action. Believed captured.'

Poor Uncle Henry! He actually cried on the phone. 'How can I tell her? What can I say?' he blubbered.

'Does she have a telephone? Can you actually talk to her? Would you like me to give her the news?'

No, no, and no. The only way to inform Aunty was via a similar telegram, which was perfectly dreadful, Uncle said, followed by a letter. Which, any way you looked at it, was awful. Aunt Silvia, in

South Africa and far from home, far from her husband, must be given the news she had dreaded all along in the most impersonal and dispassionate way possible – through a telegram.

'But what shall I say, Rosie? How can I *possibly* tell her? She's all alone out there! This will kill her!'

'But why? How, what happened?' I could only stutter stupid questions in my shock. I mean, we all knew that such an eventuality not only existed but was even probable. But when it actually hits you, you are left breathless, stunned.

'I don't know and it doesn't matter – we won't be told till it's all over. The problem is how to tell Silvia. I don't know what to say! It will kill her!' he repeated.

I had to be practical – Uncle Henry was having hysterics himself, which was usually Aunty's forte.

'I have to send a telegram but I don't know what to SAY!'

'I'll come up this weekend,' I said. 'We'll write it together.'

And that's what we did. I found Uncle in a state of complete discombobulation; rattling around all alone in that huge house, without even the comfort of his wife… but then, Aunt Silvia would not have been able to provide much comfort, I thought, and at least we had the opportunity to put thought and care into the way she received the news.

'I think,' I said, 'rather than send her a telegram, we should inform one of her friends over there and let *her* gently break the news. She should not be alone when she finds out. What's the name of the friend she travelled out with: Mrs Carruthers? Didn't you say they lived together, in Durban? We could send her the telegram and explain the situation.'

Uncle sniffed. 'Yes, that's true. That's a good idea. What an awful task to lay on her shoulders, though! Without even asking first!'

'She'll understand – what's a friend for? We haven't really got much choice. We can't risk Aunty receiving the telegram all on her own – she might faint. She needs support. Come, Uncle, let's get down to it.'

In the end, the telegram turned out to be short but to the point and, I hope, caring and even a bit hopeful:

SAD NEWS FOR SILVIA HUXLEY STOP PLEASE CONVEY TO HER KINDLY AS POSSIBLE STOP SON ANDREW MIA BELIEVED CAPTURED SO ALL NOT LOST STOP HIGHEST HOPE WILL BE SAFE AS POW UNTIL END WAR STOP KEEP COURAGE AND HOPE AND ALL PRAYING FOR GOOD OUTCOME STOP ROSIE HERE WITH ME STOP BOTH PRAYING STOP LETTER TO FOLLOW STOP HENRY

'Do you think she will understand what MIA and POW mean?' I asked. Aunty had never shown much interest in the lingo of wartime and I had my doubts, but Uncle assured me that in spite of her *see no evil, hear no evil* attitude, she was very much up to date with the movements of their boys and the possible dangers they might face.

'She knows,' he said. 'But she'll believe the worst. She always does. And anyway, we know how those Japs treat their POWs.'

'Still, we must never give up hope. It's better than that terrible *Believed Killed*. The finality of *that…*' I left my sentence unfinished. We both knew that there were two more Huxley sons out there.

Chapter Twenty-Nine

And it wasn't long before the next one fell. This time it was Graham. We all knew that Graham was a naval doctor aboard the battleship *Princess of Jaipur*, which roamed the Straits seas and had already survived two intense battles with Japanese vessels, and had narrowly escaped a submarine hit last year.

Unlike Andrew and Victor, Graham had been a regular and faithful writer since beginning his tour of duty. True, he was not allowed to say much and his letters were heavily censored, but the fact that he stayed in constant touch kept him close to our hearts and ever in our thoughts and prayers – not that the others were not in our hearts and thoughts and prayers, but Graham, by keeping himself present in our lives, had become rather a living spirit among us all. I was especially pleased and grateful that ever since our interlude at the waterfall he had simply embraced me, drawn me into the family fold, included me in his reaching out to family, whereas Andrew – to whom I was *actually* closer, who had always been my friend – was sporadic and negligent in his correspondence. I suppose that exemplified their behaviour in real life, too: Graham, always reliable, constant, mature; Andrew, dreamy, sentimental, unrealistic.

This time it was Aunt Silvia who found out first and who broke the news to us; first to Uncle, who broke it to me. Still in the throes of abject grief due to the news of Andrew, she had been unable to sleep. By now, it seemed, she was obsessed with listening to BBC reports and, in the middle of the night, had switched on the wireless. And there it was. Of course, the night was destroyed for her and all of us. She managed to place an international call through to Uncle.

'The *Princess of Jaipur* has been torpedoed!' she screamed down the line. 'It's Graham! It's my baby! My first baby! He's gone! They've taken him!'

The call was cut short by an operator but the deed was done. Uncle rang me immediately.

'Graham's ship has been torpedoed, Rosie. He's been taken from us.'

A cold chill ran through my body, top to bottom.

'Graham? No! No, no, no!'

I found myself blubbering into the phone. Uncle then told me, in a cool calm voice, word for word, what Aunty had said. Despite being someone who claimed to have little interest in the intricacies of war, she had known the exact position of her son's ship and had been living in a state of impossibly heightened anguish for weeks.

Uncle's calm was deceptive. When I hurried back to Newmeads that weekend, I found a man dissolved in pain. He paced his study, *stengah* in hand, hair dishevelled. I'd never seen him so agitated. What could I say to a man who had lost his son?

But just being there, sharing his pain, seemed to be enough. As I walked through the study door, he put down his glass on his desk, strode swiftly towards me and took both my hands in his.

'Rosie, Rosie, I'm so glad you've come. I-I don't know what to say, what to do! First Andrew, now Graham!'

'I know, Uncle, I know!' I struggled to hold back my own tears, but it was no good. I broke down. Uncle bundled me into his arms.

'There, there, my dear. Don't cry. We all have to be strong at this dreadful time.'

And comforting me seemed to comfort him. He poured me a strong gin and tonic, and we both retired to the darkness of the drawing room.

'How's Aunty holding up?' I asked once I had taken a few sips and felt in control of myself again. Graham, gone! I realised for the first time how much I cared for him, how much he meant to me. Dear, dear Graham! He was the lynchpin of this family, I realised, the strongest of them all, the one that held them all together. Myself included. If he was gone – truly gone – what would we do? How would Aunty cope?

'She isn't. She had a breakdown, Mrs Carruthers says. I got a telegram this morning.'

We talked and talked, but in the end there was nothing either of us could say that would lessen our pain.

But we weren't alone, and that helped. News spread quickly and commiserations soon poured in, from Uncle's friends, other planters, equally hit by one bit of bad news or the other, equally in the terrible position of being separated from their wives and young children. Those who had suffered losses managed to bond together in their shared agony. They visited each other, congregated at their clubs and churches and offered each other shoulders of commiseration in this time of tragedy, shoulders to cry on. I could not join in any of these gatherings; they were all too Old Boys' Club, stiff upper lip affairs, I soon found, and so I had to bear the pain of losing Graham all by myself.

But tragedy had actually brought us closer, Uncle and me. While in the past we had had a polite but distanced relationship, now our grief created a mutual emotional bubble, a sort of safe space where we could both simply talk about how we felt, express our fears and our hopes.

While for Andrew we did our best to bolster each other in the latter ('we must never give up hope!' we constantly told each other), for Graham there seemed to be not even a thread of hope left. 'No survivors,' was the bitter report. At work, too, nothing better could be confirmed. I actually worked with naval officers and, understanding my situation, everyone did their bit to investigate what had actually happened and what the chances were of survival.

Absolutely zero.

A few days later, Uncle received the confirmatory cable:

MISSING IN ACTION. BELIEVED KILLED.

That was it, then.

I was not a bit unaware of the fact that, of the three Huxley sons, the only one now known to be alive and well was the one I least liked. Victor. The one who lived the most dangerously. The one most likely to be killed, the one who actually boasted of his closeness to death, was still tempting fate. But then Victor's story took a new and devastating turn.

This time, it was Uncle who had visited me; he was down in Colombo for a meeting of some kind, and was staying at the Cinnamon Gardens flat for a few days. Continuing our ritual of sitting together of an evening at Newmeads, nursing *stengahs* and discussing war and losses and sharing our misery, we sat on the flat's balcony and once more combed through the detritus of the boys' lives. Uncle had taken to reminiscing, now, recalling the times when they were young and carefree, the differences between them, the hopes he and Aunty had for each one of them.

'Silvia always hoped that Victor would marry early,' he had told me on one of these evenings. 'He was such a wild one! She thought a calm, steady girl would do him good.' He gave a wry chuckle. 'A girl like you. She loved matchmaking, don't you know?'

'I know,' I said. 'But me and Victor? Never!'

'You don't like him much, do you?' he said in a matter-of-fact tone. I saw no need to deny it, because it was true. The quality that had been leadership and boldness in childhood had mutated into antagonism in youth and downright aggression in adulthood. There was no point in denying it, or denying that I disliked Victor's attitude of belligerence and lack of empathy. He had demonstrated it to Aunty on his last visit home – and to me. Our last disastrous encounter had left a bitter taste, and I still hadn't forgiven him. Every time I thought of Victor, that image rose up in me: that snarling, mocking face of his as he made his preposterous insinuations. I couldn't help thinking, why hadn't it been him? Wrong, I know. But there it was. I didn't like him.

But Uncle was still talking. 'I don't blame you,' he said. 'I know he's not exactly Prince Charming.'

I gave a grunt of agreement. I couldn't very well criticise Victor to his own father so I preferred to stay silent. He continued, in a rambling sort of way.

'The girls seem to like him, though. Strangely enough. He's a bit of a rake, I've heard. What is it about females that attracts them to caddish behaviour?'

I had to say something here. 'Not at all!' I protested. 'Nothing puts me off more than a man who lacks basic decency!'

'Ah! So you agree that Victor lacks basic decency.'

I gave a little shrug, and hoped that that would be enough. I could not possibly agree openly about Victor, his last remaining son. Uncle took my silence as a cue to keep on talking.

'I've been hearing some unfortunate talk about Victor,' he said. 'And I was wondering if you would mind if I brought it up. I'm not sure if it's appropriate to talk of these matters with a young girl, but – well, it's been preying on my mind and a female perspective would help.'

'Yes?'

'Well, you know, another one of the planters was talking to me the other day. He's also lost a son so we were basically commiserating with each other. But he also has a daughter, a little older than you, I believe. A former pupil of Girls' High. Victor had apparently been a suitor to this girl. He had given her hopes; they'd known each other since their schooldays in Kandy. Well, when Victor was here on leave – that last time, you know – you remember he rushed off early, leaving his mother in a state? Well, he went straight to that girl's home. It's near Nuwara Eliya, so not too far. You remember, he took the car. Of course, he was welcomed with open arms by the girl, and subsequently by her parents. The man's wife, by the way, is not this girl's mother; he married her as a widower with older children. He was of course on his best behaviour – Victor can be quite charming when he wants to be.

'Anyway, this planter friend told me that during the night he heard something like a scream. Just one little sound, and muffled. As if cut off. So he got up to investigate. To his surprise, he heard strange noises coming from his children's nanny's room – she's a live-in ayah, a Tamil girl who looks after the two toddlers. He didn't know what to do – he couldn't very well barge in – so he knocked on the door, very gently, and called her name.

'Two seconds later, who should emerge from the room but my Victor. Looking rather sheepish, tucking his shirt into his belt, apparently, which was unbuckled. And he gave my friend a very un-sheepish grin and a wink, and said, "Just between us two men, right?" As if that made everything all right.'

Uncle Henry stopped speaking abruptly. I was horrified into silence. Absolutely stunned. Finally, I found the breath to ask a single question, though I already knew the answer.

'What's the name of this family, Uncle?'

'Harrison,' he said.

The silence hung between us. As I downed the rest of my *stengah*, I was trembling with rage and horror. Uncle began to speak again.

'The thing is, my friend didn't know what to think. Had the girl invited him into her room? Had she flirted with him so that he was aroused enough to – um – take things further? Boys will be boys and all that, after all. Was she of immoral character? Should she be summarily dismissed? Or – what was far worse – had Victor forced himself on her?'

In the end, I managed one question:

'What did Mr Harrison do?'

'Well, he did nothing. The matter resolved itself. Soon after that the order came for his wife and children to evacuate and so they left, leaving the girl behind. There was nothing to be done. He never told his wife. It was just the one little incident, but he thought I should know, as Victor's father. Between friends. The story is over.'

Except that it wasn't.

Somewhere in India, that one little incident had left behind a small boy now growing up in an orphanage, and a young Tamil girl whose life had been destroyed by Victor Huxley. And I was the only one who knew the whole truth. The only one beside Usha, that is. And Usha would never speak of it.

Inside, I seethed. But I knew I had to play my cards carefully. Victor was Uncle's precious son. I knew exactly where his allegiances lay. So, choosing my words carefully, I said:

'And the girl… what became of her? Did she ever, well, you know, complain of – of misbehaviour?'

'Well, you see, my dear, that's just it. It's why I took the step of talking to you in the first place. It's such a delicate subject, one that I would not normally broach with a woman. The sort of thing men discuss among themselves. But, you see, it turns out that the girl, the ayah, happens to be the very girl who until quite recently worked here, at Newmeads. Sunita's daughter. She used to help in the kitchen. I even remember her. A pretty little thing, I recall. Now, normally I would not be involved with goings-on in the servants' department but I do remember Silvia complaining that she did not approve of a friendship developing between you and one of the servant girls, and I believe this is the very girl she was referring to. She called it an "inappropriate friendship", but there was little she could do about it at the time. And then there was that little affair with Andrew.'

'Affair with Andrew?' I had to feign ignorance. I had no idea how much Uncle knew of this 'affair', or, indeed, how much Aunty knew.

'Yes, you know. A little bit of dibble-dabble. Jiggity-jig, or whatever you young people call it these days. Andrew of course was just a lad at the time and easily tempted. So it seems to me that the girl is herself of loose morals, a bit of a tart. Tempting the lads and so on. Who can blame them, if they succumb? They don't need any encouragement. But I don't suppose you know much about that, a good girl like you.'

I seethed even more, but decided to remain silent, to see what else he had to say.

'So what I am asking here, Rosie, is do you still have contact with this girl? There was some talk of you exchanging letters with her?'

'Why are you asking, Uncle?'

'Well, because there's more to the story. It appears that, just like you, Mrs Harrison was rather taken with this girl, hobnobbed with her as a friend. Never a good idea, to fraternise with the servants. It seems that the very next morning, Victor left before daybreak, leaving a letter thanking the Harrisons for their hospitality, etc., etc. But when Mrs Harrison encountered the girl, she found her with horrific bruises on her face and neck, and, on further investigation, on her body. She questioned the girl, who at first refused to talk, but basically it was obvious that she had been assaulted quite viciously. In the end Mrs Harrison got her to admit what she herself suspected: that Victor had, in fact, forced himself on her.'

I gasped, and my shock was genuine this time. Though I had already put two and two together for myself, it was terrible to hear confirmation that Victor's rape of Usha had been committed with such appalling violence.

'Mrs Harrison was so disgusted that she began to badger her husband to take legal steps against Victor. Accuse him of raping the girl. I cannot imagine what got into her head – to turn against a valued house-guest in this manner, especially since it was only a servant involved. Thank goodness Mr Harrison, being a true friend, refused to do anything of the kind. We English have to stick together. But he thought it was only right and proper that I should be aware of the danger. Even if Mrs Harrison does not report the incident, the girl herself could.'

'And has she done so?'

I knew she hadn't. But I wanted to probe the depths of Uncle's perfidy. I could tell that a scheme of whitewashing was in the making. Should this 'incident' ever come to light, the entire blame would be shoved on to Usha's shoulders, and the judicial system, being what it was, would always be heavily weighted on the side of the English.

'Not as far as I know. That's why I'm turning to you, Rosie. I am assuming that, notwithstanding your past friendship with this girl, you will always be on the side of the family. We are, after all, your family as well, and Victor is almost like a brother to you.'

'Well, Uncle, you can rest assured that I have no contact with Usha any more.'

'So you don't know what became of her? Where she went after Mrs Harrison was evacuated? They did manage to brush the whole thing under the rug for the rest of her time in Ceylon but one can't help wondering what became of the girl, and if she harbours any resentment and intends to bring charges – one day, even, years from now. Victor is our only surviving son. Assuming that he will survive the war – which is what we hope and pray for – he will inherit Newmeads and such an accusation, even if immediately disproved, could be his ruin. So I was wondering…'

He paused. I was impatient to hear him out. 'Yes?' I prompted.

'I was wondering – if you do have contact with her…' At this junction I breathed a sigh of relief. He had not waited for my reply to his last questions: what became of Usha, where she went after the evacuation. I would have found it hard to lie. Uncle paused, waiting for my reply, and when none came, continued.

'If so, you could let her know that, for one, any such accusation would be futile, as Mrs Harrison will not be a witness in her defence.

Her husband will make sure of that. And, secondly, we as a family would be ready to make her a handsome reward for her silence.'

So, finally, we had arrived at the crux of the matter: Usha's silence was to be bought. I wondered what Uncle would think, what he would offer, for the knowledge that Usha had, in fact, given birth to Victor's child? What would the Old Boys' Network say to that? That he was grandfather to a half-caste child?

But that was a knowledge I would keep to myself. For as long as it was necessary. For as long as Usha needed my silence. Forever, if need be.

There was only one person who had a right to that knowledge, and that was Andrew. But Andrew was *Missing in Action, Believed Captured*. Perhaps dead. Most likely dead, in fact. He and Freddy both.

It seemed to me that all our destinies were wrapped up in each other's. Mine, Freddy's, Andrew's, Usha's. Victor's.

When all this was over, we would all be the wiser. *When*.

For the time being, all I said to Uncle was: 'I promise you, Uncle, I have no communication with Usha any more.'

Which was absolutely true at the time of speaking. But I knew, even as the words left my lips, that it would not be true for very long. I had grossly misjudged Usha, and it was time to contact her again. Father Bear would know where to find her. I had to apologise.

Chapter Thirty

And then it was Victor's turn to fall. And fall he did, quite literally. His plane was shot down over the Pacific, close to the Andaman Islands, is all we knew; other pilots in his squadron reported an explosion, a ball of fire plummeting to the ocean. And no pilot parachuting out.

No chance of survival. No 'believed killed', this time.

This time, too, no telegram and no hearsay over the radio.

'Hand-delivered!' Uncle reported, over the phone. 'By SEOC Headquarters in Kandy; two senior officers. They came in a jeep yesterday evening.'

His voice trembled as he spoke, and I knew he was trying hard to hold in raging emotion. We all knew that Victor was his favourite son.

By that time, knowing what I did, my feelings for Victor were less than tender and even though we had been childhood friends, my reaction to his death was complicated. I longed to mourn my old playmate, the boy who had led us all in our adventures, with whom I'd laughed and frolicked, climbed trees and plunged into the icy waters of the waterfall pool. But I could not, for that boy had been obliterated by a darker, sinister version of himself: a man so damaged by war, by senseless killing, by the numbing effect of violence, that he must have lost all sense of valour. The man who had coldly provoked me in my own room; who had brutally raped my friend – he was no longer my friend and not a single thread of grief at his passing wove its way into my response to the news.

But I *did* care about Uncle. I was able to get emergency leave, notwithstanding the fact that he was not an actual relative of mine. And I did care about Aunty, and now Uncle and I were faced with the most horrendous task of all: breaking this worst of all outcomes to her. No more *believed captured.* No more *believed killed.* This was plan, untainted *death*, staring her, us all, in the face, and it had to be broken to her.

By this time Evelyn Carruthers had proven a real friend in need to Aunty over in South Africa; in fact, they had all moved in together and lived in a bungalow with its own garden: Aunty, Mrs Carruthers and her daughter Gwen. The two older ladies had found genuine companionship in their exile from home. Mrs Carruthers had supported Aunty with all her strength and heart during the two previous calamities. This would be the final and worst trial. Not only was Victor completely, irrefutably dead, with not a glimmer of hope remaining: he was the last of her sons, the last of her children. How could any mother ever recover from such news? For Uncle having to convey the news by proxy was almost worse than hearing it himself, however skilled and compassionate that proxy might be.

I felt for them all: for Uncle, for Aunty, for Mrs Carruthers. But there was nothing to be done. I cannot imagine a worse destiny than to be the mother of men who go off to war and lose their lives. To have given birth to three perfect children, only to see them go into the belly of a conflagration: what a perfectly gruesome fate.

I thought Usha needed to know that her nemesis was gone. I also needed desperately to let her know that I knew the truth about her baby's father, and how it all came to be. And I needed to ask her forgiveness for ever doubting her.

I wrote her a long letter, saying all this. I told her of Victor's death, and of (presumably) Andrew's. I had not written to her for ages, not knowing how to address the whole matter, not knowing whether to confront her with what I knew, or to keep silent, yet longing to comfort her as a friend. It was all so complicated. We all clung to the hope that Andrew's capture would end positively, and I knew Usha would cling to that hope too. And now that I knew she had not betrayed him, I felt all the more for her. Even if Andrew survived, what future was there for him, for her, for them, for Victor's child?

I addressed the letter to her care of Father Bear at the Vellore orphanage, knowing that he'd forward it.

My dear Usha, there's so much to tell you, I hardly know where to begin. I know, Usha, I know the truth, all the truth. About what happened to you, about who Luke's father is. I know now it isn't Andrew. I never told you I knew and that I was cross with you all this time, and now I have to apologise for misjudging you. I know it was Victor. I know he raped you. And I hate him so much for that! But now he is dead. You'll be happy to hear that, I'm sure.

But, Usha, that's not all. The Huxley family has been hit so dreadfully. I hardly know what to say. We've lost Andrew as well. They say he might have been captured, but no one knows for sure. All we can do, at this point, is hope and pray. I wish I could be with you now, to support you...

She replied very briefly.

I have always loved Andrew, and I always will. I feel with great certainty that he is alive and will return to me. I live in that hope.

Yes, the child is Victor's. I have tried to purge my son from my heart, but I cannot. I do not know what the future holds. It is all in God's hands. I hope we will meet again, Rosie, for I love you.

Yes, 1943 was a year of tragedy for us all. A veritable *annus horribilis.* And not just us: Sunita, too, felt the devastation of this war. Yes, Sunita still worked for Aunty and Uncle. How could she not? Uncle had brought her family over from India when he first took over the plantation, Sunita and Rajkumar both. The drama with Usha had, apparently, been forgiven, if not forgotten, and even with me she now managed a civil and polite relationship.

But that year Sunita and Rajkumar's eldest son, Yogesh, who had volunteered with an infantry battalion of the Ceylon Defence Force, was killed in Burma. Sunita received the news in the middle of the day, delivered to her by her other son, Karthik. Her scream reached me and Uncle Henry, where we sat on the veranda; we rushed to the kitchen, where we found her, collapsed on the floor, heaving with sobs. Karthik told us the terrible news.

'He leaves a widow and a little boy, sir,' Karthik said. 'It is all devastating.'

'She must go home,' said Uncle Henry immediately, 'She can have a week off.'

'Then, sir, I will come and cook for you. I am – was – a professional cook at the Galle Face.'

'*Was?*'

'Yes, sir. I was dismissed, not so much work right now.'

'Very well. We'll be pleased to have you.' And that was how Karthik, whom I'd always liked since we'd played together as children, came to work for the Huxleys. Sunita came back to work a week later, but a different Sunita: shoulders hunched, her cheeks sunken as if she hadn't eaten in days, she was a shadow of her old self.

*

Yet the year came to an end on a good note. In Europe, the tide had finally turned and it had become abundantly clear that the Nazis were staring defeat in the face. That the Allies, in Europe at least, would be victorious.

Here in Asia it was not nearly so clear, but we clung to BBC News as to a lifeline and little slivers of hope accumulated in our hearts to make us believe that here, too, we could one day breathe again.

And then, at last, the evacuation order was lifted and Aunt Silvia, along with Mrs Carruthers, Gwen and all the other exiled mems, returned. Ships full of women and children chugged into Colombo's dockyard; husbands in droves descended on the dock to greet their long-lost wives and offspring. There was a sense of great rejoicing, jubilation, even, and the Christmas Season at the Galle Face Hotel was never so joyous.

Aunt Silvia arrived, veiled and wearing the black of mourning. I was there to meet her at the dock, with Uncle. Strangely, she threw herself into my arms first, and stood there swaying, holding me tightly, before turning to Uncle and collapsing in a torrent of tears in his arms.

She did not attend a single party. She and Uncle spent a quiet night with me in Cinnamon Gardens. The next day they returned to Newmeads, broken-hearted. There was nothing I could do or say to help them with their burden. It was a valley of shadows they would have to cross themselves. At least they were together again at last. Together, and childless. How empty Newmeads must seem to Aunty, now! I ached for her.

To my surprise, though, they summoned me. I'd thought they'd want to be alone in their grief, but the opposite was true. They wanted me at their side; although I was not a direct family member, I was close enough to genuinely feel their pain and so mitigate it somewhat. To absorb some of it. They had lost everything; for having raised three boys, only to lose them all, what had they left? A tea plantation, yes, and their own lives to live: but empty lives devoid of the family they had invested in. Nevertheless, they harboured two thin strands of hope: Andrew, Believed Captured, and, the thinner one, Graham, Believed Killed. They clung to those threads as if their lives depended on it. Especially the more hopeful of the two.

'If he was captured,' Uncle would tell us, again and again, 'he would have been taken to Changi Prison in Singapore. He'll be released at the end of the war, along with all the other British prisoners.'

'That's what will have happened,' Aunty would say, with more conviction than she'd shown when the news first burst upon us. Then, she had had no faith whatsoever in the desire of the Japanese to keep even one captured soldier alive. Now, she *had* to believe.

And I: I upheld them in their hope. 'That's probably what happened,' I told them, again and again. And so we lived from day to day, bolstering those tiny slivers of hope in each other.

I continued my work in Colombo, but every weekend, now, I returned to the place I now called home, the place where I was now truly regarded as a daughter. And I longed more than ever for this terrible war to end. For those at home, desperate for news of loved ones, it was torture.

Chapter Thirty-One

I had to do something about Aunt Silvia. It was growing worse and worse. I came home to Newmeads one weekend to find that she had not got out of bed that day. She lay in her upstairs bedroom, the sheet up to her neck, the curtains drawn. The only concession to daytime was the fact that the mosquito net had been tied up in a ball hanging above the bed. She still wore her nightie, and emitted a certain pong. The entire room had a hot, smelly, stuffy atmosphere. The overhead ceiling fan did no more than regurgitate the stale, stagnant air. It was awful.

'She's been this way for days,' Uncle admitted. 'I don't know what to do. It's as if she's given up on life.'

Uncle himself had managed to keep going; after all, he had his work at the plantation, and even if he now had, it seemed, no heir to leave it to, at least it was a distraction and something to get up for in the morning. In the evening, he'd come home, drink enough *stengahs* to forget, and retire to bed. They both sought oblivion in different ways: Aunty with sleep, Uncle with distraction and drink.

And distraction, I was certain, was what Aunty needed to lure her from the debilitating influence of sleep. A distraction: but one so potent it would take her out of the cloud of gloom that hung around her. Just walking into her room was enough to make my feelings sink. I had to do something about it. But what? I racked my brain for inspiration.

And inspiration came, not from me, but from Sunita.

Sunita looked after Aunty. Brought her meals, cleaned her room, gave her a basic wash in bed every morning. The only reason Aunty left her bed was to go to the adjoining bathroom; Sunita cleaned that, too. She brought along a six-year-old boy; her grandson, the son of her oldest son, Yogesh, who had been killed in the war. His widow had come to stay with Sunita, and worked in the tea factory, so Sunita took care of him when there was no school. A sweet little fellow who was eager to help his grandmother with her chores, his name was Kannan.

Kannan, I discovered, had a pert and eager mind, and he spoke excellent English. Sunita informed me that he attended the village school, which was English-medium, and funded by the collective of local tea planters to supply them with future workers who spoke their language.

On my first day back home on that second weekend, I heard some tinkering on the piano, Aunty's old upright imported from England decades ago, and which she had not played on since… since when? I thought back, and I realised it was since the start of the war. How could I not have noticed?

Aunty's one love, beside her family, had always been the piano. She had played it from her own childhood and had shown much talent as a girl. Back home, she had taught children piano even when only in her teens herself, and when she joined her parents in Kuala Lumpur she had been very popular with the local English wives as a piano teacher for their own children. She'd been an excellent teacher; I remembered Amma telling me about her. And Amma, with her beautiful singing voice, had soon found in Aunty an excellent partner; together they had wooed their compatriots at every party and social gathering, Aunty at the keys, Amma singing along beside her. It's how, I understood, they had won their respective husbands. Two pretty, gay, bubbly eighteen-year-old girls, one with the voice of an angel and the other with fingers that danced across the piano keys: they were the darlings of Kuala Lumpur. Lucy and Silvia: everyone adored them.

Marriage had split the duo and children had done the rest: singing and piano-playing had, over the years, become for both of them no more than hobbies, to be indulged in in stray moments; occasionally to entertain others, but, mostly, just a distraction.

And now, since the start of the war, when Victor had run off to sign up, the piano had been silent. But now I heard its voice again. A hesitant plink-plonk on the upper keys; no tune, just a little tinkering. I hurried to investigate, and there he was: Kannan, standing at the open keyboard, the fingers of his right hand bobbing on the black and the white keys.

I came up silently behind him. 'Hello, Kannan!' I said. He jumped, looked up at me in fright, and quickly – but gently, I noticed – closed the cover.

'I'm sorry, Miss!' he mumbled.

'No, no!' I quickly said. 'I didn't come here to scold you! It's nice to see you interested in the piano. Have you ever heard one being played?'

He shook his head. 'No, Miss.'

'Shall I play something for you?'

'Yes, please, Miss!'

'Very well, then!' I opened the piano again, sat myself down on the stool, and played one of the tunes Amma had taught me so very long ago, and sang along to it. It brought back poignant memories of myself and Amma, sitting at the piano at Shanti Nilayam, me playing this very song, she singing. Not so appropriate for a child, I thought, but it was the one that first came to my mind.

> Early one morning,
> Just as the sun was rising,
> I heard a young maid sing,

In the valley below.
Oh, don't deceive me,
Oh, never leave me,
How could you use
A poor maiden so?

I finished the song and looked up at him. His eyes were shining. 'That's lovely!' he said.

'Shall I sing another?'

'Oh, yes please!'

So I sang 'Country Garden', a favourite from my childhood:

How many different sweet flowers grow
In an English country garden?
We'll tell you now of some that we know
Those we miss you'll surely pardon
Daffodils, heart's ease and flox
Meadowsweet and lady smocks
Gentian, lupine and tall hollihocks
Roses, foxgloves, snowdrops,
Blue forget-me-nots
In an English country garden.

Kannan looked up at me with worried eyes. 'I don't know all those words!' he said, and seemed genuinely anxious. He meant the names of the flowers in the song.

I laughed. 'Of course you don't know them! Those are the names of English flowers.'

'Oh,' he said. 'But it's a nice song!'

'I used to sing it with my amma when I was your age, and I didn't know the flowers either, except roses. Nor did my amma. She'd learned it from *her* amma, who had grown up in England.

But, I have an idea. Maybe we could rewrite it: replace those flowers with ones we know?'

'Oh, yes! Let's do that!'

What a delightful child he was!

'Right!' I said firmly. 'Then, first let's make a list. I'll get my notebook.'

I hurried to my room and returned with a notepad and pencil. 'Now, Kannan, you tell me the names of all the flowers you know. What's your favourite?'

'Rose!' he said at once. 'But I love bougainvillea too, and jasmine smells so good, and the marigolds are pretty, like little suns, and...'

'Wait, wait, not so quick! I can't keep up!' I laughed, and quickly made up a list. He knew flower names I'd never heard of, and seemed quite a keen little gardener. Soon we had a list of at least ten flowers.

'That's enough!' I said. I perused the list.

Kannan also inspected it. 'None of them rhyme,' he said, 'so it won't work the same!'

How astute of him! 'It doesn't matter,' I replied. 'Lots of poems and songs have lines that don't rhyme. So we won't be able to make it *just* like the English song. But we can get a nice rhythm, and that will make up for it.'

'What's rhythm?'

So I explained rhythm, and beat, and metre, and he seemed to understand, nodding along as I spoke.

Together we shuffled the flower names, trying to get a nice rhythm, using the most well-known flowers; Kannan was as keen as I was, and had a good natural sense of poetic metre. He counted syllables, tapped out beats, hummed this version and that, while I played out the tune on the keys. We even had a little argument: I wanted to substitute *Ceylon mountain garden* for *English country garden*, but he said Ceylon was a proper noun and we had to use an adjective,

Ceylonese; and that these flowers didn't *only* grow in the mountains. What meticulous reasoning! In the end we came up with this:

> How many different sweet flowers grow
> In a Ceylonese garden?
> We'll tell you now of some that we know
> And those we miss you'll surely pardon
> Frangipani, forest flame
> Oleander, marigold
> Hibiscus, crocus, jasmine and rose
> Lily, lotus, ixora, bougainvillea
> In a Ceylonese garden.

'And now we have to play it, and sing it!' I said, and that's what we did. I played and we both sang; he had a sweet, high voice and sang perfectly in tune. By the time we were finished, his eyes were sparkling.

'Miss?' he said, hesitantly.

'Yes, Kannan? Oh, and why don't you call me Aunty Rosie? It's so much nicer than Miss!'

'Really?'

'Yes, really. Now, what were you going to ask?'

He hesitated again. 'I was going to ask, Miss— Aunty Rosie – if I can try playing it too?'

'Well, of course! I'll teach you!'

He beamed. 'I think I know already,' he said. 'Look!'

And he put his right hand on the keys and indeed, picked out the tune perfectly. Only one-handed, to be sure, but he'd done it.

'Why, Kannan, that's simply marvellous! How clever you are!'

He beamed even more. 'Maybe I can learn to play the left hand too!'

'Well, of course you can! I'll teach you. Or...'

And that's when it came to me: the solution for Aunt Silvia's distress. I looked at Kannan, and closed the piano.

'I'll tell you what, Kannan, let's have a proper lesson tomorrow, all right? At ten o'clock?'

His eyes sparkled so brightly, I wanted to hug him. I didn't now, but I knew I would one day.

Chapter Thirty-Two

The next morning, after Sunita had removed the breakfast tray from Aunty's room, I burst in, singing that very song. The room was, as always, dark, lit only by the small table lamp next to her bed. She liked it that way. Sunita was forbidden to open the curtains, or even the window.

But I was not.

I drew the curtains back. Sunlight streamed in. I turned to Aunty.

'Good morning, Aunt Silvia! Rise and shine!'

She rubbed her eyes and groaned. 'Don't, Rosie. Why did you do that? You know very well that I don't—'

'But today is different, Aunty. I've got a plan! You're going to love it!'

'Oh, Rosie, really! What on earth has got into you? You know I don't—'

'Yes, you do! Now, I think the first thing you should do is have a lovely shower – the water's a bit cold still but Sunita is right now heating up a big pot and she's going to empty it into the shower tank and we'll get the perfect temperature for you. You're going to love it, feeling all fresh and clean again!'

I was bluffing, of course; I had taken a bold decision, to simply ignore Aunty's doom-and-gloom disposition and simply give her no choice: infect her with the very sunshine streaming into the room, fresh air, music... Inspiration had come to me in the wee hours, thinking over my plan and how best to implement it. I knew that the right thing to do was to give Aunty no choice. To simply enfold her in the certainty of it all. Not to argue, not to give in to her gloom, but to sweep her up and straight into the new proposal.

I went to the door, opened it, called: 'Sunita! We're ready!'

'Coming, Miss.'

Sunita came in, bearing the bucket of hot water. She bowed slightly to Aunty as she rushed past and into the bathroom adjoining the bedroom. I heard the swish of water as she poured it into the overhead cistern. That done, Sunita flitted out again, back to the kitchen.

'All right, Aunty, the shower's ready. Let me help you get up.'

I walked over to the bed and stretched out a hand for Aunty. I knew I was pushing it, with my new-found bossy-boots behaviour, but it was the only way. I instinctively knew it. It was as if an inherent sense of authority had overtaken my normal nice-compliant-niece demeanour, an authority so shocking to Aunty she could only comply. It was a situation as new to me as it was to her; I was acting entirely on instinct, and perhaps that was why she did not argue.

She took my hand. She stood up! All the time mumbling: 'Rosie, I really don't think…'

'Just do it, Aunty. I know you can. If you need help, just give me a call. No, no need to put on your dressing gown, you'll be taking everything off again in the shower. But you can take it to put on afterwards, if you like. Now, come along. I'll find some fresh clothes for you in the meantime.'

I led her into the bathroom, hung up her dressing gown on a hook, made sure there were soap and fresh towels handy, and left her to it. To my delight, a few seconds later I heard water running. It was working! She was actually having a shower!

I opened her wardrobe and selected three of her favourite daytime dresses, laid them on the bed for when she returned from the bathroom. She could at least have the choice of what to wear.

Three lovely, flowery, soft cotton dresses. Who could be in a bad mood, in a lovely flowery dress? Underwear, a petticoat. All laid out and ready for her. Once, Aunty had had a lady's maid who did all this for her, but those days were long gone.

When I heard the shower stop, and then the bathroom door opening, I stepped out onto the veranda outside the double doors and called, 'I'm right here, Aunty, if you need me! I'll come when you're ready.'

After that, it was merely routine. Aunty got dressed by herself; I re-entered the room and found that she had already set herself down before the dressing table and was unscrewing a little bottle of Oil of Olay, her favourite face cream.

'My hair is such a tangle!' she was complaining. 'I so wish Anjali was still with me – she was the only one who could manage it. Do you think it needs a cut, Rosie?'

She was picking up strands of it and inspecting it. Smelling it. 'Pooh! A cut and a wash! Perhaps I should make a visit to Maybelle's in Kandy…'

I rejoiced. Maybelle's had been her hairdresser for over twenty years. 'Yes, let's think about that,' I said. 'But for today, I'll help you get it sorted out.'

'Just a bun will do for today.'

I managed to get her hair straightened out. By now, Aunty's demeanour was almost back to normal, at least superficially. She had lost a considerable amount of weight and the dress she'd chosen (the prettiest of the three, I thought, patterned with yellow flowers on green vines, on a white background) hung on her shoulders and drooped on her body, the belt much too slack. And her eyes had lost their once so energetic glow; they were dull, lifeless, devoid of any interest in anything whatsoever. That was the part I had to supply.

She knew very well that something was up, something out of the ordinary.

'So, Rosie, what is this new plan of yours? I hope it's nothing silly because I'll just get straight back into bed!'

I laughed. 'Nothing at all silly, Aunty! You're going to love it! Now, come along!'

I glanced at the clock on top of the sideboard. Ten past ten. A little late, but that was fine. Sunita would understand. I took Aunty's hand and led her to the drawing room at the other end of the house. The moment we entered, there was movement at the far corner. Sunita, sitting on the piano stool, Kannan on her lap, pushed the little boy into standing and stood up herself. Sunita looked at us with anxious eyes.

'Good morning, Ma'am, I'm sorry, but…' She was obviously terrified at this deviation from her normal duties, entirely dictated by me. But today I was in charge, and I let her know.

'It's fine, Sunita; you may go,' I told her, and she scurried away as if afraid Aunty would chase after her with a whip.

'What's going on?' said Aunty, now completely confused. 'Who's that boy?'

'His name is Kannan,' I said, 'And he's Sunita's grandson. And I want you to sit down, Aunty, right here…' I led her to the most comfortable armchair, the one next to the piano… 'and just listen.'

I sat myself down on the piano stool, gestured for Kannan to stand beside me, and together we sang and I played 'In a Ceylonese Garden'. Just the one verse; I fully intended to rewrite all the other verses, substituting Ceylonese birds and insects for English ones, but one thing at a time.

'Kannan and I wrote it together,' I said. 'And he wants to play it, too, with both hands. He's already started to learn. Show her, Kannan!'

And Kannan sat down at the piano and played the melody with his right hand, and sang as he played. He had done as I'd suggested and learned the words off by heart last night.

'Aunty,' I said when he had finished, 'this boy has real musical talent. He needs a teacher. And I thought you would be perfect. What do you think?'

I looked at Aunty. My heart was pounding away in my chest, so wildly I could hear it. This was the moment of truth. It had been easy up to now, to get her out of the lethargic slump that held her in its grip of gloom; I had simply demonstrated a natural authority that had stimulated something inside her that *wanted* the light of normality; I had got her out of bed, brought sunshine into her room, got her to bathe and dress and brush her hair. That was the easy part. Music – well, that was a different story.

Music, and Kannan.

Now, that pledge was the first hurdle. The second was Kannan himself. All the children she had taught up to now had been English. Aunty was not like Amma; she did not believe that Ceylonese people were our equals, or that they should learn the things we did. I remembered well her disparaging comments about a school orchestra from Girls' College, which consisted of brown Ceylonese girls playing violins, cellos, flutes – everything. She had wrinkled her nose and said they should stick to their own instruments.

Now, here was a little native boy I was pushing on to her. A boy with a nice voice and who had learned to play a simple tune just by watching the movement of my fingers – but she didn't even know that. She had only seen him play and sing this one verse. And she saw, now, the eager light in his eyes as he turned to look at her, begging for her approval. How would she react?

What she said next would tell me everything: had my strategy worked, the plan that had been swirling in my head and in my heart ever since we'd played that song together yesterday? A new beginning for Aunty. Music. A child to teach. Bringing back into the light the musical brilliance that lay within her, for her to pass it on to another, to awaken it in another. Had it worked?

Aunty's eyes met mine, and at once I knew. It had. Because Aunty was smiling, and that smile was written also in her eyes. I hadn't realised that I was holding my breath. Now, with a sigh that I'm sure she heard, I let that breath go. All was well. My plan had worked.

Chapter Thirty-Three

The following April – 1944, two full years after the Colombo bomb attack – I was summoned to my superintendent's office. He was a tall, straight man in his fifties, rather gruff in his demeanour but whose bark I always suspected was worse than his bite. His praise, when it came, was always somewhat measured, smile-less, and yet his voice seemed to hold a quiet warmth.

As it did now. 'Good morning, Miss Todd,' he said, after gesturing to the chair before his desk. I sat down, echoing his greeting. After a few preliminaries about some of the details of my work, all of which had to do with the typing-up of reports of the cypher work done in that department, he came to the point. He shuffled a pile of papers lying on the desk in front of him, found what he was looking for, and held up a page. I recognised it as my leaving certificate from my Madras secretarial college.

'I understand that you are not only fluent in Tamil, but that your stenotypist qualifications include a diploma as a bilingual secretary, with special merit in translation and interpretation.'

I nodded. 'That's right. I actually grew up bilingual.'

He stroked his moustache, a gesture I'd grown to understand indicated satisfaction.

'I see… I see.'

I waited; more was to come.

'Well, Miss Todd, as such you could prove to be of much use to us in that capacity. I am going to refer you to a certain Mr Henderson for a further interview. You will hear from him shortly.'

And that was it. The interview had ended as abruptly as it had been called, and I was still none the wiser as to what was to be expected of me, further than it required my knowledge of Tamil. Politely dismissed, I nodded, shook his hand again, and left.

The next day I was summoned by Mr Henderson. We were to meet, it seemed, rather clandestinely, in a private home in the Kotikawatta suburb to the east of Colombo's central business district, a residential area. Following instructions, I took a taxi there, and found myself deposited in front of a very typical, nondescript dwelling house, a bungalow set back from the road behind a tangle of non-flowering shrubs and trees, barely visible from the street. I entered through the gate, walked down a weed-overgrown sandy path and rang the doorbell. It was immediately opened by a man with a ginger beard and wearing clothes as nondescript as the house, rather tired-looking, I thought – the clothes, not the man, who had a very intense gaze and extremely bright eyes. They positively glittered.

He introduced himself as Mr Henderson.

We were alone in the house, it seemed. He greeted me politely and led me into the sitting room, which was sparsely outfitted with a three-piece sofa set: a hardwood sofa and two armchairs with reclining backrests and thick cushions that seemed almost new, arranged around a long glass-topped coffee table. On the table was a pile of files and papers. The room did not look lived in at all.

At his invitation I took a seat in one of the armchairs. He sat down opposite me, picked up a soft-covered green folder that, I could see by reading upside-down, had my name on it. It was filled with sheets of paper. He opened the file, sifted through the papers. Looked up. Thereupon an intensive interrogation began. I was astounded at how much he knew about me, mostly seemingly from memory, aided by occasionally glancing at papers he picked out of the file. The names of my parents, that my mother had died, and when; Pa's work. When and why I moved to Newmeads, my relationship with Aunt Silvia's family, her sons. When I had had holidays in Madras. Pa's disappearance. My secretarial training in Madras. My present job, where I lived, with whom I shared my dwelling.

The one thing they – I very soon began to think of him as a kind of collective, a mysterious *they* of which he was merely a mouthpiece – did not know, however, was the initial reason for my visit back to Madras in 1942. They did know I had gone with Usha and returned without her.

'So you've been spying on me,' I said jokingly, trying to break the serious tension in the atmosphere. Mr Henderson, in fact, did not seem the jocular type, or for that matter a man who even understood the nature of a joke. He did not laugh.

'Please be serious, Miss Todd. We do know that you travelled with this young Tamil girl; that you booked a train reservation to Talaimannar and paid for your two tickets, and from there took the ferry to Rameswaram, and on to Madras, where you both stayed in your own home; that the girl's name is Usha Chettiar. The Chettiar family are an Indian Tamil family who work for your foster-family, a family your foster-family took to Ceylon when they moved there after Mr Huxley's marriage to your aunt. Why did you take her to India? Did she ever return? We do need to know details.'

'Well, it's rather a private matter,' I said.

'In war, private matters must take a subordinate position to the public good,' he said sternly. 'There is much Tamil unrest going on in India, what with this Gandhi fellow and his calls for Independence. We need to establish impeccable credentials for all persons associated with you. Some of them are traitors.'

For the first time, I felt a twinge of nerves. He was so deadly serious. I needed to defend Usha, free her from even a hint of disloyalty. I told him the truth.

'Usha worked for the Huxley family until early 1942. We were friends. She found herself in a compromising situation and asked me for help. I took her to Madras and settled her in my house, where a member of my staff looked after her until – er – until her confinement. That's all there is to that.'

He seemed satisfied with that explanation. Closing the file, he said, 'Well, Miss Todd, thank you for clearing that up and confirming our knowledge of you.'

I noted his use of 'our', which confirmed the background *they* I had been imagining. He coughed, then removed another file from the pile. He now spoke about my work for the Far East Combined Bureau.

'We were wondering, and in fact hoping, you would agree to work for us in a rather more delicate area,' he said now. 'You already signed the Official Secrets Act when you joined the Far East Combined Bureau. Now we'd like you to go a little deeper into Intelligence work.'

My spine tingled. So it would be spy work, after all! I was thrilled. I smiled, and nodded my compliance.

'This is about a branch of British Intelligence called Force 136,' he continued. 'It's a cover name, originally disguised as the record-keeping branch of the India Mission. Force 136 headquarters recently moved to Kandy. It cooperates closely with South East Asia Command, your current employer. It's actually a Far East branch of the British Intelligence organisation, the Special Operations Executive, the SOE. You won't have heard of the SOE, but they've been doing stellar work in Europe helping to bring down Hitler by sending in agents to disrupt Nazi operations. Men and women were parachuted into the occupied areas to sabotage the enemy and generally scrambling their operations.'

At this point he actually chuckled.

'No need to blanch, Miss Todd. We won't be parachuting you into Burma to face the Japs. No, the work we'd like to see you doing is purely office work. Translations, typing up reports in both English and Tamil, working with our Intelligence officers in Kandy.'

'In Kandy?'

'That's right. You'll be required to move to Kandy within the coming week.'

'Where will I stay?'

'Let that be our problem. All will be arranged. But one thing you have to know: this is all absolutely confidential. Nobody, absolutely nobody, must know what you are doing. We will arrange a civilian job for you as a cover, and that will be your excuse for giving up your Colombo job. Not a word to your uncle and aunt, or your Kandy friends – I believe you have quite a few.'

I nodded. 'Yes, I went to school there.'

'And absolute discretion while on the job. No private conversations. If you recognise any of your colleagues as a former acquaintance of yours, you must ignore the fact and treat him or her as a stranger. Is that clear?'

I nodded. 'Perfectly clear.' A frisson of excitement ran through me. It was as if I was being drawn into the secret nub at the very core of the war. I would at last be playing a role in bringing down the Japanese. Maybe a small role, but a role nevertheless. One tiny but essential cog in the machinery that would end this terrible war. Just knowing that I was wanted, that I'd been chosen, gave me a much-needed lift. I returned home that evening filled with instructions, and with a new-found confidence that gave me wings.

Chapter Thirty-Four

As Mr Henderson had promised, the following week I was sent to Kandy in a chauffeured vehicle to start my new job. When I spoke to them on the phone, Aunty and Uncle were delighted that I'd be closer to home and could, presumably, visit them frequently.

I was told to keep it vague if anyone asked about my work; that a frown combined with the generalised term 'war work' was usually enough to let people know that my work was confidential, which of course was true. I was told to drop the name 'Lord Mountbatten' now and then into my conversations, and hint that I was working for, or even with, him. In fact, I didn't know it then, but just at this time plans for the invasion of Burma were being made in the Botanical Gardens at Kandy, and Lord Mountbatten himself lived at the Swiss Hotel there, though I never met him.

In fact, my workplace was in quite a different part of Kandy. It seemed to be an abandoned office building of some sort, nondescript and rather run-down from the outside. It had a main door opening on to a busy main road, under a sign that said Kandy Financial Strategies. There were two other entrances accessible from a side road, and that was where I was told to enter. Security was tight; a uniformed guard stood inside each door and inspected our identity documents, each and every time we entered.

On my first day I was escorted up a staircase and along an endless corridor whose bland walls were interspersed with several doors on both sides, all without signs except for two, near the end, with the signs Ladies and Gentlemen. My escort was a tall, thin, uniformed security guard who did not speak a word, but opened one of the doors and signalled for me to enter. Which I did. The door closed behind me.

I found myself in a large office divided into two parts; this first part was obviously some kind of reception room-cum-secretary's office. Grey filing cabinets lined the walls and a large desk was set in the middle, on which a typewriter sat in place of honour before a rather cumbersome office chair. Was this to be my office? Very different from the typing pool I had worked at before, down in Colombo! A door to the next room stood open, and through it I could see an even more imposing desk and a tall man just rising from it, and striding towards the door to greet me.

I couldn't believe it. I almost rubbed my eyes in incredulity. It couldn't be – it was impossible – but it was true!

I almost screamed, 'Pa!', but before the word could exit my lips he had placed a finger on his own lips and I remembered the first law of my new job: absolute discretion, and if I ever recognised anyone, not to show that recognition. But Pa's eyes twinkled and all of a sudden a huge load was lifted from my heart.

It was all right. It had always been all right. *This* was what Pa had been doing from the start, and judging from the layers of secrecy that had been wrapped around even me, a very minor player in this game, I understood, all at once, that he could never have confided in me back then, in 1939. He had had no option but to simply disappear, even if it left me believing the worst.

I wanted to throw myself at him, let myself be taken up into his arms, let things return to the way they were before the war, but I knew that now, I had to take my lead from him, which meant playing a part, even when we were alone together. He extended a hand for me to shake.

'Pleased to meet you, Miss... Todd, is it?'

I smiled and nodded. He went on to introduce himself.

'I'm Mr Pemberton, and we'll be working together in this office for the foreseeable future. May I add that you were chosen specifically for this job, Miss Todd, due to your fluency on a native speaker's level of Tamil and typewriting skills in the same. I'll now explain a little to you of what your work will involve.'

And he did. It turned out that my task was quite simple – in theory.

'We have a leak,' he said. 'Somebody in one of the many army, navy and RAF bases, both in Colombo and Trincomalee, is a spy. Confidential information about Allied movements, especially at sea, keeps falling into enemy hands and we have to find out where the leak is, and who's the culprit, without alerting suspicion. We have to find the mole.'

While there were highly trained intelligence officers working in situ to do the extremely sensitive detective work, he explained, there were other ways of spying, and that was where I came in.

'Your job is a basic one: to read private letters, and see if you can find any clues as to enemy allegiance. Any clues at all. Anything pointing to things not being as they seem.'

'Private letters? How are we going to do that? Surely they just, well, pop them into a post box and then they're gone?'

Pa – or I should say, Mr Pemberton – chuckled. 'We have our methods,' is all he said to that. 'Now, we have many Tamil native speakers working in our offices, and that's where you come in. We suspect that there's an enemy cell in Madras working with our man – or woman – in Colombo. As you know, the Free India movement collaborates with the Japanese and there we have the nub of our theory – that information from Ceylon is being passed on to the Madras faction. I want you to read each letter we pass to you thoroughly and look for any signs, any oddity, anything that just doesn't seem right. You pass those on to me. I'll give them a more rigorous inspection. That's it in a nutshell, Miss Todd. I think you'll do a wonderful job.'

It was strange, having Pa call me Miss Todd; stranger still, the very situation in which I found myself – with the father whom

I'd imagined to be sitting in a cave somewhere in the Himalayas, actually at the nub of a British Intelligence operation. I had so many questions! Where had he been for the first few years of the war? Surely not in Ceylon? Perhaps in India, perhaps even in England? And why was I here? How had they known, to bring us together? Had Pa, somehow, been following my movements, known where I'd been the whole time? All of a sudden anything seemed plausible. But this was not the time to ask questions. It had been drummed into me: my role here was strictly confidential. No personal conversations, no fraternisation, nothing private whatsoever. We were colleagues and no more; I was his subordinate, not his daughter.

But all in all, I felt at once secure, and honoured and delighted. I had been singled out, given, it seemed, a promotion to even more sensitive work.

My accommodation had to be sorted out. But that was simple: a small hotel had been requisitioned and repurposed as a boarding-house for single working girls, all English, 'doing their bit': a staff residence, as it were. There we slept and cooked and ate together, enjoyed our free time. The girls worked not only for Force 136 but for various other British organisations in Kandy – we were a mixed lot. I shared a small room with a young woman from Birmingham, a pleasant enough person who worked in Lord Mountbatten's office, and very proud indeed of the fact. I was the only 'locally-grown' girl, as they called me – all the others had come over from England on ships, and a few had had problems adjusting to the climate and the culture.

On the whole we got on well; I turned out to be popular with the girls since, due to going to school in Kandy, I knew some nice little cafés and restaurants – though we could little afford dining out on our salaries – and even knew where to meet English men. Except, of course, that right now there was a dearth of men of the right age for these girls.

Life that year was dreary. One thinks of wartime intelligence work as exciting and full of intrigue, but I was no Mata Hari and really, all I had to do was comb through letter after letter written in English or Tamil, sometimes translate the one into the other, and file them away. I saw little of Pa, who was engaged in higher-level work, and only visited the office next door occasionally. I was never to find out exactly what he did; I just knew it was important. I wished that I, too, could do something important, groundbreaking, for the war; find some essential secret that would pull the plug on the entire Japanese secret service, bring it all down like a tower of matches. But it was obviously not to be. That final year, 1944, was, for us civilians hunkered down in Ceylon, the calm before the storm.

Chapter Thirty-Five

The months crept by, and the only brightness on the horizon was the news coming to us from home: we all clung to the BBC reports that yes, the Nazi era was coming to an end; it would soon all be over, at least in Europe. Here in Asia, though, the prospects were as grim as ever, and the atmosphere at Newmeads was bleak, in spite of Aunty's new-found role as a piano teacher to Kannan. I began to dread going home for the weekend; Aunty and Uncle were by now ghosts of their old selves, and seemed to be relying on me to perk them up. Pa helped me to get hold of a collection of recordings: Glenn Miller, Vera Lynn, the Andrews Sisters, which I hoped would lift the mood.

I placed them, one by one, on the gramophone, and indeed, the big-band sound of Glenn Miller brought a bit of life into the after-dinner vacuum that so often set on of an evening. Uncle actually stood up and asked Aunty to dance, and I laughed and clapped as he swung her about the room. That record came to an end and I placed another on the turntable. How foolish of me! I had not looked at the label and Vera Lynn's 'We'll Meet Again' blared out. Aunty let out a cry of agony, pulled herself from Uncle's arms and rushed off to her bedroom. I ran after her and was right behind her as she flung herself on to the bed in a virtual avalanche of sobs.

'We'll never meet again! I'll never see them again!' she wept. Internally, I wept too. I wept for Freddy, for Graham, for Andrew. For the hundreds and thousands of lives lost, in Singapore, in Burma, at sea, in the air. Bombed and torpedoed and tortured by the Japanese. I did not weep for Victor. I loathed Victor. He deserved all he got. Thank goodness I would never meet him again. But for everyone else, I mourned, and that record, in all its sentimentality, brought out the tears as never before.

Aunty refused to even have 'We'll Meet Again' in the house, so I took the record back with me to Kandy on Sunday and offered it to the girls, who loved it. Three of them had sweethearts fighting in Europe; all had brothers, fathers, acquaintances in peril. All of us had known boys and men who'd fought and died. We cried together, played that record again and again; it evoked such bitingly sweet pain, the kind of yearning pain that gouges itself into your very being; a keen agony that, though it hurts, you inflict on yourself again and again.

There was also a cinema in Kandy that, for a couple of hours each time, took us all into a different world, a world in which we could forget the bleak times in which we lived, sweeping us up into the dramatic stories of *Rebecca* and *Jane Eyre*; making us laugh until our bellies ached in comedies like *The Man Who Came to Dinner* and *The Palm Beach Story*; yet the films that dug the deepest, and which we loved the most, were those that made us cry. Films that reflected our own pain and the uncertainty of our own lives: wartime films. *For Whom the Bell Tolls* and *Casablanca* were everyone's favourites. We loved to cry.

I tried to persuade Uncle and Aunty to come to Kandy to the cinema. I thought a laugh-out-loud, belly-splitting comedy would do them both good; but they refused, and in the end I realised that they didn't want to laugh. That laughter during such a time, a time when sons were being blasted from the skies in fireballs or bayoneted through the stomach in a Burmese jungle, just wasn't appropriate – at least, not for parents in deep mourning. These were insights that I, as a young girl with little life experience, had to learn for myself. I had to learn to be Uncle and Aunty's emotional caretaker.

*

The one little light in my life – apart from being reunited with Pa – was that my relationship with Usha had been resuscitated through a lively exchange of letters. Usha had by this time completed her nursing training and was employed at the Christian Medical College Hospital in Vellore, which was by now one of the very best hospitals in all of India. She worked on the men's ward, attending to casualties, sometimes casualties of war. Usha had evolved and matured so much in the last few years; it was evident in her letters.

I actually envied her: now *she* was the better-educated one. I still longed to train as a doctor, but at this time it just was not possible; whereas Usha had not only qualified as a nurse but was working as one. I was proud of her; and yet my own 'unfinished' status certainly prickled. But I put my ever-slinking-in envy to one side: it was an unpleasant side to my character that I vowed to overcome. This wasn't a competition. I was happy for Usha, but also sad for her in another respect.

She was in agony due to the son she had lost. Luke, she said, was well taken care of in Father Bear's orphanage. She had tried with all her might to tear him from her heart; he was a child of rape, a child she should not love. But she did.

'I cannot help it!' she wrote, and I could feel her bitter tears between the lines.

> I know I signed him away when he was born, but I cannot sign him away from my heart. He is there, Rosie, and he will always be there. Sometimes I sneak away and visit the orphanage, and watch him over the fence, at play with the other children, and I feel as though my heart would break. I know he can never be mine – but he IS mine, and always will be! He cannot help the method by which he was placed in my womb. I might hate his father but I cannot hate him, try as I might. I know it is wrong to hope he is never adopted, but that is indeed

what I hope; because that's the only way I can, one day, make myself known to him. When he is an adult.

Concerning Andrew, she was optimistic.

'He is not dead!' she wrote. 'If he were, I would feel it in my heart. I would know. I know he is alive, and will return to me. We are one entity. He will come back.'

I did not ask her what she thought his reaction would be, finding out that his own brother had raped his beloved. She seemed to assume it would not be a problem. But then, Usha knew very little about the ways of men. I also knew little (and what little I knew came from novels), but I knew that, when it came to other men sharing their women, they were complicated. Nevertheless, I tried to share Usha's hope that Andrew was alive; that the 'Believed Captured' part of that terrible telegram was true; that he was being held by the Japanese as a prisoner of war and would, one day, return to us safe – and be reunited with Usha. What Aunty and Uncle would say to that was anyone's guess, but I assumed they would prefer a living Andrew, even with a native wife, to a dead one. I could only hope and pray for a good outcome all round.

And I still mourned Freddy. Deeply, totally. I still hoped that he, too, would emerge alive from the conflagration and return to me. For a happily-ever-after. But I had none of Usha's confidence, none of her inside knowledge that the man I loved was alive. I only had my hope.

Christmas 1944 was a sorry affair at Newmeads. We didn't even go through the motions of celebrating, and Aunty and Uncle did not go to church on Christmas Day, for the first time in their lives, nor did they listen to the usual locally recorded Christmas service on the wireless. They both seemed to be sinking deeper and deeper into a black hole, and it seemed my duty to pull them out as far as I could. But I couldn't. They were too far sunk; and instead of taking the hand I reached out to them, I felt they were pulling me in. It is hard to be around some people. But I was all they had.

And all *I* had was Pa. Even though we maintained the charade of being supervisor and employee, even though he always formally addressed me as Miss Todd, there was something strong between us. He was my anchor, my lifeline. In him was a rope I could cling to. And once again it was the eyes that kept me grounded, his eyes. It was as if he could read me like a book, see my despair, and with a single glance pull me out of those dark depths. I wished I could invite him to Newmeads to perhaps provide a little lift to Uncle and Aunty, but that was out of the question, and in the end all I could do was organise a Christmassy lunch on the day. There were no presents, of course, let alone a tree or carols or Bible readings, all regular elements of a normal Newmeads Christmas.

And so, 1944 came to a dreary end and bled into 1945. Whereas the war in Europe was drawing to a definite end, there was no sign of a ceasefire of any kind in Asia and it seemed to all of us that it would continue month after month, year after year, with only more deaths and more mourning, and no future for any of us. The lights had all gone out, and there was no reason to ignite them again. No hope.

Part Three

The Aftermath

1945

Chapter Thirty-Six

And then, seemingly out of the blue, news bulletins started coming over the airwaves, and the news was all good. This new year was different. It was to be a year in which we clung to the wireless to hear of one event after the other taking place far across the world, in a war-torn Europe finally freeing itself from Hitler's grip. From month to month, our hopes grew as one bulletin after another reached us. Surely, with the war in Europe so near to closure, Asia would follow suit? Surely, if Hitler was losing, the Japanese, too, would be forced into surrender? We could only hope – and cling to the wireless, buy newspapers, read each story a hundred times. Every month, some new victory.

At the end of January, we heard that the German army was on retreat back into Germany. It was the beginning of the end. Then, in early March, British and American troops crossed the Rhine and later that year, the bomb that would turn out to be the last of the war, a V1, fell on Berlin.

And then it all happened so quickly: the capture of Vienna by Russian forces; in April, the news that Hitler himself had bunkered down in Berlin. And then, at last, on 30 April: Hitler himself was dead, along with his new wife, Eva Braun. Both had committed suicide by taking lethal capsules.

May was a month of glory. First, Berlin surrendering to the Russian Army, and then one surrender after the other until, at last, Nazi Germany was no more. And on 8 May, at last: Victory in Europe Day.

Oh, what a day that was! I knew very well that Uncle and Aunty, though obviously relieved, would not be in the mood to celebrate, but I certainly was, and so were the girls, and, given the day off work, we all made our way down to Colombo because that was where the action was.

We were young and vibrant and filled for the first time in years with exuberant joy. We were swept along on a tide of effervescent elation; hugged and kissed by strange soldiers on the street, swung around at this party and that, laughing and giggling as we kicked up our heels. We stayed at the Cinnamon Gardens flat, ten of us Kandy girls, though it may have been more, hardly sleeping, for two full days of partying.

And then it was back to Kandy, back to work, but now there was a new lilt to our steps, and our faces were set in permanent smiles because we knew, we felt, that the tide had turned in Asia too and victory was in the air, and it had been going on in tandem with the events in Europe.

And so it was. Month after month, new victories to be celebrated, just as in Europe. First, the three-day bombing of the island of Iwo Jima by American forces, and, days later, the landing of US forces on that island and the raising of the US flag on the summit of Mount Suribachi.

On 1 April, American troops had taken Okinawa, the last island held by the Japanese. One of the bloodiest battles of the Second World War had come to an end. The Japanese commander of Okinawa's defence – I won't even honour him by mentioning his name, which I have anyway forgotten, just as it will be forgotten by history – committed suicide rather than surrender. That was the beginning of the end for the Imperial Japanese Army.

I found it hard to rejoice over what came next – I can never rejoice over the death of innocent civilians – but it did mean the end of the end.

Once again, I heard the news through Uncle, who was forever glued to the wireless, day and sleepless night.

The call came early on the morning of 6 August.

'Rosie!' he shouted down the phone, which almost vibrated with his excitement, 'the war's over! Over!'

'Over? What do you mean? Has Japan surrendered?'

'Not yet but they soon will! They dropped the bomb, Rosie! The atom bomb! Remember I told you about it? It can wipe out a whole city at once, and that's what's happened! They dropped it on Hiroshima. The Americans. The city was flattened. The war's over.'

A shock wave ran through me. 'The city – flattened? By a bomb?'

'Yes, yes, the atom bomb!'

'They dropped a bomb on a city and flattened it?' I still could not grasp the enormity of it, the horror.

'Yes, Rosie, are you hard of hearing? The city – gone. It's all dust now.'

'Men, women and children – civilians? Wiped out?'

'Rosie! What's wrong with you? Don't you realise what this means? It means it's over. It's all over. Japan will surrender now – guaranteed.'

'Yes, yes, Uncle. I understand now.'

I replaced the receiver, stunned. Was the news that the war was over actually good news when it came at the price of thousands of people, innocent people including children, all dead, wiped out in seconds?

An estimated 200,000 people died in Hiroshima. Later, amid the celebrations of Japan's surrender, I continued to be stunned. Had mankind entered a new and very, very dangerous era, with this capability of killing hundreds of thousands, perhaps millions, of innocents with one stroke? It certainly gave me pause and I longed for a philosophical discussion with Pa, but of course that was not to be; not yet.

On 9 August, another US bomber dropped another atomic bomb, this time on the Japanese military port of Nagasaki. A further

200,000 innocent deaths. Again, I could not rejoice, though Uncle did so wholeheartedly.

And finally, on 2 September, the news we were all desperate for: Japan had surrendered.

The celebrations, this time final, began all over again: Victory in Japan Day in Colombo was like no other. The city went wild! For the second time that year, the girls and I descended on Colombo and joined in the festivities. The place swarmed with soldiers; we all had five of them on each arm! I put away my shock at Hiroshima for the time being and simply celebrated.

Oh, how we danced and frolicked! The joy of those days of celebration can never be described; it bubbled over like a bottle of shaken champagne when the cork pops out. It was exquisite. The weary years, the years of dread and hopelessness and grief and sheer waiting, waiting for an end that never came: they rolled off our backs and faded into nothing because the end HAD come and we had lived to see it. And even those of us who had lost loved ones for a while buried our sorrow and instead rejoiced in the fact that there would be no more wasted lives, no more senseless killing, no more young men coming home in coffins; or else never coming home, their bones lost on foreign soil, or sunk to the bottom of the ocean.

It was all over. And it was time to pick up the final pieces. Time to face difficult truths about our boys. Time to return to the dreary everyday. For us, it was back to Kandy; for me, back to that grey office where the only light was the possibility of seeing Pa now and again, and exchanging a cheeky wink or a twitch of half-smile.

The war might have been over, but it was as urgent as ever to unearth those traitors who had tried to undermine the Allied effort, and Force 136 would carry on as before. And there was always that file of private letters from those suspected of betrayal that had somehow been intercepted and sent my way.

One day I found a red flag. A tiny one, it is true, but a red flag all the same.

It was sent by a clerk named Ralph Baker who worked in the Colombo office at Pembroke College where I, too, had worked before my transfer to Kandy. I had met him on one or two occasions; we had not worked together in the same office, but we had now and then crossed paths and I had found him a pleasant enough middle-aged man, quite nondescript, really, with his receding hairline, thinning mousy-brown hair and thick spectacles. Not somebody you'd pinpoint as a spy. He had been in the Indian Civil Service before being transferred to Colombo a year ago; he had an English wife and three children, whom he had not seen since the beginning of the war. Mr Baker's family lived in Delhi, where he'd lived with them before the transfer. He wrote to them regularly, and in a very slow process that, I believed, involved the clandestine interception of personal letters, discreetly opening them, making copies, resealing and then delivering the originals as addressed, and passing the copies on to our office, I was sent his file; a file of letters dating back to the previous year. I had reached December 1944.

I read one of these letters, and frowned. I read it again, and felt a twinge of something. It was just… odd. It did not make sense. I picked up the letter and walked down the corridor and knocked on a door with no sign on it.

'Come in,' called a voice, and I entered. Pa, sitting at his desk, looked up and smiled as I entered.

'Miss Todd!' he said. 'What can I do for you?'

'Good morning, Mr Pemberton. It's just this letter. There's something not quite right about it.'

He gestured with one hand for me to sit, and held out the other hand for the letter. He read it, and frowned.

'I see what you mean,' he said, and began to read. '"Once again, I must spend Christmas without you, without my family. I cannot tell you how much I miss you and the children. I want you to know that I'll be right there with you when you celebrate on Christmas Eve. Little Matty is too young to understand, but I'll be imagining the light in Annie's eyes and James's when the bell tinkles and they know the Christ Child has arrived. Even writing that, I feel a shudder of excitement. How I wish I could be there in person, lighting the candles on the Christmas tree, seeing the joy radiated on their faces..."'

'That's not an Englishman,' I said. 'That's not an English celebration, or an Indian one.'

Pa looked up and his eyes were grave. 'It's a German custom,' he said. 'The Christ Child comes on Christmas Eve and delivers the presents. Well done, Miss Todd. Leave this with me.'

I left that office with a swing in my step. I might be only a little cog in the wheel of the war machinery, but in my very tiny way I had – it seemed – helped to shine a light into one of the dark corners of the underground tunnels that reinforced the enemy. To know that I had helped capture one of those who had lived in those shadows – well, it delighted me.

A few weeks later it was all revealed, and Pa told me the results: Ralph Baker was, in fact, the son of Ralf Bäcker, a German citizen who had married an Englishwoman and moved to Liverpool at the end of the nineteenth century. Herr Bäcker had anglicised his name and taken on British nationality, becoming Ralph Baker, and had managed to keep a low profile before the First World War. He had sincerely tried to integrate fully into English life, but had maintained a few German traditions after his move to England. He had also always spoken German to his children, so Ralph junior was, secretly, bilingual.

Ralph senior was entirely loyal, a patriotic Englishman to all appearances, and volunteered to fight for the British. But he had been captured early and sent to a transit camp, a *Durchgangslager*, where this first massive wave of prisoners were incarcerated and redirected to their individual detention camps. Thus he came to a transit camp for Allied prisoners of war at the former Europäischer Hof in Karlsruhe. This camp was known as the 'Listening Hotel' by the inmates; it was a camp devoted to Nazi intelligence collection.

At the Europäischer Hof, to save his own skin and in the hope of gaining for himself better living conditions, Ralph Baker senior made his German roots known to his captors. He was nevertheless sent to the internment camp at Brandenburg, where he served out his time before being released at the end of the war. But his cultural roots, and his allegiance, were known to German Intelligence.

Ralph junior trained as an accountant, led an inconspicuous and solid life, married an Englishwoman, founded a family. But like his father before him, Ralph kept a few German traditions alive; traditions that were so ingrained in him he didn't even realise they were German, not English; thus the German Christmas tradition of the Christ Child bringing the children presents on Christmas Eve. His English wife had adapted to this custom; it was normal in their family, and so he had innocently spoken of it to his wife in their correspondence.

In 1939, at the start of the war, German intelligence agents tracked down Ralph junior and recruited him. At the time, it seemed highly likely that Germany would win the war and Ralph let himself be recruited out of fear for his family. It was as simple as that.

Now, he was caught, arrested, interrogated. He confessed. He had indeed been sending, via coded wireless, information as to British naval manoeuvres in the Indian Ocean to the enemy. I had played a part in his uncovering. That gave me a lift. I had felt so inadequate; while the three boys I'd grown up with were out there, risking their lives, sacrificing their lives, here was I, safe at home and in the office, sitting at a typewriter. I often discussed this with the girls; sometimes we argued into the night.

There was no need for my guilt, they tried to persuade me. We women back home were a necessary part of the war. It was vital to keep the 'home fires burning'; necessary to maintain a solid foundation to the world the boys were fighting for; for them to actually be fighting for something, for a sane world they could return to, a world kept functioning and running as smoothly as possible by us: the women, and older men. We provided hope and solidity and continuity. We should not undermine ourselves. We were important, just as we were. There were no inferior jobs.

And in the end I had to agree. But the capture of Ralf Bäcker remained a special feather in my cap. I had removed one tiny but vital screw that had held together the Japanese war machine; the war might be over, the information now not as vital as it would have been two or three years ago, but I had helped unearth a spy. It felt good.

Chapter Thirty-Seven

September 1945

Work continued much as usual; we were winding up the war machine, and that took time. But now, new information was flooding in, information about what had happened to the men we'd lost, and one day Pa burst into my office, his face flooded with delight.

'Rosie! Rosie, darling!' he exclaimed. These days everybody was more relaxed and we no longer bothered to uphold the charade; he addressed me as Rosie, I addressed him as Pa. I looked up from my typing; immediately I saw his expression I sprang to my feet, heart racing. I could tell something momentous had happened.

'What, Pa?'

'It's Graham! Graham Huxley! He's alive!'

'No! I mean, oh my goodness! How? Where? How did you find out?'

'I put in a special request to someone I know at the Red Cross in Colombo – top brass. Gave him the names of the Huxley boys and asked him to keep a watch out, let me know if anything – good or bad – turned up. Graham's name has been found on a list of prisoners kept in Changi Prison, in Singapore. He's alive, Rosie, and he's coming home!'

'When? Oh, Pa! That's just…' I was speechless. Tears pricked at my eyes and my heart felt full to bursting; it was as if a huge cloud of relief and gladness that I'd been storing within me surged through my whole being. I simply rushed to Pa, let myself be enveloped by his open arms. I'd not even known I'd cared so much for Graham;

I'd clearly held my grief in abeyance – but now my gladness made up for that suppression.

'We have to tell Aunty and Uncle! At once!'

'Of course! Come along to my office, Rosie, and you can tell them yourself.'

There is nothing grander in life than being able to tell parents who'd believed a child dead that he is alive. Their joy reverberated through the telephone line; we shouted at each other, 'He's alive! Yes! He's coming home!'

'But when? When?' screamed Aunty over the line.

'I don't know! We just have to wait,' I screamed back. And then it was Uncle's turn and Pa spoke to him.

'According to my information,' Pa said, 'after the unconditional surrender prisoners of war from all the Japanese camps, Burma and Malaya and God knows where else were brought to Singapore. Now there are about 17,000 men congregated in and around the Changi jail compound, most of them needing medical treatment of some kind. It's only because Graham's a medic himself, and so on the staff lists, that we found his name. I can imagine it will take time for them to release him.'

For several minutes, Pa talked to Uncle but then it was me and Aunty again, Pa grinning at me from behind his desk, but finally my euphoria calmed down and, myself grinning from ear to ear, I replaced the receiver.

Now it was just a matter of waiting.

By this time I was feeling a little overly optimistic. If Graham could return from the dead, why not Andrew? Why not Freddy? Not even from the dead, but from captivity.

Graham had been *Believed Killed*. Both Andrew and Freddy had been *Believed Captured*. Surely *Believed Captured* was less serious than *Believed Killed*? Surely if Graham could survive, then so could

Andrew and Freddy, my thoughts went. I hoped. I prayed. It was all I could do.

We all went down to Colombo to receive him, Uncle, Aunty and myself. We were to spend the night at the Cinnamon Gardens flat. By this time, Eileen Grantley and her daughter Pamela had already moved out; they had received the devastating confirmation that Mr Grantley had been one of the unlucky ones: he had not survived incarceration in Changi Prison. His wife and daughter had boarded a ship to take them back home the previous month. It had been a sad farewell. Now I was alone in the flat, and Graham, it had been decided, should first come here to reunite with his parents – and me – before making the long and winding trip upcountry. I refused, however, to go down to the dock to meet him: that was clearly something that only his parents were entitled to – I would not intrude on such an intimate moment. I would wait for them back at the flat.

In spite of their insistence that I be there, I did still feel decidedly odd. This was not my place, not at all. If I'd been a real sister, it would have been different – but I hardly knew Graham; he'd always been that grand thing, a doctor, the culmination of my own ambitions, a bit like royalty to me. That one morning at the waterfall had normalised our relationship somewhat, as had the encouraging conversations we'd had thereafter; yet I'd never quite got past my rather childish hero-worship of Graham. We were not on the same level, as far as I was concerned.

How astonishing it was, then, when the emaciated, limping, wasted figure of Graham walked in the door behind Aunty and Uncle and he literally barged past his parents and hobbled towards me in a half-limp, half-sprint, and, before I knew it, I was in his arms, in a tight embrace, and he was shuddering with… with what? I didn't know, I couldn't understand it, but he was, indeed, shuddering, and if I hadn't known him better, hadn't known him for a sensible, solid, rational man, I'd have thought he was sobbing. And all I felt was gladness; a lovely warm wash of gladness that swept through me in a wave. We stood like that for what seemed ages. I have no idea what Uncle and Aunty thought of that reckless and totally incongruous embrace, inconsistent with everything they'd known about our relationship. It seemed they dispersed, taking what little luggage Graham had to his room and then vanishing into the kitchen to prepare drinks. I only know that when we separated again, Uncle and Aunty had gone. Graham took me by the hand and led me to the sofa and we both sat down, and he held on to my hand, and said to me, 'Rosie, Rosie. Rosie! My wonderful, wonderful girl!'

You could have knocked me down with the legendary feather. Since when was I his wonderful girl?

Chapter Thirty-Eight

I wasn't sure if it was just my imagination, but Aunty seemed rather reserved towards me for the rest of that day and during the journey home the following day. In fact, she did not once address me in that whole time. I put it down to overexcitement due to Graham's miraculous return. All of her conversation was directed towards Graham; she ignored me, completely, not even greeting me as we sat down for breakfast but chattering away excitedly to Graham.

Yes, the old Aunty was back. Over the past two months she had anyway made a miraculous recovery herself, ever since she had taken on Kannan as a pupil.

And such a delightful pupil he was. A bit of Andrew, in that he seemed to have a natural gift for music, and a bit of Graham, in being utterly steadfast in learning, and doing so in a disciplined and consistent way, applying himself most diligently to all the more boring aspects of his subject, such as practising scales and musical notation, both of which Andrew detested.

In addition, Kannan seemed to have simply pushed a button in Aunty's psyche, one that said *open sesame*, and almost overnight she was a different person, getting out of bed of her own accord, taking pride in her physical appearance, eating breakfast and other meals at the table with her husband and, if I were there, with me, engaging in conversation (as long as it never touched on either war or her sons) and even directing Sunita in her household tasks. And as ever, we got along famously; she was ever-warm towards me, as if I really were a daughter.

Her seeming coldness towards me after Graham's arrival thus was unexpected; but after all, this was a son practically risen from the dead and so I did not take it personally. But that evening I began to understand: there was more behind it. In all these months since her return and the end of the war she had not had any guests. Not a single dinner party, not a single tea-party; neither had she attended any such event. But that very first evening back at Newmeads, who should be invited to an elaborate dinner but the Carruthers family: her dear friend Evelyn, Evelyn's husband Frank, and their daughter Gwen.

And that's when the penny dropped. Aunty had for years made no secret of the fact that she thought Graham and Gwen a perfect match, and this dinner, it seemed, was designed to seal the deal. Gwen herself, an extremely pretty young lady whom I was sure could take her pick of suitors with very little effort, appeared flushed and enervated during the meal, chattering away about life in South Africa and what great fun all the single girls had had, despite the dearth of eligible young men, and what parties they had attended, and what a pity there'd been a war on to spoil the fun. I personally found it all a bit insensitive, to be exulting about parties and missing young men when one such young man, who had *actually* returned from hell, was right there, opposite her at the table. But Gwen, a conventionally pretty girl with fair hair in ringlets, was oblivious and chattered on, with very little discretion, practically offering herself as a prize on a golden platter.

Evelyn, as I'd found out during the time she was taking care of Aunty's emotional health in South Africa, was an eminently sensible lady with her head firmly screwed on to her shoulders, but, it seemed, she had a blind spot where her daughter was concerned and was as keen as Aunty to negotiate this match. She beamed at her daughter throughout the latter's chatter, as if her words were made of gold. Aunty, too, did all she could to applaud Gwen.

'Gwen and her mother were such a help to me throughout my ordeal during the evacuation!' she gushed. 'I don't know how I would have got through it all without the two of them – dear Gwen was a particular consolation to me – almost like a daughter!' She reached for Gwen's hand across the table and squeezed it, and the two smiled at each other as if harbouring a great and intimate secret – this, after Gwen had made such a speech of how pleasurable her stay in Durban had been.

I shrank back into my chair as she said this, but then reprimanded myself. I noted a bit of jealousy in my response – because surely I, too, had helped Aunty, after her return home especially, but also in liaising with the Carruthers family in the first place, to help mitigate the shock. But Aunty ignored me throughout the evening and, I have to say, it hurt. But I had to deal with that, and the little pricks of self-pity evoked by what I felt was the unfair centring of 'dear Gwen'. I scolded myself: *jealousy does not become you, Rosie!* I thought, and tried to be more generous towards Gwen. Perhaps she *had* been of enormous help to Aunty in South Africa – how was I to know?

Yet it was all so obvious, this matchmaking and elevation of Gwen to improbable heights; *too* gauchely obvious. Everyone understood except Graham himself; his manners were as always impeccable, but, unless he was a perfect actor, he seemed utterly oblivious to the hints dropped and the most unsubtle inferences made by the two mothers and the young lady in question – including, to my astonishment, a direct suggestion by Aunty that Graham should invite Gwen to the looming Christmas Ball at the Planters' Club in Kandy. Even I was embarrassed by that and by the lack of delicacy on her part. But Graham handled it with extraordinary grace and tact. He smiled at all three ladies looking at him with such eagerness, and with the utmost poise and charm said, 'I'm afraid I wouldn't be much of a dance partner for Gwen – my poor right leg is in absolute shambles. I can barely hobble my way across the room! She'll be much better off with a fully intact escort.'

'Oh, but there's such a dearth of young— Oh!'

Evelyn yelped in mid-sentence. It was perfectly clear that Frank Carruthers, sitting next to her, had pinched her thigh or some other concealed body part, as he coughed ostentatiously and barged in with '…but I thought that nice young man from Kandy, you know, the manager of the Royal Hotel – such a fine young fellow! – has been keen to take you, Gwen? Haven't you accepted yet?'

'Oh, but…'

But Frank grabbed this distraction and ran with it. It seemed that for him, at least, the clumsy attempt by the three ladies in question to partner off Gwen with Graham was an embarrassment, and he now launched into a veritable homage to that particular young man, one of the few of fighting age who had not run off to war due to the fact that he was in a reserved occupation.

For me, the evening was exhausting, and that night when I went to bed I felt completely drained. I couldn't explain it, as I had spoken hardly a word all evening – indeed, hardly anyone had noticed me, except Graham, who every now and then had looked my way and smiled, and always I smiled back, but in a forced, unnatural way. I felt somehow depressed, and couldn't understand it. How quickly my elation at Graham's return had vanished.

Whenever I spent time at Newmeads the highlight of my day was always my dawn visit to the waterfall with my trusty bansuri flute. The waterfall was like a magnet, drawing me in, and playing to its clean splash against the rocks was always uplifting. So it was on the day after Graham's arrival. My sombre mood from the previous evening had not melted during the night and so I rose early, hoping that an early-morning infusion of pure, sweet music would help. And so I made my way through the woods to the pool. It was still quite dark, and very cool, so I wrapped up warmly in a Kashmir shawl and carried, as well as my flute, a warm woollen blanket to place on the cold rocks as a seat. I settled down on my favourite spot, unpacked my flute, warmed it with my breath, began to play, and in no time the clear, hollow, sweet voice of the bansuri worked its magic.

I felt lifted, realigned, restored. All the frayed and spiky bits of my being brought back into harmony. All the ambiguous and unexplained distress of the night before fell away from me, and, by some mysterious process, I was made whole again by sound; sound that came from without as well as from within me, sound that echoed from silence and seemed rooted in something majestic, magnificent, and made me majestic, magnificent. Sound that was so delightfully vibrant, strong, clear it captured me and made me, too, delightful, clear, strong, wiped clean of whatever it was that had stained me last night. I sailed on the breath of music, and I was whole, and beautiful.

At last I laid the flute on my lap and rested. I took a deep breath. As always, I had played with eyes closed, and now I opened them.

'Oh!' I said, and nearly jumped out of my skin.

It was Graham, sitting on a rock opposite me. And he was smiling.

'That was magnificent, Rosie!' he said, and his voice was almost a whisper.

'Thank you!' I replied, rather embarrassed at having had an unseen audience. 'Have you been here long?'

'I've no idea!' he laughed. 'When you play, time just seems to vanish. I feel as if I've been here forever. As if you're permanently installed in this place – as if you are a part of it all.'

'Well, I always come here when I'm at Newmeads. Every morning.'

'I know. That's why I came.'

Silence fell between us as I pondered these words.

'You came – to hear me play?'

'Yes. To hear you play. You really are a miracle-worker, Rosie. Your music is healing. I came home with such wounds inside me and now I feel as good as new. Almost as if there'd never been a war.'

'Oh! Oh, that's a lovely thing to say. Thank you.'

'And it's true.'

'Thank you.'

What else was there to say? Nothing. We sat in silence for some time. I closed my eyes again, savouring the sense of pure happiness I felt, an unexplained happiness that was complete in itself. And then he said, 'Rosie?'

I opened my eyes. 'Yes?'

'I also came to see you. Alone.'

'Oh!' was all I managed, for the third time that morning. A lump rose in my throat, a lump I tried to swallow, but couldn't.

Another silence, filled only by the rush of water.

'Rosie?'

'Yes?'

'Will you marry me?'

I could not have been more shocked if the Japanese had dropped a bomb right there, beside me. I gasped aloud and I must have looked a fright, the way I gaped at him.

He chuckled. 'I'm sorry to just come out with it like that without a preamble. I don't know, I'm just no good at all this courting business, at being coy and flirting and taking it slowly and gradually. I only know it's all I want. It's all I've thought about for years, months. I've known it since the last time we met and… well… I know it's probably crude of me to just blurt it out like that. I ought to win your heart first, shouldn't I? That's the way it's done. I'm afraid I'm not a very romantic fellow and don't know much about courting rituals. But I do know, absolutely certainly, that you're the one I want. So why not just tell you? I know you've never thought about me in that way. But couldn't you start now, just with a tiny thought of it, and work forwards from there? I do love you, you know. I really do. Loving you, I think, has kept me alive. And I need you to know that. I love you, Rosie. And nothing would make me happier than for you to love me too.'

'Oh, but...' What could I say? I was shocked to the core. Never, in all my life, had Graham entered my thoughts as my future husband. Because of Aunty's matchmaking I had considered both Andrew and Victor, and had rejected them both for different reasons. But Graham? Not even Aunty had suggested him as a suitor. I had the feeling she'd be shocked. Especially after last night's debacle.

I couldn't speak. I could hardly breathe. All I could do was shake my head slowly.

Graham's face fell. 'It's no? You won't even consider it? Is there someone else? I know... I know Mother had been trying to pair you off with Victor – she can't help but talk about these things, can she? Were you in love with him? Had you two reached an understanding? Are you still grieving? But, oh, Rosie! Life goes on and—'

'No, no, no! It's not Victor! It was never Victor! Aunty was mad to even suggest it!'

He breathed out audibly. 'Yes! Because you're far too good for Victor. Andrew, then? He was Mother's other choice for you. She seemed to want you as a sort of healing salve for one or the other of them. Victor, the bad boy, Andrew the dreamer: you, the sensible one who might save them. I know you and Andrew were close—'

'No, no, Graham. It's... it's not Andrew. It's not either of them... it's... it's not...'

Just at that moment a brain-fever bird burst the dawn silence with its nerve-racking cry, loud – it sounded as if it was just behind us, in the forest beyond the waterfall – raucous and utterly unhinged. And I remembered Freddy's remarks about that wild cry of desolation: *Where's my love? Can you imagine, losing your love and being so broken-hearted you can only cry out with such utter torment: where's my love? Where's my love? Where's my love?'*

And I had lost my love, and since the day I had learned of Freddy's disappearance my own heart had been crying, as desperately as that bird now shrieked: *'Where's my love? Where's my love? Where's my love?'*

Now, I could not help it: I wept. I wept for Freddy, profusely and bitterly, more so than I had ever wept, slowly shaking my head, and murmuring to Graham, 'I'm sorry. I'm so sorry. I can't, I just can't.'

But I had to pull myself together. He deserved a coherent, unemotional answer. So I sniffed, and wiped my eyes with my hand, and once again, just like the last time, Graham pulled out a handkerchief and I dried my face properly. Why was it that both times Graham and I met here at the pond I had cried, and both times he had handed me his hanky? He must think me a proper ninny, I thought, but then I said, 'Oh, Graham, thank you so much. Those are the nicest words anyone has ever said to me. You're one of the best people I know. Thank you so much for considering me. But, you see, it's just that… I need to explain. I can't, I just can't…'

I sniffed and blew my nose loudly into his hanky in a most unladylike manner, and then I said, looking straight at him, dry-eyed and as candidly as I could: 'There is someone else, Graham, and I can't even consider what you asked. Not now. Not till I… not till I know.'

'Ah,' he said, and nothing more. The brain-fever bird launched into its cry again, mild at first, then spiralling out of control, louder and more frantic with each new sequence, and it was all I could do to control my own cry of desperation, in tandem with the forlorn bird.

We sat there for a while, neither speaking. The water plunged over its rock and the splashing, gurgling, flowing sound it made was somehow soothing, comforting, smoothing out my frayed feelings and, hopefully, allaying whatever disappointment I might have caused Graham. There was something so companionable about our silence; no urge from either of us to break it. It was as if the breakage of my own heart was somehow, slowly, undergoing an operation of some kind, an invisible surgery that could be felt but not seen. A silent commencement of healing. No longer the searing, desolate agony of not knowing where Freddy was or what had happened to him, but a kind of acceptance. Acceptance that whatever his fate, my own hurt would not help but only my *overcoming* of hurt. As if my own healing might, in some mysterious esoteric process, help him. Wherever he was. Dead or alive. In a way that the constant nurturing of my inner wound could not. This was an insight that dawned on me slowly, as the two of us sat there doing no more than listening to the waterfall.

And then a new insight dawned on me. I picked up the bansuri lying across my lap and began to play again. My fingers danced lightly over the flute and my breath entered it and my very spirit, my entire being, poured itself into that long hollow reed and the music that emerged was something so exquisite, so fine, so searing in its fragility, so ephemeral and yet so eternal – it lifted me out of my pain and I knew I had reached a turning point in whatever it was that bound me to Freddy. It was the antidote to the delirium of the brain-fever bird. A melody so exquisite it gave me goosebumps; a melody that came not from me but through me, a melody I could not claim as my own; bittersweet, poignant, transcendent. As unique and as evanescent as a rainbow. I did not compose it, could not claim it as my own. It was its own.

The music came to its end. I lowered my flute and met Graham's gaze, and it was good, so good. He smiled, and then moved to get up. 'Shall we go and have breakfast?'

I smiled too, and nodded. He reached out a hand and pulled me up. Together we walked back to the house.

Chapter Thirty-Nine

That haunting music stayed with me all day and lifted me completely out of the melancholy I had felt previously, echoing on in my heart long after I replaced the flute case on its hook on my bedroom wall. Graham and I enjoyed breakfast together with Uncle and Aunty, and after that, I retired to the back veranda with a book. After a while, Graham joined me there. I put my book down and we talked.

It was as if he had never proposed to me, and was not the least affected by my rejection of his proposal. Talking to him seemed so natural. Our talk drifted naturally to Andrew, the brother we still all hoped had somehow survived. Graham's own return to us had, of course, renewed all our hopes for Andrew, confirming that anything was still possible. The bonds of war were slowly loosening and some names had not yet filtered through, names of survivors, names of losses. All we could do was wait.

'Andrew is such an unlikely soldier,' I sighed. 'He should never have gone off to war. He should have stayed here and helped Uncle. But nobody could have stopped him.'

'Andrew has a stubborn streak,' Graham agreed. 'But I believe there was a girl involved this time.'

'Yes.' I paused. 'Usha.'

'Usha.' He thought for a while, then said, 'That's the Tamil girl, yes? The one he claimed he was going to marry?'

'That's her.'

And then it all came out. Oh, the relief, to speak about her and Andrew to someone who not only knew them both but would not condemn them, vilify her, blame him, condemn them both! I had been carrying this burden alone for so long. Not only the burden of their forbidden love; the burden of her pregnancy, his shock, her faithfulness. Her rape.

I had to tell Graham what Uncle had told me about what Victor had done. It was a load too heavy for me. Sharing it would not only relieve me of a great weight, but give me the chance to discuss the consequences with someone who would not condemn Usha, as Uncle had done. I knew in my heart that Graham would be fair. And indeed, he was.

'What a despicable… what a cad!' he spluttered. 'I can't believe that a brother of mine would do a thing so appalling!'

'Victor is not a very nice man,' I said. 'He was always a bit aggressive, and being in the war for so long seems to have only made him worse. He was very rude and callous to me as well. Made some totally tasteless comments.'

'War brings out the best in some people, and the worst in others,' said Graham. 'It creates heroes – but also criminals.' He shook his head in frustration. 'That poor girl! Have you kept in touch with her? What's she doing? How is she? What about the child?'

I told him what I knew. 'The little boy is well cared for in an orphanage near Vellore,' I said. 'He must be about four now. And she's actually done well for herself. Usha was always a bright girl, and she's now a qualified nurse.'

'How does she feel about the child?' Graham asked then.

'Well, understandably, as a consequence of the rape she tried to reject him,' I said. 'To cast him out of her mind. But she tells me it's just not possible. She's still his mother, he's still her child. She says she thinks about him day and night, goes to the orphanage to stand outside the fence and watch him play.'

'Heartbreaking,' Graham said. 'And he's my nephew! I'll have to look into it, whether or not Andrew returns to us.'

'But even if Andrew *does* return, we don't know how he'll react when he finds out the story,' I replied. 'Men are – men can be funny about that sort of thing. You know, jealous.'

He chuckled wryly. 'Says a young lady who's an expert on men!'

I sniffed. 'I read a lot.'

'Well, you may actually be right about Andrew. He's the very opposite of Victor, isn't he? Oversensitive, if anything. This great love of his might not survive the real horror of knowing his beloved's been raped, by his own brother, and given birth to a child.'

'But it's a lot better than believing she'd been unfaithful.'

'Better for him, maybe. Not better for her. But we need to do something. Victor's dead, so she can't press charges. But that child – left to grow up in an orphanage. How terrible. When all this has settled I must go to him. I'd like to meet her, too, if possible. She deserves help.'

We were both silent for a while. Then Graham said: 'Rosie, would you come with me to India? To visit them both – the child, what's his name? – and Usha? I think I need to do something. Make sure they're both all right. I feel a sense of – of duty. Would you do that?'

'Luke's his name, and I'd love to!' I said at once. 'But, you know, you don't really have a duty.'

'I do. Just as Victor would have had, had he survived. Being a father, if only in the physical sense, is a responsibility, and since Victor's not alive then we, the family, have to look out for Luke.'

I realised right then and there that Graham was the best of the three brothers. The best of the Huxley family. That he would make some woman, one day, a fine husband. Had I been foolish in turning him down outright? And for what? For an experience years ago that had lasted less than an hour; for a man I'd known less than three days; for a man who was, in all probability, dead?

*

For the rest of that day, I thought about these things. I thought about Freddy, my feelings for him. Even if he had survived, I wondered; even if he returned to me; even if we could continue where we'd left off, was I not being a bit of a foolish, sentimental girl, the kind of lightheaded girl who, in Aunty's novels, invariably fell head over heels in love with the dashing stranger who turned out to be a rake; which every reader, myself included, could see from a mile away so that you shouted in silence at the heroine to 'give it time, get to know him! Beware!'

Shouldn't one get to know the man one had chosen, before declaring him 'the one, the only one'? Was passion, head-turning, once-in-a-lifetime euphoria, enough foundation for the long term? I began to doubt, seriously doubt. To wonder…

And so I was relieved when, the next day, Graham himself brought up the subject. He had not joined me that dawn at the waterfall, and I'd been curiously disappointed. I enjoyed having him as an audience, revelled in his appreciation of my playing. Before now, I'd always only played for myself. It had been wonderful to play for him, to know the music that came from my heart touched his.

Now, as we once again sat in the wicker chairs on the veranda, Graham said, out of the blue, 'So, Rosie, would you like to tell me about this *someone else*?'

I must have looked shocked, because he chuckled. 'Well, you know. I'm curious. Who is this rival of mine, vying for your hand?'

I blushed and felt warmth spread through me. It was so lovely, hearing him speak of himself and Freddy in those terms. As if he was somehow the rejected suitor; and yet not defeated by rejection, but keeping his sense of humour about it. No wounded pride, just unassuming dignity. I liked that. And perhaps Graham was the last person on earth I should confide in about Freddy, but – well, he might be the last person but he was the *best* person. There was no one else who might be able to help me sort out what I really felt, what I should do; I knew instinctively that whatever I said about Freddy, Graham's thoughts on the matter would always be fair, impersonal, not clouded by his own private stake in the matter.

'He's a friend of Andrew's,' I began. 'Andrew brought him to visit when they both had leave, back in 1942.'

And then it all poured out. Right from the beginning. The immediate magnetism between us; the edging towards each other climaxing in that magnificent, utterly spontaneous, physical union beside the waterfall, a union so otherworldly to this day, years later, it reverberated in my mind as the epitome of love; the apex of love's expression. Nothing could ever equal that.

And after that, the silence between us; a comfortable silence, a silence born out of the knowledge that there was nothing more to say. And then goodbye. And then: the news of Freddy's disappearance.

'I see,' said Graham. 'And you feel you must be loyal to that experience of love. Love with a capital L, so to speak. Whether or not he's alive.'

'Yes,' I said. 'Because, Graham, what if he *is* alive, and thinking of me? Clinging to that memory, and it is that that's keeping him going, keeping him alive, even? Just as you said the memory of me kept you going while you were clinging to life in Changi? What if?'

'Indeed! It's true that just a thought, a memory, of a sweetheart can be a lifeline to a man clinging to life. And it speaks so much for you, Rosie, that you know this and are staking your whole future on it.'

I felt he wanted to say more, yet the silence lingered.

'I feel there's a *but* in there somewhere. Some reservation or other.'

He shrugged and gave a grunt of acquiescence. 'You're right. There's a *but*… But…' Here he grinned, 'I'm not going to say any more. As a man with a stake in the outcome of this story, it's not my place to speak out.'

'Oh, but I'd like you to! I value your judgement, Graham!'

'Sorry, no. It's not my place. But I do have one question…'

'Yes?'

'You said he's from… South America?'

'Yes. British Guiana.'

'And he has family there?'

'A large family. He's one of eight brothers, he said!'

'So, Rosie, assuming the best of outcomes, and he comes back to you, and you marry – will you move to South America, or will he move to Ceylon?'

I was silent at that. He had caught me out. This was the one stumbling block in the narrative I kept running in my head. The scenarios I painted for Freddy and myself: they always ended with our glorious reunion – the two of us, flying into each other's arms. Sometimes, a vision of a wedding, me in a white gown, flowers everywhere. But a life together: where we would live; the reality of what would happen then… I invariably blocked it out.

Now, I said, rather stuttered: 'We'd cross that bridge when we came to it.'

He seemed to accept that. He nodded. And then, out of the blue, he struck the final below-the-belt blow: 'When I was last here, Rosie, before I went off to war, before you met Freddy, you were so keen to start studying medicine. I do hope that you don't abandon that plan – you'd make a wonderful doctor.'

And with that remark I was completely and utterly floored by Graham Huxley. But he must have sensed my utter discombobulation, because he fielded it smartly by leading directly into a change of subject.

'Father told me how much you helped Mother overcome her depression,' he said. 'He said you simply gave her a meaningful task that distracted her from her worries. It's that kind of sensitivity to the needs of others that makes a good doctor. You have it. I've always noticed. It's what I love most about you. Mother appreciates you too, even if she doesn't always show it.'

And hearing that, I glowed. Praise from Graham was a wonderful thing.

Chapter Forty

But the glow was short-lived. A slight stroking of the ego was not enough to smooth away the waves of doubt, the surges of questions that crashed against the certainty of my love for Freddy. Because yes: what I had experienced with him was doubtless extraordinary; doubtless a coupling of souls, of spirits, of whatever it is that makes us human, had occurred in that short space of time. But would it be enough – even assuming he had survived the war unscathed, returned to me ready to pick up where we'd left off – assuming, in other words, the very best of outcomes – would it be enough to sustain us through a lifetime together? Was it enough of a foundation to build a marriage on? Is a perfect physical union, one so complete that it includes a spiritual union, an indication of a perfect future together, bestowing maturity, perseverance, patience, strength; all the things I knew by now were vital to the quality of a marriage?

One thing I knew for sure: in the days and years before I met Freddy, even as a young girl inexperienced in the nuances of love and romance, I would have poo-pooed that very notion. How I had rolled my eyes at the sentimental nonsense spouted by the girls I'd known, when they sailed off into baroquely vivid descriptions of the feelings evoked by whichever young swain had caught their fancy. How I had reasoned with them to hold the reins of their emotions tightly, so as not to gallop off on unicorns into rainbowed pastures. How I had argued with Andrew, trying to convince him that no, what he felt for Usha could never, ever be love.

I was the sensible one. Wasn't that, after all, the reason why Aunty had thought I'd be a good match for either Victor or Andrew?

I was the 'good' girl, the one on the straight and narrow, the one with her head tightly screwed on, not likely to be captured by an over-flamboyant imagination. I'd have been a 'cure' for either of her younger sons. (Her oldest son, obviously, did not need such a 'cure'. She had other plans for him. A more light-headed sort of girl, judging by her choice of Gwen.)

But I had fallen. For Freddy. If my life were a novel, I'd have derided *that* development as being completely out of character. Artistic licence taken a step too far, I'd have said. But in this case, life had imitated art; the impossible had happened, reality captured and overthrown by an extravagance of inner experience I could never have imagined, not in my wildest dreams. Human consciousness is indeed a miracle. What depths are hidden within it, depths we cannot even begin to be aware of? My union with Freddy was of that extraordinary calibre.

I could not deny the uniqueness of that depth. It had happened. But was it enough? And – as Graham had intimated – was it enough to vanquish my one-time burning desire to become a doctor? And I realised now how much that very ambition had faded in tandem with my obsession with Freddy. And yes, it was an obsession. And an obsession, no matter what its object, is not healthy.

I pondered these matters. Turned them around in my mind. Turned them inside out and back to front. And I found, to my astonishment, that I was not as captured by my obsession as I'd thought. I found myself taking a step back, away from the mental situation of 'Rosie loves Freddy'; observing it as if I were a neutral entity, a scientist looking at an interesting microbe, for instance, or a doctor examining a wound. I placed distance between me and the thing, the 'Rosie loves Freddy' thing. Not judging, just observing. But in the very act of observing, I felt the obsession fading, growing weaker, its grip waning.

That night I tossed and turned, plagued on the one hand by a compulsive need to cling to Freddy, a need made complex by various intruding emotions such as guilt, habit and sheer loneliness; not to mention a newly discovered need to be that woman, that loyal, long-suffering beloved who stays true to her soldier-man through thick and thin; whose faith keeps him alive; whose very strength of devotion is the vessel that will bring him through. Yes, that is the vessel I had clung to. A self-enhancing, self-indulgent vision of myself.

I found it impossible to confront Graham at this time. I had to think this through. It was too complex, and the self-enquiry required needed to be without influence of any sort. Graham confused me. I needed space.

When I returned from my dawn session at the waterfall, I was, therefore, relieved to find that Aunty and Graham had had an early breakfast and then gone out for the day. Aunty had left a note for me: they had gone to Kandy, where they'd be meeting up with Evelyn and Gwen. They planned some shopping, and lunch at the Club. I was grateful. A day to myself was just what I needed.

I decided that what I needed right now was prayer. I would have cycled to the usual chapel, but discovered that my bike had a flat tyre. Bother! And then I remembered another place of peace: a small shrine, just a fifteen-minute walk from Newmeads on a side road between the main Colombo–Kandy road. It was a Hindu shrine, to the elephant-headed god Ganesh, and Usha had brought me here a few times. I'd never felt odd, worshipping in a Hindu temple; Pa had shared his belief with me that all religions were only paths leading to the same universal power we call God; and that all worship was in essence the same: a yearning of the self for inner peace, and love, and security; and that all prayer, no matter to whom it was apparently directed, was at its core a plunge within for peace.

And so, dressed appropriately, I walked down the Newmeads drive and turned in the direction of the main road. Finding the shrine, I removed my shoes and stepped inside. Someone had been here shortly before me; a few sticks of incense still burned in their holder before the stone effigy, releasing white tendrils of smoke curling upwards, filling the close air of the shrine with an intensely sweet sandalwood fragrance. And flowers, marigolds and jasmine, were arranged at the statue's foot. It was quite large, the effigy, the elephant head being as big as the pot-bellied body, its trunk reaching down to curl in its cross-legged lap. Usha had explained to me that the gods of Hinduism weren't really gods in their own right; they all represented only aspects of the single power known as Brahman, and provided comprehensible paths to something that was beyond human comprehension. Ganesh, for example, represented the removal of obstacles.

I placed my palms together as Usha had taught me, closed my eyes and dropped to the stone floor of the shrine, where I sat, cross-legged, settled back against the wall. And prayed. Prayed with all my might that all obstacles, all the heavy, unbearable burdens that had settled on my shoulders, on the family's shoulders, on our country and on the world itself, might be removed. Burdens I was incapable of carrying. In my mind I lifted them up and placed them all in greater, more capable hands; and gradually, slowly, something shifted. It was as if I had stepped on board a train, bearing that unbearable burden, and set it down; and the train continued as ever, bearing both me and the burden. That deep sense of unburdening slowly, gradually settled into a deep inner peace. This was what I had sought. I settled into it.

Two hours later, renewed and restored, I was walking back home along the narrow main road when an army truck overtook me. To my surprise, it stopped, and a rather dishevelled-looking man got down; someone inside the truck handed him a crutch, so his back was momentarily turned to me. The truck drove off, and he turned round and began to hurriedly hobble towards me. Even now, with his face hidden beneath a heavy beard, his clothes – khaki shorts and a faded blue shirt – hanging limply and loosely on a tall, bone-thin body, I didn't recognise him. Yet somehow the ragged figure lumbering towards me reminded me of Graham as I'd first seen him only days before, when he had stepped into the Cinnamon Gardens flat and rushed to embrace me. Except that Graham had been clearly Graham, his face not half-concealed by a ginger beard, as this fellow's was. But then, this fellow, too, propelling himself in a shambling half-run, half-limp towards me even as the truck drove off, called my name: *Rosie! Rosie!*

And then I was in his arms and it was Andrew, and my heart was bursting with joy, just as it had burst days before on Graham's return. It was too much to bear – I had no words; I fell into his embrace and let myself be transported by the utmost relief and gratitude and I knew the meaning of the word grace because that very thing flooded through me with such vigour and such power that I was lifted up by *it*, and it was a joy beyond description.

Andrew was home again.

Later, after a meal and a bath and a shave and a change of clothes, Andrew was ready to talk. He came out to join me on the veranda, almost tripping over a delighted Flopsy, who was curling around his legs.

'I don't understand,' I said. 'Pa had lists – Red Cross lists, army lists, Changi Prison lists – he combed them all for your name. He found Graham, but not you.'

'I know,' said Andrew, lifting Flopsy on to his lap. 'I didn't make it on to the lists – not in my real name. Somewhere along the line, maybe when somebody with atrocious handwriting was transcribing the name from my dogtag, someone else transcribed that scrawl as Haxley instead of Huxley. And since then I've been known as Haxley. I was in hospital, unconscious, for months, so I couldn't object. Nobody realised. I didn't even know it myself until they were doing a roll-call on the ship and I wasn't on it, and the chap they called Haxley, A. was nowhere to be found. Anyway, here I am.'

'And how are you, Andrew?' I asked. What a stupid question; I'd asked it out of polite British convention and already I knew he wouldn't give the conventional 'I'm well, thank you!' answer. It was obvious: this wasn't the same Andrew I'd known, the carefree, handsome, healthy young man whom I'd known almost as well as I'd known myself. This man was almost a stranger. An uncomfortable silence slid between us. And then he said: 'I'm a wreck, Rosie. A total wreck. I've been half-dead for months, unable to even open my eyes. And that's just my body...'

'Oh, Andrew!' was all I could sigh. I didn't nudge him further. He'd tell his story, what of it he was willing and able to tell, later. There was no hurry.

We sat, now, on the wicker swing on the veranda, before us, on the table, a jug of nimbu pani and slices of mango as well as a variety of Ceylonese snacks. It was plain that Andrew needed feeding up, and Sunita – who, it seemed, had forgiven him completely for his transgression with her daughter – was happy to supply sustenance of all kinds, coming out again and again with a plate of something new and even more delicious than the last. Andrew helped himself as he told his story.

'I've been working on the railway,' he said. 'The Burma Railway. Hell on earth.'

I had heard rumours about the Burma Railway; Pa had informed me of the 258-mile railway connecting Thailand with Burma, under construction since 1940 by the Empire of Japan to supply troops and weapons in their Burma campaign. Pa had told me how appalling the conditions were for Allied prisoners forced to work on it; they fell like flies, he claimed once the information reached Intelligence. He had, of course, checked those lists, too, for Huxley sons.

'It was hell on earth,' Andrew repeated, 'I'll just leave it at that for now. I'll tell you all, when we're all together again,' he went on. 'I don't want to go through it twice, I want to hear *your* news. Any news of Graham, Rosie? Of Victor? Did they survive? How's Mother? Is she back from South Africa?'

I laughed at his eagerness. And told him the good news first: that Graham, like him, had returned from captivity, had survived.

'He came home just three days ago,' I told him, and related a little of Graham's war journey. 'We couldn't believe it – we had given him up for dead. And you too, Andrew, almost. Aunty will die and go to heaven when she comes home and finds you here!'

'I can't wait to see Mother,' said Andrew. 'And Father. I'll go over to the factory later and surprise him.' He paused. 'And Victor? He didn't make it?'

I shook my head. 'No. Victor's plane was shot down. He's dead, Andrew.'

A moment of silence descended on us as Andrew digested this news. He did it dry-eyed but obviously intensely moved. He and Victor had been so close as boys. Victor had been his hero, the big brother he'd looked up to.

Then he gulped, audibly, as the terrible news sank in, buried his face in his hands. I placed a comforting hand on his back, let him have his moment of reflection. He was holding back the tears, I knew. But then he shuddered, as if physically pulling himself together, and said, 'It's what we all expected, isn't it? That Victor would be the one to go. Of all of us, he was the one who took the most risks. Although on the other hand you'd almost expect him to be the one to survive, to cheat death.'

'Victor challenged death every day from when he joined the war,' I said. 'He held up a red cloth to the bull of war, and said, *take me if you dare.* I think he thought he could get away with it. His bravado wasn't just empty air – he really thought his name was a sort of lucky charm.'

Andrew nodded, and I thought, *yes, Victor really had believed he could get away with anything. That regular rules and laws, even the rules of life and death, didn't apply to him. That he could take what he wanted, without consequence. Even Usha.*

As if he could read my thoughts, Andrew broke the silence. 'And Usha?' he said. 'Have you kept in touch with her? Where is she? What happened about the baby?'

And *that's* when tears came to his eyes. 'I can't forget her,' he said. 'I loved her throughout. Through every ordeal, through every agony. Even when I had no hope, when I thought I couldn't go on, I thought of her and somehow I found the strength to carry on. I don't care what she's done, I just don't care. I love her, Rosie. And I just can't believe she betrayed me. But it doesn't matter. I love her. And if she still loves me… I must go to her, tell her that.'

I hesitated. Should I tell him what Victor had done to his beloved? No, I couldn't. *Not now*, I thought, it wouldn't be right, so soon after the news of Victor's death. Let him mourn in peace first. And anyway, it was not my secret to tell.

But then another thought: *He had to know what had happened to Usha. Usha had to be exonerated.* It was enough that he knew what had happened to her, not who had done it. Not today. Not while he was still mourning his brother. It was enough that Usha's faithfulness be known to him.

And so I said it: 'Usha didn't betray you, Andrew. She was raped.'

Andrew gasped. 'What? No! Who did it? How? When?'

'It happened at that house,' I said. 'Plantation Somerset. Soon after you left.'

'But how? Who? I'll kill the bastard!'

Fat chance, he's already dead, I thought to myself, but aloud I only stuttered something about a house-guest being the perpetrator, and not knowing all the details. Thankfully I was spared any further explanation by the familiar crunch of wheels on gravel.

I jumped up. 'They're back!' I cried. 'Andrew, Aunty's back! Come on!' I leapt down the veranda's low staircase, ran to the car and flung open its rear door.

'Aunty! Aunty!' I cried. 'He's back! Andrew's back! He's alive!'

Aunt Silvia almost fell flat on the driveway in her haste to get out of the car; she shrieked his name as I helped her to her feet and then they rushed to each other, Andrew hobbling on his crutch, Aunty sobbing as she ran, open-armed, towards him; and then they were together, her arms cradling him, swaying him, rocking him as if he were a tiny baby while sobbing and crying his name, again and again. Tears pricked my own eyes, and something tender welled up within me. I felt a hand on my shoulder and looked up. It was Graham, who had left the car and walked up beside me.

'Now that's a sight I'll never forget!' he said, smiling down at me. 'Mother and son reunited.'

'It's a miracle!' I said.

Aunt Silvia , dissolved in tears, kept sobbing: 'The second son come back! My baby!'

She clung to him as if she would never let him go, swaying back and forth.

Later that day, Andrew went over to the factory to let his father know the good news; his homecoming was far too precious an event to relate by phone. Graham drove him to the factory, and Aunty went too – it seemed she could not detach herself from Andrew for even a second.

That evening, after dinner, we heard the story Andrew had been saving all day so that he could tell us all at once, just once, and would never have to speak of it again. Later, he described it as pulling a smouldering coal out of the fire, red-hot to the touch, searing the fingers. It had to be done, he knew; the door to that horror had to be opened that night, to give us all a censored glimpse, before he slammed it shut forever, locking it, throwing away the key.

'It was absolute hell on earth, that railway,' he said again. 'Beyond imagination. We – my group of prisoners – had to carve a way through the jungle and prepare the ground for the next group, who would lay the rails. We had a camp, but, well... It was just a clearing, mud floor, no protection against the rain. In the jungle, in the horrible dense, stinking jungle. Few of us survived. If fever and septicaemia didn't get us, the Nips killed us. They killed us as if we were flies, a nuisance. We lived basically in miserable hovels. We had no tents, no nothing. They gave us a little rice to eat and that was it. I never want to eat rice again, Mother. Don't ever serve it at a table if I'm there.

'The worst of it was having to carry the heavy teak trunks we'd felled to the improvised sawmill to make sleepers. Backbreaking work, but if you were slow or faltered the Nips beat you, kicked you, forced you to just carry on even if you couldn't.

'I don't know how many diseases I got. Beriberi, pellagra, dysentery, malaria, dengue fever, blackwater fever, tropical ulcers – you name it, I've had it.'

'I'll take you to Kandy Hospital to get you checked out,' said Graham, concerned. 'It was the same in Changi.'

'So many died! So many!' Andrew carried on. 'And you know what? The worst of all was carrying a dead body to a grave where he'd be buried without ceremony, without a prayer or a hymn, without his parents or his sweetheart knowing. Reduced to a corpse, an empty destroyed body, all hopes and dreams extinguished.'

Andrew began to cry, then. I could not imagine what he had gone through, how he had suffered. His mother slipped onto the sofa next to him, placed an arm around him. Flopsy, too, tried to comfort him, patting his face gently with a paw. That only made him cry all the more.

Graham said, 'The trouble was, the Japs had so many prisoners of war – thousands and thousands – they didn't know what to do with them. They were totally overwhelmed – where to put them? How to maintain them? So they invented these terrible and useless tasks just to get rid of them. They *wanted* their prisoners to die in their thousands. They torpedoed ships carrying mothers and children, just to get rid of them. They made them suffer just so they'd die, just to get them off their hands. Ships raised white flags of surrender, and still they were bombed. The camps were absolute chaos, men getting sick and dying like flies. I was one of the lucky ones. The only reason I survived was that as a medic I had it slightly better than the others.'

Andrew continued: 'They were convinced they'd win. You can't imagine the cruelty, Father. It's a different cruelty to the Nazis, I've heard. Hitler's methods – that was a premeditated brutality, a coldly planned thing. Japanese viciousness was more brute savagery unleashed on a spur-of-the-moment impulse, here today, gone tomorrow. You could be beaten mercilessly by a guard one day, the next day he'd offer you a cigarette. But towards the end of the war it got better because they knew they were losing and would have to face an international court.'

Andrew stopped crying and blew his nose on a handkerchief his mother had supplied. 'Towards the end I was such a wreck I couldn't even walk, couldn't talk, couldn't think. I was a living corpse. I didn't know the war was over and didn't care. After Japan surrendered I was taken to some hospital camp, Tamarkand Bridge, I found out later. I came back to consciousness for a while; I was on a makeshift cot in an atap hut. A sunburnt Englishman wearing nothing but white shorts came up to me and told me everything was going to be all right. I didn't believe him. I don't even know what I had at that point. I kept falling in and out of delirium. Pain all over my body, sores, an open ulcer. They told me I was out of danger but I didn't care. Frankly, I wanted to die. I stayed there for weeks and weeks. Months. I lost count. That's where the mix-up about my name happened; I didn't know that officially I was known as Andrew Haxley, because I wasn't conscious most of the time.

'They transferred me to another camp; a long train journey through Siam. Eventually I ended up in Changi. The war was long over but organising the thousands of PoWs, sorting them out and sending them back to wherever they'd come from – that took time. But now I'm here.'

'Home again,' said Aunty. 'Back where you belong.'

Flopsy patted his face again and once again he dissolved into tears. 'I want to go to bed now,' he said. 'I could sleep for a thousand years.'

'Sleep as long as you like,' said his mother. 'We'll be waiting when you wake up. You're home now. Safe at home.'

Chapter Forty-One

It was many weeks before Andrew was halfway himself again, and weeks more before he could go anywhere. On his second day home he suffered a mental breakdown. It was as if, having consciously and permanently locked the door on his ordeals, a thing hidden in the dungeons of his mind rose up in protest, pushing past the walls and veils and doors to invade the shallow peace he had found, to haunt and harass and torture him. He cried out as if in utmost agony; he writhed, screaming, on his bed; he curled up into a ball like a foetus, his face distorted as if he were holding back a scream of pure terror. Nothing we could do helped him, nothing we could say brought relief. Aunty, distraught, paced the corridor outside his room, brought him his favourite dishes, wept, stroked his hair, his back, his cheeks; he batted her away, yelled at her to keep away. I, too, went to him, but me, too, he rejected. I knew it was best to stay away; that it would pass.

It was Graham who, in his own way, helped. Graham simply sat in Andrew's room, in an armchair away from the bed, and waited, a glass of water on a side table beside him.

Around midday, Andrew, gasping as if dying of thirst, demanded water, and Graham handed him the glass. After that, Andrew slept.

'What did you do?' I asked when Graham emerged from a room now silent.

'I gave him a sedative,' he said. 'It will take some time, but he will eventually get past this. We must be patient, and not try to force him.'

It was wonderful to see Graham's care for his little brother. The two in fact hardly knew each other. Graham had already been at boarding school in England when Andrew was born, and apart from a handful of trips to Eastbourne with his mother, Andrew had not known him as a child; then, as adults, they had only met on a few occasions between the time Graham returned to Ceylon and the outbreak of war in 1942, when both went off to defend the Allies.

Over the next few days, Andrew slept. He woke and cried and, eventually, came out in his pyjamas and, unshaved and unkempt at first, slowly, gradually, made his way back to the land of the living.

Under Graham's supervision, both he and Andrew were slowly built back up physically, thanks to Sunita's cooking and vitamin supplements Graham ordered from Kandy. They both attended physiotherapy sessions in Kandy once a week; both needed it. At home, Graham led Andrew in daily exercises designed to restore his lost muscles. They went swimming, and running up and down hills, cycling. Both put on weight, and by the end of the second month both began to look like healthy men once again.

During this time, Graham and I became closer. We had so much to say to each other. It was good, so good, to have a true friend, someone with whom I could share my every last thought, my doubts, even my dreams. Graham did not judge. I could tell him anything, everything; things I'd normally share only with a close female friend, without shame, without embarrassment. I could speak to Graham about Freddy without evoking the slightest hint of jealousy, in spite of knowing of his attachment to me. He truly tried to help me navigate through my doubts, my sense of loyalty, my need to simply do the right thing. Graham understood that I could not open myself up to a future with him before finding closure regarding Freddy.

'It sounds awful,' I said, 'but even to know he was dead would be better than this hanging in limbo. Because what if he were indeed to return, just as you did, just as Andrew did, only to find out I had given up on him? What would you have done, Graham, in that position?'

'Frankly, I don't know,' he replied. 'But I'd like to think I'd be man enough to understand. To understand that you cannot wait forever, holding on to a vague hope. I'd like to think I'd be noble enough to accept that you have a life to live, and to wish you well in whatever decision you'd made.'

And I knew, even as he said the words, that that was exactly what Graham would do, no question; but he was too modest to lay claim to such a high-minded reaction. And I knew I was a fool to cling to Freddy; and not even to Freddy, but to the idea of Freddy, the memory of Freddy, which I now had to make an effort even to keep alive. I knew that the only sensible thing to do was to let go, move forward, understand that here before me was the sort of man I'd never even imagined would come my way, and he was waiting for me, and he understood me as no man ever had, and no other man could. What more could I wish for? With whom else could I ever build a future? And if I had not experienced the same passion with Graham as I had with Freddy – for the long term, what use was passion anyway? Here today, gone tomorrow. Just as it had been with Freddy.

I also knew that I loved him. Had always loved him. Loved him without knowing it.

And that love was more, a lot more, than a moment of passion. And yet…

Still, I clung to the memory of Freddy. Or else the memory clung to me, twisting itself back into awareness the moment I tried to cast it off. I could not disentangle myself. It was a question of guilt, of morality, of duty, even. I could not let go. Because: *what if Freddy came back?* It was like clinging to a phantom; an apparition, with no physical reality, yet as visible to me as if he stood before me. I could not strip him from my mind. I just couldn't. He was there, within my mind, as clearly as if etched into it.

'I need time, Graham,' was all I could say, and he nodded in agreement, and in patience.

In the meantime, he helped me sort out another aspect of my future: my application for medical studies. I hoped to start that very September, when the University of Ceylon returned to its full academic function. Thinking about this was a welcome distraction from both Freddy and Graham. It was a clear path my future could take, no matter what. Except... except. If Freddy did return, what then? Again and again, these doubts and indecisions plagued me.

The three of us, Graham, Andrew and I, spent hours getting to know each other again, each learning how much the others had changed, inching forward into new, solid and enriching relationships with each other. And one day, the unspeakable was spoken out. I had to say it.

'I take it you have no news of Freddy,' I said to Andrew, a question disguised as a statement.

He shook his head. 'No. But then I wouldn't, would I? How would either of us know anything?'

'Well, I asked Pa to have his name searched for among the various survivors. Changi, and the railway, and all the other camps. Nothing.'

'The people to ask,' Andrew said, 'would be his family. They'd know the latest, if there were any good news. His mother, in British Guiana. His—' He stopped abruptly, something rather strange in his eyes.

'What were you going to say?' I asked, when he did not continue. The sentence seemed unfinished.

Andrew sighed. 'I'm sorry, Rosie. It kind of slipped out. I have to tell you. It's unfair. I promised I wouldn't tell, but I have to.'

A chill went through me. 'Tell what?'

'I was going to say his wife. Freddy is married, Rosie. He's got a wife back home.'

I was stunned. 'Married! How can that be? He's so very young! You said he was sixteen when he ran away to war!'

'Yes – that's just it. They were both sixteen, childhood friends who fell in love and got married in haste when Freddy signed up. The whole hasty marriage was driven by her, apparently; he did it as a favour to her, to save her from her parents, to make sure she could live with his mother. He wasn't in a hurry himself. It was for her protection.'

'But… then why did he, with me, start…?'

I was beyond shocked. I couldn't even put a clear sentence together. My voice shook with devastation.

'You have to understand, Rosie. It was war and Freddy had lived through the most horrendous situations, bravely, and alone. For years, he had had no home leave, no one close to him, no one touching him lovingly. He was starved for love, for touch, and then *you* were there, giving him more than he could ever dream of. And this: he told me that he knew he had married far too young, and that if possible, he wanted to dissolve his marriage. He asked me not to tell you; you'd feel deceived, he said, and he hadn't meant to deceive you. He did… he does care for you, Rosie. It wasn't just ships passing in the night. He'd contact you if – if he were alive and able to do so, I'm quite sure of it. That's why I'm quite sure he's not alive. That he fell, and died, unaccounted for, in some remote Burmese jungle. I'm sorry to be so blunt but I think you need to know. He did intend to come back to you. But first, he was going to have to take care of things at home.'

I took a deep breath. In a matter of minutes, Andrew had swept away all my indecision and doubts, and I was not going to mourn Freddy one second longer. Yes, perhaps he'd had valid excuses for everything, but if I'd known, if Andrew had not kept his secret, how liberated my life would have been! I'd spent years yearning for a phantom that had never existed; Freddy had never been mine to pine for, mine to hope for. Another woman was doing that for him. All those selfless, self-sacrificing thoughts I'd been sending his way: he hadn't needed them, for he'd had them from her. Righteous indignation washed through me, dispelling every thought of Freddy along its way, as well as the very notion that this had been love. It hadn't. I gave a wry chuckle as the last of my illusions dissolved as mist in sunlight, so rapidly it was almost obscene.

'I'm sorry,' said Andrew now. 'But then again, I'm not really sorry. I hadn't known you'd been so obsessed with Freddy over the years. I thought you'd forgotten him. But Graham... Graham spoke to me.'

'Graham? Graham told you my secrets?'

'No, no, don't get upset. It wasn't anything like that. I was questioning him, you see. I could see the way he looks at you. It's most revealing, you know. And I asked him if there was anything going on between you, and he said no, you loved someone else. After that it was easy to see just who it was you loved. It didn't take much detective work. I guessed at once. Don't be cross with him, Rosie. I think you should... you should give him a chance. It would be a wonderful thing – for all of us! You'd really be my sister then, part of the family.'

'Hmmph,' was all I could say to that.

'And it would get Mother off both our backs. She's at it again, you know! She just can't help her matchmaking. She's on my back to court you, and on Graham's to court that Carruthers girl. She's secretly planning a double wedding for us.'

'I can't see her rejoicing if Graham and I— well, if anything were to develop between us. She's got loftier plans for him.'

Andrew made a dismissive gesture. 'Take it from me, he'll never marry that girl. He told me in so many words. He's just too nice to tell Mother outright.'

'And when she finds out about you and Usha, she'll have a fit!'

He shrugged it off. 'Can't help that.' He never spoke of Usha these days. 'But, Rosie, will you really not consider Graham now?'

I, too shrugged. This was all too private to discuss, before I'd sorted out and rearranged my feelings, cast the dead embers of what

I'd once called love from my heart, found the energy to ignite new ones. It was a path I had to walk alone.

And so, slowly, slowly, Andrew found his way back to himself, back to his feet, and his voice, and even his laughter; and to Usha. After five weeks had passed since his return, he was ready. He repeated the words he'd spoken on his first day: 'I must go to her, Rosie. Will you come with me?'

'Of course I'll come!' I said. 'I can't wait to see her again.'

I remembered that Graham, too, had wanted to travel with me to India, but to see Luke. But that was before Andrew's return, when we'd believed the little boy to be without a father. Now there was no need for his presence; Andrew and Usha would sort matters out themselves, and I would mediate if necessary. As far as those two were concerned, the path seemed clear. The next hurdle, of course, would be Aunt Silvia's horrified reaction, but, as Andrew declared, we'd cross that bridge when we came to it.

The night before Andrew and I left for India I said goodbye to Graham. Nothing had changed since my conversation with Andrew; he had not made any attempt to court me again, and certainly hadn't repeated his proposal of marriage. In fact, he was so much the friend, the brother to me, I'd started to wonder if he had in fact changed his mind and feelings towards me, just as I was beginning to change mine towards him. How ironic, if that was the case! Now, he took me in his arms and held me close, so close. I wanted to stay there forever. It just felt right; a wellspring of tenderness, of warmth, rose up within me, and a sense of a vacuum waiting to be filled – by him. I wanted him to kiss me, but he didn't. Finally, he chuckled and we drew apart, and he said, 'Bon voyage, Rosie, and God speed. I hope it all works out for Andrew. He deserves some joy.'

Don't we all, I thought. But aloud, I only said, 'Goodbye, Graham, and thank you for everything.'

Chapter Forty-Two

We went first to Shanti Nilayam, where we spent the day catching our breath after the long hours on trains, first up the Ceylonese coast from Colombo and then up the Indian coast to Madras. It felt like another homecoming. I realised then that Shanti Nilayam, even without Pa there to welcome me, was home in a way that Newmeads never could be – unless I married one of the Huxley sons and settled in there as the new mistress of the house; and the only Huxley son left to marry was Graham, who had no interest in the tea business and so would never become the heir to the estate. That could only be Andrew. And now we were on our way to sort that future out, in a way that would be most problematic for Aunty. But it had to be done.

At home we were, as usual, well catered for by Thila; and then off we went to Vellore. Andrew was visibly nervous. He had not written to Usha to let her know he was coming. I had wanted to write to let her know, but in the end thought better of it. I had interfered too much in these young lovers' story. Let them find each other in their own way. Let them write their own story. I did show Andrew Usha's letters, the words of confidence she'd written in her last:

'I know he's alive, Rosie! I would know if he were dead. I would feel it. It is a faith and I have to keep faith.'

Andrew had been overwhelmed. 'I think it's her faith in me that kept me going, Rosie. It gave me strength even across the ether.' And though he did not write, he kept that letter close to him, rereading it again and again; it was his main solace during the weeks of his recovery, and I believe a source of strength that helped to pull him back on to his feet. He would always have the scars of his captivity, always have a limp, but he had Usha's love, and that was his anchor. There were more hurdles awaiting him; would Usha tell him what his brother had done to her? It was up to her. I vowed to myself to stay out of it. Now, though, as we boarded the train from Madras that would take us to Vellore, he had his doubts.

'She has a different memory, Rosie. I'm no longer the healthy, strapping young man she once knew. Look at me, I'm a wreck! She'll be disappointed, I know it. That railway has aged me about twenty years. I don't know what to say to her.'

And I smiled and squeezed his hand and told him all would be well. Because I believed it. It had to be well. There had to be a happy ending for these two. Yes, there'd be a long and bumpy road ahead of them, but the worst was, hopefully, behind them. No, not hopefully. The worst *was* behind them, for what could be worse than the Burma Railway?

We had a hotel booked, but before that Father Bear, whom I had telephoned from Madras, met us at Vellore station and took us to his home in an ancient Morris Oxford. It was his first meeting with Andrew, and the two formed an instant rapport, Father Bear folding him into one of his big-bear embraces even before I could introduce them formally – for which there was then no need. I should have remembered that Father Bear had no use for pointless formalities.

He lived in a small, rather ramshackle bungalow in its own overgrown garden. He immediately apologised for the state of both garden and house. 'I've no time to do all this,' he said, waving a hand at the tangle of rose bushes that needed pruning and the bougainvillea hanging low, needing support. He turned the key in the lock and the front door creaked open.

'…and I'm my own maid and cook and not a very good one – can't afford a boy with me wee salary! You'll excuse the mess!'

The living room was shabby, the walls needing a coat of paint, the furniture old and worn, and a layer of dust lay on the sideboard and little dining table – and yet it all had an atmosphere, a sense of homeliness, as if imbued with Father Bear's huge personality. Andrew and I sat down on the flat and faded cushions of the two armchairs, and Father Bear, after serving us tea and Milk Bikis, plonked himself down on the third such chair.

'The reason I wanted to bring you here first,' he said, 'instead of taking you to the hotel, is because I'm after having a little conversation, to prepare you a little.' He looked at Andrew.

'Usha's a fine young woman,' he said. 'I've kept in touch with her over the years and she is – she's…' He held up a hand, thumb and finger touching in a sign that said 'top notch'. 'I know her story,' he continued. 'I know everything. She has converted to Catholicism and she's accepted me as a mentor. I know what happened to her. She's grown up past that and made the best of a bad situation. I know she loves you, Andrew, and has waited for you all these years. But there's one thing you need to know.'

He paused, looking from Andrew to me and back.

'You need to know that she has a child. And you are not the father. And she is not to blame for that child's conception: she has not cheated on you, because she loves you. But even more than her love for you, Andrew, even more than her faith in your survival, Usha has prayed for one thing: that she can claim her child as her own. The boy is a delight, a lively wee young thing, and very smart. She can't visit him, but she comes to watch him playing over the fence and she loves that boy more than anything. You need to know this, Andrew, because however you feel about that boy will affect how you and Usha can continue. You need to think about this before you meet her.'

Andrew was shaking his head slowly even before Father Bear finished speaking. Now, he said: 'I know. I know she has a child and I'm not the father. I know she loves that child. I know she's a mother and the child is innocent and she loves him and he's not to blame for how he came into being. If she will have me, Father – I want them both.'

Father Bear rose to his feet, pulled Andrew to his and gave him another bear hug, this time lifting him off his feet and swaying with him.

'That's what I wanted to hear,' he said. 'So, let's go.'

Father Bear had booked two single rooms for Andrew and me in a downtown hotel, where we went to check in and deposit our luggage. It was lunchtime by now, so we had a thali meal of rice and sambar in the hotel's restaurant, after which Father Bear drove us to the nurses' hostel where Usha had lived for the past few years. He knew her schedule, he said; she now worked night shifts at the CMC hospital, coming home at dawn and sleeping in the mornings.

'She'll be up and awake by now,' said Father Bear as he parked the car on the road outside the hostel. 'Rosie, you come with me. Men are not allowed inside the hostel – not even me, a respectable Catholic priest!' he guffawed, and continued, 'But you, Rosie, you can go in. Tell you what, don't tell her Andrew's here. Andrew, you can follow us and wait in the garden.'

The hostel was a rather sad-looking building that, like Uncle Bear's bungalow, could have done with a new coat of paint. It was a tall building, six or seven storeys high, with balconies out to the front from which hung items of clothing drying in the sun, saris of all colours draped in zigzags on cords tied to the balcony rails, sheets, pillowcases. At the front was a small garden with a seating area beneath a pergola covered in bougainvillea: a small metal table, three uncomfortable-looking chairs. 'Sit here, and wait,' Father Bear told Andrew, and, 'Come along, Rosie.'

Father Bear pressed a button on the front door, and soon the door was opened by an older woman wearing a nun's habit. She beamed when she saw him.

'Father Bearach!' she exclaimed, giving him his full name, a name I'd practically forgotten over the years. 'How good to see you! You look well!'

'And yourself, Sister Magdalena!' said Father Bear. He gestured towards me. 'Now this wee lass, she's an old friend of Nurse Ruth.'

I looked at Father Bear in astonishment. 'She changed her name when she converted,' he said. 'But she won't mind…'

He didn't finish what he was about to say because Sister Magdalena had already grasped my arm and was leading me into the building's hallway, chattering as she went. I turned and smiled at Father Bear still standing in the open doorway, giving him a wave to let him know I understood: Usha would always be Usha to me.

The sister led me into a generously proportioned sitting room, and gestured vaguely for me to take a seat. Around its floor were placed small groups of tables and chairs, where, it seemed, the nurses could receive their visitors. 'I think she's up. Probably still in the dining room with the other nurses, having her breakfast. I'll fetch her. What did you say your name was?'

'Rosie,' I said as I sat down. She nodded and disappeared, leaving the door open. I heard her footsteps clattering up a wooden staircase at the back of the hall.

After less than three minutes I heard them clattering down again, and voices, and then, there at the door, stood Usha.

'Rosie!' she cried, and flung herself into my arms. It was a reunion that brought tears of joy to my eyes; I had not seen Usha since I'd left her, a young girl, pregnant and worried, at Shanti Nilayam years ago. Now she was a woman, a mother, a nurse. A different being altogether, and it showed. After our warm embrace I pushed her away to behold her.

'Usha!' I said. 'You're more beautiful than ever!'

She laughed, and that made her yet more lovely. 'Thank you, Rosie, but you too have blossomed! How wonderful you look! How lovely to see you! Thank you for coming! What brings you all the way from Ceylon? Did you come to see Father Bear?'

So many questions! Instead of answering them all, I took her by the hand. 'Usha! Just come with me. I've a surprise for you.'

I led her into the hall, out the front door, into the garden. You could not see the interior of the pergola from the door. Usha let herself be docilely led across the scrubby overgrown lawn. We reached the pergola's entrance. Andrew stood up.

'Oh!' exclaimed Usha, and then no more words fell from her lips. A moment later, she was in Andrew's arms.

'Come,' said Father Bear, and led me discreetly out into the road.

Chapter Forty-Three

Andrew and Usha spent the entire afternoon getting to know each other – at last. Father Bear drove us back to our hotel, Usha having received permission from Mother Agnes, her superior in the hostel, who ran the institution rather like a nunnery. It was only after Father Bear had given his solid word that he would chaperone her at all times was she permitted to leave in Andrew's company. I was with him at the time, and I saw the wink he, Father Bear, gave the Mother.

'I have been *in loco parentis* for Nurse Ruth for many years,' he told her, 'and it is high time for her marriage to be arranged. This is a good boy of high-standing family,' he went on. Like many of the nuns, Mother Agnes – he told me later – had converted from Hinduism and understood that language, that tradition. She had nodded acquiescence. And so off we drove.

'The two of you need to talk things out,' he told Andrew and Usha, who were seated on the back seat holding hands, gazing into each other's eyes. 'Unfortunately, Vellore has little to offer in the way of parks or gardens you could stroll around, so we'll just return to the hotel.'

The hotel, called Broadlands Lodge, was, Father Bear told us, a former nawab's residence, built in the mid-eighteenth century. I'd already noticed, during our hasty check-in and deposit of luggage earlier in the day, that it had a certain old-world charm, reminiscent of a more genteel era when Indian royalty reigned supreme, an era of elephants and bejewelled, besworded, turbaned princes on magnificent stallions, and veiled princesses, swathed in gorgeous silks, swaying in howdahs on elephants' backs. It was in this now tree-shaded courtyard, Father Bear informed me, that the elephants were kept in those days.

The hotel rooms were located around three sides of the building, three storeys high, and opened on to wooden, blue-painted balconies that overlooked the beautiful courtyard and garden, with a small pond and spouting fountain in the middle, and even a small play area for children. The fourth side of the hotel faced the driveway and road, and the arched, ornately carved entrance of stone was indeed high enough to allow an elephant to pass under.

And it was in this glorious courtyard, beneath the red flame-of-the-forest and the yellow golden rain and the blue jacaranda, among the hibiscus and the fragrant oleander and bougainvillea shrubs, beside the spouting fountain, surrounded by fluttering butterflies, serenaded by a bulbul bird, that Andrew finally proposed to Usha, and Usha accepted. Even a peacock strutted by; this garden had everything a courting suitor could desire. It was perfect.

Father Bear and I, sitting in the hotel restaurant on the ground floor that opened up to the garden, were witness to it all. Andrew actually got down on one knee. He had purchased a ring before we left Colombo, and as he showed it to Usha, and she stretched out her hand for him to place it on her finger, her face bathed in smiles, Father Bear and I exchanged a grin of triumph. We'd done it! Together we'd reunited this so-deserving couple. A few other restaurant guests at the other tables also noticed, and clapped, and no one, not a single one of the white-skinned patrons, seemed in the least offended by the fact that Usha was Indian. Indeed, we all knew at that moment that love truly conquers all and melts the heart.

Later, when Andrew and Usha joined us at the table, we spoke of the practicalities. Usha's driving desire, now, was first and foremost to visit Luke, the son she had not held in her embrace since he was a babe in arms, and introduce Andrew to him. And then there were other serious, formal matters to be dealt with.

'You should get married as soon as possible,' said Father Bear. 'I'll marry you. I'll be needing a few days.'

Andrew frowned in astonishment. 'So soon? I thought it would take ages! What about the banns, and all those formalities? Don't we have to wait?'

Father Bear only chuckled and shook his head.

'Let me deal with that,' he said, and explained: it was always possible, if there were good enough reasons, for the Bishop to grant dispensation from the banns. He knew the Bishop. He'd talk to him, he'd get that dispensation.

And so it happened. The speed at which the wedding was prepared was almost dizzying, but Father Bear was right; they had both waited so very long, both gone through such harrowing times, why should they wait even a day longer than was necessary? What would be the point of a long engagement? Surely the past several years – since 1942 – had been, de facto, a period of engagement, since both had been absolutely certain – apart from Andrew's lapse when he had doubted Usha's fidelity.

'But I never stopped loving her!' he said now with some finality. 'It was heartbreaking, yes, but only because my heart knew, so very strongly, that we belonged together. I simply could not fathom it.'

The necessary preparations made, Usha and Andrew were married in a small chapel in the grounds of the CMC hospital. Usha wore a simple white dress she had bought off the rack at a Christian bridalwear shop in Vellore; Andrew wore a new suit from a tailor friend of Father Bear's. Father Bear, to use his own words, looked grand, and very impressive, in his black and white habit. The pews were empty except for me and three of Usha's best friends, all nurses who lived in the hostel with her.

I had been to very few weddings in my life: a few in Madras when I was a child, and two or three of friends of the Huxleys, all rather grand affairs that had left me unmoved. But here, now, was my best friend Andrew, speaking the sacred words: *I, Andrew David*

Huxley, take you, Ruth Maria Chettiar, to be my wife. I promise to be true to you in good times and in bad, in sickness and in health. I will love you and honour you all the days of my life.

After so much sorrow, so much tribulation, so much faith, it was done. A tear escaped my eye and a surge of emotion rose up in me in a wave so mighty I feared I'd actually start to weep. But I didn't. It was over, and there we were, bundling back into Father Bear's car, a Father Bear back in civilian clothes with just his white priestly collar hinting at the exalted role he had just played. He truly was a priest like no other.

There was no question where we'd head for. Usha had waited patiently for this very day; she had been patient enough, now, to wait four more days to not only meet Luke, hold him in her arms at last, but to take him away. 'I couldn't bear to visit him, hold him, and then leave him behind at the orphanage,' she said, and so she had waited.

As we drove up in Father Bear's clunker of a car and parked outside the orphanage gate, a host of screaming children rushed out of the open door of the building, swarmed towards us, holding out their arms to us, laughing, trying to hug us all at once. A nun bustled behind them, calling out: 'Children, children! Behave yourselves! Do not annoy the sahib and his wife or they won't pick any of you!'

But we had not come to pick a child. Usha looked around, frowning. 'Where is he?' she asked Father Bear. 'Where's Luke? He's not here!'

The nun said: 'Oh, that naughty little boy! He doesn't want to be adopted! He's inside, with Anna-Marie.'

'Take us to him, Mother Maria,' said Father Bear. She gave a quick *follow me* hand signal and led us all into the building, along a short corridor, and into what was obviously a schoolroom, with long, low desks and benches arranged in rows. A teacher, also in a grey nun's habit, sat at a larger desk at the front, reading; she was obviously used to this kind of drama and was just waiting for the children to return. At one of the desks near the back sat two children: a boy of about three, and a slightly older girl. The boy had that colour of skin the Indians describe approvingly as 'wheatish'. The girl was dark: tamarind-brown.

Another lump rose in my breast as, hand in hand, Usha and Andrew made their way to the children at the back of the room.

'Hello, Luke!' said Usha, in the gentlest of tones. 'I'm your mummy! I've come to take you home!'

'No! No, no!' cried Luke, and cowered away from her, into the protective arms of the little girl. She clasped him tightly, and glared at Usha. 'You're not to take him!' she cried. 'He's mine!'

Father Bear, coming up behind me, sighed. 'I feared this would happen,' he said. 'Those two are inseparable, always have been.'

He turned to me. 'Better leave them to it. Usha, stay here and talk to them both. Explain to Anna-Marie that she has to let Luke go. Come with me, Rosie.'

He led me away from the classroom into a little office at the end of the corridor.

'What's going on?' I asked. 'Why doesn't he want to be adopted? I thought all orphans wanted a proper home?'

'It's Anna-Marie,' he sighed. 'Anna-Marie who put the fear of adoption into his little head. He'd have gone long ago if not for her.'

'And Anna-Marie,' I said. 'She's your…'

He nodded. 'Yes, she's my daughter. And I promise you, I never showed favouritism. I never let her know she was special to me. I never singled her out. But…'

He took a deep breath, and then sighed. 'It was always clear to me that I wanted to keep her here. I think now it was a selfish decision; but it was also not an outlandish outcome. As you may have noticed, about half of the children here are Eurasians, fair of skin. They are the ones chosen first, the ones Indian parents choose, and even the few English parents who want to adopt. Fair of skin, and a boy: they are the ones who go first.'

He paused, and wiped his forehead, which had broken out in sweat. 'Anna-Marie, though she's Eurasian, is dark. That happens sometimes: you can't tell some of the little ones are half European. They are indistinguishable from native Indian children. They are second choice. And nobody wants the girls. So, she was dark – and a girl: third choice. That was all in my favour, and at some point, when she was three or four, I made a mistake. I told Anna-Marie that she'd never be chosen, that *this* was her home, and that I'd always look after her. That was the nearest I ever came to telling her the truth. "I'm Father Bear!" I said. "Your father." I said it as consolation for the fact she'd probably never be chosen, but she took it literally. Almost as if she sensed it was true. She never wanted to go, she accepted that this was her home. But then Luke came along. And I made another mistake. I brought Luke here as a tiny baby. Anna-Marie came rushing up: *Father Bear! Father!* she called, '*Let me see the baby!* And I bent down and showed her the baby, and from that moment she was besotted. She claimed him.

'The first time prospective parents came looking for a child – oh, she was so naughty! She had been very involved in looking after him, cleaning and feeding him, and she simply took him from his crib and hid with him! Until they were gone. Over the years, she developed this hiding routine to perfection – not only that, she persuaded Luke to behave so badly when parents came looking that they wouldn't choose him. He'd throw tantrums, throw things at them, climb up trees, run away. He even urinated on a couple once! We despaired of ever finding a home for him. In fact, we gave up. But now, of course, he has to go. She'll be devastated, but it's time she faced reality. She can't cling to him forever. She has to let him have a life of his own. And now his real parents are here – well, that seals it. He has to go – kicking and screaming, maybe, but he has to go.'

'Oh, Father!' I sighed. It seemed to me that Father Bear, so wise in many ways, had tripped when it came to his own personal life. He had let his own needs triumph over the needs of his parishioners, in this case a little child, his own daughter. He had shown favouritism. He had let her know, in a way not obvious to anyone but the two people involved, that she was special to him. His daughter. I had no idea what his superiors in the Church would make of all this, but I was pretty sure that, in the eyes of his religion, he had fallen. It was all a tangled web, and I was not in a position to sift through it all, and had no right to judge, but I felt in my heart that Father Bear was wrong. And that right now, Usha – and Andrew – were paying the price.

If Usha had thought she could simply swoop in, collect Luke and go off on her honeymoon, she had to think again. During my conversation with Father Bear in the office, Usha and the two crying children had been escorted by Sister Maria to what seemed to be a visitors' room, fairly comfortably outfitted with a sofa and a play area, and she was kneeling on the floor before the two children, who clung, still crying, to each other. An open packet of Milk Bikis lay discarded on the tiled floor; we had brought a bagful for all the children, and Usha had taken out a packet for Luke and Anna-Marie to share; they had obviously not been bribed. An anxious Sister Maria stood wringing her hands in the background.

Usha looked up in despair as we entered the room.

'He won't leave – he won't be separated from her!' she cried out, before turning back to the little boy. 'Luke!' she pleaded. 'I'm your mummy! Your real mummy! And look, you have a daddy too!' She gestured towards Andrew. Luke clung all the more fiercely to Anna-Marie, burying his face in her chest. And she – she glared at Usha: 'I'm his mummy! And that's our daddy over there!' She pointed to Father Bear, who had the grace to blush.

Sister Maria said, 'It is very difficult, Father. We could force them apart, of course but I'm sure that would only cause more problems for the future. But neither of them…' She didn't finish, just gestured to the two children huddled together.

And yet, I couldn't help noticing the way Luke, every now and then, glanced away from Anna-Marie and was that doubt I saw in his eyes? I couldn't tell, not knowing him at all, but it was clear that the ringleader in this childish rebellion was Anna-Marie. Now Father Bear stepped forward, kneeled in front of his daughter.

'Anna-Marie!' he said, 'you have to let Luke go. His real mummy has come to fetch him. You have been such a good girl, looking after him just like a mummy, but—'

'I'm his mummy! I *am*!'

Father Bear looked at Usha apologetically, 'She's looked after him since he was a baby, helping the nuns. He was like a live little doll to her. Unfortunately, it's gone to her head a bit. My fault, probably. I indulged her. We all did.'

'But he's not, and she has to realise that!' said Usha, irritation giving an edge to her voice. Turning to Anna-Marie, she said, this time quite strictly: 'Anna-Marie, you are not Luke's mother. You are only a child and he needs a proper mother now. I'm sorry, but I am taking him with me. You must let go of him and say goodbye.'

'No! No! No!' Anna-Marie screamed and clutched Luke all the closer to her.

Usha looked up at Father Bear: 'Can't you do something?'

'Can we have a word? Alone?' he replied. Usha nodded, and looked at Andrew.

Father Bear said: 'Andrew as well. This involves him.'

The three of them left the room, as did Sister Maria, nodding at me to let me know that I, now, was in charge in here. The two children relaxed, let go of their hold on each other. I sank down to the floor, sat there cross-legged beside them.

'Hello!' I said, smiling from one to the other. 'My name is Aunty Rosie, and I'm an old friend of Father Bear.'

Anna-Marie looked at me suspiciously. 'You're not old!' she said. 'You haven't got white hair!'

'Ah, but I've known him a long, long time! Since before you were born, even!'

'Did you come to take Luke away? Because you can't!'

How does one argue with an adamant five-year-old convinced of the absolute truth of her argument? I didn't even want to try. I picked up the discarded packet of Milk Bikis. It was open at one end, but none of the thin rectangular biscuits had been removed. I took out the first one and handed it to Anna-Marie; she hesitated, obviously deliberating as to whether she should make a concession and enjoy the treat, then finally took it, which was the cue for Luke to take his, too. They both munched their biscuits, staring at me in silence.

I made the split-second decision to get involved. Sometimes a neutral third party can be helpful as a mediator. And mediation had been my role in this family's story from the start.

'You see,' I tried to explain, 'That lady – she really is Luke's mummy. She always was, but she couldn't come for him before now. But she loves him with all her heart.'

'I love him too!'

She started to cry, bitter, heart-wrenching tears of utter desolation. Spontaneously, I held open my arms and, as if in complete capitulation, Anna-Marie fell into them. Just like that. She fell into my arms and began to cry; no longer a mother protecting her child, but a child herself, hungry for affection, for personal, individual, maternal affection; flinging herself, a helpless bundle, at someone who in her eyes could give it.

'I want a mummy too!' she sobbed. 'It's not fair! I want my mummy! Where's *my* mummy? Why does Luke have a mummy but not me? Why doesn't *my* mummy come to get me?'

Something lurched within me. Something enormous, a wave of complete and utterly perfect comprehension; call it an instinct, or a perception, a knowledge, a knowing. Perhaps it was this thing, this wonderful, beautiful *insight*, that had first swept through Usha and Andrew that day so many years ago, telling them that this *just had to be*. I simply knew it.

But we'd all have to be patient. Now, I whispered in her ear: 'I think one day your mummy will come for you too, Anna-Marie. You just have to be patient a little while longer.' I laughed then, and it was a laugh of delight. I wiped her eyes with a corner of my shawl, and kissed her on the forehead.

She sniffed. 'You promise?'

'I promise!' I said.

'Cross your heart and hope to die?' She made the accompanying gesture, crossing her heart, and so did I as I repeated: 'Cross my heart and hope to die.'

And in that moment she relaxed completely, turned into a totally different girl. We sat on the floor, the three of us, playing with the scattered toys, and the two children finished the packet of Milk Bikis between them, which I probably shouldn't have allowed but it was a small packet, and a special treat, and a special day, because both of them had found their mummy; and every second I loved Anna-Marie a little bit more.

Father Bear, Usha and Andrew returned a few minutes later. Whatever they had spoken of seemed not to have resolved a thing; all three were frowning, and Father Bear began to speak sternly as he walked in the room:

'Anna-Marie, you have to let Luke—' He stopped abruptly as I leapt to my feet, beaming, gesturing towards the two children playing happily on the floor.

'It's all right,' I said. 'Luke can go with you, Usha.'

She looked at me, understood; she squatted down, opened her arms. Luke leapt up from his toys and rushed across the room towards her.

*

Later, back at the hotel, once Father Bear had gone home and Usha was putting Luke to bed up in their room, Andrew and I sat on the hotel terrace sipping *stengahs*, reviewing the tumultuous day: a wedding, a small war, and, finally, an adoption. That's when he told me what the three of them had discussed, or had tried to discuss.

'Father Bear wanted us to adopt both children,' he said. 'He wants Anna-Marie to have a home as well, a family. I don't know why he's so invested in her – there's a bit of favouritism there, I think. He tried to persuade us, but Usha said no. She said it wouldn't be fair to Anna-Marie, because she'd only be an afterthought; it's Luke she wants and she doesn't think it's right to adopt another child as a sort of duty. She was sorry for Anna-Marie, she said, but it just wasn't right. But it seems— I don't know what magic you worked, Rosie, but we came back ready to tear them apart forcibly, and found you'd done all the work; we found a little boy only too eager to come with us.'

I smiled at the memory. The smile across Luke's face when, back at the orphanage, Usha swept him into her arms, had melted all our hearts.

'So,' I said, 'And now the three of you can enjoy your honey-moon.'

Chapter Forty-Four

I left the three of them at Shanti Nilayam, the perfect place for them all to get to know each other. Two weeks, they had decided to stay; perhaps longer.

'Stay as long as you like,' I said.

I stayed two days with them, and on the second day, while Andrew took Luke down to the beach, Usha and I had a chance to catch up, to truly talk things over, renew our friendship. We had not had such a long talk for years, not since 1942 when I'd left her here, pregnant with Luke. It was as if we'd come full circle.

The first thing I did was to apologise for ever thinking ill of her, for believing she had fooled me, Father Bear, Thila, all of us into thinking that Andrew was the father of her baby, a fallacy that was sure to come out anyway if Andrew survived.

'I should have known better,' I said, as we sat on the coolness of the veranda. 'Asked you to explain, instead of jumping to the first conclusion.'

'It's all right,' she said, 'it was the most logical conclusion to jump to. Who would ever have guessed…' She shuddered visibly and didn't finish the sentence.

After a short silence, I asked, tentatively: 'Are you going to tell Andrew… you know. Tell him who it was?'

She shook her head. 'No. What's the point? It would only upset him all over again. Victor was his brother and he is mourning the memory of what they had. Why should I spoil that for him? There is no advantage and it will just leave a taint on everything. Maybe even spoil his relationship with Luke.'

'But knowing Luke is actually his nephew? Isn't that worth it?'

Again, she shook her head. 'No... why? I think he'll love Luke just the same, even without the blood tie.'

'And what if he asks you directly? Asks you what happened?'

'If he asks, I'll tell him it was an English guest at the Harrisons' house, and that I want to put it all behind me. That I don't want to speak about it, ever again.'

And I left it at that. Usha would cross that bridge if ever she came to it. We spoke of other matters: of Anna-Marie, Father Bear, my future as a medical student. Of her nursing past, her nursing future, her return to Newmeads as Andrew's wife; of Aunt Silvia's reaction, and meeting her mother again, and her father, and her brothers, Satish and Karthik; hopefully, reconciling with them all, patching up the family rift.

She already knew of her eldest brother, Yogesh's, death. I told her of Kannan, her little nephew; she looked forward to meeting him. For her, returning to Newmeads would be a return home. As it was for me. But only in a way.

Home? Home? Where was my home, really? Truly, I felt it was right here, at Shanti Nilayam, and one day, hopefully, Pa would be here again, and I'd be back regularly. For now, though, it was Ceylon that was calling, for reasons of my own, and I was quite excited to return.

First of all, Cinnamon Gardens. I arrived towards evening to find the flat empty, though there was evidence that someone was living there. I knew who that someone was. I could actually smell him; Graham had always seemed steeped in the very fragrance of Ceylon, that indescribable melange of cinnamon and lemon and cardamom and ginger that infused the island. Or perhaps it was just my imagination. Perhaps what I smelled was not an actual fragrance. Perhaps it was the atmosphere of him that filled the flat, that made all my senses race, now, in anticipation. Graham, I knew, was back at work at the hospital. Sooner or later, he would come home. I waited for him, cooked a delicious meal, and listened.

At last, at about ten that night, I heard the key turn in the lock, and the light in the living room switched on. I'd been sitting in the darkness, waiting, planning, dreaming, hardly able to contain my excitement. The happy ending to Usha's and Andrew's story had left me thirsty, panting for my own happy ending. And it was, hopefully, about to happen. Unless— but no. Graham was a waiter, not a player. I knew it would all be fine.

Now, I rose to my feet. Graham, walking into the room, stopped suddenly, and the exclamation of surprise died on his lips. I locked eyes with him, asking him not to speak. And then I stood before him. And then I sank down on one knee, and held up my hands in a namaste. I didn't have a ring. Just as Graham had not played this courting game according to the established rules, neither would I. He had proposed the first time; it was my turn, in my own way. I lifted my namaste hands a little higher, and, holding his gaze, said: 'Graham, I know I'm a bit late with this. But, will you *still* marry me?'

And he laughed and laughed, and pulled me to my feet, and then I was in his arms and this was my happy ending; except it wasn't an ending, it was a beginning.

We stayed up all night, talking. Over the celebratory dinner I'd cooked I told him about Usha and Andrew and Luke. I told him about Anna-Marie. I had not had a single worry that Graham would stand in my way in this. When I had promised Anna-Marie a mummy, I had also, silently, promised her a daddy, and spoken, silently, for Graham. Now, he confirmed my decision.

'Of course we must adopt her!' he said. 'As soon as possible. As soon as we're married, we'll go over and get her.'

Excitement tingled within me. 'I can't wait to tell Father Bear!' I said.

'I can't wait to meet this Father Bear of yours!' he teased. 'D'you think he'll marry us too?'

'Why not? There's nothing I'd like better. A small wedding, at Shanti Nilayam, maybe. And Pa has to be there.'

'And Mother, and Father, and Andrew. And Usha.'

We made plans, far into the night. I would enrol to start my medical studies in September. It was all perfect. We'd have an ayah for Anna-Marie. And a house with a garden. Maybe right here: this house, converted back into a family home; it already had a lovely back garden where she, and our future children – we wanted more – could play. Weekends, and holidays, at Newmeads. Andrew would take over the plantation. Usha would be the mistress of the house.

'Though I don't see Aunty being terribly happy for now. Not at Andrew's wedding, and not at yours. You both married the wrong wife.'

Graham made a dismissive gesture. 'Oh, Mother will come around. Her bark is worse than her bite. The main thing is, two of her sons survived. Who cares what wives they choose?'

'Maybe you're right,' I said. And then: 'Oh, I just had a thought! Kannan!'

'Who's Kannan?'

Kannan had been back at school when Graham came home, and had not visited the house. Graham had not met him, and I had not thought to tell him – there'd been so many other stories to tell, from both him and Andrew. Now I told him; that Yogesh had been killed in the second year of the war; about Kannan's mother, Yogesh's widow, living with Sunita and Rajkumar, working in the tea factory.

'Kannan and Luke are cousins,' I said. 'Kannan's a few years older, but we have to make sure they stay in touch.'

And so we talked into the night, laying down plans, dreaming our dreams. Had we never heard the saying: *Man proposes, God disposes?*

So very true, so very pertinent, as it all turned out. But that night we dreamed on, caught up in the euphoria of our happily-ever-after aspirations. In the wee hours after midnight, we went to bed and I fell asleep in his arms. More was not necessary; we could wait. A lifetime of married life lay before us. Rosie-and-Graham was going to be at the other end of the spectrum from Rosie-and-Freddie. The grown-up version of love.

Chapter Forty-Five

Graham and I took the train to Kandy that Saturday, and from there the bus down to Newmeads. I felt not a little trepidation: we had not only to confront Aunt Silvia with the news of our own soon-to-be wedding, but also had the difficult task of preparing her for the fact that Andrew was already married to Usha. How would she take it? Both she and Uncle disapproved most strongly of mixed marriages, and to make matters worse, Usha came from the servant class. Already two taboos broken.

But we had underestimated her, underestimated them both. 'So be it,' she sighed when Graham broke the news about Andrew and Usha that night. 'Who am I to complain, when my prayers have been answered and my son has been returned to me, alive? Perhaps it is all, indeed, God's will and I have only to be grateful, a thousand times grateful, for the blessing of his safe return.'

Uncle Henry nodded. 'Indeed, indeed. The main thing is, he is alive.'

Graham and I exchanged a glance. This was so much better than we'd expected. But Aunt Silvia wasn't finished. 'I think, Rosie, in the end perhaps your mother was right. And your father. I suppose it's because they both grew up in India, with Indian ayahs, speaking the language like natives. Lucy used to tell me she loved the scent of India, the sound of it. It was in her blood. The people were her people. She saw no difference whatsoever, and learned from them whenever she could. She always said we had so much to learn, we English, and rejected the idea that we were a superior race. We argued along those lines many a time, and I always walked away from those conversations feeling ill at ease, feeling that, somehow, she had won, even though I was the one with the more forceful arguments, the louder voice. It was the same with your father. How I used to openly mock Rupert! But now, I know he helped us win the war, in his own way, precisely due to his Tamil contacts and language skills. Rupert once said to me that all people were simply people, and we must look far deeper if we are ever to understand our purpose here on Earth. This dreadful, horrid time behind us – it has forced me to look deeper. And if Andrew has found love, well, we must accept it and move forward.'

'I'm not sure if the rest of the planter set will agree with you on that, dear!' said Uncle, 'But we will see. There's a job waiting for him and this will all be his. You, Graham – I assume you don't want it, and will continue in Colombo.'

Graham nodded. At last, he and his father had reconciled. That was when we told them the next bit of news: that Graham and I were engaged. Again, I wasn't sure how Aunt Silvia would take it, but here, too, I had underestimated her. She was happy for us, and so was Uncle. In fact, they popped open a bottle of champagne.

'I always wanted you to marry one of my boys,' said Aunty as we clinked glasses, 'I just didn't think it would be Graham. I had other plans for him.'

'You and your matchmaking!' said Uncle, and we all laughed, and Aunty blushed, and once again that sense of perfect well-being washed through me.

'So when, and where, is the wedding to be?' asked Aunt Silvia, sipping at her glass. She, of course, loved weddings and I knew without being told that, having been confronted with a fait accompli in Andrew's case and not given the chance to organise it, she would be all guns blazing in trying to plan Graham's – all the more so because she was also, in a way, the mother of the bride.

I was sorry to disappoint her, but it had to be.

'We're going back to Shanti Nilayam,' I said. 'Pa is moving back there next week, and, well, I just think there's no better place for us. And I want Father Bear to officiate.'

'*What*? That Catholic?' exclaimed Aunt Silvia. 'Bad enough that Andrew had a Papist ceremony! You too, Graham?'

'It doesn't matter,' I said. 'Not to me, at any rate. I'd have a Hindu wedding, if it was in Father Bear's hands!'

'Humph!' grunted Uncle. 'I heard that old rascal is anyway half a Hindu.'

'I haven't met him yet,' said Graham, 'but I'm looking forward to it. From what Rosie says, he's a fascinating man.'

'Your father came to visit while you were away, Rosie!' said Aunty. 'He was disappointed not to find you here, but we had a good little chinwag. He's changed so much. I always thought he was a bit of a fuddy-duddy, but he isn't.'

I laughed. 'That was your wrong perception,' I said. 'You put Pa in a box. He's a lot more than that!'

'I can't wait to meet him,' said Graham.

I reached out and squeezed his hand. He squeezed mine back. The most wonderful thing in the world is having a partner who is entirely tuned in to you. And you to him. I knew Pa would love him, and so would Father Bear, and that it would be mutual in both cases.

'We'll marry as soon as it all can be arranged,' said Graham. 'You're both welcome, of course, but it's going to be a very, very small affair.'

'You see,' I said, 'there's a little girl I made a promise to. I can't keep her waiting for long.'

Again, Aunty grunted. 'Well, I'll come over to India for this miniature wedding, of course.'

'I too,' Uncle Henry said. 'There is no force on earth that will keep me away from my daughter's wedding.' And my heart swelled at that.

'And we have to have a big party, later, here, when you're all settled,' went on Aunty Silvia. 'I insist. This will be the wedding of the year among the planters, marking the end of this terrible time as well; we have to celebrate with all my friends. They'll never forgive me if I deny them a party. Or even a ball…'

And I could see her mind whirling as she sped off in that direction.

Chapter Forty-Six

So many plans to be made!

The next thing I had to do was inform Father Bear, who still had no idea of what was in store. It was not possible to make phone calls to India, and anyway, I could explain better in writing.

> She's such a dear little girl, Father Bear, and when I held her in my arms I knew that that was where she belongs. You saw, and understood, I think, that she needs someone of her own, someone to love and cherish her, someone special. That's the reason she was so attached to Luke, and it wasn't healthy. You are not capable of that, and, from what you proposed to Usha and Andrew – that they should adopt her – you must know that now. Even the best orphanage cannot replace a family, and that's what Graham and I can offer her. I made her a promise, and I shall keep it, as soon as possible. But first, Graham and I must marry – can you arrange this as speedily as you did Usha's wedding? Let me know what documents you need, and perhaps it can be done at Shanti Nilayam, in a week or two.

Father Bear replied by return of post, and his excitement bounced out of his letter. We laughed at his eagerness to see us married, to give Anna-Marie a home. He proposed a date two weeks from the date of his letter, and we agreed.

Next, we had to write to Andrew and Usha to let them know, and to ensure they stayed on at Shanti Nilayam at least till then. They, too, responded with much joy.

Then there was the matter of our clothes, and the rings, and Aunt Silvia's clothes, and Uncle's. And they, they proclaimed, were going to take over all the costs for the wedding.

I tried to argue. 'Really, it's just a tiny affair, hardly worth the effort and any expenditure!'

'Nonsense, my dear! Just because a wedding is a small one, it doesn't have to be drab!'

'No, but I can just go a day early and buy a nice new dress from Spencer's in Madras. They had all the latest fashions, and managed to keep going all through the war. And—'

'I won't hear of it! A lovely wedding dress for you, Rosie darling! I know just the woman who can whip it up in a week. You deserve the best!'

'Really, I don't want—'

'Nonsense, dear! This is a once-in-a-lifetime event, and only the best is good enough. We've suffered this dreadful war for so many years, we all deserve a bit of extravagance. And Graham is to have a new suit.'

And so she dragged me along to her seamstress, and we leafed through a catalogue of styles and inspected various old copies of bridal outfits, until we'd made up our minds; and I had to admit the proposed dress was gorgeous. Several trips to Kandy later, several fittings later, it was packed away in a special bag along with the veil, and we were ready to depart for India. In a fit of overwrought generosity, Aunty also sent money to Andrew to purchase suitable wedding outfits for Usha, who was to be my matron of honour, and himself; he was to be Graham's best man. I was not happy with this extravagance – it was not at all what Graham and I had planned – but Aunty would not hear of anything else. It was her last chance to plan a wedding for one of her children, and that I was to be the bride exceeded all her expectations. No, it might not be a big wedding, but we were all to be dressed as if it were, and we were to have photographs, and flowers, and a feast.

Since we seemed to be going all traditional, I wondered if Anna-Marie could be a flower girl, but Father Bear said no, it would all be far too much for her. It would be better for her to simply sit back and be a witness. Thila would look after her during the ceremony.

And so Graham and I were married. A tearful Pa walked me up the aisle. My dress was a delight, and even I, so indifferent to fashions, couldn't help but exclaim when I saw myself in the mirror. It was of exquisite white Pochampally silk, from the eponymous Andhra Pradesh town famous for its silk weavers; the bodice was of intricate ikat styling, ivory on white. It had a sweetheart neckline and three-quarter lace sleeves, a long veil and a full skirt, and it fitted me like a dream. As I walked down the aisle to greet my new husband and to exchange vows with him, I believed myself to be walking on air. How could I ever have doubted that this was the man with whom I'd share the rest of my life? I grew wings in that moment.

It was all over so quickly. Apart from the extravagance of the dress we had indeed managed to keep everything small, thanks, most probably, to the fact that we were in India. Had we been married in Ceylon I doubt that Aunty could have restrained herself from inviting every one of her planter wives, her bridge club ladies and the ladies of the choir, as well as all their daughters. Here in Madras she knew no one, and that was a godsend. The feast she had ordered from the caterers at the Connemara Hotel was sumptuous but small, as the only participants were the family, Father Bear and Thila.

The big moment of the day – almost, but not quite, the biggest – was the reunion of Luke and Anna-Marie, before the ceremony. They quite literally catapulted themselves into each other's arms, and stayed that way for the whole ceremony, looked after by Thila.

Luke had changed: he had put on weight so that the pinched look of a waif he'd worn before his adoption had completely disappeared, as had the empty look in his eyes. Now, they shone with a brightness that reflected his smile, and he chattered away with all and sundry. Anna-Marie, on the other hand, was still too thin and her eyes darted around in suspicion and, I guessed, anxiety. It was a big day for her too. When I saw her, I squatted down to her level, took her in my arms and whispered in her ear: 'After today, I will be your mummy.' I laughed, then, when she did not want to let me go, and signalled for Thila to come and help.

'I can't be your mummy until I get married!' I said. 'And you have to let me go to get married.'

And she did.

Later that day, after we were all sated and Aunty and Uncle had gone for a walk with Andrew and Usha, after Father Bear had removed his cassock and looked himself again – a spruced-up, tidy version of himself – Graham and I signed the adoption papers and became Anna-Marie's parents. And a new life for us all began.

Just like Andrew and Usha before us, Graham and I were to stay on at Shanti Nilayam for our honeymoon, and just as their honeymoon had been shared with Luke, ours was spent with Anna-Marie. It was a time of not only growing into each other as husband and wife, but of expanding out to embrace this little girl who had so suddenly fallen into our lives.

I had been worried about tearing Luke from her once again, when Andrew and Usha departed for Ceylon, but it was no bother at all: Anna-Marie was now completely dedicated to being in a proper family, and would not leave us alone for even a second, except when she slept. She seemed fearful that I would leave her; I reassured her again and again that I would not, that I was here for her forever, and so was Graham; that she now had real parents.

It was a gentle process, requiring much patience, but an eminently rewarding one.

'You're not going to send me back?' she asked, again and again, and again and again, I reassured her: 'No, Anna-Marie. We're your mummy and daddy. We belong together. We'll never let you go again. We're going to our new home, soon, and you'll be our daughter.'

Our new home. For the time being that would be Cinnamon Gardens; we would occupy just one of the flats until such time as we could convert it into a family home, and redesign the garden into a smaller replica of gardens we had known. But we'd visit Newmeads often, for there was Luke, and Uncle Andrew and Aunt Usha, and her new grandparents. Anna-Marie had gained not only new parents but a complete family.

And then the honeymoon was over. Graham had been granted extraordinary leave due to the wedding, but only for a week, and it soon passed. We moved into Cinnamon Gardens, made it our home. The second weekend, we all three made the journey up to Newmeads. I thought it would be nice for Anna-Marie to have some time with Luke, and for us all to be together as an extended family looking towards the future.

And so we were all there on that fatal night. That literally fatal night.

We were all sitting on the veranda, sipping our *stengahs*, chatting as usual about this and that; that is, Uncle and Aunt, Andrew and Graham, and me. Usha was not with us yet. She and I took it in turns to put the children to bed: they both slept in the nursery, and both enjoyed a bedtime story before they fell asleep. It was early, not yet eight, but night was already upon us. The night creatures had started up their incessant cheeping, croaking, chirruping night choir. Suddenly a new sound broke into the familiar, but comparatively muted, chorus. A high-pitched, raucous, three-tiered cry: the brain-fever bird.

'That bird!' said Aunty. 'It's back again.'

To be sure, we had not heard it for ages. I shivered. I did not like this bird. There was something foreboding about that cry, spiralling up into the heights of frenzy. *My eyes are gone! I'm going blind!* Or some such desperate lament. So loud, this time, it must be right outside the veranda, hidden in one of the frangipani trees, perhaps.

But it did not stay long. We heard a flutter and a crashing of wings and then, a few minutes later, the same cry, but much further away.

'Thank goodness it's gone!' said Aunty. 'Once, one of them stayed outside my window for a whole hour and I could not sleep a wink.'

'It used to wake me up when I was a child!' I said. 'In the middle of the night. I used to be so frightened. I'd run to Amma's bed for safety. One came the night before she died.'

Andrew looked towards the door, and then at his watch. 'I wonder what's keeping Usha,' he said.

'One story after the other,' I laughed. 'She's telling them the entire *Mahabharata*, I think. Or else she's fallen asleep.'

Just then, one of the dogs began to bark wildly, crossly, just as they did when anyone opened the gate to the grounds.

'I hope that's not a visitor,' said Uncle. 'I'm not really up for entertaining.'

But the barking turned to the whining, whimpering sound dogs make when they're greeting a friend.

'Who on earth can that be?'

The cluster of bells at the veranda stairs jangled. Three times, the way Victor always announced his arrival. Everyone else just jangled once.

'Now, that gives me the creeps,' said Aunty. As for me, it was as if a light-footed spider ran up my arm. Goosebumps. Footsteps – heavy ones, for you couldn't usually hear feet on the hard veranda tiles.

And then a voice. A voice too familiar for my liking. A voice that should not exist in this world. My entire body cramped, as if shrunk into itself, a stiff, rigid effigy. It was Victor's voice.

And then it was Victor. In person. Standing before us, in brown corduroy trousers and what looked like the kind of black leather jacket pilots wear, and a corduroy cap on his head, and heavy, worn boots, and a huge grin plastered all over his face.

'Well, well, well – the whole family, gathered in welcome!' he announced. The same old smug, arrogant tone that nobody except me seemed able to detect. Still frozen, I watched as Aunty shrieked and propelled herself into his arms. Uncle, too, rose, but waited his turn because once Aunty had had her hugs Andrew was the next, grinning broadly as he embraced his big brother, clapped him on his back. Graham glanced at me and rose, obviously reluctantly, to his feet. This was his brother. Like it or not, he had to join in the welcome back from the dead. But he knew I wouldn't like it. I stayed obstinately seated.

Exclamations on exclamations. *We thought you were dead! They told us you were dead! How did you… when did you… where were you… what happened?*

But Victor wasn't finished with his greetings. He looked straight at me and with that same old mocking, derisory grin, he said, 'And you, Rosie, you're not going to say hello? Not glad to see me? Don't I get a hug from you?'

I rose reluctantly and held out my hand, sat down again, not saying a word. No point making a scene now. Luckily, Victor, waylaid by Aunty by a deluge of new questions, made no further remark.

'Let me get you a drink,' said Uncle, and disappeared into the house. I wanted to get up, run inside the house myself, go to Usha, warn her. But it was as if I were glued to the chair, held down by a sense of intense, illogical terror. As if I knew what was to come. And I was curious to know how he had survived.

Settled on to the double sofa next to his mother, Victor began to tell his story.

'I was stationed at Trincomalee,' he began, and immediately Aunty cried out, 'Trincomalee! You were right here, in Ceylon, all these years?'

'Well, not exactly, Mother! My base was the China Bay Airport – it's where the RAF established their base to fight the Japs. So I might have been stationed there but mostly I was out flying missions. I flew Spitfires – best little plane in the world!'

'You were so close, all these years! And you never came to visit!'

Victor chuckled. 'Trincomalee isn't exactly Colombo, is it? It's on the other side of the island. I couldn't just come home for the weekend!'

'You must have had leave! You did come on leave, once!'

'Yes, but that ended badly, didn't it? To be quite honest, Mother, nothing really drew me back home. I spent my leave with my mates in Trincomalee. Mostly Australian chaps, they had no family nearby. Trinco's a good place to let off a bit of steam.'

He laughed, then, as if to let his mother know he had had better things to do than visit her. But it was a hollow, empty laugh. I hated him more than ever. Uncle protested: 'You had your poor mother to think of. Here she was, worrying her head off about you, and then the news of your death…'

'Well, I couldn't help that, could I? You should know I've got nine lives. Kept the faith!'

Another mocking laugh.

'So, what happened?'

'I was getting to that, Father. Patience!'

'So, we were on our way over to Burma, my squadron of Spitfires,' he began, 'We were somewhere over the Bay of Bengal when the Japs attacked. It was a vicious attack. I saw two planes go down. My mates Howard and Duncan, Australians.' He stopped speaking and gulped as if holding back emotion. Even I felt a moment of empathy for him. His mother reached out to hold his hand, but he pulled it out of her grasp, took a deep breath and began to speak again. 'My plane was hit too. I managed to release my aircraft canopy and scrambled out of the plane. Just in time; it started to plummet to the sea in a ball of fire, spiralling down.'

'Good Lord!' said Uncle. 'That was lucky!'

'Oh, Victor!' gasped Aunty. She was in tears. He ignored her and continued. 'I tried to release my parachute but the rip cord refused to deploy until I was very low – just a few hundred feet away from the water. I suppose that's why the other pilots didn't see the chute opening: they were looking high. I came down in the sea and freed myself of the chute. I was lucky – it happened pretty close to the Andaman Islands. I saw the outline of land and I was able to swim to shore.'

'But didn't the Japs find you?' asked Uncle. 'The Andamans were crawling with them!'

'Well, if they did, I wouldn't be here to tell the tale,' Victor replied. 'The Nips killed downed airmen without a second thought, and yes, they'd already occupied the Andaman and the Nicobar Islands; it could have been a leap from the frying pan into the fire. But this was one of the smaller, remote islands. The Japs hadn't bothered with it. I was lucky.'

He relaxed palpably as he came to this part of his story. He told it in bits and pieces, interrupted again and again by Aunty and Uncle, and, occasionally, Andrew. 'I managed to survive on coconuts for a day. But I had a few burns and I was worried they'd get infected, so I went in search of help.'

'Dangerous!' exclaimed Uncle. 'What if you'd run into Japs? You should have stayed in hiding.'

'Let him talk!' scolded Aunty. 'Go on, darling.'

'Well, I explored the island – cautiously, of course. I'm not *that* stupid, Father!' He shot Uncle a filthy look. 'But there were no Japs on that island. Not a one. I found a village. The villagers took care of me. They had herbs that healed my burns. They had no contact with the other islands, no contact with the Japs. Nice people.'

He chuckled. 'They even offered me one of their daughters as a bride. Obviously, I accepted. I'm a married man, now, you know! Time for some congratulations. And for that matter, I'm a father!'

Graham and I exchanged a knowing look. I raised my eyebrows, he shook his head, slowly as if in reproach. I couldn't stand Victor's flippancy, his facetiousness. It was so disrespectful of his parents, who had grieved so heartbreakingly, and to spring news of a wife, a child, on them in such a way!

But once again they seemed not to care. Neither of them reacted to that bit of news; that Victor was *alive* was all that mattered. I suppose I had to understand: that's what it's like to be a parent. You overlook a child's faults, or excuse them. That's the power of love, and all children need love. Sometimes, though, as in the case of Victor, if such excusing is done without discernment, it can make a child a monster.

'But why didn't you let us know? Why didn't you get a message to us? Surely you must have known when the war ended…? Why didn't you…?'

'Well, for a start, like I said, the island was isolated. We had no idea what was happening in the outside world. No idea the war had ended. Eventually news filtered through: about the big bomb. That the Japs had surrendered. That was about four months ago.'

'Four months! Why didn't you send a message? Come home?'

Victor brushed away the question with a quick wave. 'I told you, I had a woman. She was pregnant at the time – I wanted to see the baby, watch her grow a bit. My daughter. Yes, Mother, you're a grandmother!'

'But you should have at least let us know you were alive! We *mourned* you, Victor!' It was the nearest Aunty could get to a rebuke, but even that slid off Victor like water off a duck's back.

'Oh, Mother! What a waste of energy! You should have kept the faith. You named me Victor – you should have known!' He guffawed and gave his mother a rough hug, pulling her to him and kissing her forehead. 'You should know I'm indestructible!'

At that moment the door to the living room opened and Usha appeared in the doorway.

'So sorry!' she said gaily, turned away from us as she closed the door behind her. 'I fell asleep!' She turned to face us. 'And those childr—' She stopped abruptly. I jumped up, ready to usher her back inside. I should have gone to her ages ago, warned her, but I had been transfixed, rendered almost immobile by Victor's overpowering presence.

A look of sheer horror implanted itself on Usha's face. Of utter contempt, revulsion – and terror, all these emotions mixed in together. She, too, just like me, seemed transfixed, stuck there on the spot wearing that mask of horror, a mask that said everything. Victor ignored it.

'Well, well, well, who's this come to join the party? My little friend Usha – that's the name, isn't it? Don't tell me Andrew's been dipping in his paintbrush as well?'

Andrew was the third person who now seemed turned to a statue. I looked at all of them; while Usha and Victor seemed locked in a mutual staring contest, Andrew looked from one to the other and I saw his face change as he slowly put two and two together and came out with a resounding four, writ large and shining. Andrew grasped it all. Usha turned and fled.

In the next few moments everything descended into chaos. Andrew flew at Victor:

'I'll kill you! I'll kill you, you beast! You monster! I know what you did! I'll kill you!'

He yelled it in a frenzy of utter desperation, and I knew he meant every word. I lunged towards him, trying to drag him away, but he flung my arms off. Uncle, too, leapt up, saying, somewhat ineffectually, 'I say, I say! What's going on?' Graham, meanwhile, tackled Victor from behind but was quickly thrust away as if he were no more than a pesky mosquito. Victor was strong, so strong!

Aunty screamed and threw water at them from a nearby jug, but they both ignored it. They were fighting properly, now, wrestling each other to the floor, getting up again, pulling each other down. Arms stuck under armpits, legs twisted around bodies – I could not bear to watch, but had to, my hands over my mouth, crying out, as ineffectually as Uncle had, 'Stop it, stop it! Andrew! Stop it!'

They ignored us all. Flung aside all attempts to intervene. This was a serious fight, not the kind of wrestling match they'd engaged in as boys. Their faces, when occasionally visible, were grim with deadly intent. Arms, legs, heads, bodies, all in a tangle. On the floor, and standing: it seemed to go on forever, the four of us onlookers all yelling our useless pleas to stop.

Usha, hearing the tumult, appeared again in the doorway. She gave a shriek of terror, rushed to Andrew and tried to pull him away. Victor shoved a muscular arm between them and flung her to the floor as if she were a matchstick.

It was, in truth, an unequal fight. Victor had obviously gained weight and muscle over the years of his exile, but he was no longer the strong, strapping man he'd always been, perhaps due to lack of training. He even seemed to have gained a bit of flab.

Meanwhile, Andrew, although still quite thin and much depleted physically, was much stronger than he had been. But it wasn't a physical strength that now launched him into the fray. Andrew was on fire, fuelled by a rage so strong it seemed even to outrank Victor's sheer brawn. He was a young god of revenge, a powerhouse of might. He had obviously been trained to fight well, and had quite a few techniques up his sleeve; previously, Victor, with his superior physique, could have snapped him in two, but not this time.

Victor must have noticed that mere muscle could not vanquish the power derived from an almighty wrath motivated by pure, unadulterated vengeance. He must, in that moment, have inwardly surrendered. He pushed Andrew away, but the latter only staggered a little and lunged forward once again like a tiger on the attack, a tiger set to kill. Victor neatly sidestepped him, as if he'd given up the fight, refused this last challenge. But then he struck.

His hand flashed, a hand as straight and hard as a thin wedge of wood, a hand slashing at the back of Andrew's neck. It was a lightning-quick chop. But afterwards, when I kept seeing it again and again, it was in slow motion.

Andrew fell. He lay on the ground, a limp heap of rags. Victor, breathing heavily, stood above him, gazing down, a look of disbelief across his face. Uncle, Aunty and I all screamed. Usha ran to Andrew's prone body in a volley of shrieks and bent over him, putting her ear to his chest. Shaking him, crying out: 'Get up, Andrew, get up! Please! Get up!'

Victor's immobility lasted less than three seconds. In the fourth second, he turned and ran. The dogs raced behind him, barking, no doubt thinking it was a splendid game.

In a blink of an eye our castle in the sky collapsed into dust.

Chapter Forty-Seven

What had been chaos a minute ago now descended into pandemonium. Graham plunged into the darkness after Victor. Uncle seemed shocked into immobility, standing there pulling at his hair. Aunty and Usha were on hands and knees beside Andrew, slapping his face, calling at him to come back, bending down to listen to his heart, bawling and crying and shrieking all at the same time.

Graham returned in less than thirty seconds. 'No point chasing him in bare feet,' he said, and he too got down and bent over Andrew, lifted a limp arm to feel his pulse. Uncle came to life: 'We have to call an ambulance! A doctor!' he cried.

'I *am* a doctor,' said Graham calmly. He sat up on his haunches. 'I'm sorry, there's nothing anyone can do.' I watched in utter horror as he stood up, his face white as a sheet, his hands shaking. Yet he remained calm.

'Usha and Mother, you have to stop screaming,' he said quietly. 'You'll wake the household.'

Indeed, now Sunita appeared at the door, summoned by the commotion. She, too, stood staring in horror, then padded silently up behind me, whispered in my ear: 'Miss, what can I do?'

'Maybe a drop of brandy for everyone,' was all I could think of, and she slipped away again. My mind had turned completely numb. I could hardly speak, much less move. I was confused. It had all happened so swiftly, in the blink of an eye.

'What did he do? How could he…? I didn't see!' I moaned, to anyone or everyone.

'A karate chop,' said Graham. 'Do you remember, years ago, Victor had studied it in Kandy? And Father had thought it was being disloyal, learning a Japanese skill? It was that. A quick chop to the back of the neck. If you know how, it's deadly. Victor obviously knew how.'

'But... but why – did he mean to kill...?'

'I think it was a reflex,' said Graham. 'Why would he want to do that? But Andrew was a powerhouse, and Victor was losing. I think he just lost his head and delivered the chop.'

He spoke calmly, matter-of-factly, staying above the fray, and that helped to calm us all a little. Sunita emerged from the living room with a tray laden with small glasses half-filled with amber liquid. She passed it around. Everyone took a glass.

Graham gently pulled his mother, now sobbing quietly, away from the corpse, then, even more gently, took hold of Usha, cradling her under her arms. He sat them down next to each other on the sofa and turned to Uncle.

'We have to call the police,' he said.

'Now, now, not so hasty,' stuttered Uncle. 'We can't just jump into this. We have to get the story straight. We have to have a valid explanation.'

Graham frowned. 'What more of an explanation do you need? A fight turned lethal. A man killed another man. What bloody story do you want to get straight?'

The two stared at each other for a moment of silence, and in that moment a dreadful wall of discord dropped between them. An invisible wall, inherently programmed to split this family in two.

Uncle, who had obviously been thinking up his story, said, 'All we have to say is that it was a stranger, some vagabond, a burglar, maybe, who surprised us. Nobody knows that Victor came back. He's officially dead. Nobody would suspect him if we all keep quiet. We're the only witnesses to his presence here tonight, to... to... what just happened. We could say that Andrew tried to fight him off, and was killed. Nobody would argue with that. We all have to stick together, as a family, and Victor can come back later when it has all died down.'

Graham glared at him. 'A cover-up, then? You want us all to lie?'

'Well, it's the only way, isn't it? Victor is your brother, Graham. Our son. We can't pull him into this. Totally unnecessary. Why create havoc when there's a perfectly plausible explanation?'

'Lying about a crime is in itself a crime. I'm going to call the police. Now.'

Uncle threw his brandy into his mouth, threw the glass into the garden and stepped into Graham's path, blocking the door. 'I am not going to deliver my own son to the police!' he bellowed. 'We can't bring Andrew back from the dead, and now we need to rally together to protect Victor. Your brother, Graham!'

'No. Victor must face justice. He has killed a man – his own brother. We can't let him get away with murder.'

'Murder!' screamed Aunty. 'He'll be hanged!'

'Not murder. Not murder. Manslaughter! Self-defence!' shouted Uncle. In his own way he was as distraught as Aunty; he just didn't weep and wail. His eyes were wild and his brain was, evidently, working overtime, grasping desperately at this logical straw and that. 'But even that'll be years in prison! I can't send my son to prison!'

Graham yelled back: 'Your son killed his brother, my brother, your son! He's a killer – why can't you see that?'

This was a Graham I'd never seen before. His eyes on fire, he seemed to tower over Uncle, who shouted back: 'How can you say that? He's your brother! It was self-defence! You can't put your brother behind bars! Your only remaining brother! You're a traitor!'

'Shhh!' I said, ineffectually. 'The children!' I signalled to Sunita, standing stunned on the sidelines with the empty tray. She rushed off to take care of them. They could not be allowed to see Andrew's body, prone on the floor.

Rage now overcame Uncle, and that gave him new strength. He had roared those last words at Graham, who roared back: 'And always your favourite! Always the manly, dauntless, virile one of your sons, the shining example of what a man should be like, and Andrew and me the weaklings, the pansies! But I tell you what, Father, Victor was cruel and brutal and underhand and malicious. He always was and you always ignored it, spoiled him silly.'

Now it all devolved into a full-blown row, the two of them shouting blue murder at each other. I'd never seen Graham like this: it was a side of him kept under cover till now, only revealed under extreme provocation. I called to him now and again to stop, to calm down, but for once he ignored me. Aunty screamed the place down, telling them both to stop.

But then Usha stood up.

'NO!' she said. She said it quietly, calmly, but with great authority. She had stopped screaming as the quarrel began, stopped weeping, and had been listening, watching, wide-eyed, as Uncle and Graham tore themselves apart verbally. Her single word was a spike into their dialogue. And her eyes spoke daggers.

'No, I am not going to lie. Victor killed my husband. I want this to be known. I want him punished.'

Considering her near-hysterical condition only minutes ago, Usha spoke with astonishing calmness and clarity. Aunty, who had subsided into quiet weeping, began to shriek all over again. Sunita reappeared with another tray bearing more small glasses and more brandy. A moment of silence while we each took a glass. The brandy stung, but it helped. I immediately felt more in control of myself. I spoke up.

'I agree with Usha,' I said. 'We can't lie. Justice must be done.'

Graham nodded. 'Moreover, he could very well be tried for more than manslaughter. If Usha speaks up. Father, you know exactly what I mean. He's committed more than one crime. He has to face justice. He's not above the law.'

He glared at his father, who immediately sank into himself, finally defeated.

Graham and I exchanged a glance, and smiled wryly at each other. It was good to know that he was on the side of truth. I stepped over to Usha, sat next to her and placed an arm around her. She reciprocated the gesture. We pulled each other close. I felt her shiver, and placed my own shawl around her, though I know she was shivering not from cold but from shock. From utter devastation.

Aunty, who had been quiet for a few seconds as she downed her brandy, began to shriek again: 'Justice! What justice? It was self-defence! Andrew started it!' and then, realising that Andrew, too, was her beloved son, and was dead, broke into a volley of sobs. 'My son!' she gasped. 'Both my sons! The death penalty! They'll hang Victor! Oh, God help me! And somebody, cover up Andrew! I can't bear to see him like that.'

'I'm going to call the Kandy police headquarters right now,' said Graham firmly. He unfolded one of the thin woollen blankets that lay on the wicker swing in anticipation of chilly nights, spread it over Andrew's body.

'Let's all go inside,' he said then. 'Come, Mother.'

He helped his mother to her feet and led her, stumbling as she wept, into the living room. I felt so sorry for her: one son dead, the other son returned from the dead and now, perhaps, facing the ultimate punishment. But right now, Usha came first. Arm in arm, we too moved to the living room. We sat next to each other on the sofa.

It was going to be a long night.

The police arrived before dawn. They came in an unmarked car, with a police van right behind it. The body was bundled into the van and they drove off. We were all questioned, one by one. Uncle and Aunty refused to give statements. Uncle spoke for both of them: 'We need to speak to a lawyer first.'

Graham, Usha and I told the truth, leaving out a chunk of the backstory. Later that day, the three of us, with the children, returned to Cinnamon Gardens. The family split was complete.

On the basis of Graham's, Usha's and my statements a massive manhunt was set in motion, covering the whole island. All the ports and airfields were put on high alert. The newspapers printed front-page articles with large pictures of Victor.

Four days later, the telephone rang: it was Uncle. He spoke to Graham.

'They found him,' said Graham as he replaced the telephone receiver. 'They found him, cowering at a former girlfriend's house. In her father's shed.'

The Huxley name was now a bad word; no girlfriend, former or not, would want to protect him.

Shanti Nilayam, three months later

A wound had been slashed right through the Huxley family that dreadful night, gouging it in two: Uncle and Aunty on the one side, Graham, me and Usha on the other. In the end it was Graham who, finally, stopped the bleeding. Usha had, all this time, kept quiet about her rape by Victor. There was no need for that story to come out, she said, but if it did, the Huxley name would be more than a bad word: It would be in tatters. Victor would be tried not only for manslaughter but also for rape.

As things stood, his lawyer was going to plead self-defence – Andrew had, after all, instigated the fight. If it came out *why* exactly Andrew had attacked Victor – well, there'd be little sympathy left for him. He had raped his brother's fiancée: a despicable act, a despicable man.

And it was now more than likely that the Harrisons, who could be called as witnesses in a rape trial, would speak out, and the whole thing would be made public. Nobody wanted that; not the Huxleys, not Usha.

'Usha is not going to speak up,' Graham told his parents now. 'She could, but she won't. You must respect her for that. It's her husband who was killed, your son who killed him, your son who raped her. She could go straight for revenge, but she won't. You need to understand that, and be thankful. If she were to speak up, our name would be dragged through the mud. Surely you care?'

As it was, it was the scandal of the year, but at least the family could hold our heads up. A vicious fight between brothers that had turned ugly and ended fatally, by accident. That was the final version. Self-defence; who knew why Andrew had attacked Victor, out of the blue! Probably there was a woman involved. But not rape; rape was never mentioned.

And slowly, over time, the poisoned blood between Aunt and Uncle on the one side, and Graham, myself and Usha on the other, began to heal. With Andrew dead, Victor awaiting trial, Graham busy as a doctor, the Huxley parents had only us left. There was no son left to take over the plantation. Eventually, they sold it to the Carruthers, the neighbours who had always wanted to expand, and planned their retirement. And where should they retire to? Eastbourne, perhaps?

No, they decided. Here in Ceylon was their last remaining family: Graham, and me. Now that they knew of Usha's rape, and resulting pregnancy, there was also Luke, Victor's son, their first grandchild, and another grandchild – for Usha was now pregnant with Andrew's child – on the way. They chose to stay, and make it up with Usha, and with us.

When Graham and I declared that we would be moving to Shanti Nilayam, and Usha with us, the future was sealed: Aunty and Uncle, too, would move to Madras, buy a bungalow there not far from Shanti Nilayam. They would bring the Chettiar family with them, Sunita and Rajkumar and, if they wanted to, Satish and Karthik.

And so the lot of us moved to Madras. Graham and I and Anna-Marie moved in with Pa, who by now was back at home, and set about renovating the derelict building at the back, which had once served as a servants' residence, into a pretty three-bedroomed cottage for Usha and Luke, who stayed with us in the meantime.

Three-bedroomed, because we'd had an idea: Kannan and his mother, a widow like Usha, could also move in. Luke and Kannan were first cousins; how wonderful for them to grow up together! Their two mothers could share childcare, if and when they found work. And with Anna-Marie living with us in the bungalow at the front, all three of the children would be together.

*

Peace on the surface, but that superficial quietude seemed to bring out an inner disturbance in me that kept me awake at night, all night.

'You need to digest the past,' Pa told me. 'You can't forget it with a wave of the wand. Consolidate it within you. It has invaded your subconscious mind: you need to work through it all; step back from it and regard it all as distant from you. Look at it all as a story, as a novel, with a main character going through all the things you did, right from the beginning.'

'The whole story?'

'Yes. The whole story, right from the beginning. Write it down.'

So that's exactly what I did.

Four months later

And now I've done it. Written it all down. And here it is, my story in tangible form, a pile of pages five inches high, sitting there right next to my typewriter. I've a great sense of achievement, of peace. Pa was right: writing it down was a form of therapy for me. It is as if I have sloughed off the past, and there it sits, separate from me, in that pile of paper.

Pa taught me more ways to deal with all this, and it all helps. My heart stops its wild beating, and my breathing slows into a quiet rhythm, and I know it is all over.

Writing it down has calmed my spirit, and put everything into perspective. I'm less bothered by thoughts and anxieties, and sleep is better. Now it's all about moving forward, building a new life out of the ruins of the past. War is a terrible thing, but it is never the end. Life continues; the new lives we build out of the old, out of the remains. This story might be over, but it continues. It always continues, doesn't it?

Graham is now working as a doctor at Madras Central Hospital, and soon will be recommencing his training as an orthopaedic surgeon, the training he had to pause because of the war. And I, at last, can start my own medical training. Yes, I'm going to be a doctor, too!

Soon after we moved back home – for this *is* home – we received a letter from Father Bear:

> …well, as I told you in my last letter, I've been thinking of making some big changes myself. I need a new task, a new challenge, a new mission. And I had a grand idea, inspired by you and the terrible events of the last years.
>
> So many women have been widowed, and left destitute by this war. Widows have a desperate fate in India. Not to mention single mothers, left destitute through no fault of their own, seduced and abused and discarded. The very reason I came to India was because of the terrible fate of these poor mothers in Ireland, the way the Church has treated them there. I tried to protest but all they did was pack me off to India. So, on a personal level it's time to come full circle.

I've been looking around and found a grand old building in Tindivanam, which just needs a lick of paint and some plastering and a new kitchen and some bathrooms and hey presto, we'd have it as good as new, a home for widows or single women with children, where they can all support each other and look after each other's children, just as you are doing for Usha and Sita. Tindivanam is not so far from Madras so I'll be nearby and – with your permission, of course – stay in touch with Anna Marie…

Pa roared with laughter when he read that letter.
'That old rascal!' is all he said.

I still occasionally find it hard to sleep at night, but it's so much better now. When the brain-fever bird pelts out its eerie cry, I still sit up in bed with a jolt, and I weep, for them all, for the pain we have all endured. I still mourn Andrew, but nothing will bring him back. I still hate Victor, but he will surely get his comeuppance when the court deals with him. I even still wonder about Freddy, and what became of him.

Now that I've written this all down, Pa says I must now take this pile of paper, this story of mine, and throw it on the bonfire. Put everything behind me. And I will. Perhaps. Or maybe not. Or not *yet*. Graham wants to read it first. But my story is over: there it is in that neat heap of paper, and I am free to move on.

And yet… There is still one tiny, niggling, loose end that tickles me within. Perhaps I'll never snip it off. Perhaps I will.

Epilogue

Six years later

Dear Rosie,

I hope you are well, and your life has turned out well.

I suppose the last thing you're expecting right now is a letter from me. You have surely forgotten all about me. But I did promise you I'd write – those were my last words to you; I do remember that! And so, here I go. I've never been good with words, but I'll try and explain. I'll keep it brief.

I asked Andrew not to tell you this. Not so as to deceive you, but because I was going to make everything right: I am married, Rosie, and was married when we met. She's a girl I've known from childhood; a close friend, a bit like you and Andrew, except that we married just before I ran off to war, aged sixteen. She was the same age; and she needed to marry so she could move in with my mother. My mother protected her. Marriage protected her. Under normal circumstances we would not have married. We were much too young.

When I met you, I knew I would end that marriage when the war was over. I was thinking along the lines of annulment. By this I want you to know that you were not just a passing whim. I was sure I'd return to you, a single man, having sorted out the matter. But the war put an end to all that. As for what happened to me, why these years of silence…

There's no need for detail – I just want you to know that I was in a brutal attack and left for dead by the Japanese, bleeding from a head wound. But I wasn't dead. I was found by local Burmese and nursed back to health. But I had lost my memory. It was a case of severe amnesia. Everything, my whole past, wiped out. My childhood and youth, the girl back home – and you.

You might think that I am not telling the truth but that's what happened. It lasted six years, in which time I built a new life with a new identity, even learnt a new language. And then, something happened that triggered my memory, and it all came back. I made myself known to the British authorities, and was repatriated.

I met that girl again – and, Rosie, I could not abandon her. She had waited, loving me all this time. How could I let her down? Love begets love, and here I was, a married man in my home country. And I still am that. I know that this all sounds glib and maybe unbelievable but it happened, and was a most dramatic process. I can't give you more than a brief summary. I hope you accept that, and forgive me.

I trust that you, too, are now happily married to someone deserving of you. He is a very lucky man. It was not to be. But I will never ever forget you.

Love,
Freddy

A Letter from Sharon

Thank you so much for choosing to read *Those I Have Lost*. I hope you enjoyed your time in Rosie's life; if so, you might like to keep up to date with my latest releases, which you can do by just signing up at the following link. Your email address will never be shared and you can unsubscribe at any time:

www.bookouture.com/sharon-maas

And if you did enjoy it, I'd be very grateful if you'd tell your friends, family and social media contacts, and perhaps write a review to share your impressions with other readers.

I love hearing from my readers, and you're welcome to stay in touch through Facebook, Twitter, Goodreads, or my website. I'd love to hear from you, and promise to reply.

Thanks,
Sharon Maas

Acknowledgements

It was not easy to find research material relating to life in Sri Lanka during the war in Asia; though there's enough factual information about what went on in terms of warfare, bombing, evacuation and so on, practical everyday life back then is quite shrouded in obscurity. And so I was delighted to come across the book *Baggage Reclaimed* by Alastair Sutherland, whose parents actually lived through this period. Not only was Alastair able to reconstruct their tragic –and very moving – experience through documents and letters left by his parents, but he agreed to correspond with me and fill in some of the gaps in my knowledge. I'd like to thank him for taking the time to do so. Any errors of fact are mine, not his – though I do admit to making use of creative liberty in one or two tiny details.

And of course, I'd like to thank the busy staff of Bookouture who work behind the scenes to make this book the best it can be. In this year of Covid-19, they were all working from home, and yet managed against the odds to bring it up to scratch and help it out in the world. In particular, my thanks go out to my brilliant editor Lydia Vassar-Smith, but thanks also to Jacqui Lewis, Jane Donovan and Ami Smithson. Last, but not least, my thanks to Sarah Hardy for her invaluable work in bringing it out to my readers, as well as Kim Nash and Noelle Holten.

And last of all: thanks to my family, daughter Saskia, son Miro, son-in-law Tony: my secret support team. I couldn't do it without you all.

Printed in Great Britain
by Amazon